A Lady Wears Pearls

Hope Page

Published in the United States of America

ISBN 978-1-961507-44-9 (SC)

Hope Page Books
222 West 6th Street
Suite 400, San Pedro, CA, 90731
worksofadrianna@gmail.com

Order Information and Rights Permission:

Quantity sales. Special discounts might be available on quantity purchases by corporations, associations, and others. For details, contact the publisher at the address above.

For Book Rights Adaptation and other Rights Permission.
Call us at toll-free 1-888-945-8513 or send us an email at admin@stellarliterary.com.

Acknowledgements:

Charmaine Kennedy

&

Geneva Gaither

This experience would not have been possible without you.
I am so grateful for your help and support. Your insight and thoughts
were instrumental to my creativity and motivation.

Table of Contents

Chapter One: Anniston

Nestled in the arm of the love of her life, Lexington sits on the pew between her husband and four of her five children. Sitting up straight like a lady, as always, with her legs crossed toward her husband, happiness surrounds Lexington. She listens to the pastor preach with one hand resting on her husband's lap, and the other hand interlocked with her husband's hand resting on her shoulder.

Anniston glances at her mother, admiring the happiness on her face accented by the shine of her pearl necklaces.

Lexington catches Anniston looking at her; she whispers, "Are you okay?" Anniston shyly nods yes. Lexington winks at Anniston. Anniston quickly turns her head just as

Khryssa leans over to whisper, "They're so embarrassing," peeking at their parents. Khryssa says, "They can't even keep their hands off each other in church." Anniston smiles at her sister.

After the service, Lexington meets with and a group of young women in the sanctuary while Anniston, Khryssa, and the twins sit outside the sanctuary playing on their phones. Michael talks with the men of the church, planning their next community service event. Anniston glances at her mother through the windows in sanctuary's doors. She wonders what Lexington is saying to the group of young women.

When the meeting is over, Anniston sees the group of young women doting on Lexington as they walk toward the door. Anniston knows the women of the church adore Lexington. She has watched the women of the church love and praise her mother all her life. Anniston admires her mother's beauty as her mother walks toward the sanctuary's door. Just before the women exit the sanctuary, they hug and say goodbye.

Lexington walks out of the sanctuary and straight into Michael's arms. They don't speak, Michael and Lexington embrace and walk toward their children.

"My children let's go home," Lexington says, getting her boys to stand up. Lexington wraps her arms around her daughters as they leave the church.

As Michael drives his family home, the kids are fixated on their phones. Anniston looks up to see her mother caressing the back of her father's head and neck while he drives with one hand on the wheel and the other hand on Lexington's thigh.

Anniston quickly looks down when she sees Lexington turning around to ask the teenagers, "Did you all enjoy the sermon today?"

They say yes.

She asks, "What did you learn?" No one answers.

Lexington says, "That awesome sermon and you all took nothing away. Come on, someone had to learn something."

Anniston says, "The importance of making good choices, wise decisions."

Jaxon says, "We need an understanding of our choices to make the best decision."

Nexen, Jaxon's twin brother, says, "When we make bad decisions, we learn from them."

Khryssa says, "We become better, wiser from our mistakes, but we also must live right, not making decisions loosely or taking opportunities lightly."

Anniston says, "We should first get an understanding and pray for guidance and wisdom before making decisions."

Lexington says, "Michael, did you hear our babies?"

"I did," Michael says.

Lexington continues, "I'm so proud of you all. Michael, God really blessed us."

"Amen!" Michael says.

The kids go right back to their phones. Lexington says to Michael, "Baby, you've done a wonderful job," as she touches his beard.

He replies, "As have you," as he takes her hand and kisses it.

Khryssa scoffs at her parents' display of affection, but Anniston thinks the way they show affection is cute. Anniston admires the way her father looks at her mother. Khryssa and the twins see their parents' affection for each other as embarrassing. Anniston thinks it's cute and sweet.

As soon as they arrive home, the boys say they're hungry. Lexington promises to start cooking in ten minutes. Lexington goes to her room to change her clothes. Anniston walks into her parents' bedroom and stops at the closet door. She sees her mother's journals and scrapbooks sitting on a fire/waterproof lockbox as she peeks around the doorway. "Mom," she says.

Lexington walks out of the closet, putting on her shirt, and says, "Yes, Baby Girl."

Anniston says, "I need to talk to you," as she stares at a mark on Lexington's lower abdomen.

Lexington says, "The boys," as she touches the area where she was cut to birth her twin sons before she pulls her shirt down. Lexington is prepared to give Anniston her undivided attention.

Lexington asks, "What's on your mind, Baby Girl?"

"I have a question," Anniston replies.

Lexington says, "Ok, have a seat."

Before Anniston can sit down, Michael enters the room. He says, "Babe, I'm going to catch the game with the fellas. Are you going out?"

Lexington answers, "No, after I cook, I have a ton of stuff to do around the house."

He says, "I'll catch up with you tonight."

Lexington says, "Ok, have fun!" Michael embraces and kisses his wife.

Anniston begins to walk away. Lexington says, "Baby Girl, come back!"

Anniston says, "I'll talk to you later."

Lexington asks, "You promise?"

Anniston says, "I promise," as she exits the door.

Michael says, "One more kiss before I go!" They kiss again. He says, "I love you."

She says, "Twenty years of marriage, five kids, and I am still in love with you."

He says, "See you tonight!"

She winks and says, "See you later, Baby!" Michael walks out of the room.

Lexington goes to the kitchen to prepare dinner. Khryssa and Anniston come to the kitchen. Khryssa says, "Mom, we'll help you cook."

Lexington says, "Awe, you girls are so sweet. I appreciate you, both. Get in here! We can cook and talk."

Anniston washes her hands and starts cutting vegetables. Khryssa washes her hands and starts making the salad. Lexington says, "Anniston, Baby Girl, did you want to talk, now?"

Anniston says, "It's okay, we can talk later."

Khryssa says with a mocking tone, "She probably wants to talk about her boyfriend."

Lexington pauses. She is shocked. Lexington says, "Boyfriend?"

Khryssa says, "Mommy, guess what his name is."

Lexington asks, "What's his name?"

Khryssa says, "Michael, just like Daddy. He plays basketball. He's tall, handsome, and chocolate just like Daddy. They say girls like men who are like their fathers."

Anniston says, "Khryssie, you are not helping me, at all."

Lexington asks, "Do you like this boy?" Anniston shrugs her shoulders. Lexington asks, "Is he your boyfriend?" Anniston shyly nods her head, yes.

Lexington asks, "Why didn't you tell me you have a boyfriend? Baby Girl, you know I want to know everything going on with you, and you know you can tell me anything, always. We can talk whenever about whatever, and I promise it'll be okay. Okay, Baby Girl?"

Anniston nods, yes. Lexington sternly says, "Middle girl, that goes for you too," pointing her finger at Khryssa.

Khryssa puts her hands up and says, "Hey, you made yourself clear last year when we had our talk. You and I have full disclosure; I promise!"

Lexington asks, "No secrets?"

Khryssa answers, "No secrets!"

Lexington turns back to Anniston, and asks, "Baby Girl, how long has this been going on?"

Anniston says, "A couple of months."

Lexington shockingly asks, "Months, and I'm just now hearing about this!"

Anniston says, "I didn't want you to think anything bad. It's not easy to tell my mother I'm breaking a rule."

Lexington says, "I get that. I really do understand how you feel, but I want and expect open, honest communication with my girls. If you're thinking of breaking a rule or you are actually breaking a rule, it is what it is, and we should talk about it. I never want to hear anything about you from someone else. Got it?"

Anniston says, "I got it."

Lexington asks, "Khryssa, how long have you known about this?"

She answers, "I found out when I saw them talking in the gym after practice a few weeks ago."

Lexington says, "And, you're just now telling me?"

Khryssa says, "She swore me to secrecy."

Khryssa says, "Mommy, Michael was her first kiss. He kissed her after the basketball game a few weeks ago. She was all smiles and giggles after he kissed her. Charly and Simone were standing there like cheerleaders." Khryssa makes kissing noises looking at Anniston.

Anniston says, "Khryssie, stop snitching!"

Lexington is shocked; she says, "Kiss! You kissed him?"

Khryssa says, "It was a long kiss, too!"

Anniston says, "Mommy, it wasn't a real kiss."

Lexington asks, "What is a real kiss?"

Anniston answers, "You know!"

Lexington says, "If his lips touched your lips, it was a real kiss."

Anniston says, "Mommy, it was quick."

Lexington asks, "Did you like the kiss?"

Anniston answers, "It wasn't anything to like."

Khryssa says, "I don't know about that, Sis. You two were hugging and very close to each other. It looked like you both liked it."

Anniston says, "It wasn't a big deal!"

Lexington says, "I'm your mother, but I know when a girl likes something a boy did. I think you liked the kiss."

Khryssa says, "You were geeked."

Anniston keeps chopping vegetables; she says, "Khryssie, you're exaggerating!"

Khryssa says, "I'm having a casual conversation."

Anniston says, "You're selling me out. No loyalty!"

Khryssa says, "Mommy needed to know, and you needed the courage to tell her. I'm a means to an end."

After they cook, everyone sits at the table to eat. They talk about school. Lexington checks their grades on the parent portal. She tells each child that she is proud of their grades. The girls just had exams, and they achieved an A on each one. Lexington asks everyone about their activities for the upcoming week, so she can add their activities to the calendar in her phone.

After dinner, Lexington goes to her room to fold and separate laundry. She takes the kids their clothes and tells them to get ready for the school week. Lexington walks into Anniston's room as Anniston puts her phone down.

Lexington asks, "Were you texting your boyfriend, Michael? What's his last name?"

Anniston answers, "Bateman is his last name. No, that was Charly and Simone."

Lexington came to Anniston's room last because she wants to talk. Lexington sits on Anniston's bed, she asks, "What do you think of me?"

Anniston says, "You're my mommy. I love you."

Lexington asks, "As a woman, what do you think of me? Am I a good mother? Am I nice? Am I mean? Am I trustworthy? Do I listen well? Do you like me? If I weren't your mother, am I the type of person that you would hang with?"

Anniston says, "I think you're nice and I love that you're my mother. Sometimes I feel like you're closer to Khryssa and Michelle. You three are like best friends because you're always laughing and talking with them. Sometimes, I feel like the left out middle child, especially since the boys are always hanging with dad. I wish you and I were closer." Lexington is saddened by Anniston's honesty, but she accepts her truth.

Lexington asks, "Am I correct, I heard you say, I don't give you enough individual attention?"

Anniston says, "Yes, I want more of you to myself without Dad and the other kids. I want us to talk and laugh more."

Lexington says, "Out of my five children, you have the most of me. You think like me, you look like me, and you're short like me. You remind me so much of me that I feel like I know you are good, your chores are done, and your schoolwork is done correctly, on time, but I apologize if I ever made you feel left out that was never my intention. I assumed you felt that connection, and I was wrong for not communicating that to you. I want to fix it. One day out of every week is a day for you and me, and we can do whatever you want. How does that sound?"

Anniston says, "It sounds good!"

Lexington says, "Today, hearing you had a boyfriend that you didn't tell me about made me feel left out. I don't want any space or secrets between us. You can tell or ask me anything, and we will have a calm, open, honest discussion. I'll keep your secrets. I'll wipe your tears. I'll help you fix your mistakes. I will help you correct your wrongs. Just promise to always talk to me."

Anniston says, "I promise, no more secrets." Lexington makes her pinky promise.

Anniston says, "May, I ask my question, now?"

Lexington says, "Please do."

Anniston says, "Michael asked if I could go to the dance with him on Saturday. I know I can't date until after my birthday, but can I go just this one time? I promise, I won't ask to go out with a boy again until after my birthday."

Lexington says, "Wednesday after school, I'll take you to buy a new dress. Yes, you can go!"

Anniston is so excited; she says, "Thanks, Mommy!" Anniston leaps into her mother's arms. Anniston says, "Daddy is going to kill me if he finds out about the dance. Please, don't tell him."

Lexington says, "He will kill us both if I don't tell him. Don't worry, I'll work my magic."

Anniston says, "And, Mommy, I would be your friend if you weren't my mother because I think you're fun, smart, and beautiful. All the kids at school and church always talk about how pretty and stylish you are, how cool you are, and that makes me proud. The people at church always talk about how kind and sweet you are, and that makes me proud. And to see how much Daddy loves you makes me proud. I feel like I am connected to a remarkable person. I am so thankful that you are my mommy."

Lexington hugs her daughter and says, "Awe, I think you're intelligent, caring, loving, adorable, responsible, trustworthy, and you're absolutely breathtaking. I am so honored that you chose me to be your mommy. I look at you, and I see all that is good in me and about me glorified and multiplied. I know in my heart you're going to be better than me. I love you so much, Baby Girl."

"I love you too, Mommy," Anniston says as she hugs her mother.

"Before I leave, I want to know if there's anything else on your mind," Lexington says.

Anniston asks, "Can I wear makeup, get my nails and hair done even though I am not allowed until I'm sixteen?"

Lexington answers, "Friday after school, we'll get your nails done. Saturday morning, I will take you to get your hair and makeup done, ok?"

Anniston says, "Ok!"

Lexington kisses Anniston on the forehead, and says, "I love you, Baby Girl!"

Anniston replies, "I love you too, Mommy!" Lexington leaves the room.

Anniston texts Charly and Simone to tell them that her mom said she can go to the dance.

Wednesday after school, Lexington arrives to pick Anniston up from school. Anniston gets in the car, she says, "Hey, Mommy!"

Lexington says, "Hey, Baby Girl, how was your day?"

"It was okay," Anniston answers.

Lexington asks, "Did you see Mr. Michael Bateman?"

Anniston answers, "Yes."

Lexington asks, "How did you meet Michael?"

Anniston answers, "One day, we started talking in the gym."

Lexington says, "What do your friends think of Mr. Bateman?"

Anniston answers, "They think he's cool."

Lexington says, "That's a good sign." Lexington asks, "Did you tell Michael he has to meet your parents before you can go to the dance with him?"

Anniston says, "Yes, he's coming over tomorrow night for dinner."

Lexington asks, "Are you nervous about your dad meeting Mr. Bateman?"

Anniston says, "Yes!"

Lexington says, "I know how you feel. I was grown when Michael met my dad, but I was so nervous. There's nothing as nerve-racking as your father facing the fact that you are growing up."

Anniston says, "How old were you when Papa met Dad?"

Lexington answers, "I was thirty-four, but I felt sixteen. I intended to introduce him to my parents earlier, but I didn't want to press the issue. We were stressed flying back and forth to see each other."

Lexington explains, "Walking to their door, I felt excitement and anxiety. Excited because I hadn't seen my parents in a while. In that while, I had gotten married and pregnant without having a conversation with my daddy, so I was full of anxiety."

Evaluation

When Lexington saw her mother, she said, "Mommy!"

"My baby's having a baby," Mrs. Lear said with a voice full of love and happiness. "Come in here!" she added as Lexington walked toward the door. Lexington and Mrs. Lear hugged.

"Mommy, I missed you so much," Lexington said.

"I missed you too," Mrs. Lear said. Mrs. Lear closed the door; she said, "Give me those," as she took Lexington's luggage.

"Mr. Lear, your daughter is here," Mrs. Lear sternly shouted. The way she said it let Lexington know he was not happy about the situation.

Mrs. Lear said to Lexington, "He's in the kitchen. Go! Talk to your dad." Mrs. Lear took Lexington's bags to the guest room. Lexington went into the kitchen to see her father.

"Daddy, I missed you," Lexington said with a smile on her face.

He turned and said, "Daughter! It's good to see you." They hugged.

"Where's your husband?" he asked.

"He'll be here, Daddy, I promise. He's excited to meet you," Lexington said.

"You know the father of the bride should get a chance to talk to the groom before the wedding, not months after the wedding, and there is a baby on the way," Mr. Lear said, giving Lexington an unapproving eye.

Mrs. Lear came into the kitchen to join the conversation. Lexington said, "Daddy, I know you're not happy that I didn't talk to you before getting married, but things moved fast after the car accident."

He said with a slightly sarcastic tone, "Well, Daughter, you're grown, you're smart, you're responsible, and you're capable of making your own decisions."

Lexington said, "Daddy, don't be like that. Once you meet Michael, you will see why I married him."

Mrs. Lear grabbed Lexington's chin to see how her face and forehead had healed. She said, looking at the scar on Lexington's forehead, "The doctor did an excellent job. I can barely see the scar."

Lexington said, "I'm so thankful."

Mrs. Lear asked, "How have you been, Little Girl?"

"Mommy, life is good," she answered.

Mrs. Lear asked, "So, tell us about this husband of yours. Where is he? What does he do? How old is he? How does he treat you? Is he a Christian?" Mrs. Lear knew all the answers to the questions, but she was trying to encourage a conversation between father and daughter.

"Well, honestly, he's amazing. Right now, he's with his family, and I know you both are going to love him," Lexington said.

Mr. Lear asked, "Why isn't he here with his pregnant wife?"

"Daddy, he is doing something I asked him to do. Whatever I need, he gives me. Yes, he is a Christian. He's a real estate broker. He's forty, and he's good to me always," Lexington said.

Mr. Lear said, "Forty! He was damn near a grown man when you were born. I mean, he's close to my age."

Lexington said, "Daddy, he's only six years older than me, and trust me, I benefit from his maturity. I wouldn't have married him if he was not exactly the man you've always wanted me to marry. I promise, Michael is a good man and you're going to approve once you meet him."

"If you say so. We will trust you. We've always trusted you," Mr. Lear said.

"Have I ever disappointed you," Lexington asked.

"No, you haven't, and you never will," Mrs. Lear said with her hands gently on Lexington's cheeks. Mrs. Lear looked directly into her daughter's eyes and said, "I love you so much, and I'm going to love your husband because you love him. He's a part of this family, and he is a part of my granddaughter."

Lexington asked, "You think it's a girl?"

Mrs. Lear said, "Yes, you're definitely carrying like it's a girl," as she rubbed Lexington's stomach.

Lexington said, "I was hoping for a boy for Daddy, but Destiny and Michael think the baby is a girl."

Mrs. Lear said, "You're young enough to try again, so don't feel pressured. We'll let your father cook. Let's go talk."

Mrs. Lear and Lexington went into the den to talk. Mrs. Lear asked, "A baby on the way, a new husband, a new house, that's a lot of change in a short amount of time. Mrs. Moore, how are you handling all that change?"

"Honestly, I've been feeling a way that I can't explain. It's not about Michael, the house, or the baby. Mommy, lately, mistakes I made before I met Michael have been haunting me, and I don't know why. I thought I had moved on," Lexington answered.

"What is going on in that pretty brain of yours," Mrs. Lear asked.

"I had a few weird dreams, I ran into a few people from the past, and there's this gnawing feeling that I betrayed Michael with things that happened before we met. After we were married, I told Michael my whole truth. Mommy, I felt terrible telling my husband my secrets. He hasn't said anything, and nothing has changed between us, so whatever it is that's bothering me is in my head," Lexington said.

"What secrets, Lexi," Mrs. Lear asked.

"Men," Lexington answered. She added, "The men before Michael. The other day, I ran into Raymond."

Mrs. Lear scoffed. Lexington said, "Mommy, I was so glad that you never liked him because you affirmed that he wasn't the one. Everyone thought I was crazy for breaking up with him."

Mrs. Lear said, "What did he say?"

Lexington said, "He told me this is supposed to be his baby. He wanted a family with me."

Mrs. Lear said, "I was so glad when you broke up with him. Do you know why I hated him so much?" Lexington said no.

Mrs. Lear said, "You went against me for him. It hurt me so badly when you moved in with him after I told you not to. I cried so hard."

Lexington said, "Mommy, I'm so sorry."

Mrs. Lear said, "It hurt, but I had to let you learn the hard way and see for yourself."

Lexington said, "I did learn the hard way!"

Mrs. Lear said, "And, we survived!"

Lexington said, "Mommy, Michael asked who bought the jewelry I wear, so I told him about Camren, Raymond, Roman."

Mrs. Lear cut Lexington off when she heard Roman. Mrs. Lear asked, "Who is Roman?"

"A guy I dated for a while before I met Michael," Lexington answered.

"Did you like this Roman," Mrs. Lear asked.

"Mommy, I say I didn't, but I did too much. It was complicated," Lexington answered with a bit of shame in her voice.

"What was complicated, Lexington?" Mrs. Lear asked.

Lexington answered, "I knew he wasn't good for me, but I was very attracted to him."

Mrs. Lear asked, "How long did this go on?"

"Three years," Lexington answered.

Mrs. Lear asked, "If he wasn't good for you, why did you let it go on so long?" Lexington silently stared at her mother. Mrs. Lear quickly heard everything she needed to hear in the silence. "Ok! I got it, loud and clear," Mrs. Lear said.

Mrs. Lear asked, "So, what happened between you and Mr. Roman?"

Lexington answered, "Mommy, we had a good time until it was time to move on."

Mrs. Lear asked, "How did you feel ending things?"

Lexington said, "Like I had done the right thing."

Mrs. Lear responded, "Well, you did, so you should feel at peace. It was what it was, and now it's over."

Lexington said, "That's exactly what I am telling myself, but it's not working. I want to focus on my baby and husband, but the past is really bothering me. That's kind of why we're moving." Lexington injected that comment into the conversation to see how her mother felt about her moving.

"Moving? Where? Why?" Mrs. Lear shockingly asked.

"We're moving to Michael's hometown to be near his company and family. Right now, I'm going to work for ten to twelve hours per day while Michael is working from home. I don't want a stay-at-home husband. He needs to go to work, so I can be home with the baby. Destiny is going to run things at Lear Accounting for me. Mommy, if we move, I can have a fresh start to concentrate on my husband and my baby," Lexington said.

"Baby, you can run from your mess, but that won't reconcile it. I hear all you're saying, and it is understandable, but running won't make those emotions go away. Whatever it is you're feeling, you have to deal with it immediately and appropriately, especially with that baby growing inside you. Your pleasures, your desires, your afflictions, your propensities, your shame, your fears, and your demons are like your eyes. They are traits your daughter can inherit. You don't want to pass those demons or burdens on to her, so you have to get rid of them now," Mrs. Lear said.

Mrs. Lear grabbed Lexington's hand and said, "Come here, let me show you something. (They walked up the stairs.) When we carry a baby and burden, it's not good for the baby. As a new wife and a first-time mother, it is common to feel anxious or uncertainty. Your life is about to drastically change, and you are growing up to deal with that change."

Sitting on a cushioned bench in the attic, Mrs. Lear pulled out two scrapbooks from a fire/waterproof lockbox. She hands the scrapbooks to Lexington.

"What's this," Lexington asked.

"It's my mother and grandmother's prayers. When they passed, I read their prayers. And one day, you'll read my prayers," Mrs. Lear said.

Mrs. Lear said (handing Lexington two journals), "Here are some of my old journals. Read them to see I was no different than you when I was a new mother. I had to pray as a new mother and work things out in my mind."

"I remember you writing at night, but I had no idea what you were writing," Lexington said.

Mrs. Lear said, "I think you should read my inner, most personal thoughts during that time. It may help you. Sometimes we need to know the demons our mother, grandmothers, and great-grandmothers fought to get perspective in our own fight."

Lexington became curious to know what was in the journals and scrapbooks. Lexington said, "Mommy, thank you for sharing this with me."

"Take the journals and scrapbooks home with you, so you can take your time to go through them, and when you've read everything, let's talk about what you learned," Mrs. Lear said.

Lexington said, "I will!"

Mrs. Lear said, "Daughter, I know it is easier said than done, but you can't let what happened in the past interfere with what will happen, that'll only give the devil a victory."

Lexington said, "Mommy, you're right!"

"Mommy, may I ask you a personal question," Lexington shyly asked.

"Go ahead, Baby," Mrs. Lear answered.

Lexington asked, "Did you wait for Daddy?"

"I did, and so did he," Mrs. Lear replied.

Lexington said, "See, Mommy, I wish I could say that to my baby when she asks, but I can't. I feel bad about that."

"You'll have a beautiful story to tell your daughter. Everything you tell me about you and Michael is beautiful. Don't beat yourself up," Mrs. Lear said.

Lexington said, "If only I listened to you about Camren. Mommy, I felt so bad when I came home crying about him cheating on me. You were so supportive. You never said I told you so."

Mrs. Lear said, "One mistake doesn't define a whole life. You made an unwise decision, but you were and still are my good girl. I'll always support you."

Lexington said, "Camren and Raymond I can live with, but Roman and Chad…"

Mrs. Lear interrupted to ask, "Lexi, who is Chad?"

Lexington answered, "Mommy, Chad is one of the "Camelot" boys."

"How did you meet one of the Hudson boys," Mrs. Lear asked.

Lexington, feeling shame, answered, "We met at the gym."

Mrs. Lear asked, "Which one is Chad?"

Lexington answered, "The youngest one."

Mrs. Lear said, "Lexington Michon Lear!" Lexington cringed listening to her mother say her full name, which meant her mother was disappointed in her behavior.

Mrs. Lear asked, "So you met Chad after you ended things with Roman?"

Lexington said, "It was while."

Mrs. Lear excitedly asked, "Lexington, what were you thinking?"

Lexington answered, "I was bored and lonely. Roman fulfilled my physical needs, but I knew he saw other women and that made me feel lonely. When Chad approached me, I felt like he was a good, safe option to not feel so lonely."

Mrs. Lear said, "Lexington, when did we ever teach you that it is okay to play with some woman's son to feed your ego? Because that's what you did with that little boy, right, and, you know that is never okay. That is not how I raised my good daughter to treat people. Akera, I don't know what to expect, but I expect better from you."

Lexington said, "I know, Mommy!"

Mrs. Lear said, "Now, you want to run away to get away from the mess you created. Let me guess how the story went. They both fell in love with you, you didn't feel the same way, and they both got their feelings hurt because they wanted more and you didn't."

Lexington said, "Mommy, how do you know everything?"

Mrs. Lear said, "I am your mother." Mrs. Lear added, "You had your fun with them, and when you were done, it was over. It didn't matter how they felt."

Lexington said, "Mommy, don't rub it in."

Mrs. Lear said, "You won't find peace looking at a half-truth. Tell yourself the whole truth about your behavior, the antecedents, and the consequences."

Lexington said, "Mommy, you're telling the truth."

Mrs. Lear asked, "Lexington, so Chad is the last one, right?"

Lexington answered, "Yes, mommy, those four men are it outside of my husband, I swear."

Mrs. Lear asked, "And the experience of those four men makes you feel?"

Lexington answered, "Guilty, regret, remorse, and shame."

Mrs. Lear asked, "In all of that, did you learn anything?"

Lexington answered, "Mommy, I learned so much."

Mrs. Lear said, "Maybe the purpose was the lessons." Mrs. Lear asked, "Did you experience another man during the relationship with Michael?"

Lexington answered, "Never!"

Mrs. Lear said, "Life, before you met him is the past, and that's all it is: the past."

Lexington said, "I feel like I cheated him by not waiting for him. I gave so much of myself to other men. What does that leave for him?"

"Did Michael wait for you," Mrs. Lear asked.

"I never ask about his past," Lexington answered.

Mrs. Lear asked, "Lexington, you don't ask about his past? You know I've always told you to get to know a person before you pursue anything. Have you taken the time to really get to know him?"

Lexington answered, "Yes, I know him."

Mrs. Lear asked, "So, based on what you know, has he been with other women?"

Lexington answered, "Yes!"

Mrs. Lear said, "So he has given himself to other women. I bet any amount of money he has been with way more women than you have been with men, and what is left for you? Do you feel loved, protected, honored, desired, respected? I know you think it is different because you are a woman, but it is not.

"See, Baby, times are different than they were when your father and I were young. Back then, waiting was the norm, but now young women are out in the world, working like men, desiring like men. You've made mistakes. You've recognized them. You've felt convicted. You've confessed your sins to your husband, and now, it's time for redemption and testimony.

"I believe Michael understands that people lose their way and make bad choices. You don't ask, and he doesn't disclose his past says something. I'm one hundred per cent sure he's done some dirt and he doesn't want you to know that's why you don't talk about his past. And I'm one thousand per cent sure, his dirt is a million times bigger than yours.

"I bet he learned from his past, and you benefit from those lessons. It's the same for him. He benefits from what you learned. He knows that you're a good woman, and he knows with you he is and will be honored, loved, respected, protected, desired. I guarantee, he's not thinking about Roman, Chad, Raymond, or Camren because neither of them can affect anything in his household. Yes, it would've been ideal for you to wait.

"Maybe there was something HE wanted you to learn in those experiences that prepared you for Michael. When you think about those experiences, you have a greater appreciation for Michael. You've learned something. You're a better wife and woman. You've grown. You've changed. You'll forever do better. You will teach someone what you learned. That's what life is about: learning from your mistakes and teaching someone the lessons you learned.

"Before the baby is born, you need to establish a prayer ritual for the morning and night. In the meantime, you need to take a deeper dive into God's word to find the spiritual meaning of your journey. Look at what you've been through: your lowest to your highest point. Find the victory and celebrate it. Thank him for the change. God is always pleased when we change for the better.

"Looking closely at those prayers and journals may help you develop your rituals. Getting to know us as women will help you make sense of your journey. Get a journal, start writing out your feelings and thoughts, find Bible verses that address your thoughts. When you move, find space in your home to carry out your prayer ritual. Be sure to keep your area sacred. Teach your husband and your baby to respect your space and to stay out of your space."

Mrs. Lear touched Lexington's hand and added, "Little Girl, what you did with Roman and Chad, well I am not condoning, but it is nothing to carry with you. That innocent little girl you're carrying doesn't need to be in your womb crowded by guilt or shame. She needs a clean, clear space to grow appropriately. You need to figure out how to let that go. You shouldn't feel guilt or shame about loving a man. Did you love them?"

Lexington hated to admit it, but she answered, "I did." Mrs. Lear hated to see her baby sad.

Mrs. Lear said, "Roman, Chad, and Raymond may have gotten their feelings hurt, but trust and believe they don't regret knowing you or spending time with you because you're that woman, and I know because I made you.

We all have things we want but can't have. That's not necessarily a bad thing. They'll be alright!"

"Thanks, Mommy," Lexington said as they hugged. Lexington asked, "Mommy, you keep saying, girl. How do you know it's a girl?"

Mrs. Lear said, "It's a girl, and she looks just like her daddy. I'm your mother. I just know."

Lexington said, "Michael thinks she looks like me. What makes you think she looks like him?"

Mrs. Lear answered, "You love that man. I can tell by the way you talk about him. You light up when you say his name. She looks just like her daddy."

Lexington said, "Mommy, I think you are right."

As they leave the attic, Mrs. Lear said, "You better wait to tell your father about moving; he is still stuck on you marrying Michael without Michael talking to him first."

"Would it help if I asked Michael to marry me," Lexington asked.

Shocked, Mrs. Lear asked, "You asked him?"

Lexington shrugs her shoulders; she said, "Long story!"

Mrs. Lear, looking bewildered, said, "Uh! No! Never mention that to Mr. Lear."

Mrs. Lear added, "When Michael gets here, let the two men work it out amongst themselves, and you stay out of it. The men will respect each other more if they come to an understanding without your intercession. They are men, and they will figure it out. The way you speak of Michael, he sounds like an amazing, intelligent person. I'm sure he knows what needs to happen. Now, let's go eat!"

(Present Day) Anniston says, "Now, I know why we can't go in your closet. It's your prayer space."

Lexington says, "That's right!"

Anniston says, "Did Papa hate daddy when they met?"

Lexington says, "You know your father is charming. He won Daddy over within minutes."

Anniston asks, "Did you feel better after talking with Nanna?"

Lexington answers, "Yes, I did. I did everything she told me, and I learned so much. I learned Akera and I were reaping and benefiting from their prayers. A praying grandmother makes a difference. I am a witness."

Anniston asks, "Mommy, did you and Nanna talk about men when you were growing up?"

Lexington says, "Mommy is reserved; she believes ladies don't talk about sex. She told me what not to do. She taught me to always be a lady, a good person. In college, I was naïve and got hurt. I want my daughters to be prepared. When Michelle and Khryssa turned sixteen, I sat them down and we had a deep, long talk about men and sex. And now, my baby girl is interested in boys."

Anniston says, "Mommy, you were right, I should've told you about Michael Bateman as soon as we started talking."

Lexington said, "I should have introduced Michael to my parents as soon as it was clear we were in a committed relationship, but I didn't want Michael to think I was pressuring him. It's karma."

Anniston says, "Mommy, I never meant to hurt you."

Lexington says, "I know you didn't. We never mean to hurt the ones we love."

Reception

Lexington saw the car as it pulled into the driveway. Lexington waddled outside to greet Michael. When he stepped out of the car, Lexington said to herself, look at my handsome husband. He walked over to her, dropped his bags, and picked her up. She kissed him and said, "I missed you!"

"I missed you, too," Michael said.

She whispered, "Did you get the stuff I told you to get for Daddy?"

"Yes, I did," Michael said.

Michael put Lexington down to grab his bags. Lexington wrapped her arm in his, and they walked toward the house; she said, "Good, you're going to have to butter Daddy up. He feels like we cheated him because he didn't meet you before we got married," Lexington said.

"Don't worry, Baby. I got this," Michael said. As soon as they walked through the door, Mr. and Mrs. Lear greeted them.

"Mommy, Daddy, this is Michael," Lexington said.

Michael shook Mr. Lear's hand first; he said, "It's a pleasure to meet you, Mr. Lear."

Mr. Lear, still being stubborn, said, "Uh-huh! It's nice to finally meet my daughter's husband."

Michael reached for Mrs. Lear's hand, but she hugged him and said, "Son, welcome to the family."

"Thank you, Mrs. Lear," Michael said.

"Mom, call me mom, you're my son-in-law," Mrs. Lear said. Michael thanked Mrs. Lear for the warm welcome. Lexington elbowed Michael.

Going in his bag, Michael said, "Mr. Lear, I brought some things I thought you might like. Your daughter talks about you all the time. She swears these are your favorite things."

He handed Mr. Lear a box of expensive cigars, expensive bottles of whiskey and bourbon, and season baseball tickets. Mr. Lear was impressed, he said, "Thank you, leave your bags here. We'll get them later. Let's go to the man cave, have a smoke, a taste, and get to know each other. Leave the women to have their girl talk."

Reconnection

Lexington was asleep when a tipsy Michael entered the room. He looked at her and he was filled with desire. It was mainly the bourbon and whiskey that had him on ten. He took the small decorative pillows and put them between the wall and headboard. He got close to her to rub her exposed thighs. He whispered, "I missed you," as he kissed her neck. She was too deep in sleep to hear him. Michael whispered her name as he moved her panties to the side.

He put his legs between hers. He wrapped one arm around her chest, and one hand covered her mouth. She opened her eyes. He whispered, "I missed you," as he slid inside her. She made a little noise. He whispered, "Shh! They'll hear you."

Michael held her so tightly she couldn't move or reject him.

She whispered, "Michael!"

He whispered, "Baby, I need you!" She reached to push him away, but he pinned her arm behind her back.

She was in a fit on the verge of an orgasm; she whispered, "Shit!"

He covered her mouth. He whispered, "You have to be quiet!"

He rolled on his back and pulled her on top of him. He tightly held her to his chest, and he used his legs to keep her thighs open, locking her ankles behind his calves. Michael made her take the whole thing with each stroke.

Michael was trying to make up for each day that he hadn't seen his wife. He missed her. Lexington felt the rapture of his emotions. Her whole body shook as Michael moved inside her. Lexington decided it would be easier to let him finish than to fight it. She tried to be quiet, but it was hard to control her reactions. Michael stuck his thumb in her mouth to keep her quiet.

Michael hugged her as he felt a release of tension.

She whispered, "Baby, let me go back to sleep!"

Michael whispered, "I need you, Lexi," but he let her go.

Lexington went to use the bathroom; she hoped he would fall asleep while she was in there. As she washed her hands, he came through the door.

She said, "Go to sleep!"

He said, "Fuck me to sleep!" She shook her head, no. She dried her hands and tried to walk out. Michael stopped her.

Michael backed her against the sink. She put her hand on his chest, but he walked closer. He picked her up. He wrapped her legs around his waist.

Michael said, "I can't tell you don't want it. Look how wet you are!" He kissed her. He leaned against the wall. He grabbed her camisole and wrapped it in his fists. He had her across him like she mounted a horse. She held onto his chest as she slowly slid down him. It felt so good; it took his breath away.

He whispered, "You're so wet. I can't stop, Lexi." He used her camisole to hold and control her movement. She breathed heavily and moaned. He whispered, "Shh!"

She asked, "Why are you fucking me like this if you expect me to be quiet?"

He whispered, "Because it's so sexy!" He puts his thumb in her mouth to muffle her moaning. She sucked his thumb. Michael stopped moving to let her experience her orgasm. He whispered in her ear, "Let me get it from the back!"

She whispered, "You owe me for this one. I can't believe you, right now!"

He replied, "Baby, it's the alcohol. Your daddy got me tipsy."

She whispered, "You better hurry up."

Michael said, "Baby, you can't rush art."

Lexington said, "You have fifteen minutes."

Michael said, "I can work a masterpiece with that."

(Present Day) Lexington tells Anniston, "Michael went from his daughter's husband to his son by dinner that day. You know what's funny, my dad always wanted a son, so Michael fulfilled that adult son comradery he longed for. When I had you girls, my parents visited for a few weeks. When I had the boys, my parents moved here. The twins gave him a chance to know what it is like to raise boys."

In the boutique, they look through the racks. Lexington asks, "Have you and Michael Bateman picked a color?"

Anniston says, "All the basketball players are wearing white suits with red accessories to represent our school colors."

Lexington says, "So, we need to find a fabulous red or white dress."

Anniston says, "It would be cute to coordinate colors."

Lexington says, "You know, this reminds me of being back home with my friends hanging out and shopping every Friday night."

Anniston says, "Shopping every Friday sounds like a dream come true for me. I want that life as an adult."

Lexington says, "Be careful what you wish for. Yes, it was definitely fun and glamorous to cloth myself in luxurious, fine clothing. I had every material item a girl could ask for, but really, I had nothing of real value."

Anniston says, "Mom, what makes you say you had nothing if you had everything?"

Lexington says, "Having a lot of stuff that I love was very gratifying for my flesh. I guess you can say my flesh was satisfied, but my soul was searching for something. I didn't know what I was missing at the time, but the expensive clothes, shoes, and handbags did not fulfill the internal longing. I had all this stuff, surrounded by people I love, doing the things I love, but I was longing for something more before I met."

Tradition

Lexington and her friends looked through the racks as Akera, Destiny, and Kendra talked about sex. Kareen and Lexington were on the other side of the rack listening. Akera asked Destiny how sex has changed in twelve years of marriage. Destiny said, "We know each other and are more comfortable to try different things." Kendra asked if they use toys. Destiny answered, "The marriage bed is for the giving of one's body. I do a lot for my husband."

Akera asked, "So what is the perfect little wife doing?"

Destiny said, "She's doing a lot, and after twelve years, she is doing those things like a professional."

Akera and Kendra said, "Damn!" as they high five.

Akera asked, "What that head and neck do?"

Destiny replied they are taking it all. Destiny whispered to Akera and Kendra while Kareen and Lexington talked on the opposite side of the rack. Kendra's and Akera's jaws dropped as Destiny whispered.

Akera said, "Damn, Destiny, that's hot."

Kendra said, "I must agree by the reaction in my panties."

Akera said, "Who knew the quiet, perfect wife was so blazing?"

Kendra asked, "How do you handle that."

Destiny answered, "It takes practice."

Akera said, "It definitely takes a combination of relaxing your muscles, controlling your breathing, and producing excess, thick saliva like mucus."

Lexington said, "Sometimes, I don't believe we have the same mother."

Akera said, "Shut up, vitamin D is good for you."

Lexington said, "The kind from the sun!"

Akera said, "Lexi, stop ruining my fun because you get none."

Lexington said, "I get good and plenty!"

Akera said, "That's child's play!"

Lexington said, "I haven't had a marathon ran through my shit."

Akera said, "But practice is how you learn to work that ass."

Lexington said, "All that practice is how your numbers got higher than your age. All of us are in single digits."

Akera said, "That's why they call me the G.O.A.T!"

Kendra said, "Don't start on Lexi. Not everyone is as comfortable as you with their sexuality."

Lexington said, "Well, when you start getting to centers of Tootsie Roll Pops when your twelve-years-old, you are more comfortable talking about it than most."

Akera said, "One time, and you can't let it go."

Lexington said, "One time on the church bus and one time in the church's bathroom."

Akera said, "He did me in the bathroom, twice! You're just mad because you didn't get got!"

Lexington said, "Not at twelve!"

Akera said, "We were all smashing in college, so there are no saints here!" Destiny smiled at smashing in college and asked Kendra about Professor Nathans.

"That's a good question. You never talk about that night," Lexington said.

Kareen asked, "Who is Professor Nathans?"

Destiny answered, "A fine ass professor of political science who had a thing for Kendra."

Kendra said, "He took my virginity, and I want my shit back."

Akera asked, "Best Friend, what happened with this professor? I thought Kadeem was your first."

Kendra said, "He always made an excuse to talk to me whenever I saw him. He knew most of the girls on campus had a crush on him, so maybe he assumed I did too. I thought he was cute, but I was with Kadeem at the time.

I wasn't trying to kick it with him at all. He lured me off-campus for dinner. I knew it wasn't a good idea, but I didn't follow my first mind.

"We ate; everything was cool. When we were driving back to campus, he pulled over at a nearby park. He pounced on me like Tigger pounces on Winnie the Pooh. I said no, stop, get off me. I can still remember the smell of his cologne. I wanted him off of me. We tussled, but my wrists were so slim he could hold them both in one hand. I had on a skirt, so he had easy access. Twenty minutes of hell! It hurt so badly.

"There was blood all over the seat. It was so embarrassing. It took months to scrub his scent off my skin. He never asked me out again, but he continued to speak and smile like nothing happened."

"Oh my God, Kendra," Lexington said.

Destiny said, "I am so sorry that happened to you. I never imagined he hurt you."

Lexington said, "Kendra, why didn't you say something. I can't believe we didn't pick up on something tragic happening that night. I thought you never mentioned going on a date with him because you were embarrassed about something that happened. I never thought you were raped. Little Sister, you should've have told us, so we could've comforted you. I'm so sorry."

Destiny said, "Yes, I wasn't expecting you to say that. I'm in disbelief."

Akera said, "So when you said he took your virginity, you literally meant he took it. That bastard. You never told me that, Best Friend. I would've fucked him up. Did you tell anyone?"

Kendra answered, "No! Never! This is the first time I ever told the story."

Kareen said, "Sister, you should have told someone. You carried that heavy burden by yourself for all these years? You didn't tell Mom or Dad?"

Kendra answered, "No, I wanted it to go away. I pretended like it didn't happen. I had sex with Kadeem and pretended like that was my first time, not that it was much better. He was a virgin. He didn't know what he was doing. I still don't know how he got cum in my hair."

Akera laughed, she said, "What? Were you…"

"Akera, please," Lexington interrupted her.

Akera said, "You are only offended because you don't do it. The grown ass women understand it can be messy."

"I can't take you," Lexington said.

"Apparently, you can't take a lot of things, so what's your point," Akera said.

"Ignore her and finish your story, Kendra," Lexington said.

Kendra said, "No! He jumped when he was landing the plane, and it shot all in my hair. I had just gotten my hair done, too!"

Akera said, "I know you were pissed!"

Kendra said, "Livid!"

Lexington said, "Kendra, my heart goes out to you."

Kareen said, "You're my sister, Kendra! Why didn't you tell me? I would've helped you."

Kendra said, "I didn't know how to tell you." The other four women felt devastated for Kendra. They surrounded her with a group hug.

Akera said, "Lexi, you and Raymond had to do something exciting? I mean, he was like ten years older than you."

Lexington said, "Why bring up Raymond. He was boring. His clothes were boring. His conversation was boring. That was boring. I thought his being older would teach me something, but no. I faked it a lot just to get it over with. I was inexperienced and didn't know how to make it better. Toward the end of the relationship, I would vomit after sex. One time he caught me, and that fool asked if I was pregnant. I was thinking, hell no, I'm not having your boring kids."

Destiny said, "Awe! Lexi, Raymond was so cute and sweet, but I get it. You can't build a relationship without passion and desire. But wait, you threw up after sex, it was that bad?"

Lexington said, "Four years in the same positions, saying the same thing with the same unexciting cat lick head. He never tried anything new."

Kareen asked, laughing, "Lexi, what the fuck is cat lick head?"

Lexington answered, "He literally licked it like a cat drinks milk (mocking a cat's movement licking milk)."

Destiny said, laughing, "Lexi, cat lick head!"

Akera asked, "So you didn't enjoy yourself at all?"

Lexington said, "Not until Roman. Roman isn't shit, but that is incredible."

Kendra said, "Why is it like that? He ain't shit, but the dick is the shit, or he is an awesome person, but it's lackluster?"

Destiny said, "I bet it's because Eve ate that apple."

Kendra said, "Why didn't Adam shake the shit out of her and smack the damn apple out her hand?"

Kareen said, "He should've put her ass in a chokehold."

Lexington said, "Punched her ass in the throat!"

Kendra said, "Despite Eve ruining humanity, I believe Lexi's, Kareen's, and my husbands are coming very soon. This is our year. Akera's ahh…whatever the hell you like on that day, a man, woman, or unicorn, is also coming soon. They will fulfill our minds, bodies, and spirits."

Destiny said, "A woman, she always liked women more than men."

Kendra said, "Akera's her and Lexi's, Kareen's and my him are coming soon. I'm going to fast and pray on it."

Kareen said, "Amen to that!"

Lexington followed, "Amen!"

(Present Day) Anniston says, "Rape, that's devastating!"

Lexington says, "Extremely."

Anniston says, "It sounds like you all had fun back then."

Lexington says, "We did. When I moved, I was so lonely without them. I felt better when Kareen moved here after marrying Amir. It's not the same, but one best friend is cool."

Anniston says, "Uncle Amir is what dreams are made of; Aunt Kareen is the luckiest woman in the world."

Lexington says, "Amir is an awesome man, and as fine as mulberry silk."

Anniston laughs and says, "Right! We have got to continue this conversation later. I want to know how Aunt Kareen met Uncle Amir."

Anniston holds up a white dress and says, "I like this one."

Lexington says, "That's really pretty. Try it on. We'll talk later!" They buy the dress, a pair of shoes and a handbag. After dress shopping, Lexington and Anniston sit down to eat.

Sitting across from Anniston in the restaurant, Lexington says, "I'm going to ask you a question, don't freak out."

Anniston says, "Okay!"

Lexington asks, "Are the kids at school having sex?"

Anniston says, "Some are!"

Lexington asks, "Do they talk about it?"

Anniston answers, "Some do!"

Lexington asks, "Have you?"

Anniston hurriedly answers, "No! Mommy, absolutely not."

Lexington asks, "Has Michael mentioned it?"

Anniston says, "No!"

Lexington asks, "Have you thought about it?"

Anniston answers, "Sometimes, I wonder about it."

Lexington asks, "What do you wonder? Be honest and say whatever is on your mind."

Suddenly, Anniston is nervous, but she manages to say, "I wonder what it feels like, does it make you happy, when should you do it, and why you do it. I get that the purpose is to make a baby, but what makes a person say you are the one, and this is the time."

Lexington says, "There are so many consequences of sex, so to answer the question when: you are ready to have sex when you are capable of managing the consequences of sex on your own. There's no guarantee your partner will stay around to deal with the outcomes with you.

"Don't let anyone make you feel obligated to give them your body or allow someone to pressure you into having sex. Sex will not make a man like you, so don't think sex will change things. Don't have sex because you can't control your body or desires. We are supposed to control our bodies and minds to resist temptations and manage our desires. That's not easy, but that's our task. When you are in love, everything will let you know.

"Don't ever compete with a woman for a man. If a man wants you, you don't have to worry about another woman. Fitting in is not a good reason to have sex. Just because all the other girls are doing it, doesn't mean you are ready.

"Sometimes people have sex to get over a breakup. The best way to deal with a breakup is to take time, so you don't carry unhealthy energy into your next relationship. Being emotional can increase the need to be close to someone, but it's not a good time to make decisions.

"Sex can be a vice to boost your self-esteem. If you didn't love yourself before sex, you won't love yourself after sex. Sex won't slay any demons or resolve unaddressed issues. Sometimes sex fills gaps and spaces in your life. It seems like so much fun when people are talking about their sexual experiences. People get bored with life, and sex can help them feel alive.

"When you're in love, you give your body as an expression of love to your partner. As a woman, I can promise you that sex with love and commitment is not the same. If you wait for love and commitment from the man you are supposed to be with, it will be so much better. The morning after sex can be the loneliest morning of your life. The man that loves you won't leave you feeling lonely or regretful, and the morning after will make you smile.

"Sharing yourself with a man is so serious. Once you do it, it can't be undone. You can't take sex back. You can't erase it. It's a permanent decision. We make poor judgments and bad decisions when we take sex lightly. I hope you know that you and your body are so precious. I hope you love yourself. If you love you, you will require the man in your space to respect you.

"I'm not trying to control you, so don't think that's what this conversation is about. You're my baby girl, and I want the best for you. I don't want you to experience sex until you're married, but that's my hope for you. I want you to be with a man in that way because you want to be with him. I hope you make that choice because you love him, and he loves you.

"I hope you choose a man that you can trust, that will make you feel safe and protected, a man that takes his time, and will do anything to satisfy you."

Anniston asks, "Mommy, you want that for me because you have that with Daddy?"

Lexington smiles: she says, "Because you deserve love like that when you are ready."

Anniston asks, "What advice would Lexington give a young woman starting her first serious relationship?"

Lexington answers, "I would say you need to take your time, know who and what you're getting into, be clear about what you want and expect in the relationship. You must clearly communicate what you want and expect, and he should do the same.

"If you are considering making sex a component of this relationship, you have to be prepared for all of the possible consequences. If you are not equipped to deal with all the possibilities, it is not the right time for a sexual relationship."

Anniston asks, "Like what kind of consequences?"

Lexington says, "Being lied to or used, getting your feelings hurt, or your heart broken. Men can be like the enemy. They come to steal, kill, and destroy. You have to watch how they move and react. Listen very carefully to everything they say and pay even more attention to what they don't say.

"You can get pregnant, and being a parent is demanding. Becoming a parent means putting someone's best interests before your personal goals. You want to make sure you choose the right man to father your children."

Anniston says, "In health, we watch videos, and they show us pictures. It is so scary."

Lexington says, "So, you understand how important it is to protect yourself."

Anniston says, "I definitely understand."

Anniston says, "Sexual relationships sound difficult."

Lexington says, "If you think sex is simple and easy like it seems in the movies, it is not. It can hurt like hell. It is messy. It takes a greatly skilled effort of a man to satisfy a woman. He has to work her mind, emotions, and body to induce pleasure. Making love is an all-day, everyday event that starts in the mind. It starts with the little things: the communication, the touches, the kisses, the doing nice things for each other."

Anniston says, "So, that's why you and Daddy are always all over each other."

Lexington says, "When the mind and emotions are involved, the body is more likely to get involved. You, Anniston, have to know Anniston's body and what it likes, needs, wants. You can't leave it to a man to figure out how to please you. If you don't advocate for yourself, your needs will go unattended.

"It's exhausting trying to please a man. You must stroke his ego and reaffirm him constantly. And you can't be afraid to ask for what you want and how you want it because a man will ask for what he wants. Touch this, move this, grab this, say this, move here, hold this, do this, put that right here, arch your back, lift up, open up, relax, scoot back, don't move, come here, take it, let it out, let your hair down, put your hair up.

"Men need to be intrigued visually and verbally. You have to have desire in your eyes and pleasure on your face. That can be hard when you're tired from working all day or just had a baby. They need to hear that you are enjoying them. Every time you're with the man you love, you have to perform with a high level of energy and intensity.

"Both participants have to be vested in his/her partner and pay attention to what their partner's body responds to. You have to listen and watch to see what brings pleasure to the other person."

Anniston says, "I guess it's way more complicated than I thought."

Lexington says, "It's very complicated. Think about it: you invest a ton of time and energy into a man, and the relationship doesn't work. He cheats, lies, leaves, or one day you realize he is not the person you want.

"Being with the wrong man can mess your whole life up: your money, mind, and body can be damaged. When you meet someone, you have to question their motives. Some men will be honest, but others won't. You have to look out for your best interest. Dating is like playing chess: you have to be several steps ahead of your opponent."

Anniston says, "I need to learn to play chess."

Lexington says, "Your dad is a great chess player, he beats me every time we play."

Anniston says, "Mommy, how do you know if he's the wrong man?"

Lexington said, "There are signs: he's unavailable, doesn't keep his word, too hard to read, inconsistent or sporadic, very needy, or he drains all your energy."

Anniston asks, "Why is dating so difficult?"

Lexington says, "Because everyone is looking to get what they want. That selfishness can drive someone to hurt another person."

Anniston says, "Give me an example."

Lexington says, "Well, Kendra was dating this guy, Rodney, who was perfect on paper. He was smart, had a great career, and physically perfect. The boy was fine. He hung out with us a couple times. I thought he was so cool, and the relationship was going well until Rodney told Kendra he was married with children. Kendra would've never slept with a married man. He took her choice away to get what he wanted."

Anniston says, "What did Aunt Kendra do?"

Lexington says, "There was nothing she could do. She left and never saw him again."

Anniston says, "Aunt Kendra just left?"

Lexington asked, "What do you think she should've done?"

Anniston says, "Hit him! Yell at him! Break something!"

Lexington says, "Anniston, never worry about getting revenge; it's not your duty. God has a way of serving justice, and trust he'll do a better job than you."

Anniston says, "I feel so bad for Aunt Kendra. She didn't deserve that."

Lexington says, "Tell me about it! That's why you have to be careful. You never know someone's true intentions. Predators can be cold and purposely vengeful. It's like they get even more pleasure from humiliating the woman, especially when she's beautiful and innocent like Kendra.

"Rodney's deceit didn't change Kendra. Kendra held on to her faith. Like a child waiting on Santa Claus, Kendra believed her one true love was coming soon. She was true to her faith, and as always, God provided for Kendra."

Anniston asks, "Is that when she met Uncle Bishop?"

Lexington says, "Yes! I love them together."

Anniston says, "Me too! They are so cute together."

Lexington says, "Everything about Bishop is perfect for Kendra."

Anniston asks, "What if you know he's no good, but you like him?"

Lexington answers, "There three things you cannot waste on the wrong man: your time, your money, and your body."

Anniston asks, "Not even if it's just for fun?"

Lexington answers, "As long as you can handle it. You can't confuse sex with love. Men like Rodney come with a lot of sex and fun, but that's not enough if your desire is love. Bishop was the love Kendra desired."

Chapter Two: Kendra

Invalidation

Kendra, full of desire, knocked on Rodney's door. Rodney opened the door and pulled Kendra into his apartment. He closed the door and pulled Kendra close to him. He leaned his forehead against hers. She wrapped her arms around his neck. He wrapped his arms around her back. Rodney relaxed, closed his eyes, and breathed her scent. He smelled the coconut and vanilla oils in her hair, her perfume, and strawberry-melon-kiwi lotion.

Rodney looked at her in a way that let her know just what he was thinking. She was thinking the same thing. Rodney began to caress her body as they kissed. Rodney got closer to her. Their bodies collided as they kissed.

Their kisses were full of passion. She felt so much desire that a fish could swim through her panties. He carried her over to the table. He snatched off her boots and threw them on the floor. He took off her jacket and shirt; he flung them on the floor.

Rodney reached for one of the burning low-temperature candles sitting on the table. He slowly dripped small specks of wax on Kendra's chest and abdomen. The heat turned Kendra on even more. Kendra tenderly exhaled as the trickles of hot wax slightly burned her skin.

He grabbed a chilled bottle of champagne and popped the cork. He poured champagne over her chest and abdomen. The stinging followed by the chill titillated her senses. He licked the champagne from her chest and abdomen before he sipped the champagne from her navel.

He dripped more hot wax on her then poured more champagne on her. The warm then cooling sensation made Kendra's nipples hard. He kissed from her lips to her neck. He continued kissing down her chest to her stomach as his hands caressed her breasts.

He gripped her thighs as he kissed her through her tights. Rodney didn't have time to take her tights off; he ripped a hole in the crotch like the hulk rips off his shirt. He pushed her black lace panties to the side, poured champagne on her, and sucked her.

He pulled himself over his pants and pulled a Trojan Magnum XL condom in a golden wrapper from his pocket. He put the condom on as he kissed her second set of lips. He was ready to dive knee-deep into Kendra's love. He wrapped her legs around his waist. Kendra's thick sticky icky clang to the condom like cheese clinging to pasta. He tore into Kendra like Cookie Monster tears into a bag of cookies. He beat the atrium of Kendra's womanhood like a drummer at the peak of his solo. The sound of their bodies colliding against the table sounded like airplane turbulence.

He picked Kendra up with her legs over his arms; it was like she was in a swing. He pulled Kendra back and forth onto him while her arms were wrapped around his neck. They stared into each other's eyes as excitement shot up their bodies. He had total control of Kendra. She had no choice but to relax and let the sex flow.

As Rodney walked toward the bedroom, the back and forth turned into up and down. He felt so good that he had to stop walking. He held her against the wall to take a moment to feel her. Rodney and Kendra moaned as Rodney felt every bit of her surrounding him.

When they entered the bedroom, he undressed her before hurriedly undressing himself. Smack! Slap! Clap! The sound of his body hitting against her body. Boom! Boom! Boom! The sound of the bed colliding against the wall and floor. Kendra was so wet that Rodney swam through her like a hungry shark hunting for food through the ocean. Kendra's brain experienced a high equivalent to a hit of heroin.

Kendra turned around to face Rodney. She put the tip of him in her mouth while holding him with both hands. She moved her head up and down with her lips around him. All lips and mouth no teeth, Kendra sucked her own juices off the condom. Rodney enjoyed the overwhelming sensation of Kendra's tongue and lips engulfing his manhood.

Kendra pulled Rodney to the bed and straddled Rodney's lap. She eased down onto him as she bit her lip. With her hands on his chest, Kendra moved her body back and forth, up and down. As Rodney inched closer to the edge of fulfillment, he had to take control.

When he was done, Kendra laid her head on Rodney's chest and cuddled in Rodney's arms. Kendra curiously asked, "What's up with us?" Rodney paused. His face changed from pleasure to concern. He lifted her from his lap and sat her on the bed. He hopped up putting on his shorts.

He said: "I thought you knew I have a wife and kids, so there is no us."

Kendra was shocked. She quickly hopped up to put on her clothes. She exited the room. Rodney followed. She said, "Of course, I didn't know you are married. You never mentioned a wife."

He interrupted, "I figured you knew."

Kendra gathered her clothes as she walked toward the door. "Well, I guess it's time for you to leave," Rodney said. Kendra didn't even look at him before she walked out of the door. Rodney stood at the closed door, laughing. He said, "She was mad!" He ran to take a shower.

(Present Day) Lexington says to Anniston, "After the thing with Rodney, Kendra did the work to pull herself together. She didn't date or look to date. She focused on improving herself inside and out. She worked out at the gym and worked within by praying and fasting."

Introduction

Kendra stopped at a coffee shop after work. She read a report as she sipped her coffee. A firefighter approached her table. He said, holding a cup of coffee, "It must be important." Kendra looked at him. He clarified, "What you're reading must be important."

Struck by his handsome face, muscular body, brown skin, and tall stature, Kendra smiled, and said, "It is important for work."

He asked, "Am I disturbing you?"

She said, "No, not at all!"

Kendra told him to sit down. He asked, "Are you expecting anyone to join you?" She said no. He reached out his hand and said, "I'm Bishop Lawrence."

Kendra took his hand and said, "I'm Kendra Caine."

Bishop said, "It's a pleasure to meet you."

Kendra said, "Same here!" Kendra asked, "Is Bishop a title or a name?"

He answered, "Now, it's a name, but maybe one day, it will be a title."

"It's a nice name," she said.

"Thank you," he replied.

"Ms. Kendra, what do you do for work?"

Bishop asked. Kendra said, "I'm an architect."

Bishop said, "You like what you do?"

Kendra said, "I love it! What about you, do you love what you do?"

Bishop said, "Actually, I do, probably too much."

A little voice in Kendra's mind said: that explains why you are so physically fit, but she said, "Going out every day knowingly risking your life to save others is a noble and honorable profession, and I bet you are great at it."

Bishop checking his watch, says, "Thank You! Ms. Caine, I wish I could stay, but I have to get to work. If you're not seeing someone, I would love to talk to you again."

She said, "I'm not seeing anyone," as she handed him a card.

He said, "I'll call you." He reached out his hand. She took his hand. This time when their hands met, she felt the warmth of the sun and the softness of the clouds.

She said, "It was nice meeting you."

He said, "The pleasure was all mine."

That night, he called from the station. The conversation put a huge smile on her face. They talked until Bishop heard the alarm. He said, "I have to go save the day!" She told him to be safe.

The next morning, Bishop called before she left out for work just to wish her a good day and to tell her that he would call her again after work. Kendra told him to rest well, and she looked forward to his call.

It was something about him that she liked. He was handsome, but he seemed sincere. His approach was gentle, but full of strength. He was kind, but he was confident. His physical and social charms were intriguing. Kendra prayed to ask God if pursuing Bishop was a wise choice. She asked God to guide and protect her from any ill-intentions.

Bishop and Kendra agreed to meet for lunch on the third day of their acquaintance. When Kendra walked into the restaurant, she saw Bishop sitting at the table. Their eyes met, and they both were immediately captivated. Bishop was taken by the way Kendra's thick, long hair moved with each step she took and the way her brown skin absorbed the sunlight. Kendra loved the way he looked at her.

In Bishop's mind, she moved in slow motion. Bishop was so captivated by her appearance that everyone in the restaurant disappeared. Bishop stood up to watch Kendra walk to him. Kendra looked at Bishop, looking at her. Bishop smiled at her. At that moment, heaven came to earth.

When Kendra reached the table, they greeted each other with a handshake, Bishop said, "How are you?"

Kendra said, "I'm well and yourself?"

Bishop said, "I'm well! I'm glad you came."

Kendra said, "I'm glad you invited me." Bishop pulled out her chair as a gentleman should. He helped her sit and pushed her chair closer to the table. She thanked him. He winked at her. When he sat down, they looked at each other and smiled. He tried to conceal his shyness and nervousness, but Kendra saw it and was attracted to him even more.

Bishop said, "I know your free time is limited, so I'm honored you're sharing it with me."

Kendra said, "You're worthy, so it's worth it."

"I'm worthy," Bishop jokingly asked, smiling.

"I think so," Kendra said with a smile.

He said, "You have a beautiful smile," which made Kendra shy and smile even more.

Kendra said, "Your smile should be the topic of conversation."

Bishop said, "So, I have at least one thing working in my favor." Kendra winked at him.

Bishop asked, "So how does a woman as beautiful and successful as you manage to stay single?"

Kendra answered, "I don't know." She giggled and continued, "I'm currently working to figure that out myself."

Bishop said, "I can see your light, kindness, intellect, goodness. Those character traits shine so brightly from within you. I can only imagine that God has kept you for me. I can't think of any other reason."

Kendra smiled and said, "That's really sweet, thank you!"

Bishop said, "So, I'm just going to put my story out there. I lost my wife five years ago. We met in the tenth grade and married in college. She was a teacher. She taught high school English. I majored in business, but after college I felt the call to be a firefighter. We had a perfect life together. When that drunk driver killed her, my entire world came crashing down. I hadn't prepared for our life together to end so quickly.

"It's been a long road to get to this point where things have settled down. I have two boys. Christian is fourteen; Bradley is ten; and 1 girl, Chase, who is six. They're the fuel that keeps me going. Chase has been my biggest challenge. Trying to raise a baby girl without her mother is a daunting task. My wife's family helps me a lot. Honestly, I wouldn't have made it without them. My parents are deceased, so I really don't have a support system.

"I was faithful to my wife every day of her life from the day we met in high school. I have never dated another woman. I never thought about dating another woman until I saw you. I said to myself, she looks like an angel, and I could really use an angel in my life. When I approached you, you seemed so calm and warm. Calm is something I really want. It is something to watch little boys grieve their mother and care for their baby sister.

"You were sitting there, and I had to meet you. I was so nervous. Something about you gave me the courage to approach you. It was like we were opposite ends of magnets; a force of nature pulled me to you. (Kendra smiled.) And here I am, still extremely nervous and very rusty at this dating thing. I probably sound lame, pouring my heart out five minutes into our first date."

Kendra said, "My deepest condolences. That's the most touching, inspiring story I've ever heard. You and your children have an incredible amount of courage and strength. I can't imagine what it takes to survive something of that magnitude. And for the record, you do not sound lame. I thought what you said was flattering." As Bishop told his story, Kendra's heart opened to him.

He asked Kendra what inspired her career path. She told him all about her dad and how she wanted to do everything he did. She said, "My father takes pride in everything he builds. I take pride in everything I design. We work hard, and our reputation is our biggest asset." Bishop congratulated her success. She asked Bishop what caused the shift from business to firefighting. He told her he felt a sense of purpose and service as a firefighter.

After lunch, Bishop took Kendra to his church. She observed him lead the weekly bible study class. She was impressed by his knowledge of the Word of God. His faith was something Kendra hadn't experienced in any other person. As she watched him teach, she truly saw Bishop's goodness. She has never met a man who was so honest, pure, and decent. She liked him already.

(Present Day) Lexington says, "Kendra and Bishop have such a cute love story. He is really a man of faith. He made sure their love story was decent and in order."

Anniston asks, "What did he do?"

Lexington says, "They waited until they were married. That's the proper order: love, marriage then sex."

Anniston asked, "Did you and daddy do things in order?"

Lexington answered, "Your father tried, but I needed him."

Anniston asks, "Mommy, are you serious, you needed to, you know?"

Lexington says, "Desire!"

Anniston asks, "Desire?"

Lexington answers, "It can be hard to deny desire. The first four months, when I would visit him, I slept in the guest room. One night, desire wouldn't let me sleep. I was in love with him. I was attracted to him. I wanted him to touch me.

"Humans are made to procreate, so a woman's body naturally goes through a cycle to encourage procreation. After you experience pleasure, your body wants more of that pleasure, especially when you haven't experienced that pleasure for some time. The feeling of sex can be as addictive as a drug. That night all of those factors were working against me."

Anniston asks, "Mommy, you couldn't fight it?"

Lexington says, "I couldn't!"

Anniston says, "How did Aunt Kendra control her desire?"

Lexington says, "Bishop was the key to her success. Bishop had self-control. His self-control helped her have self-control."

Anniston says, "Daddy's self-control couldn't stop you?"

Lexington says, "He couldn't say no to me."

Seduction

After four months of dating, Kendra thought it was time to make a move on Bishop. She thought Lexington and Michael waited four months, and all is well. Kendra was sure that sex would secure their relationship. Kendra planned every word she'd say, every move she'd make, and the clothes she'd wear. Kendra fantasized about being with Bishop over and over again since their first date. She planned to live out each and every one of her fantasies, tonight.

Kendra and Bishop went out for dinner after work four months to the date of their first date. Bishop had been a perfect gentleman, but she was hoping she could bring out his inner warrior. When Bishop walked her to the door, Kendra invited him in to catch the game. Bishop said, "My kind of girl!" Bishop sat on the couch. Kendra turned on the TV and handed Bishop the remote. Bishop said, "Thanks."

Bishop became totally preoccupied by the game. She sat close enough to feel his energy, but not close enough to alert Bishop that she was up to something. Kendra watched the game for a little while before excusing herself. Kendra went into her bedroom and slipped into white lace lingerie and a white silk robe. She fixed her hair, refreshed her make-up, and confidently strutted back to Bishop in heels. Kendra stood next to the couch and called his name. When he looked up, she dropped the robe.

Bishop was so caught off guard, he nearly choked on the lemonade he was drinking. His bottom lip dropped to his chest. His eyes widened. He was speechless. Kendra said, "Bishop, come kiss me." Regaining his senses, Bishop managed to sit the glass of lemonade on the table. He got up and walked over to her.

Their desired filled eyes were locked on each other. Kendra tried to kiss him, but Bishop bent down to pick up the robe. He took one last look, he said, "Damn!" Bishop didn't normally use profanity, but Kendra's beautiful body hit a nerve. Bishop wrapped the robe around her as he said, "You're beautiful, absolutely beautiful! I am flattered, tempted, but I'm saving myself for marriage." Kendra was shocked that he turned her down.

Kendra said, "I'm so embarrassed!"

Bishop said, "Don't be embarrassed. I would love to live in my flesh, but…" he took one last look at her and continued, "I have to stay true to my faith." He hugged her and said, "You're a good girl, and you deserve more than a man trying to fulfill his flesh. The man who taught you this was the way to build a relationship was wrong. On his behalf, I apologize." Kendra collapsed in his arms, crying.

Kendra exhaled and let her weight fall onto Bishop's chest. Bishop continued, "God didn't make you this beautiful and perfect from your silky, glistening brown skin to your pure, caring heart to your big, intuitive brain to your glowing, creative spirit to spend your life capturing a man's emission in vain. He made you to love and be loved by a man that sees all of your beauty, cherishes you, and appreciates you." He sat Kendra down; he said, "Let me pray for you."

Invocation

Bishop prayed: "God, I pray Kendra's heart is healed and filled with love, joy, courage, and strength to endure a long life. Give her heart peace and clarity to reconcile the past and endure the future. Open her eyes to see her truth, her own beauty, and purpose in her journey. Make her eyes attentive to your work in and around her. Let your words ring loud and clear in her ears, even when it is quiet and still.

"God, give her the capability and capacity to do the work of your desire. Give her patience to use sweet words, kind words, godly words of love and wisdom. God, I pray her feet will support and sustain her as she walks and not faint and as she travels and not tire. I pray she has the strength to carry the blessings and burdens without wear and tear on her body.

"I ask you to rebuild and restructure her mind to get rid of old ways of thinking. God, I pray you will renew her spirit. Make her spirit as innocent and free as it was when she was a child. In Jesus' name, I pray, Amen!

As he prayed and held her tightly, Kendra wept from her soul. He wiped Kendra's tears and kissed her forehead, he says, "You're okay, God has you!" She held onto Bishop as if she was holding on for dear life. Bishop looked in her eyes and said with a remorseful tone, "I'm so sorry, some man hurt you." He hugged her before he jokingly said, "Now, go put on some clothes before the devil comes up in here, and we have to repent." Kendra laughed.

Bishop watched her walk away. He whispered, "Jesus be with me! That girl is gorgeous, and she doesn't even know it. God give me strength." Bishop went back to watching the game. Kendra returned dressed in jeans and a T-shirt, without make-up and her hair in a ponytail. When she sat on the couch, Bishop looked at her and said, "Your natural beauty is breathtaking."

He looked into her eyes, and said, "Either men have been blinded by your beauty, or you've only shown your beauty to blind men. It's a shame either way. Beauty like yours is a gift from God that should be admired."

Kendra smiled, "You're a good man," she said. She asked him, "How do you stay so faithful after all you've been through?"

Bishop said, "We were never promised a comfortable life. Trials will come. God uses trials to mold us into what he wants us to be. We're supposed to come through stronger, better, more beautiful, and more prepared to fulfill our purpose. I've learned that only God gets you through the things that should've killed you or made you crazy. I believe every event has a purpose, even if I don't understand. I praise Him in good and bad times, and he gets me through both."

Kendra said, "Wow, that's really inspiring!"

Bishop asked, "Did that make sense?"

Kendra answered, "It made complete sense. Thanks for sharing."

Bishop said, "Kendra, (She said yes.) I really do like you, so don't misread that situation. (She smiled.) I just want us to do things rights."

Kendra said, "I really like you, too."

He asked, "So we're still cool, right."

Kendra said, "Absolutely."

Bishop said, "Kendra!"

"Yes, Bishop," she answered.

Bishop said, "It took every fiber of my strength to resist. I want you more than the air I breathe. When I get to have you, I want us to lay together on a foundation of love, trust, commitment, and understanding. I want you to know me, and I know you. I want something lasting with you. I think it will work if we take our time."

Kendra listened overjoyed with his words; she said, "I want that too! I am so honored you want that with me. I support your commitment to God. I know you're right. We should wait."

Bishop asked, "Are you cool with taking this relationship one step at a time?"

Kendra said, "I am!"

Bishop asked, "So I can officially call you, my girlfriend?"

Kendra said, "I'd love that!"

Bishop said, "Can I tell you something as my girlfriend?"

Kendra said, "Yes!"

Bishop said, "You looked amazing. I am so blessed that I can call you, my girlfriend. I'm asking myself how I did that!"

Kendra said, "Bishop, you are fire from head to toe. Everything about you amazes me."

Bishop said, "You're so sweet, Kendra."

Kendra replied, "As are you!" That night, they slept fully clothed on Kendra's bed in each other's arms.

Realization

Kendra invited Bishop over for dinner. She cooked, set the table with her grandmother's crystal, and lit candles. Kendra prepared her words and filled her heart with courage. When he knocked on the door, she took a deep breath. She opened the door, they smiled and embraced.

Bishop said, "You look beautiful!"

Kendra said, "Thank You! You are so very handsome yourself."

Bishop said, "Thank You!"

Kendra led him to the table. Bishop said, "It smells good in here. Did you cook everything?"

Kendra said, "Yes, and I hope you like it."

Bishop said, "I am impressed. It looks like you know what you're doing."

Kendra said, "My grandmother taught my sister and me how to cook. It wasn't optional. She believed a woman should know how to keep her household running. She taught us how to sew, garden, hair care, and all about God. She made us read the bible with her. We never missed Sunday service. She always said: Prayer was a woman's duty."

Bishop washed his hands. He said, "She sounds like an inspirational, wise woman."

Kendra paused and said, "Saying that just now made me realize how far I had strayed away from what I knew to be true."

Bishop replies, "It happens to so many people, but it glorifies God each time a lost soul finds its way back to God."

Kendra said, "You think so?"

Bishop said, "You should consider that everything that has happened was all in his plan for you. The victory is in you finding your way back to him."

Kendra put the food on the table. She sat across from Bishop; she said, "I have to tell you something. I've been reading, and I've come to understand that confession is necessary for forgiveness and redemption. I want you to know me, so you understand me. I grew up in church, and I was a good girl who did everything right. My intention was to do life right, but fate wouldn't have it work out that way.

"I lost my virginity in a rape in college, and I never told anyone. I went on with my life with my boyfriend, who became my fiancé. When he cheated on me while we were planning the wedding, I lost something, maybe a piece of my mind or my peace. I don't know what it was, I just know I wasn't the same. The fiancé and I met at church when we were children. We started dating in high school.

"I think he only asked me to marry him because people thought we should get married, not because he loved me and wanted to be with me. Cheating was his way out. I was the bad guy who ended it, but he was really the one who wanted the relationship to be over. I was so embarrassed. I couldn't go back to church. I had to pick myself up, dust the fragments of him off, and move on with life. But not life like before the rape and betrayal, life in survivor's mode.

"Two years later, I was engaged again, and it didn't work. Truthfully, we really didn't love each other. We both desperately wanted a connection. Before we could start planning the wedding, he told me he was in love with someone else.

"Before I met you, I dated this wonderful guy for almost six months. He was kind and charming until he coldly told me he had a wife and kids. Honestly, I never learned what love is or how it feels. I learned men like sex. Men like sex with me, but I don't know that men like me.

"The night I tried to be with you, I thought the emotions I felt for you meant it was time to have sex. My experiences had me so confused, but I want to thank you for helping me find my way back. Your decency taught me that there's still good, caring humans. I was vulnerable, and you didn't take advantage of me. Bishop, thank you!"

He walked over to her and said, "I'm glad you feel comfortable enough to trust me with your story." He wrapped his arms around her. Bishop said, "Rape! You were raped, and you never dealt with it. I want you to take a deep breath. Relax in my arms and breathe. That's a very heavy burden, and you've carried it around by yourself for so long. I'm here now. You'll never have to deal with anything alone ever again."

Kendra said, "I appreciate that."

Bishop said, "A real man has you now, and I'm not letting go."

Kendra said, "That makes my whole life better."

He kissed her forehead then her lips; he said, "I'm your resting place, Kendra. You can lay your burdens and baggage down. You don't have to carry them any further. Those failed relationships were a course. I will teach you all about love." With tears flowing from her eyes, Kendra kissed him.

Confirmation

At their annual Halloween get together, the girls talked as they carved pumpkins. Kendra decided to tell her secret, she said, "In my Toni Braxton voice, I got a boyfriend. We've been dating for six months. He's a widower, a fireman, and an assistant pastor. He has three adorable children. He's a good person. He's good to me. I like where we are and what we're doing."

Akera said, "When did we start keeping secrets?"

Kendra said, "I took a page out of Lexington's book. I waited for the commitment to be there before I spoke on it."

Lexington said, "I'm happy for you, Kendra."

She replied, "Thanks, Lexi."

Akera said, "Now, really tell us about him."

Kendra said, "It's not like that. He doesn't believe in relations outside of marriage."

Destiny said, "That's what I'm talking about, a man of faith."

Kareen said, "I like him already."

Lexington said, "Me too."

Akera said, "Six months and he hasn't touched it, smelled it, tasted it?" Kendra shook her head no.

Lexington said, "Akera, relationships are more than sex."

Akera said, "But it's a big part of it. You can't agree to spend your life with someone without knowing how it's hitting."

Lexington said, "Waiting is the right thing to do, and you can teach him to please you."

Destiny said, "Love can conquer all obstacles."

Akera asked, "So, if Michael wasn't knocking that shit all the way back, would you still have married him?"

Lexington said, "Why do you make everything about me?"

Akera said, "Because you're my big sister. You are how I relate to the world. I look up to you, so everything is about you."

Lexington said, "Cute! Stop!"

Akera said, "No, I can't stop. Ms. Raymond couldn't make me cum. You didn't marry Raymond, and he loved you so much."

Lexington said, "You always come for me. No matter what we are talking about, you throw shit at me. Kendra clearly likes this guy, and the body will follow the mind. Besides, I married Michael because he loves all of me and I love all of him."

Destiny said, "Amen to that!" Lexington and Destiny high five.

Akera said, "Who wants to spend the rest of their life bored in their bedroom? No one."

Lexington said, "You need more than good sex to make a marriage work. You can be incredible, and things can fall apart."

Destiny said, "That's true!"

Vanessa said, "I can attest to that."

Kendra said, "I know that won't be a problem. I can see through those sweats when he goes to work out. It's not little, and I highly doubt I will be bored with all that!"

Destiny said, "Love my man in workout gear. Those damn basketball shorts get to me every time."

Akera said, "They make you want to trip and fall on his dick. Like oops, I've fallen, and I can't get up!"

Akera said, "So how long has it been since his wife died?"

Kendra answered, "Five years."

Akera said, "There's no way possible he hasn't had sex in five years."

Kendra said, "He hasn't even dated since her death."

Kareen said, "Sister, that's really deep and sweet. A tragedy led him to save himself for you."

Destiny said, "That's a man that will be faithful. If he can hold true to his values like that, you can trust him. Kendra, this is it for you."

Akera said, "Girl, he is going to go caveman, ape shit, savage on your ass when he does get it. You're going to call me after the wedding night saying he broke it. You're going to come home from your honeymoon with your pussy in a sling."

Lexington said, "Girl, start your yoga classes now; it will help your situation handle that sexuation."

Destiny said, "We are about to play the next game: Bobbing for Apples, but it's not really apples; it's vibrators. Lexi, you're going to have to sit this one out. It's alcohol in the tubs.

Akera said, "She can't suck dick, anyway!"

Vanessa said, "Babe, you can be so vulgar!"

Destiny says, "Akera, you have to stop picking on Lexington; she's happily married now. Besides, every time I see Michael, he has a huge smile on his face, so Lexi is doing something."

Lexington said, "He got that good, and I know what to do with it!"

Akera said, "I almost bought that shit. Project it like you mean it. From your pussy to your chest, Sis, say that shit."

Lexington laughed and said, "You know I hate you, right!"

Akera said, "I can't buy it if you don't sell it."

Destiny said, "Lexi, say it in Oprah's voice."

Lexington seductively said in a sultry, low voice, "What keeps my man satisfied is I am a lady in the streets, and I am exactly what he needs between the sheets."

Destiny said, "There you go, Lexi!"

Kendra said, "Nailed it!"

Vanessa said, "Akera, I think she sold it. I mean, I'll buy it."

(Present Day) Anniston says, "Uncle Bishop was her knight in shining armor. Mommy, why would someone mistreat Aunt Kendra when she's so sweet?"

Lexington says, "Because they can!"

Anniston says, "She sowed in tears, reaped in love, and all she had to pay was patience."

Lexington says, "Baby Girl, you are so right. I'm blessed to have a daughter full of wisdom."

Anniston asks, "Do you ever regret not waiting to be with dad?"

"Any decision I made regarding Michael, I will make a million more times and still have no regrets," Lexington answers.

Anniston says, "I hope I can say the same thing twenty-one years into my marriage."

"I pray you and your husband will have a love story like Kendra and Bishop's love story. Man, I missed the proposal. I hate that I missed Kendra's big moment," Lexington said.

Confederation

Eighteen months after Bishop and Kendra met, Bishop invited Kareen, Amir, Destiny, John, Akera, Vanessa, and Kendra's parents to his pastor's twentieth anniversary celebration. Kendra knew how important it was to Bishop that everything was perfect, so she worked tirelessly and vigilantly to ensure everything went the way Bishop wanted.

Bishop and Kendra stood at the altar before the ceremony holding hands, lovingly looking at each other. Bishop said, "I appreciate you and all you've done to help me pull this off."

Kendra said, "You're welcome."

Bishop said, "Did I tell you how beautiful you look today?"

Kendra said, "I don't think you did!"

He said, "Remind me to tell you later."

Kendra laughed; she said, "Sure!"

Bishop kissed her forehead; he asked, "Are you ready?"

She answered, "Let's do this."

At the end of the celebration, everyone congregated in the dining hall for dinner. As everyone ate, Kendra noticed Bishop and his kids were missing, but she figured they needed a family moment, and she carried on talking and enjoying the meal with her family and friends.

Bishop walked into the dining hall with his daughter in his arms. Chase held a dozen red roses and a letter she wrote to Mr. and Mrs. Caine. Bishop and Chase were followed by his sons holding two ring boxes. Bishop and his kids approached Kendra's parents.

Bishop put Chase down then handed her the mic. She began to read her letter: "Dear Mr. and Mrs. Caine, My name is Chase. Bishop Lawrence is my daddy. He and I love Kendra and enjoy being with her. We play games and watch movies together. She helps me with my homework, she reads stories to me, and gives me big hugs when she drops me off at school. My big brothers love Kendra, too. She takes me to their games, and she packs the best snacks.

"When she makes my lunch, she gives me all my favorite things to eat. She makes delicious spaghetti and macaroni and cheese. I really love her, and I love that she makes my daddy happy. If you allow us to ask for your baby daughter's hand in marriage, I promise we will be kind to her. We will respect her and love her. My brothers and I will be good and have good manners. Thank You, Love Chase."

Chase ran to hug Kendra and gave her the flowers. Christian and Bradley walked over to Kendra. They opened the boxes and got down on a bended knee. Bishop walked over to Mr. Caine, and said, "I know it is not the situation you desired for your daughter: a man with three kids. I understand you may be skeptical of all the responsibility your daughter would be taking on by marrying a family.

"I cannot promise life will be easy with us, but I can guarantee that your daughter will be loved, honored, appreciated, protected, respected, covered in prayer, and I will provide for her. Mr. Caine, I humbly ask for your blessing to ask for your daughter's hand in marriage."

Mr. Caine stood up and shook Bishop's hands; he said, "A man, a father, could not ask for more. All I want is for my girls to be happy, and you make her happy. I am very confident that you will hold true to your word. I happily give you, my blessing. Welcome to the family, Son."

Bishop and Mr. and Mrs. Caine hugged. Chase clapped and hugged Mr. and Mrs. Caine again. Bishop walked over to Kendra. He held her hand and he got down on one knee between his sons. Chase jumped into Kendra's lap. Kendra wrapped her arms around Chase. Chase wiped her tears; Chase asked Kendra if she was sad because she was crying. Kendra told Chase the tears were tears of joy.

Bishop said, "Kendra, my sons and I have discussed life and our future, and as a unit we decided we want you in both. You have been a breath of fresh air for us. We cannot promise you a life of luxury, but I promise you joy, love, dedication, appreciation, and sincerity. I promise you as long as my body is able, I will work to provide for you. I promise to keep you covered in prayer, appreciate you, love you, put forth an effort to fulfill your heart's desires. I promise I will be faithful, and you will never question or doubt my love. Kendra, it will make us happy if you would be my wife."

Kendra hugged Bishop and said, "Yes."

Bishop explained, "We have two rings, one is from me, and the other one is from the boys." Bishop slid his ring on her ring finger. The boys slipped their ring on her index finger. Kendra hugged Christian and Bradley. She thanked them for putting so much thought into the proposal. Kendra's friends and family happily joined in the hug and welcomed Bishop to the family.

Consummation

After their beautiful wedding ceremony and reception, Kendra and Bishop flew to Hawaii for their honeymoon. As they walked along the beach enjoying the night sky over the water, Kendra held her husband's arm and admired the beauty of the beach. The sight of his wife in her bikini and sarong filled him with desire. Bishop led his wife back to their room.

Bishop picked her up and said, "I am so glad you are my wife, and I get to spend my life loving you," as he carried her across the threshold of their honeymoon suite.

Kendra said, "It's so amazing to say you're my husband." She kissed his cheeks. He walked over to the bed and laid her down.

Bishop sat down to massage her feet; he said, "I have thought about this night since we met: making love to you as husband and wife. The time is finally here, and I want you more than you know."

Kendra straddled his lap and said, "Do you want the good, innocent wife, or do you want the sexy, naughty wife?"

Bishop caressed up and down her back, he kissed her, and said, "I'll take both, please."

Kendra laughed, she lovingly looked at her new husband, and she said, "You want both, huh?"

Bishop said, "Absolutely, give me half the night with one and the other half with the other. I don't care which order."

Kendra, staring in her husband's eyes and caressing his face, said, "I love you, and I love being married to you already."

Bishop removed her sarong to touch his wife's legs and thighs, he said, "I love you more, Kendra."

Kendra said, "Kendra is the good wife; call me Keke when you want the naughty wife."

Bishop kissed his wife and said, "Well, Keke!"

Kendra put her finger on his lips and said, "Ssshhh!"

Kendra pushed him, she said, "Mr. Lawrence lay back. Keke has this handled," grinding gently against Bishop as she kissed him while caressing his shoulders and chest. Bishop took off her bikini top. Bishop's hands took hold of her breasts as they kissed. Kendra pulled off his shirt to lick from the top of his abs to his shorts.

When her tongue reached his shorts, she put her hand in her husband's shorts and pulled him out. She stared in her husband's eyes as she slowly slid her lip down him while she circled the tip of him with her tongue.

Bishop inhaled as he watched his wife slowly move her hands and lips up and down him, he said, "I get to have all this for the rest of my life. I'm so thankful." Kendra pulled his shorts completely off, so she could rub his exposed thighs.

Kendra crawled off the bed to kneel on the floor. She pulled Bishop to the edge of the bed. Kendra kissed all over his manhood. She stared in his eyes as she squeezed him with rotating hands before pushing the tip of him to touch her tonsils. She moved her face side to side, rubbing the tip of him around the back of her mouth.

Bishop said, "Oh my God!" Bishop moved Kendra's hair and held it to the side. Kendra held the base of him with one hand and massaged him with the other hand. Kendra's head moved up and down as she sucked him. The slurping sound filled the room. Kendra slurped so hard she turned herself on. Bishop's mind exploded with the first orgasm of his new marriage. Bishop said, "Oh! Kendra, I love you," as Kendra slurped and swallowed Bishop's vitality.

Bishop laid back on the bed and Kendra got on top of him, she said, "Husband, call me Keke when we get nasty."

Bishop said, "Alright, Keke," as he sat up and regained his composure.

Kendra said, "Baby lay back and relax, let Keke do her thing. You don't have to do anything but enjoy the ride."

Bishop said, "Keke, I can definitely do that!" Bishop relaxed as he watched his wife take a ride on his escalator.

He put his hands behind his head and said, "Well, Keke, go for what you know!" Kendra slowly lowered onto him, making Bishop feel her inch by inch. Bishop felt a burst of enchantment as he entered his wife for the first time. The wet, warm, tight sensation shocked his nerves and overtook his entire being.

She rocked and rolled her hips as she completely surrounded him and stroked him in all directions. The swishing sound of her soaking wet, slippery flesh rubbing against him filled the room. Bishop said, "You feel so good, Baby!"

Kendra said, "You do too, Husband." Bishop's face said his mind was gone to a happy place.

He longed to feel more of the friction of him and her sliding against each other. He grabbed Kendra's thighs to control her movements. Kendra's moans inspired Bishop to love her harder. The sound of the bed escalated from a settle squeak to pounding.

Kendra said, "Yes, Baby! I like that! Bishop, Baby! Don't stop!" Bishop's bottom hung off the edge of the bed as he rapidly thrusted upward into his wife. Kendra said, "Baby! Yes! Just like that! Right there!" Sparks and tingles flooded Kendra's whole body.

Bishop said, "That's where you want it, Baby, that's where it'll stay."

Kendra said, "Thank you, Baby!"

Kendra's body began to shake as she saturated Bishop, she said, "Bishop, you got my whole body shaking."

Bishop said, "I want to make you feel good, Baby. Do you feel good, Baby?"

Kendra said, "Yes, Baby! I feel so good." The sound of their bodies smacking heightened the sensation they both felt. Bishop breathed heavily as Kendra felt butterflies in her stomach.

Her eyes lowered as they twitched and twinkled. Bishop stopped to watch his wife climax. Bishop said, "You're so beautiful when you feel that way. The faces and sounds you make are so sexy." Bishop sat up and wrapped his arms around Kendra. Kendra tightly held onto Bishop, and moaned out, "Ah! Baby!" Bishop enjoyed the feeling of his wife's excitement.

Bishop laid his wife on the bed. Kissing, touching, caressing her, Bishop was all over his wife. She watched her husband get acquainted with her body. He told her, "Mrs. Lawrence, you are so beautiful."

She said, "Thank you, Husband!" He kissed her belly button then licked down to the middle. Bishop's whole tongue swiped up and down Kendra.

Kendra touched Bishop's head and back as his tongue moved between her thighs. She controlled her breathing to intensify the sensation she felt. Kendra laid back, relaxed, cleared her mind as she existed in the pleasure her husband was giving her. Bishop licked and sucked Kendra as if he was searching for black gold between her thighs. Kendra breathed and moaned as her husband's tongue penetrated her deep enough to taste their future. From his point of view, life was going to be sweet.

Bishop pulled Kendra to the edge of the bed to wrap her left leg around his waist. He rubbed himself against Kendra before he slowly entered her. Bishop introduced himself to his wife, making a lasting impression. Bishop's stroke was spellbinding and delightful.

She cried out, "Oh my God! Baby! You're giving it all to me!"

Bishop said, "It's all yours! Take it all."

Kendra said, "I can take it, Husband."

Bishop said, "I'm going to enjoy giving it to you."

Kendra said, "Just like that!"

Bishop said, "You like that?"

She answered, "Yes, I love it!"

The back of Kendra's eyes and her forehead felt it first. Then, the tenderness moved to her toes. Kendra's body shook as a creamy satin covered Bishop. Bishop loved the way Kendra's love felt.

Bishop asked, "Are you enjoying yourself?"

Kendra said, "Yes! Baby!"

Bishop asked, "Is it everything you thought it would be?"

Kendra said, "It's more; it's so amazing!"

Bishop pulled Kendra to the side of the bed with her legs spread wide. He locked his hands around her back, pinning her between his body and the bed. With nothing blocking him, Bishop was able to reach every part of his wife. She wrapped her arms around his neck. Kendra inhaled and exhaled, holding each breath for a few seconds.

Kendra said, "I love you so much, Bishop!"

Bishop said, "I love you, too!"

Bishop felt his longing and loneliness melt away. Kendra gave him life back. Bishop picked up his wife and laid her in the bed. He caressed her exhausted body. He kissed her forehead and asked, "Are you ok?"

Kendra answered, "I'm extraordinary."

Bishop asked, "I wasn't too aggressive, was I?"

Kendra replied, "You were perfect!"

Bishop said, "You were too!"

Kendra said, "You put in work on the side of the bed."

Bishop responded, "I had seven years of pent-up energy to work off." Kendra and Bishop laughed.

Bishop said, "When I met you two years ago, I knew we would get married. Talking to you on our first date was like talking to an old friend. You made me so comfortable. Putting on my tux and preparing to walk down the aisle to become your husband, I thought to myself, I am so blessed to be given a second chance at real love. When I saw you walking toward me as I stood at the altar, I said to myself, Bishop, you have the most perfect bride. Laying here next to you, I know that my life with you will be great."

Kendra asked, "How do you know?"

Bishop said, "If I knew Keke got down like that, I would've married you on date two." They laughed. Bishop said, "Seriously, I know because you are everything I could ever ask for in a wife. I love you!"

Kendra pulled him on top of her and said, "Bishop, I love you, too!"

She slowly, passionately kissed him as she caressed his back. Bishop caressed her hips. Kendra said, "Mr. Lawrence, it's Kendra's turn to know her husband!"

Bishop asked, "What does Kendra like?"

Kendra answered, "Kendra likes it slow and sexy."

Bishop replies, "It is my duty to please my wife and give her what she wants."

Kendra said, "The pleasure will be mine!"

(Present Day) Anniston says, "That's the cutest proposal ever. Their relationship could be made into a movie."

"I was so happy for her when she called and told me what happened," Lexington says.

Anniston asks, "What happens if you wait, and you get the storybook proposal and wedding, you're happy in your marriage, and he doesn't keep his promise to love you and be faithful or somehow you're not happy?"

Lexington says, "It doesn't have to be the end. It may be a tunnel you have to go through to get to the other side. Couples have to renovate their marriage to make it work as they grow, and things change."

Anniston asks, "Would you stay?"

"I can't say I'd leave, especially if my husband was trying to work it out," Lexington answers.

Anniston asks, "You think a marriage can survive something so devastating?"

"I know it can," Lexington answers.

Lexington says, "Let me pay the bill, and I will tell you all about Destiny's revelation year in the car." As Lexington starts the car, she says, "Baby Girl, let's stop at the bakery."

Anniston says, "Yes, I'd love some cupcakes and a brownie."

As Lexington drives, she says, "You know how much Uncle John loves Aunt Destiny?"

Anniston says, "Yes!"

Lexington says, "One time, John stepped out of his marriage, and Destiny was devastated. John had never done anything like that before, but you know people get comfortable, curious, and it doesn't help that some women openly tempt and pursue married men. Melanie knew John was married. Melanie didn't personally know us, but she knew of us, and she knew Destiny and John were married. She didn't want John; she wanted to disrupt Destiny's household."

Anniston asks, "Why would a woman hurt another woman knowing how devastating cheating can be?"

Lexington answers, "A woman can desire to take your happiness not because she wants your man, but because she doesn't want you to have what's yours. They watch you and plot on you while they smile in your face. Baby girl, you have to watch women. Unfortunately, many women age but don't grow up. They live their entire lives with the maturity of a high school female."

Anniston says, "That's deep. The girls at school can be a bit much."

Lexington says, "It doesn't change in college, your career, at the club, or in church."

Anniston is shocked, she said, "Uncle John, though! They've been married like forever. He always so you know over Aunt Destiny. They have more public displays of affection than you and Dad."

Lexington says, "Thirty-two years of marriage and thirty-six years together, they have a reason to be all over each other. They have survived."

Chapter Three: Destiny

Tribulation

Destiny went to the check-in receptionist. Destiny told the receptionist that she and her husband checked in earlier, and she left her key in the room. She showed the receptionist her driver's license and a credit card with John's name on it. It had the same number as the card he used to check-in, so the receptionist gave her the key card with the room number on it.

Rage and anger rose in her chest as she approached the room. As quietly as she could, she put the key in the card reader and opened the door. The sound of sex filled the room. John was so distracted by the woman bent over before him that he didn't notice his wife creeping up behind him, holding the vase that was sitting next to the door.

She quietly swung the vase with all her might. She struck John with so much force that his naked body tumbled out of bed. John crashed into the wall and fell onto the floor between the bed and the wall. John laid unconscious with his socks and the condom still on. One side of the vase shattered into pieces, leaving the other side in Destiny's hand.

She flung the remaining piece of vase against the wall above the bed, making broken glass rain over a naked, cowering Melanie. Destiny told Melanie, "If you know what's good for you, you will get the fuck out of here, now." Melanie hopped up and quickly grabbed her clothes. As she ran toward the door, Destiny said, "Keep your fucking hands off my husband."

Destiny walked over to John. Destiny stomped him in the head and back, screaming: "John, you, nasty son of a bitch. I'm at home with your kids, doing your work, and you're here, fucking some bitch and on a school night. Get your ass up, John, and go wash that bitch off you."

John woke up and grabbed his head. She kicked him one last time, she yelled, "I hate you so much, right now!" She grabbed the lamp from the nightstand and hit him in the same spot where she hit him with the vase.

She found his keys in his pocket. She took the house keys off the keyring, threw his car key against the wall, and yelled, "Find your ass somewhere else to live. You are not welcomed in my house."

When Destiny got home, she frantically walked through the house, packing anything that belonged to John in garbage bags. Kendra tried to stop her and keep her quiet because the kids were sleep, but Destiny was a woman scorned. Destiny fussed as she packed the bags. Destiny threw the garbage bags full of John's belongings on the back lawn.

John frantically drove into the driveway, bleeding profusely from his head. He hopped out of the car and screamed for Destiny to come outside and come talk to him. From their bedroom window, she screamed, "Hell No! I have nothing to say to your nasty ass."

John begged Destiny to open the door and let him into the house. Destiny told him to go stay with your bitch or run back to your momma's house. She said, "Get your shit out of my backyard, and get the fuck away from my house." She closed her bedroom window.

Destiny fell into Kendra's arms, crying. The twins came running to see why their mother was crying, but John Jr. slept through the whole event. Kendra intercepted the twins and tucked the girls into their beds. She ensured them that their mother was okay.

Destiny ripped the sheets off the bed. Destiny said, "I don't want to see him; I don't even want to smell him." Destiny threw the sheets in the garbage.

With every trace of John packed in garbage bags, Destiny lamented her happy marriage on her bedroom floor. Kendra sat next to her and wrapped her arms around Destiny. Kendra held and rocked her as Destiny cried from her soul.

The next morning, Kendra got the kids up and cooked for them, she made their lunches and took them to school. Kendra offered Destiny breakfast, but Destiny couldn't eat. They talked about what happened in the hotel room, what she saw, and how she felt. Kendra tried to be supportive, but she was so tickled by the thought of Destiny stomping a naked John after she knocked him.

Kendra asked, trying to hold in her laugh, "You knocked him out?"

Destiny said, "I was mad." They laughed.

Kendra said, "So, old Johnny boy went nighty-night, huh?"

Destiny said, "You should have seen the way his feet dangled in the air."

Destiny and Kendra burst into laughter. Destiny said, "I wanted to beat the hell out of Melanie, but I didn't want to give her the satisfaction of knowing she bothered me."

(Present Day) Anniston says, "I can't believe Uncle John cheated on Aunt Destiny. She's so beautiful, and they are so googly-eyed and all over each other. You'd think she'd be the last person to get cheated on. Uncle John, though? Man, if he cheated, does any relationship stand a chance?"

Lexington answers, "Sometimes, good men make bad decisions."

"Has dad ever cheated on you," Anniston asks.

Lexington says, "I don't know. I don't want to know."

Anniston asks, "Do you think it's possible?"

Lexington says, "Anything is possible!"

Anniston asks, "Have you ever asked him?"

Lexington answers, "Never ask a man a question that you really don't want answered. He may tell the truth, and then what? If you leave, you lose your man. If you stay, you lose your power. Now, he knows what he can get away with.

"Honestly, I love my husband, and I don't want to leave. He's never given me any reason to doubt or distrust him. He comes home on time; he's always available; he doesn't hide anything, and I don't go looking."

Anniston asks, "If he did, and you found out, how do you think you would survive?"

"Probably, the same way Destiny and John did: prayer and time," Lexington answers.

Reconciliation

Destiny sat alone at the top of the bleachers watching the twins play in a soccer game. John walked up the bleachers and sat next to Destiny. He tapped her thigh with his knee to get her attention. When she looked, she saw her husband not the cheater who hurt her. It was obvious they missed each other.

He said, "What's up with you?"

She said, "The usual. How are you?"

John responded, "I'm Well!"

Destiny added, "And, Melanie?"

"I don't know," John answered.

"You don't know how your mistress is doing," she asked.

He said, "I don't have a mistress. Seriously, I haven't spoken to that girl."

She asked, "Is there someone else?"

In their time apart, Destiny had been dieting and exercising. She also changed her hair. As they talked, John noticed she looked slimmer and more radiant. John wanted his wife back.

John looked in her eyes and said, "Absolutely not! I've been alone every day, every night. Honest!" John touched the back of his head and said: "I think a brother learned a lesson."

Destiny said (touching the scar she left on his head), "Looks like that really hurt."

John replied, "It hurt like hell. I had to get twelve stitches."

Destiny said, "One for each year of our marriage."

John said, "God is great with symbolism. My flesh was broken and repaired by twelve stitches."

Destiny said, "I don't want to see you hurt."

John said, "Destiny, I never want to see you hurt. I know it's crazy to say that after what I did, but I never meant to hurt you. It kills me knowing I hurt you. We aren't supposed to be here: not speaking, and it's all on me. I broke us. I changed us from the us we've known all this time. I wasn't thinking about you. A husband not thinking of his wife is not good. I failed, not you. Destiny, I am so sorry. Forgive me. My behavior wasn't about you or anything you did or didn't do. It is all on me. You did not deserve any of this. All you ever did was love me. I took you for granted. I never imagined you would put me out. I never imagined a time in life when we wouldn't be together."

Destiny said, "Thank you for that! I needed to hear that. I mean it."

After spending the day as a family, John walked Destiny and the kids to the door. Destiny sent the children in the house. She and John stood, staring into each other's eyes. Sparks flew! He leaned in and kissed her. Destiny kissed him back. He tightly grabbed her hips and pulled her closer to him. She put her hands on his cheeks. John didn't want to leave, but Destiny pushed him away. As John walked to his car, Destiny blew a kiss. John caught it and put it on his cheek.

Absolution

John came over to watch the kids, so Destiny could go to a concert with her friends. When she came home, John was asleep on the couch with the kids. Destiny put the kids to bed and let John sleep on the couch. The next morning, Destiny took the kids to school. When she returned, John was making breakfast. It was nostalgic.

As Destiny moved around, she was quiet. John asked Destiny if she was okay. She said yes. He said, "You're distant."

Destiny said, "I'm lost in my thoughts, I guess."

John said, "Maybe, breakfast will put a smile on your face."

She smiled and said, "It smells so good. I think it will." She sat down at the kitchen table. John placed her plate in front of her then he sat across from her. John said grace to bless the food. As they ate, John stared at Destiny.

Destiny said, "These are so good. I've missed your pancakes."

John said, "I've missed making them for you." John asked, "What's on your mind?"

Destiny said, "My life and where it goes from here. The things I need to do to for the next leg of my journey."

John asked, "Any ideas?"

Destiny answered, "When the time is right, we'll talk about it."

He said, "Well, I wish you whatever your heart desires because you deserve it," as he grabbed her hand.

"Thank you," she said as she smiled at him.

He said, "I am here for any and everything you need."

She said, "Good to know!"

John makes small talk as they eat to gage her thinking. John asks about her parents and family. They talk about the kids and their upcoming activities.

After they ate, Destiny grabbed the dishes to wash them. As she made the dishwater, John was intrigued by the way she filled out her tight jeans. Destiny looked so good to him that he couldn't resist. He walked up behind her. He caressed her hips, and as he brushed himself against her.

He whispered, "Let me make you feel good!" Destiny paused and stared out the window above the kitchen sink. John said, "Do you miss me? I miss you so much!"

He softly kissed her neck as his hands touched all over her body. His middle finger clutched the trigger. John handled the frame and the barrel like an expert marksman. The touch of John had her conflicted, and his kisses had her afflicted. The smell of his cologne sent her into a trance. His familiar smell and voice made her weak in the knees. Longing and need burrowed through his chest.

She cut off the water and closed her eyes. She felt John rubbing his fully loaded clip against her. Memories flooded her mind. She felt him and the memories of him completely surrounding her body. The memories and emotions held Destiny captive, and she wasn't trying to break free. John kissed and touched her like a man full of remorse.

She relaxed in John's arms as he kissed the back of her neck. The heat of his body pressed against her and the softness of his lips on the back of her neck sent desire throughout her body. The energy flowed like the coil pushing the bullet out the barrel of the gun. John whispered, "I missed touching you like this and kissing you like this. I missed smelling your shampoo as I kiss your neck."

John caressed her body so lustfully through her jeans and T-shirt that she felt naked. She had to be honest with herself, she wanted this just as much as he did. She had never been away from John this long. The need in her was giving in to him. Seeing Destiny falling under his spell, John took his position as a sharpshooter and aimed at the target. He said, "Destiny, you look so good!"

John whispered in her ear with a deep voice, "I've missed you! Let me show you how much." He unbuttoned and unzipped her jeans. Her body responded to years of his touch; years of his kiss; years of his voice whispering in her ear. He stuck his hand in her panties. The feeling of his breath on the back of her neck made her river flow all over John's fingers. He rubbed Destiny's sensitivity. He got high, listening to his fingers slide through her wetness.

Her defenses melted. Piece by piece, the newly built walls around Destiny's mind and heart made of pain and reinforced by disappointment quickly tumbled down. He said, "Tell me it's okay. Say you want me like I want you." He repeated his request as he kissed the side of her neck with one hand still down her panties, and the other hand up her shirt, in her bra, rubbing her breasts. He seductively whispered, "Let me taste you? Can I taste you, huh?" It wasn't about the sex. John wanted his wife back.

He said, "Say yes, Bae!"

Destiny, filled with desire, gave in; she whispered, "Yes! baby," rubbing her hands over his head as he stood behind her nibbling on her neck. John turned Destiny around and sat her on the edge of the sink. He slowly pulled one leg out of her jeans and panties. He stared in her eyes the entire time. John felt guilty about his indiscretion. He wanted to make his wife feel good. John was filled with a mix of emotions that triggered his animal nature.

John lifted Destiny's legs over his shoulders. He kissed Destiny's thighs continuing upward to suck her like a juicy peach. Destiny bit her bottom lip as she supported herself with one hand gripping the sink while the other hand caressed John's head. John was like a leech on Destiny. He sucked her so tightly that there was no possibility of separating the man from his wife. The intensity of John's performance flooded her body with passion and pleasure.

John's soft lips and tongue delighted Destiny, awakening the sexy wife she had been up until that night. The pleasure made her body temperature rise, and her skin became lightly moistened with sweat. Her toes crinkled and curled as she leaned her head back to exhale. She exhaled the hurt, the pain, the burden of that night. She breathed deeply, letting go of the baggage and weight of his indiscretion. Love and adoration replaced pain.

Destiny relaxed her whole body, including her mind as John used his scintillating lips to give her passionate kisses in the direct middle of her thighs. Destiny felt good from head to toe. John confidently gave his wife what she wanted just the way she wanted it. Destiny felt that familiar feeling she always felt when John loved her. She missed that feeling in the three months he was away.

Destiny's body was aquiver, she said, "Baby, it feels so good." Destiny said, "Ah! John! Please, don't stop," as a surge of heat and pleasure rushed through her core. John wanted Destiny to feel good, so he dared not stop. She made John, the kitchen floor and the cabinets under the sink glisten and sparkle like the stars in a clear, cloudless night sky.

John knew exactly what he needed to do next. John knew Destiny's body like a head coach knows his playbook. John stood up and wrapped Destiny's legs around his waist. He slowly entered Destiny, she said, "Baby!" The sensation of Destiny's wet, warm flesh sent a surge of pleasure through his nerves. Destiny pulled his face close to hers to kiss his lips.

John was finally at home after three months away. Taking his place as the king of the castle. John rested, relaxed, and enjoyed the coziness of home. The sensation of him resting in her made her body react by squeezing him with all her might, he said, "Oh! I missed that! The way you got me, feels so good!"

Destiny said, "I missed you, too!"

Destiny pushed her hips forward and squeezed him tighter. John said, "Don't ever let me go!"

When she relaxed her muscles, he began to move. Destiny exhaled and moaned from the sensation of him slowly sliding in and out of her. He knew she loved the pullout. He slowly pulled himself out of her, waited for a second before sliding back into Destiny. He repeated that several times causing pleasure to erupt inside her. She gripped his shoulders and nibbled on his neck.

John knew that was the cue to give it to her the way she liked it. Destiny felt the pressure building up in her stomach. Warm blood rushed through her body with an explosion bubbling below the surface. John knew how important this moment was, and he took full advantage of the opportunity. John was in it to win his wife back.

John turned Destiny around; he bent her over the sink. He locked his forearm over the small of her back as he maneuvered through his wife in alphabetical order going from a to g. Destiny felt so good that she began pushing back on him.

He said, "Destiny, baby! I know you feel how much I missed you. Can you feel it, Bae?"

Destiny said, "I feel it, baby!"

John's love was a force of nature, making her feel adored. Destiny's senses were completely overwhelmed. Destiny's body tingled from the sweet sensation of her husband inside of her.

John felt the tide rolling in; he said, "Cum for me, baby!"

Destiny said, "Stay right there, and you'll get exactly what you want." John stayed on that spot until Destiny's flood gates opened, and the high tide rushed in.

"It feels so good when you cum on me," John said.

John enjoyed touching Destiny's firmer, tighter curves. John, on the verge of an orgasm, strokes became faster and deeper. Feeling a complete release, John rested on Destiny who was still leaning over the sink. Trying to catch his breath and regain his energy, he said, "I love you so much!"

Destiny resting her head on the sink, said, "I love you, too!"

He picked her up and carried her to their bedroom. He gently laid her in the bed. He completely undressed her then himself. He crawled on top of her and kissed her. Destiny put her hands on his cheeks. He said, "Destiny, you're so beautiful. You're so perfect. I love you." He kissed the curves of her body pass her hips to her thigh.

He wrapped Destiny's legs around his back. He put his arms under Destiny's shoulders as if he never wanted to let her go. He gently slid into her, sending warm electric pulses up his nerves. John enjoyed the feeling of his wife surrounding him. The slippery friction sent a rush of adrenaline and relaxation to his brain. John felt jolts of pleasure surging through him, making John want more.

Destiny drowning in passion tried to get air. Her heartbeat as if it was trying to escape from her chest. Her pulse throbbed in her ears. She could feel him somewhere between her rib cage and her soul. Destiny got wetter with every stroke John took.

She said, gasping for air, "John! Baby!"

John said, "Baby! I know!"

She cried out, "Baby!"

John said, "I know, I feel it too," as his body merged with hers, becoming one in the sunlight shining through the window.

Destiny's fingertips pressed into John's back; she said, "Wait a minute, baby!"

John said, "I can't!" Destiny tried to run, but John's grip was too strong.

He said, "No, baby, don't run from me. I need you."

John rolled Destiny over and put a pillow under her stomach. Destiny's face was tilted to the right side with her arm over her head. John braced himself against the mattress. John fiercely shook Destiny's body, working her mind into an influx of emotions, memories, dopamine, and oxytocin. John fell into a trance focused on getting what he wanted: his wife's love back.

John was overtaken with passion. John said, "Destiny, baby, cum with me."

Destiny on the cusp of an orgasm, said, "Okay! Baby!"

John, with all his might, loved his wife. He said, "Here we go!" John repeatedly slid against Destiny's g-spot. A strong wave of heat and energy rushed over them as they simultaneously experienced a mind-blowing orgasm.

Out of breath and exhausted, they embraced. John said, "Bae, damn! That was hot," as he rested his body on hers.

Destiny said, "It was," as she wrapped her arms around him, trying to catch her breath.

John said, "Every time with you is amazing, Destiny. You amaze me with the tricks you pull out the bag. I swear that's how we got those twins."

Destiny said, "Baby, you never disappoint!"

Destiny laid there thinking about the Saturday they conceived the twins while John went to take a shower. They were so in love back then. There had been no secrets, no pain back then. Their love was strong and innocent. After college, Destiny put her dreams on hold to help John build his company. Destiny's and John's hard work manifested success. With the company thriving, the young couple was open to starting a family.

Conception

On a seemingly normal Saturday afternoon, John and Destiny flirted as they completed chores. They caught glances of each other through the window as John cut the grass. He winked and waved at her. She blew kisses at him. Every time John walked past her, he smacked her on her butt, making her laugh. When his chores were complete, Destiny was so pleased with John's efforts that she wanted to treat him to a warm bath.

She massaged his back and neck. He relaxed and enjoyed the touch of his wife's soft hands. She washed from the top of his head to the bottom of his feet. As she washed him, she seductively touched his sensitive places. The touching led to kissing, and the kissing produced desire. Destiny could see John was aroused by the end of the bath. She softly patted the towel on his head and worked her way down.

When she dried his leg, his erect penis brushed across her cheek. She smiled and winked at him. When she dried the other leg, his penis brushed against her other cheek. She slowly grazed her lips against his penis as she wiped his feet. She seductively stared into his eyes, tempting him with glances. John was charmed by her touch and enchanted by her eyes.

John stood in suspense, trying to figure out what she was going to do next. Destiny wrapped the towel around him. Destiny held the corners of the towel with her fingertips. She softly kissed the tip of him as she stared into his eyes. John became so excited.

She slowly pulled the corners of the towel, pushing him through her lips. John flinched when her tongue and inner cheeks completely surrounded him with a firm grip. His facial expression spoke her high praise. She winked at him as she relaxed every muscle in her body.

He said, "Damn, Bae, you're taking it all like that!" She let him stay in her mouth for a while. Little beads of sweat formed on John's forehead. She lightly released the towel, slowly pulling her head back while firmly sucking him as her lips and tongue slowly rolled over him. The pop sounded loudly as the tip came out. He said, "Damn! Bae, it's like that?" She smiled at him while she softly licked and kissed the tip of him.

She pulled the towel toward her taking him half-way into her mouth. She sucked and slurped until she made it disappear. She used the towel to hold him in place as she intensely sucked him. The pleasure was overwhelming. "Girl, you have me running," he said, but she gripped the towel tightly preventing him from moving.

They stared into each other's eyes as she relaxed the towel and slowly let him slide out of her mouth. He was anticipating what she was going to do next. She paused for a moment just to mess with him. She pulled the towel toward her again, inserting him into her mouth so far down her throat she couldn't breathe. Her eyes watered. Destiny nearly gagged herself, but she handled it. John was close to tears, he said, "Destiny, Baby, this feels so good."

She dropped the towel to put both hands on him. She firmly caressed him with her hands going in opposite directions. She rubbed him across her lips and told him, "Husband, fuck my face!" She opened her mouth and leaned her head back.

John did as he was told; he said, "You're just going to drink that shit?" She nodded yes and winked at him.

John lifted her from the floor and pushed her against the wall. John wrapped her legs around his waist. He locked his arms around her shoulders, bouncing her body on him. She said, "Baby, Fuck me!"

"I got you, Bae," John said as he kissed her neck.

She said, "Yes! Baby, yes!"

He asked, "You like it, baby?"

She said, "I love it, baby. Don't stop!"

He said, "Trust me! It's too good to stop!"

She said, "Keep it right there, just like that!"

He said, "Like that, baby?"

Destiny said, "Uh-huh! Baby!"

John asked, "You're cuming for me? You know I love it when you cum on me."

She whispered in John's ear, "Cum in me, Daddy," and he did again and again and again. Thirty-nine weeks later, the twins were born.

(Present Day) Lexington says, "Destiny and John gave each other time, and time is the best medicine for an ailing relationship. She said the best thing for them was not arguing. They waited to talk until they both could speak with calm, leveled heads. When they were over it, Destiny never threw it in John's face to shame him."

Anniston says, "Aunt Destiny is so smart. She played her cards right. I am so glad they made it. I love them as a couple."

Lexington says, "Me too. Destiny has been my marriage instructor. She always handled being a mom and wife while working with style and grace. I think back to my mom, and I remember her being so peaceful and polite with us even when Akera was acting up, which was pretty much all the time. She never yelled although she was stern, and you knew when to quit talking. Destiny and my mother handled motherhood and being a wife very similarly.

"I love that Mommy made me think for myself, but she supported me. She set goals for me and made me believe I could achieve them. When I would say, Mommy, I can't do that. She would say, 'I know my daughter can accomplish whatever she wants.' That's how Destiny was with her kids, and that's how I am with my kids."

Anniston says, "Mommy, you do a great job at being a working mom and wife."

Lexington says, "Thank you, Baby Girl. It's one thing to look at your mother and see a supportive, dutiful wife, but to watch your peer do it makes you genuinely understand what being a wife and mother is all about. Sometimes that means forgiving your husband, being patient with your husband as he grows, and it also means nurturing and adjusting as needed to maintain your marriage."

Anniston says, "Mommy, you always have a smile on your face when you talk to us."

Lexington says, "My children make me happy, so I always have a reason to smile. I love to see them, hug them, spend time with them, and hear them call me, Mommy. It all makes me smile."

Anniston says, "Mommy, you make me smile. I love to spend time with you, I love your hugs, and I love that I get to call you, Mommy."

Lexington says, "Awe! Baby Girl, that's so sweet."

Anniston says, "Mommy, you're so sweet!"

Lexington says, "See, that's how you deal with the people you love even when they don't deserve it. Talk sweetly, calmly, listening more than speaking are how you get to someone's heart."

Anniston says, "I get what you mean."

Concession

After his shower, John happily walked back into their bedroom dressed for work. He tried to kiss Destiny, still laying in the bed. She stopped him, "Don't you have to go to work," she asked, smiling. John began to slowly massage her feet. Destiny said, "You're such a sweetheart, but you're already late."

He said, "Destiny after I leave the office, I would like to come home. I want my family back. Before you speak, let me get everything off my chest. Let me be clear and hear what I say. I never had any intentions of being with that girl. It was a one-time thing. I never thought the consequence of my actions was losing my family. I was weak and stupid. I was with her because it was a convenient, easy way to feed my ego. Feeding my ego was all it was because you gave me no reason to cheat. She was throwing it at me, and I fell into her trap.

"When you put me out, I was shocked. That night, I laid prostrate, begging the Lord for forgiveness. I'm praying that you forgive me. I swear you know the whole truth. If you let me come home, we will never be here again. I will never hurt you again."

Destiny said, "You have my forgiveness, John. I want you home with us. I want to see the sunrise across your face when I wake up every morning. I want to feel you reach for me in the middle of the night. I love our family together, but if you come home, things have to be different.

"Our marriage has been all about you. I need space to put me first. I want to go to work, and not for you. I want my own money, my own career, and my own identity outside of you. You can come home and have our marriage, but not the way it was before."

They shake hands, as John said, "I can accept that. You're right. You've had my back since the day we met in college freshmen year. You put your dreams aside for this family. You worked for years to build my business. I have been selfish, taking you and your loyalty for granted. You deserve all of that back. I heard you, loud and clear. Whatever you want, whatever you need, I am fully committed to doing my part. Just tell me what you need."

Destiny replied, "We talk and communicate openly and honestly. I'm your wife, if you need something, you come to me to fulfill that need. We take turns cooking and cleaning."

John said, "I can handle that!"

Destiny reached out her arms to hug him. Destiny added, "If I'm going to get a job, I will need your help with the kids."

John said, "I'm their father, I'm supposed to do those things. I apologize for letting you handle the burdens of parenting all by yourself. I realize that wasn't fair. I have, in the past, shown up for the easy, fun stuff. I want to be the kind of father and husband my wife and kids can rely on and trust I will show up for everything.

"You never complain. You never call me selfish or bring up my bullshit. That's very commendable of you, but you deserve more participation from me. I will wholeheartedly support you in everything you need. I understand why getting a job is important to you. Destiny, whatever you need to do for you, I want you to do. We will make it work; I promise. Destiny, this whole situation has opened my eyes. I recognize what and how I need to change."

John wrapped his arms around Destiny and said, "I love you! I will do anything to make this work. I want my life and my wife back."

Destiny said, "You'll always have your wife."

John kissed her forehead and said, "See you tonight!"

Destiny replied, "See you tonight!"

(Present Day) Lexington says, "When I was pregnant with Michelle, I was full of a variety of emotions. I was trying to make sense of some things, and I needed to make some tough decisions. As always, I turned to Destiny. She cooked for me. We talked while we ate, and in that conversation, I made some important life decisions.

Cultivation

As Lexington waddled toward the door, Destiny said, "Best Friend, look at you. You're pregnant! You're so cute."

Lexington said (rubbing her belly), "Thank you! It's weird, huh?"

Destiny said, "It's Beautiful!" As they walked into the house, Destiny said, "I am so happy for you. It's an amazing journey, and you're going to love every step of the way." They hugged, and Destiny rubbed Lexington's stomach; she said, "My little niecy-pooh."

Lexington asked, "You think it's a girl? Michael thinks it's a girl."

Destiny said, "I do. I think he's right."

Lexington asked, "How are your big kids?"

Destiny said, "They are great." She pulled out recent pictures.

Lexington said, "They are adorable, Destiny. Growing up way too fast."

Destiny said, "We are blessed!"

Lexington asked, "Where are my godchildren?"

Destiny answered, "John took them out for some dad time." Lexington and Destiny walked into the kitchen arm in arm. Lexington washed her hands and sat at the table. They talked as Destiny fixed plates. Destiny asked, "So, Michael wants a girl?"

"Yes, he already made up his mind on the name Michelle," Lexington said.

Destiny said, "He's going to get his wish; it is definitely a girl: Michelle Moore. How is he?"

"He's well! He keeps talking about five more. I'm like five more, boy, that's a lot of kids," Lexington said.

Destiny said, "You'll see when she gets here. It's so amazing to see yourself in something so innocent. It's like the best parts of you and your husband wrapped into a tiny, little baby."

Lexington asked, "Do you want more?"

Destiny said, "If it happens, I wouldn't hate it."

Destiny sat down, said grace, and they started eating. Destiny asked, "How are you enjoying married life?"

"You know, I never thought I could be this content with the simple things we do. He's good for me. He inspires me to pray," Lexington said.

Destiny said, "I'm so happy for you. You deserve this."

Lexington said, "We all do!"

"You're right about that," Destiny replied.

Lexington says, "I'm rethinking my life now that I'm a wife and a soon-to-be-mother. I've been single for so long, being my own man and doing what I want. It definitely feels good to just be the woman in my life. I get nervous that I'll mess it up. It's hard to believe, but I'm trusting and believing in Michael to be the leader and provider. Destiny, I really want this to work for him, the baby, and myself. I'm trying to figure out how to make this work for us all."

Destiny said, "Just make sure you keep a balance in your marriage. You want to support your man, but make sure there's a balance in your identity between Michael's wife, Michelle's mom, and Lexington. As much as you want to support your husband and care for your baby is as much as you need to take care of you and nourish your wants, needs, and desires. Lexington is a woman inside and outside of this marriage, and she has needs and wants.

"Trust me, you'll both be happier if you are happy independently of him. I want you to be clear and honest with yourself about what you want. I didn't do that. I suppressed those things in me, thinking I was doing what was best for my family. But if I'm empty, I can't pour into my children. I was so young when I took my vows, and I didn't realize I was going to grow older, and things would change.

"Even if you think he will get upset, be confident that what you have to say is valid. Don't be afraid to express what you want and what you need. Yes, he is the man, but your needs are just as urgent, and you have to spell it out to him in plain English. Don't make him guess or read between the lines.

"Honestly, Lexi, you'll be fine because you and Michael have a lot of advantages working in your favor. Michael is mature in his faith. He knows the word and his responsibilities as a husband, a father, and a lover. You're young enough to grow together but old enough to have grown so much already. You are both already whole, complete, established people who have succeeded, traveled, and explored.

"All you've been through and all he's been through was preparation. You're ready for this; he's prepared for this, and you both want this. He is spiritual and a little older than you; I'm sure he gets it. He's a good dude. He seems focused and that makes a difference. You and he have the makings of something really special, and it'll work out. Things are changing really fast for you, so it is very reasonable for you to have questions and emotions. I think you two will be fine. In fact, I know you two will be fine."

Lexington said, "Destiny, you always know what's going on with me. There's something I want, but I've been afraid to disrupt our home."

Destiny said, "Lexi, I've known you since we were five. You think things through. You would not have married Michael if he couldn't handle you or your truth. Whatever is on your mind is important, and Michael can handle it. You said you're trusting him! If nothing comes of it, at least you had a conversation. Remember to stand firm and clearly state what you need and why. Don't back down. Michael can handle whatever is on your mind. He loves you, Lexi."

Lexington said, "That's good advice."

Destiny said, "That's real life."

Lexington asked, "Are you and John good?"

Destiny answered, "We have mended things. You know it was one of those things that you wish didn't happen, but you're better because it did happen. I wish I could've gotten the message without the pain, but the truth is we couldn't continue living the way we were living before his indiscretion.

"I was suffocating, and I didn't even know it. The thought of John leaving made me realize outside of him, all I had was three kids and no way to provide for them on my own. Everything I did and every decision I made was all about him. Our marriage was out of balance and definitely tilted in his favor. I was sowing, and he was reaping all the benefits. Until that night, I thought things were perfect. I had no clue that I gave up so much of myself to be a wife and mother.

"The enemy attacks the things that comfort us, and God doesn't like when we idolize earthly things. My marriage made me very comfortable, and I made it an idol. I hadn't even realized that I admired my husband so much. Was I supposed to get a divorce after his indiscretion? I don't know the right answer.

"I thought to myself, Destiny, you surely don't want another woman reaping the harvest from all the sacrifices you've made. I invested too much in him to let him go play house with someone else. I had to quickly get clear about what I wanted and needed to move forward. I needed to bring balance into our marriage for my own sake."

Lexington asked, "How did you two get here?"

Destiny answered, "I was mad as hell initially, but in the time apart, we both had time to think, calm down, and reflect on what went wrong. In the silence, there was no arguing or saying things to hurt each other. I didn't want to hurt John or be mean to him that has never been a component of our relationship. Words hurt, and once you start beating each other with words, where does it stop?

"The time apart gave me a chance to separate anger from pain. I chose my words carefully when I expressed what I needed. We had productive conversations. He had an opportunity to say this is what I want. I got a chance to say this is what I want. We agreed that those things were reasonable. We made a commitment to make those wishes a reality.

"I didn't pressure him to do anything, and he didn't pressure me to do anything. When he was ready to talk, we talked. When he was prepared to put it all out there, we put it all on the table. When he was ready to come home, he did. I can't dwell on it or harbor those feelings. I actually worked really hard to deal with the situation and let it go.

"I don't hold it over his head or throw it in his face. When he came home, that was the end of that and the beginning of working on our new marriage. I can't worry, and he can't give me a reason to worry. We have to have trust, or we have no union. We set rules about our communication, our household duties, and we clearly defined our expectations of each other. We had a good laugh about it and left it in the past.

"Lexi, I cannot stress how important it is to be clear within yourself and to clearly express yourself to Michael. You can't be vague or clean it up because you think he'll get mad or hurt. You have to stay in touch with you and be so specific when you communicate with him. I didn't do that. I was so busy building John, John's business, and John's family that I didn't realize I was neglecting me.

"In the time apart, I saw live and in living color what I needed. When John said he wanted his marriage back, I told John exactly what needed to change to make it work. The killing part is he knew I was letting him get away with too much. He admitted that I gave, and he gladly took. He acknowledged and affirmed me in his apology. He agreed to make things happen. He's been upholding his part of the deal, and things have been working well for us."

Lexington said, "Thank you for being open and honest with me. I needed this conversation. It made me think. I've never spoken my wants in any of my past relationships, and I realize that's why they didn't work. I locked my feelings inside and became resentful. I don't want that to happen with Michael."

Destiny said, "Anytime you need to talk, I'm here."

Lexington said, "I'm glad you said that. There's something I need to talk to you about."

Destiny said, "I'm all ears!"

Lexington said, "I have been trying to figure out how I want life to look for the next five years. I want to raise my baby, and not for a few months. I want to be present for all the special moments. The whole concept of me going to work while Michael is at home is not going to work for me. I want to be the one at home with the baby. I need him to go to work, so I can stay at home to take care of the baby."

Destiny interrupts: "Your daughter. It's a girl, and she has a name: Michelle Moore."

Lexington said, "Okay, my daughter, Michelle. I was hoping if we move, you will take over for me at Lear Accounting. You don't have to answer now. Take some time to think about it."

Destiny asked, "Are you sure you want to leave your whole life?"

"My man did it for me, and now I have to do what's best for Michelle. Working until one or two in the morning four or five days out the week is not the mommy I want to be to an infant. When she's older, I'll go back to work. I've been running on ten, trying to succeed my whole life, and now I need a chance to enjoy my life. I like my new personal life, and I want to be there to see it," Lexington answered.

Destiny said, "That's the same way I felt when I had the twins. Lexington, Best Friend, I hate to see you leave, but I will support you because I want the best for you. Talk to Michael to see how he feels. If he's down, I'm in."

They hugged, Lexington said, "No one has best friends like mine!"

Destiny said, "You better know it!" Destiny added, "I miss you already."

Lexington said, "Leaving you is going to be the hardest thing I ever did."

(Present Day) Lexington says, "I so appreciated that conversation with Destiny. It really helped me frame my approach to communicating with Michael: completely open, honest conversations where we both are free to say exactly what we need. When I got home, I told him we needed to have a conversation. He had this puzzled look on his face, but he said ok. I sat down at the table, and he sat across from me. I said to myself, Lexington, tell him what you want."

Preposition

Lexington told herself to be brave. The words flew out of her mouth, "If you ever cheat on me, I do not want to know. Promise me you'll wear condoms and cover your tracks. Keep your car clean, all your electronics put away, and if you need to get a second phone."

"I'm not cheating. I'm not going to cheat," he said.

"Just promise," she said firmly. She gave him a look that let him know she meant business.

"I promise," he said.

She said, "You're not leaving me ever, so whatever we need to do to make this work, that's what we will do. Do you hear me?"

He answered, "I hear you!"

"Mr. Moore, I am not just talking. I mean every word I said," she said.

"I don't want any problems with you. I heard you, and I'm not messing this up, Mrs. Moore," he replied.

She said, "So, you understand as long as you live is as long as this marriage will last."

He said, "I understand!"

Lexington said, "Mr. Moore, trust me, you don't want any problems with me."

"You are tough now?" he jokingly asked.

She answered, "When it comes to my husband, you're damn right. So do not try me because you don't want to see me, Mr. Moore."

Michael said, "Okay!"

She said, "I'm serious, Michael. You're not leaving me, so you better make that clear to any and all the females that come at you."

Michael puts his hands up; he said, "I got you. Anything else?"

That was the easy part. She had to gather courage for the next part; Lexington said, "There is something else, and don't get angry before you hear me out. I am mentally preparing for our baby. I need to reconcile things in my mind, and I need two things from you. First, I need your blessing to go visit my mother. I'd love for you to come even if you only stay for a few days.

"Secondly, I think we should move to your hometown after the baby is born and I'm able to travel. I want you to go to work, so I can stay home with the baby. When I'm ready, I'll find a job. Destiny can run things for me here. I know you went through a lot to make this house our perfect home. I appreciate everything you did, but I want to raise my baby. Don't be mad, Michael, or think I don't appreciate all you have done for me."

"Baby, whatever you want. Go visit your mom! Stay as long as you want. I'll work on some things before I come down. It'll give us a chance to get to know each other," he said.

"Come here," he calmly added. She walked over to him and sat in his lap. He added, "I like your plan. I will always support you. I won't ever be mad at you for telling me what you need or want. Everything you want is reasonable. You should spend time with your mom, and you choose to work and when.

"I'm not leaving you. I'll never cheat on you. The vows we took, I take them to heart. I meant every word. I never want to hurt you; I only want to love you. I will always have your back. Go call your mom and tell her you are coming and then pack." He kissed her forehead. She asked him three times if they were good, and he said yes. She thought okay, Destiny was right.

(Present Day) Anniston asks, "Mommy, do you miss your old life?"

Lexington answers, "I miss seeing Destiny and Kendra every day. I met Kareen and Destiny on the first day of kindergarten. We were together almost every day from the day we met until I moved. It was hard leaving them. Honestly, I needed some space from my actual sister. Before Vanessa, Akera was a trip. I love her, but she was hard to take. Akera was one of those people who believed in always saying and doing whatever they wanted no matter who they hurt or disappoint. That drama gets old fast. She was an inconsiderate person until she met Vanessa.

"She found peace and happiness when Vanessa came into her life, or at least I had peace and happiness because she grew up and became conscious and considerate. She met Brock first. I think she liked him more than any other man she dated, but the age difference was an issue for her. She liked Brock, but Vanessa was her one and only true love."

Chapter Four: Akera

Predilection

On the first night of the cruise, the girls sat on the deck, sipping wine, talking, and enjoying the scenery. Akera said, "Remember that time those guys followed us from the club."

Destiny said, "I remember that night."

Kendra said, "Akera was driving like a maniac."

Akera said, "I wasn't about to get raped or shot because Lexington didn't want to give that dude her number."

Lexington said, "Don't make it seem like it was all my fault. None of us wanted to talk to any of them."

Kareen said, "They were so mad. How can you be mad because a stranger doesn't want to have a conversation with you?"

Kendra said, "Akera brought them a round of drinks and told the waitress to tell them to sit there and drink about it."

Lexington asked, "You did that?"

Kendra laughed and said, "Yes, she did!"

Lexington said, "You couldn't let things ride."

Akera said, "Well, they were upset because you dissed them. I was trying to help them feel better."

Destiny said, "But, did you really have to point at the tall one, laugh, and say pick your lip up."

Akera said, "It was hanging so low it was bumping into his chest."

Lexington said, "I can't deal with you."

Akera said, "Lexington, sit there and drink about it," as she sipped her wine.

Lexington said, "I swear Mommy must have let you fall and bump your head really hard."

Akera said, "She probably did because she was so enthralled in two-year-old, perfect you."

Lexington said, "Is that it? You're a psycho because you didn't get enough attention as a child?"

Akera said, "All both parents ever said is why can't you be more like Lexi. Lexington is boring and lame, and no one wants that life."

Lexington said, "I hate you. If you weren't my sister." Lexington gestures a punch in the eye.

Akera said, "You always have to let me know you only mess with me because we're sisters."

Lexington said, "Did I hurt your feelings?"

Akera said, "Yes, you know that comment bothers me."

Lexington said, "I mess with you because I love you!"

Akera smiled and said, "I love you, too! Smooches!" They blew kisses.

Lexington said, "I still hate you, though."

As Akera laughed, her attention was high jacked by a tall, slim, beautiful woman with hazel eyes walking pass. Akera was love-struck by the woman's long, golden legs. Akera imagined her legs felt like silk. Akera felt butterflies in her stomach as she slowly looked the woman up and down. The woman smiled at one of the women she was talking to, and Akera's whole heart ran away.

Once the woman captivated Akera's mind, Akera couldn't care less about the view, the ship, her friends, or the conversation they were having. Akera was consumed by the thought of woman. The woman never looked Akera's way as she continued walking. The fact that the woman didn't notice Akera, turned Akera on even more. She thought to herself: Damn! Who is she? I need to get her alone to see what's up.

The next morning, as Akera and her friends were walking into the dining area for breakfast, the woman and her companions were leaving the dining area. Akera stared at the woman as the woman walked toward her. Akera's friends were talking to her, but she was too preoccupied with the woman to hear a word they said.

The woman felt Akera staring at her as they passed each other, but the woman purposely didn't make eye contact with Akera. Seeing the woman up close was even more impressive. It was love at first sight for the first time for Akera.

The woman's hazel eyes with a green accent were bold like the eyes of a cat. They struck Akera like lightning drawn to metal. The woman's thin pink lips looked soft. Akera imagined the woman's lips on Akera's neck. Akera turned to watch the woman walk away. The sway of the woman's hips and the bounce in her step had Akera's full attention. Akera thought to herself, "Damn, she is so pretty!" Akera made up her mind that she was going to get that girl.

Throughout the day, Akera found herself looking for the woman at every turn. While her friends enjoyed the beauty of the island, Akera watched for the woman. Akera couldn't stop thinking about her. Akera could see the woman's smile and hear the woman's laugh playing on a loop in her brain.

On the third night on the ship, Akera went to the bar to get a round of drinks when she heard a soft voice say, "I noticed you've been watching me."

Akera turned and saw the woman. The woman said, "I guess you like what you see."

Akera said, "What makes you think I was looking at you, Pretty Girl."

The woman jokingly asked, "So, you think I'm pretty?"

Akera said, "I think a lot of things. I have one of those minds."

The woman stuck out her hand, she said, "I'm Vanessa."

Akera accepted her hand, and replied, "I'm Akera." They stared at each other as they shook hands.

"For the record, you've been checking for me," Vanessa said.

Akera replied, "The only way you could know that I was watching you is if you were watching me watch you."

Vanessa said, "Maybe or maybe someone saw you and told me."

"So maybe I was watching you, how would you feel about that," Akera asked.

Vanessa answered, "Flattered!"

Akera asked, "Oh, really?"

Vanessa shrugged her shoulders and smiled at Akera. At this point, they had confirmation that they were flirting. Vanessa said, "Well, if you're interested in what you see, meet me later, and we can talk about it."

Akera asked, "Meet where?"

"My suite, we can have a drink and talk in private. That is if you aren't afraid to be alone with me," Vanessa said.

"I am never scared," Akera said.

"You're sure because there's a look of fear on your face,"

Vanessa said. "Why would I be afraid of such a sweet, pretty face like yours? You look like a harmless, pretty princess. What could you possibly do to me, rape me?" Akera asked.

"Pretty princess won't have to take it, you'll give it to me: free and willingly," Vanessa said.

Akera said, "You're sure of yourself!"

"As sure as I am that you were watching me," Vanessa wittingly replied.

"You're damn right, I was watching you," Akera said.

Vanessa winked and said, "Midnight, suite V-7, bring those looking eyes of yours."

"If you bring that pretty face and nice ass of yours, I'll bring my eyes to look," Akera said.

At eleven p.m., Akera made an excuse to get away from her friends to go back to her suite. She showered, freshened up her makeup, and fixed her hair. She wanted to be appealing to Vanessa, who was also back in her room, getting ready for the pending rendezvous.

Midnight came, and Akera secretly made her way to Vanessa's suite. She knocked on the door, trying not to be seen. Vanessa opened the door, and she reached out her hand. Akera took her hand and walked into the room. They complimented each other. Vanessa led Akera out to the balcony. Vanessa fixed drinks, and said, "So Akera, tell me about yourself."

Akera said, "Lawyer, single, no kids that's about it for me. What about you?"

Vanessa says, "Twenty-one-year-old daughter on her way to med school. Nineteen-year-old son studying to be an engineer like his father. OBGYN, married for twenty-three years before my ex-husband decided he wanted a younger version of me. It's crazy how much she looks like me: the twenty-year-old me."

Akera said, "I can't imagine what fault he found with you at any age. You are physical perfection, right now."

Vanessa smiled at Akera; she said, "Thank you!"

The attraction and energy between the two of them radiated as hot as the July sun. Akera asked, "Do you…you know…men and women?"

Vanessa said, "Twenty-five years of the d is enough for me. The d in divorce was the last d I needed. I take it, you still ride the D?"

"I have a now and then friend, but I prefer women," Akera said. Akera asked, "Did you…you know…women before your marriage?"

"Nope, never even considered it," Vanessa said.

Akera asked, "So you looked at it all day for all those years, and you never?"

Vanessa answered, "I never even thought about it until an encounter one night with a friend."

Akera said, "She rocked it, huh?"

Vanessa answered, "She did. It was gentle, passionate. I was numb, and she made me feel something."

Akera said, "I always knew. Even as a little girl, I knew my admiration for beautiful women wasn't just admiration."

Vanessa asked, "So, Ms. Akera, did you enjoy watching me?"

Akera answered, "I liked what I saw."

Vanessa said, "Maybe, there's more to see."

Akera said, "Maybe, I want to see more."

Vanessa said, "If you're sure you're ready to ride this ride, bring your ass in here," as she walked into the room.

Akera followed her. Akera said, "Maybe you can't handle me since you're pretty new at this girl thing. I do this shit for real."

Vanessa said, "There's nothing you can throw that I can't handle."

"Ok! You're testing me. Alright, I'm all on your pretty ass," Akera replied.

Vanessa replied, "But, can you stay on it?"

"Oh! I can stay on it," Akera said.

"I'm a grown-ass woman, so you can't half step with me," Vanessa said.

Akera walked over to her and said, "I'm stepping all the way to your pretty ass, now what!"

Vanessa said, "You do understand, pussy is my profession, so I know what I am doing."

Akera said, "I've never gotten any complaints."

They kissed like familiar lovers as they moved toward the bed. When Akera sat down, Vanessa straddled her thighs. Vanessa took off Akera's shirt as they kissed. To touch and be so close to Vanessa was gratifying for Akera. Akera's hands slowly became acquainted with Vanessa as she touched all her private places.

Vanessa said, "Are you ready for your life to change? After tonight you'll never be the same."

Akera said, "I could use a change!"

Vanessa finished undressing Akera slowly. Vanessa said as she slowly kissed down Akera's body, "You're an alpha like me. It gets tiring and lonely. You're used to being the aggressor and in control. Who knows what you want? Who is pleased to please you? Who takes care of you? Who knows every inch of your body and what it desires? Who can spend day and night tending to your every want and need and never tire? You need that. You need someone that can match your intensity. You need someone that can handle you. I know, I need it too."

Akera knew Vanessa was right. Akera didn't have anyone to tenderly care for her, and she did deeply desire that from someone she loved. All the sex in the world cannot cure loneliness or fulfill the desire for love. Vanessa said things to Akera that Akera longed to hear, and that's how Vanessa worked her way into Akera's head. Akera let go and enjoyed the feeling of Vanessa.

Vanessa, sitting between Akera's legs, reached for her makeup case. The top shelf, filled with makeup, concealed the bottom compartment, which was neatly filled with Vanessa's favorite sex toys. Vanessa took out a blindfold and a silk scarf. She smiled at Akera and said, "Want to have some fun?" Akera said, "I'm down for whatever!"

She put the blindfold over Akera's eyes before she traced the silhouette of Akera's body with the silk scarf. She teased Akera's nipples with the scarf. Vanessa grazed down each of Akera's thighs with the silk scarf as she softly kissed Akera's neck. Vanessa made figure eights with her fingertips on the back of Akera's knees and thighs as she kissed Akera's breast. Vanessa lightly scratched down the back of Akera's calves with her fingernails as she kissed Akera's inner thigh.

Akera bit her bottom lip as she relaxed. Wanting to have complete control of Akera's pleasure and attention, Vanessa took the scarf and tied Akera's hands to the bed. For the first time, Akera completely relinquished control to someone else. Akera felt relieved.

Vanessa's kiss made Akera feel the feeling she had been chasing all her life. The blindfold heightened Akera's sense of touch. So entuned to Vanessa's touch, Akera could feel the ridges of Vanessa's fingerprints as her fingertips slowly rolled over Akera's skin. Vanessa's body heat and soft touch sent sparks up Akera's body.

The attraction between them was unlike anything Akera ever experienced. Finally, Akera met someone who matched her willingness to explore. The closeness of Vanessa sent Akera on a high, making Akera vulnerable. Akera never wanted anyone as much as she wanted Vanessa.

Akera said, "Every part of you is so sexy! From the minute I saw you, I wanted you," as she slowly kissed Vanessa. Akera's hands continued to get acquainted with Vanessa's body. Her fingertips rolled over Vanessa's nipples in circles.

Vanessa asked, "What do you want with me?"

Akera said, "Everything! I want all of you!"

Vanessa smiled; she said, "Take what you want!"

Akera lightly bit Vanessa's neck with her vampire teeth. Vanessa's fingertips ran over Akera's back as Akera encased Vanessa's breast in her lips. Akera's fingertips slowly became acquainted with Vanessa. Akera's thighs held Vanessa's thighs open so Akera's fingers could infiltrate Vanessa while her thumb circularly rolled over Vanessa's pearl.

Akera whispered in her ear, "You're so beautiful. Every part of you turns me on." Vanessa smiled and placed her hand on the side of Akera's head as her head slowly moved down the curve of Vanessa's body. Vanessa held Akera's hair as Akera kissed every inch of Vanessa's body.

Vanessa was like strawberries and whipped cream to Akera's senses. She savored every sip she took of Vanessa. Vanessa's body jerked from the stimulation of her most sensitive self. She relaxed as Akera brought her pleasure. Akera's tongue slid over Vanessa like an experienced skier on slopes. Akera gripped Vanessa's hip with one hand while the other arm laid across Vanessa's belly so her fingers could rub Vanessa's treasure.

Vanessa and Akera fell in love as they made love. Vanessa gave as much as she took, and Akera took all she wanted until the sun was breaking through the night sky. The next morning, they made plans to meet again before Akera secretly made her way back to her room.

On the last night of the cruise, Akera told Vanessa she wanted to stay in contact despite the fact they lived in different states. Vanessa told Akera, Vanessa's children don't know about her personal life, and she wasn't ready to share that part of her life with them. Akera understood and consented to be Vanessa's secret.

Akera told Vanessa about Brock and promised that Akera's friendship with him would never supersede or interfere with their relationship. Vanessa and Akera acknowledged long-distant, secret relationships could be difficult, but they both were interested in pursuing the relationship.

Brock-Nation

Akera was giddy like a schoolgirl who had a date with her crush. When Kendra asked why are you so happy, Akera shocked everyone with her secret.

Kendra said, "You bagged R&B Superstar, Brock Blair?"

Akera said, "He is not lying in those songs. I recorded it if you want to see it."

Lexington said, "So you recorded yourself letting a twenty-two-year-old boy fuck the shit out of you?"

"That's right. It was good, too," Akera said proudly. Akera said, "The video is right here!"

Kendra and Destiny hurriedly grabbed it. Kendra said, "Well, damn!"

Akera knew exactly what Kendra was referring to, she said, "I know!" Lexington looked at Akera with a disapproving face as Kendra and Destiny watched the video. Akera said, "What!"

Lexington responded, "Don't leave evidence of your bad decisions. Be a lady, even when you're a bad girl."

Akera said, "I act like a lady when I fuck like a man!"

Kendra, laughing, said, "I think the latter cancels out the whole statement."

Destiny said, "Can one really act like a lady if said one is fucking like a man?"

Akera said, "It can be achieved." Destiny and Kendra, still watching the video, admire Brock's demonstration of the skills he sings about. Lexington looked at Akera in disbelief.

Akera said, "You mess with a younger guy."

Lexington asked, "If I jump, you're jumping too?"

Akera said, "Yes! I can't live without you."

Lexington said, "So leave Mommy without any daughters? Who will take care of her if we both die of bad decisions?"

Akera said, "Is that supposed to make me not want to jump? I don't want to live with old people. I left as soon as I could to get away from them, and I'm never going back. If you want someone to take care of your parents, you better get your life together. They're your responsibility." Akera went on telling the girls about her night with Brock.

Play-Station

After meeting with his lawyer, Brock saw Akera walking down the hall toward her office. He saw a pretty face followed by a big ass. His attention was hooked like a boy with a new video game. He followed her into her office and closed the door. When she heard the door close, she looked up and into his face. She asked, "May I help you?"

He took one of her cards from her desk, read it, and asked if he could call her later. She said, "Put that card back because I'm not trying to be in some shit from messing with your young ass."

He put the card in his back pocket and said, "I'll sign a non-disclosure agreement."

Akera said, "Boy, I could be your mother, get out of here."

Brock responded, "I bet you're not even thirty, are you?"

Akera said, "No, but I'm still too grown for you."

Brock said, "I can handle you."

Akera said, "I'm not trying to be one of the groupies that you brag about bagging in your songs and interviews, talking about she has joined the Nation."

He said, "That's for show and stunting. Those hoes want it to be known. I can recognize the difference between a young hoe and a grown woman. I wouldn't do that to you."

She asked, "How do I know I can trust you?"

He sat in the chair; he said, "I got time. Type that non-disclosure. If I mention you, your name, or your likeness in anything, ever, you can sue me. Now, say I can call you, and I will sign a non-disclosure, right now."

Akera paused and looked at him, silently debating to let him call. Akera said, "Give me the card." He didn't want to. She told him the number on the card is the office number, and she'd write her personal number on the back. Brock handed her the card. She wrote her personal number on it and gave it back.

He called a few times while he was on tour. The conversation was cool. He was talking shit like how good he is in bed and what he is going to do to her. When he came back her way, he called after his show. She said, "Alright, fuck it, you know what, come over! Watch me put it on your little, young ass!"

At about three a.m., his driver dropped him off with his eyes almost closed, smelling like he smoked a bushel of weed. He was holding a huge bouquet of long-stem red roses, two bottles of Dom Perignon, a bag of burgers, and a gift box. They popped the first bottle, ate the burgers, and listened to his upcoming album.

He opened the gift box to reveal a gold necklace with a diamond-filled key-shaped charm. He put the necklace around her neck; he said, "I'm giving you the key to my heart." She thought the whole thing was cute, so Brock earned some brownie points. They talked and killed the next bottle. The alcohol was kicking in, so she knew things were about to sexcalate.

They kissed. She was shocked that he was such a good kisser. He touched all over her as they kissed while sitting on her couch. He looked at her like he had to have it. She couldn't believe it, but she was feeling him, too.

She led him to her bedroom. He walked through the door and was stunned when he saw the swivel swing over the bed, lit candles around the bed, the oils and toys on the dresser, wedge/ramp pillow in the center of the bed, and the Take Me Thigh Cuffs sitting on the bed.

He said, "Damn" with the damn face: mouth wide open and eyes bugged out.

She said, "Oh! You thought this was going to be that regular sex like you have when you're with those young girls. Oh, no! Baby! I'm about to run a pussy-a-thon on your young ass!" She told him, "You need to turn the lights off and me on."

He cut the lights off and started ripping his clothes off. He said, "Get ready for this dick-ath-lon!"

Down to his underwear, he walked over to her and stripped her down to her secrets. He laid her down and massaged her neck and back. He told her she was so sexy, and he loves her looks and her body. He called her the girl of his dreams. She thought what he said was sweet, so it lowered her inhibition even more. She felt really good from the Dom Perignon and his sexy, young ass all over her.

Brock said, "Dance for me, Mama!" She told him to sing to her. He started singing his song, *Take It All Tonight*. She started dancing really sexy. She pulled out her naughty dance moves. She danced on him, while he touched every part of her. She bounced her ass in his face. He was hypnotized by her fat ass popping and bouncing up and down.

She reached into his underwear to discover he was packed like luggage for a long, family vacation. She said, "Boy, what are you doing with all that!"

He replied, "I'm a grown man." She asked if this is how all his dates go. He said, "No, baby! Honestly, I don't get to date much. This life on the road can get lonely." She felt bad for him because she understood loneliness.

At this point, they were completely naked. He slipped the condom on, and shit got real. She asked if he ever had a woman in the swivel swing. He said, "This will be my first."

She said, "Let me show you something. You're going to love it!" She got in the swing, leaned back, and let go. She gently bumped into him. He grabbed her thighs and held her against his naked body. His thing sat between her thing while she taught him how to operate the swing.

He lowered her head onto the bed, but her lower back was elevated enough for her body to reach his manhood. He traced her with his manhood like a kid tracing with a fat crayon. He used the handle to lift the swing, raising her to meet his face. His lips and tongue were so soft as he French kissed her lips between her thighs. He did it so well, she was impressed.

For his first time with the swing, he mastered it quickly. He put her flat on the edge of the bed and put her leg over his shoulder. They stared in each other's eyes while he took slow, long, deep strokes. He kissed the backs of her calves with his soft lips and tongue as he stroked right into the spot. She was about to blow, but he said, "Not yet!"

There was so much energy and intensity in everything he did. He sucked the life out of her and brought her back to life with his stroke. Like a python moving through the jungle, he slithered in and overflowed her. He got her out of the swing and put her onto the wedge pillow. She threw it back on him like her very life was depending upon his gratification. The way she was bouncing back on that python had him tripping. They couldn't hear anything but her dripping wet, gushy sliding on him and her ass smacking against him. It felt so good to her that she was ready to blow, but he said, "Not yet!"

He rolled her onto her back. He put small passion marks up and down the backs of her thighs. The shit was so hot, she had to record it. She wanted to watch the shit up close and personally. He was like, "I see you, girl. You don't hold them up."

She said, "Sure, don't, baby."

All the pent-up energy flowing through her body was pressing her for a release. She was in heat, and he knew it. He slowly pulled himself out of her. He whispered in her ear, "You feel so good." He rolled her on her right side, bent her left leg, and he slid deep into her.

He rocked her body with such strength and confidence that she forgot he was only twenty-two. She could feel him pushing and moving her whole core. The sensation of him brushing against her made all of the energy in her body boil. When her whole body began to shiver, he whispered in her ear, "It's time!" He rolled her onto her back, and he turned savage.

He was hyper-focused. Every stroke smashed into the right spot. Hot energy rushed from her scalp to the bottom of her feet, her eyelids twitched, her toes curled, her back jerked, all resulting in a complete release of energy.

(Present Day) Lexington says, "Two years into Vanessa and Akera's relationship, Akera called me hysterically crying like a child who Santa forgot on Christmas. She was screaming. She found out she was pregnant, and she wasn't sure how Vanessa would handle a baby.

"After Nasir was born, Akera and Brock settled into co-parenting. Vanessa's children were accepting of Akera and Nasir. I love Vanessa. She's become a big sister to me. She has made a great addition to our circle of friends. Akera and Brock turned out to be great parents, so it all worked out. Akera was blessed because not all sticky situations smooth out so easily. Thank God, Brock is a responsible father."

Chapter Five: Kareen

Anniston says, "Aunt Akera met Aunt Vanessa, Aunt Kendra met Uncle Bishop, and Aunt Destiny reconstructed her marriage the same year you married Daddy, so I am guessing that's when Aunt Kareen met Uncle Amir." Lexington gives a thumbs-up as she bites her cupcake. Anniston says, "I have got to hear how Aunt Kareen got the finest man in the world."

Inception

Kareen explained, "Back in April, Kendra, Akera, and I went to the sports bar to watch a game. Lexi was out of town. Destiny was with John. Kendra was a little shook up over Rodney, so she left early, leaving me alone and very drunk with Akera.

When Kendra left, the man of my dreams took her seat. Somehow, we started talking. We were sitting at the bar talking, eating, sipping shots, and I fell head over heels in love. The conversation flowed. Everything about him was attractive. He's tall, well-dressed, has caramel skin and a bald head with a perfectly groomed beard. He has these shoulders that drive me crazy. His chest, his back, and his voice are so sexy. Not to mention, he's smart.

Destiny said, "Fine and smart!"

Kareen said, "So fine! Incredibly intelligent! I was so drunk that I let things get out of hand."

Lexington said, "Too much alcohol plus alone with Akera equals bad decisions."

Triplication

After about two hours of talking and drinking, Amir offered to walk the girls to their car. Akera invited him over to her house, but Kareen was unsure about the invitation.

Akera said, "We are going to have a little fun." When they reached Akera's house, she took a picture of his license plate. She told him, "If any of my shit comes up missing, I will hunt you down like the FBI looking for a terrorist."

Amir held up his hands; he said, "Your stuff is safe with me."

They went into the house. Amir took a seat on the couch in the living room. Kareen sat on the love seat across from Amir. Akera fixed drinks and put on some music. They vibed to the music and drank a little more. Akera pulled Kareen up to sing and dance in front of Amir. Amir sipped his drink and watched. Akera seductively rubbed and touched all over Kareen as they closely danced. Amir looked a little shocked, and a lot excited. Akera pulled Kareen over to the couch.

One girl sat on each side of Amir. They rubbed and kissed all over him. He returned the favor. The attraction between Amir and Kareen was electric. Akera could tell Kareen was the one he really wanted. Akera pulled Kareen onto his lap. Akera watched as she softly caressed Kareen's hair as Amir and Kareen kissed. Amir's hands touched all over Kareen's secret places.

Akera unbuttoned Kareen's pants as Kareen and Amir Kissed. Akera put one hand down Kareen's pants and one hand down her own pants. Kareen held his bald head in her hands. Amir wrapped his arm around Kareen's back, holding her so his manhood could bump into her.

Akera said, "Let's take this upstairs."

Akera led them to her guest bedroom where she had a California-king round bed with a white leather headboard and white silk sheets. She reached in the condom-filled candy dish on the nightstand and handed Amir a condom: Trojan Magnum extra-large, Amir said: "You are prepared!"

Akera replied, "I refuse to get caught slipping."

Akera took off Amir's shirt.

She said, looking at his abs with glee on her face, "I hope you're as good as you look, sexy mother fucker (rubbing his stomach muscles)."

Amir smiled, he said, "I think you'll enjoy yourself."

Amir watched Kareen walk into the bathroom as Akera pulled Amir's pants down, she said: "Damn boy, your daddy has got to be part horse because you're hung like a purebred thoroughbred. Look at this dick, Kareen. This thing is huge. It's so cute."

He smirked as he watched Kareen pinning up her hair with a clip in the bathroom. Akera led Amir to the bed and laid him down, she asked him, "Do you have a woman at home?" He said no.

She replied, "Good, we don't have to worry about leaving dick for anyone; we're taking all this dick tonight. It's so much to take. This thing could move mountains. Kareen, look at this thing." The length and circumference of Amir were in a weight class that impress both women.

Kareen came into the room to see Akera kneeling between Amir's legs rolling a condom onto Amir's manhood. Amir stared at Kareen as Akera slid him into her mouth. Kareen stood at the bathroom door watching as Akera sucked Amir like a melting sour popsicle. Despite Akera performing fellatio like a porn star, Amir couldn't keep his eyes off Kareen.

Akera slowly lowered herself onto him. Amir's ineffable manhood subdued Akera's eager energy. Amir supplied Akera with a surplus of goods, but he kept an eye on Kareen. Akera signaled for Kareen to join them. Akera pulled Kareen onto Amir. Kareen laid back on his chest. Amir immediately started kissing Kareen's neck and caressing her breasts. Akera lifted Kareen's hips to meet her face. Amir said, "Damn," impressed by Akera's daring willingness to get the job done. Amir was intrigued by the sight of Akera licking Kareen.

Akera pulled Amir out of her and slowly pushed him into Kareen. Amir began to slowly stroke into Kareen, who immediately moaned from the presence of him inside her. As Amir stroked into Kareen, Akera sucked him and licked Kareen. Kareen's tight, wet flesh surrounding him coupled with Akera's mouth sucking him made him cum.

Akera gave Amir a new condom as they walked toward the shower. He stood directly in the center of the shower. The women knelt before Amir sucking him as the water poured over their heads. Amir experienced a sexual high watching two women suck him.

Akera sat Kareen on the bench. She bent over in front of Amir putting her face between Kareen's leg, kissing up Kareen's thigh. Amir knelt behind Akera. Amir felt so good to Akera that she couldn't keep her mouth on Kareen. Amir made her cum so hard that she had to tap out.

Once Akera tapped out, it was time for Amir and Kareen to explore their attraction. Amir reached out his hand to Kareen. He was afraid she would reject him. She did the unthinkable. She accepted him. She walked over to him and slowly lowered herself onto him, crowning him as if he were the king, and she was the majesty queen taking her position on the throne.

Amir touched every part of Kareen as she rocked his body in strong circles. Kareen moaned from the overwhelming pleasure. Amir was so filled with desire he couldn't let her stay in control. He grabbed the back of her neck, pulling her face to his while he pushed up into to her as hard and as deep as he could.

Akera grabbed her hand-held shower head massager to pleasure herself as she watched Amir and Kareen. So filled with lust, he needed more room to get Kareen how he really wanted her. He carried her into the bedroom. He laid her wet body on the edge of the bed, pinning her thighs to the bed. He slowly pushed into Kareen. Kareen couldn't stop panting and moaning as Amir hit her with the best stroke she ever experienced.

The thrusts of Amir rippled through Kareen's chest. Amir crossed her legs at the knees, putting her ankles by his ears. He rocked her body, making an x across his chest with her legs. He rolled her from side to side, making sure he hit every spot. He was so deep that she couldn't feel her legs.

Akera stood in the door, watching Amir and Kareen. Amir was on Kareen like a starving lion attacking a gazelle. Amir flipped Kareen over to hit her doggie style. Amir put his palms on the small of Kareen's back, making her body bounce onto him.

Kareen came so hard that a blaring ringing sound blasted in her ears. She couldn't open her eyes or move her body. Amir was so excited by Kareen's beauty that he couldn't hold his orgasm. He grabbed Kareen, and stillness came over them. Akera looked with admiration as Amir held Kareen's hips, letting himself sit inside her.

Amir kissed Kareen, and she kissed him back. As soon as she regained the ability to move, she hopped out of the bed and ran to the shower. He followed her. As they bathed, Amir struck up a conversation. He said, "I hope I can see you again." Kareen looked at him and smiled.

Amir said, "Can I call you?"

Kareen nodded her head, yes.

Amir said, "You're a very beautiful woman, and I would like to get to know you better."

Kareen said, "You really can't know me any more than you did tonight."

Amir said, "I want to know more about you as a person."

Akera overheard their conversation. She wrote Kareen's number on a piece of paper. After Amir got dressed, Akera handed him the paper and said, "Her number! She's a good girl, and I can tell she likes you. Be good to my friend!" Amir looked at Kareen's number. He said thank you. He said bye before leaving.

Consideration

Kareen said, "I don't know if it's a good idea to pursue something with him. It would be awkward knowing Akera was feeling him, too."

Lexington said, "Don't base life decisions on Akera. She has hoe tendencies. She loves to find herself in hoe situations so she can hoe her way out. He's pursuing you; he wants you."

Destiny said, "I think you should go and have a good time. Give the brother a chance. You may be shocked by what happens. Akera is happy with Vanessa."

Lexington said, "Maybe he's telling the truth when he says he's not focused on that. He already got that, so the only thing left is you."

Destiny said, "Why would he lie? He's already dug out the ditch."

Kareen said, "All the way out!"

Affirmation

Kareen walked through the ER on a Saturday morning in September when a nurse leaned toward her to whisper, "He's fine, tall, no ring, good insurance, and he needs stitches in two of his big, long fingers that he cut playing basketball this morning. If I weren't married, I would be all over him." Kareen laughed and said, okay. She grabbed the chart and walked into the room.

When she walked through the door, Amir's mouth dropped. Kareen opened the chart and saw the name. She thought to herself, please, not that Amir. She looked up and dead into his face. She thought to herself, damn, it's him! They stared at each other as if they were looking into the eyes of ghosts. Kareen broke the awkward stare by going over to the sink to wash her hands. She put on gloves and walked over to look at his fingers.

Amir read her name tag: Dr. Kareen Caine. He whispered, "You didn't tell me you're a doctor?" Kareen ignored him and focused on sterilizing his finger. Amir whispered, "Why don't you answer my calls?"

Kareen said, "Mr. Hill, let me stitch your fingers."

Amir whispered, "Kareen…"

She cut him off. She said, "Mr. Hill, your fingers, that's why I'm here." Kareen gave him a shot. Amir reacted to the pain. Kareen asked, "Are you okay, Mr. Hill?"

Amir said, "No, you see this really pretty woman has my heart, and she won't give it back. She won't even talk to me. Do you think you can write a script for that? It really, really hurts."

Kareen said, "No, I can't write a script for that, but I can give you some really good pain meds for your fingers."

Amir asked, "Can you at least ask her to give my heart back? I can't live without her or my heart."

Kareen said, "I think you'll live."

Amir replied, "Life without either won't be a life worth living." Kareen looked at him. He hit a nerve with that remark.

After she stitched and bandaged his fingers, she gave him instructions before rushing to the door. Before she could get out the door, Amir said, "Dr. Caine!" Amir rushed over to where she was standing and grabbed her arm. He whispered, "Kareen, please, talk to me!"

Kareen whispered, "What, Mr. Hill?"

He said, holding her arm, "If I call, say you'll answer the phone."

Kareen said, "I have to go, Mr. Hill. You need to let me go."

Amir whispered, "Please!"

Kareen said, "If I say ok, you'll let me go?" Amir let her go. Kareen said, "I leave here about six o'clock. Give me an hour or two, and you can call then, but if you don't call tonight, don't call at all."

Amir whispered, "Thank you, I'll call." Kareen rushed out the door.

When Kareen got home, she took a bath and ate. As soon as she laid across the bed, the phone rang. She hesitated, but she reluctantly answered the phone. "Hello!" she said.

Amir said, "Thanks for letting me call you. How have you been?"

Kareen said, "I've been well. How do your fingers feel?"

He said, "They're good! I had a really good doctor."

She said, "Really!"

Amir said, "She was gorgeous too!"

Kareen said, "You like her, huh?"

Amir said, "Yes, I do! It's something about her."

Kareen said, "When you figure it out, let me know."

Amir said, "Definitely!"

Kareen said, "Are those pain meds working?"

He answered, "Yes, probably a little too well." They laughed.

Amir asked, "So what have you been up to besides saving lives and fingers?"

Kareen said, "My usual: work. How about you?"

Amir answered, "I manage to get some work done here and there, but mainly all I do is think of you."

Kareen said, "Is that right?"

Amir said, "I can't get that beautiful face and that pretty smile out of my mind. I wonder what you are doing. I want to know everything about you."

Kareen said, "Give me some specific things you're curious about."

Amir answers, "I wonder what's your favorite holiday, do you like mac and cheese, what's your shoe size, what's your favorite color, do you drink coffee or tea, do you like me, and do you think about me."

Kareen said, "I like Christmas, but Independence Day is my favorite. I'm usually on summer vacation in some foreign or exotic place with my friends. My favorite color is blue because I like the sky and the ocean. I do like mac and cheese. I wear a nine. Let me see, I'm trying to remember what else you asked. Oh yeah! I don't drink coffee or tea. I prefer juice or water."

Amir said, "What about those last two questions? I need to know."

Kareen said, "You need to know, huh?"

Amir said, "Need those answers."

Kareen said, "Can a woman have some secrets?"

Amir said, "I want to know all your secrets!"

Kareen said, "Well if you must know. I think about you, and I like you, too."

Amir said, "Good! I'm so relieved!" Amir continued, "I really want to see you again."

Kareen said, "I don't think that is a good idea."

Amir said, "I think it is a good idea,"

Kareen said, "I don't know if it is."

Amir said, "One harmless dinner. No string attached."

Kareen said, "No, Amir, it wouldn't work."

Amir asked, "Why?"

Kareen said, "What happened the night we met, that's why. The way you start something is the way people expect you to keep it, and I'm not that girl. I don't know what I was thinking that night."

Amir said, "I'm not asking for anything like that. I want to get to know you, spend time with just you, and I want you to know me."

Kareen said, "So you think it's a good idea to pursue a woman who had a one-night stand, which was a threesome with a complete stranger?"

Amir said, "Excuse my lack of knowledge of the English language, but hell, yes! Hell yeah, it's a good idea!"

Kareen said, "Why would that be a good idea?"

Amir answered, "I had the time of my life with you. You will not scare me away, hiding behind a drunken night."

Kareen said, "You don't see that as a sign."

Amir said, "I see this beautiful woman who is smart and fun. She's accomplished, caring, tall, sexy, and good with her hands, and to be honest, she is incredible in so many ways."

Kareen said, "I can't imagine what you think of me, doing that on the first night we met."

Amir said, "I think a lot of you, and not one thought is bad. I like Kareen, and I want Kareen to like me. I want Kareen and I want Kareen to want me. I'm focused on Kareen, and I want to intrigue Kareen so much that she is focused only on me. I promise you, today, tomorrow, twenty years from now, I won't hold that night over your head. We never have to talk about that night."

Kareen said, "I don't want to be with a woman in that way again. If that's what you want, I can't give you that."

Amir said, "Kareen, I was feeling you from the moment I walked into the bar. I came and sat next to you, hoping to get a chance to talk to you. I was interested in you, then. I'm interested in you, now.

"Maybe I should've stopped what happened, but I saw an opportunity to get close to you, and I took it. I am sorry, but no one could blame me for wanting to be near you and touch you. Look at you! What man could resist you?

"It's as much my fault as yours, but I don't regret it because I got a chance to be with you, and it was so amazing. I promise to never bring up that night if that will make you feel more comfortable. I'm not going to lie. All that night did was make me want you even more. Not just sexually, but all of you."

She said, "Amir, I was feeling you too from the moment you walked through the door. We were vibing, so I thought you were feeling me too. You and the alcohol, maybe I was feeling you too much, and the alcohol pushed me. I can't blame the alcohol for everything. I blame you, too. When we were kissing on the couch, you did something to me."

Amir said, "I can say the same thing."

Kareen said, "I don't know where this could go with the way we started, but I'll try it."

Amir said, "I know one thing for sure."

Kareen said, "What's that?"

Amir answers, "I want you, and nothing will stop me."

Kareen said, "What do you want to do with me?"

Amir said, "My carnal nature wants to kiss and touch you. My emotional nature wants to hold and love you. My spirit wants to connect with yours. My mental wants you to want me too!"

Kareen said, "I like that, Mr. Hill. Honestly, I want that, too."

Amir said, "I'm glad to hear that. So, tell me, Dr. Caine, what does a brother have to do to win your heart?"

Kareen says, "Brother, you have got to pass the test. You need more checkmarks than x's."

Amir said, "Checkmarks, huh?"

Kareen said, "Lots of checkmarks."

After talking for several hours, Kareen felt better about pursuing a relationship with Amir. Before hanging up, she agreed to meet him the next night at six in the park.

Unification

After meeting Michael for the first time, Kareen left Michael and Lexington's house to meet Amir in the park. He greeted her with roses and a calendar keychain with the date encased in a heart and an attached heart engraved with the words: Our first date. She read the keychain and looked at Amir and smiled. Kareen was impressed by Amir's thoughtfulness.

Kareen said, "The flowers and keychain are really cute. Thank you."

"You're welcome," he said.

She put the gifts in her car, she said, "I love that you put so much thought into our first date. I really appreciate it."

"I'm glad you like our first date, thus far," he replied.

"So, why here, why now," she asked.

He grabbed his bag from the car, he said, "I thought I'd introduce you to something I do and maybe on our next date you could introduce me to one of your hobbies."

Kareen said, "Okay, (smiling) okay, Mr. Hill very thoughtful; you have a deal."

Amir said, "I appreciate that (smiling at Kareen), come on." He led her to the water. He said, "When I was in high school, I needed an elective. My counselor said try photography that should be an easy A. I absolutely fell in love. My teacher, Mrs. Rowe, mentored me, and I won several awards and scholarships. Now, I take photographs to relax. I thought I'd teach you to capture my favorite sight: the sun setting over the water."

Kareen said, "Wow! Amir, I love that. Do you have a darkroom at home with everything?"

Amir said, "Yes, ma'am!"

Kareen said, "That's cool."

Amir said, "Okay, so I have a checkmark."

Kareen said, "Yes, it shows character."

Amir asked, "So how many checkmarks do I need to get a passing grade?"

Kareen said, "Ten out of ten is excellent, but if you can get eight or nine out of ten, you can pass with a high B or low A."

Amir said, "I need one hundred per cent, so you make sure I stay on track."

Kareen said, "I am sure you can achieve a perfect score."

Amir taught Kareen how to use natural light to enhance the image. Kareen looking at the sun's reflection in the water through the camera lens, said, "The reflection of the sun is so beautiful."

Amir said, "It doesn't compare to your beauty." Amir had a way of saying things that got to Kareen. When the sun set, they took pictures of each other as they walked along the hiking trail. They took pictures of nature and pictures of each other enjoying nature.

When Amir walked Kareen back to her car, she said, "This was the best date I ever had, thank you!"

Amir said, "You're welcome, so we can do this again?"

Kareen asked, "Are you free on Thursday night at seven?"

Amir said, "I will be."

She said, "Bring your dancing shoes!"

Amir said, "Oh, ok! I see you." He smiled at her as he opened her car door. As she got in the car, he asked, "Did I get ten out of ten?"

She smiled and said, "You passed with one hundred per cent."

He winked at her and told her, "Drive safely." She waved as she pulled off. He waved.

Accession

Amir walked to Kareen and greeted her with a gold box wrapped with a blue ribbon. She hugged him. "A gift for me, thank you! I'm so glad you came. Hope you enjoy my hobby," she said as they walked into the hall.

Amir said, "I will enjoy anything as long as I am near you."

Kareen smiled, again his words touched her. They sat down. As she opened the box, she said, "You have a habit of saying things that hit me right here," pointing to her heart. Amir smiled.

Her face lit up when she saw the scrapbook of the photos from their first date. She said, "This is so beautiful, thank you," as she looked at the pictures. "These shots are amazing," she said.

He leaned over and whispered, "You're amazing!"

She told him, "You're amazing!" She asked, "Have you tried ballroom hustling?"

He smiled, "I don't dance, but I'll try anything to be close to you." Kareen led Amir to the dance floor, where he enjoyed being close to Kareen.

After dancing, they went to Kareen's favorite restaurant to get her favorite foods and juice. Amir said, "So you eat like this often and stay that slim?"

"On Thursday and Friday nights, I indulged myself. The rest of the week, I'm a disciplined doctor. I eat fresh fruit and salad all day the other five days of the week," she answered.

Amir said, "It's paying off because you're in great shape."

Kareen said, "Amir, you're in great shape."

She asked, "We always talk about me. You never talk about you. What do you do for a living? Where did you grow up? Where did you go to school? When is your birthday? I want to know everything about you."

He said, "Ok. My birthday is on November third."

She said, "No way, mine is the eighth."

Amir said, "Okay, something we have in common."

Kareen said, "Do I get a checkmark for that?"

He said so far you have like six out of ten." They laughed, and he continued, "I'm thirty-eight. My parents were in the army when I was born, so I have no home. I grew up on army bases all over the world: Germany, Italy, California, Georgia, and Texas.

"I'm the youngest of three boys. My brothers live in Texas. They are also computer geeks. I went to Columbia. I moved here to work as a computer software engineer. My parents are retired. They live in Florida. I have no kids but would love some if God sees fits. My favorite color is blue, and I really like you. That's my entire life."

Kareen said, "The million-dollar question: do you have a girlfriend, wife, significant other?"

He said, "The one-dollar answer is no. I've been divorced for about three years. I was married for about eight years."

Kareen asked, "What happened?"

Amir answered, "She didn't want to be married, at least not to me. She's remarried now. I've been single since the divorce."

Kareen asked, "What happened between you and her?"

He answered, "One day, the only woman I ever wanted didn't want me. I was so caught off guard. I was happy, and I thought she was too. She said she wanted something else, and if I loved her, I'd let her go, so I did. What about you? Is there a special man in your life?"

Kareen answered, "I just haven't found the man that makes me feel that way, you know."

Amir said, "A beautiful girl like you deserves a true love story."

Kareen said, "So are you going to help me write my true love story?"

Amir said, "I always wanted to be an author."

Kareen said, "Mr. Amir Hill, computer software engineer and future author, there's a lot I don't know, but I do know one thing for sure. If I had you as my man, I would do a lot of things, and I mean a lot, but leaving is not one."

Amir responded, "Is that right?"

Kareen smiled and winked at him. She added, "I can't see falling out of love with all that you are. From over here, things look amazing."

Amir said, "From over here, things look amazing."

Acclamation

After a long day at the hospital, Kareen stopped by Amir's apartment. She rang the buzzer. Amir said, "Who is it?"

"It's Kareen," she answered.

"Get up here, girl," he said as he buzzed her in.

When she reached the apartment, he stood at the door. She said, "I wanted to see you." She reached out her arms to hug him.

She closed her eyes and rested her head on his chest. She said as they embraced, "I had a really long, emotionally draining day. I'm going to go home. I'm going to sleep for a few hours before I have to go back to do it all again." She kissed him, and said, "I needed to see you, touch you, kiss you," before she turned to walk away.

"So, you're not coming in," he said, stopping her from walking any farther.

"I don't want to disturb you," she answered.

He pulled her close to him, "Stay," he said. He pulled her into the apartment and closed the door.

She asked, "Are you sure you weren't busy?"

"Never too busy for you," he said.

"I didn't call, and that's really not cool. I needed to see you before I went home," she said.

"And now, I need to see you," he said as he pulled her in for a kiss. He took her purse and sat it on the table. He sat her on the couch and took off her shoes. He massaged her feet and said, "Tell me about your day."

She said, "Amir, that feels good!" Kareen relaxed and said, "As a doctor, you know death is a part of the job, but when you lose a child, it's hard to take. A beautiful little boy and his mom died from a terrible car accident. A fifty-year-old man died from a heart attack because he continued to drink and smoke after the first two heart attacks. I was able to bring him back the first two times, but today he died with my hands on his chest. That was my day."

Amir said, "I can't imagine how hard losing a patient is for you. I can listen to you, make you a warm bath, massage your back, make you something to eat."

"You would do all that for me," she asked.

"Absolutely," he said.

"I accept your offer," she said. Amir ran her a bath. He helped her in the tub. He washed her legs, feet, and back as she relaxed in the tub. He massaged her neck and back as they talked.

Kareen said, "Thank you! You give a great massage."

"You could have this every day, any day you would like. I would love to take care of you. Think about it while I cook," Amir replied.

"I'm so hungry," Kareen replied.

He asked, "Are you in the mood for breakfast or dinner?"

She said, "Surprise me!"

"There's a brand-new toothbrush in the medicine cabinet, and there are t-shirts and shorts in the second drawer in my room," Amir said.

Kareen finished her bath, wrapped herself in a towel, she cleaned the tub, and brushed her teeth. Kareen got a t-shirt and pair of shorts out of the drawer and made her way to the kitchen. "It smells good," she said.

"Wait until you taste it," Amir said. Amir asked, "Juice or water? I purchased organic pineapple and cranberry juice just for you."

Kareen said, "Awe, that's so sweet. Juice, mixed, please!" She tasted the food; she said: "This is delicious."

Amir bit into his food, he says, "So good."

Kareen asked, "So you're saying, I can have this all the time."

Amir said, "That's what I'm saying."

Kareen asked, "Are you ready for all that?"

Amir winked at her, he said, "I think I need it."

After they ate, Amir told her to go to bed and get some rest. He laid down on the couch. She asked, "You're not coming with me? Come, hold me!"

Kareen reached out her hand. Amir got up and took her hand. He whispered, "Are you ready for all that?"

Kareen said, "I think I need it." Amir picked Kareen up and carried her to his bed. He gently laid her down. He took off his shirt, got in the bed, and wrapped her in his arms. He played in her hair until they fell asleep.

Kareen woke up about an hour later. She looked at a sleeping Amir. She bit her thumb as she thought about how good he looked. She lifted the sheet to see him bulging through his boxer-briefs. Kareen debated in her head if she should make a move.

Her body reacted before her mind could complete the thought. Her fingertips slowly rubbed down his chest and glided down to his abs. Suddenly, her mind found her hand kneading his manhood under his boxer-briefs. He jumped and opened his eyes to see her kissing his chest. Kareen asked, "Did I scare you?"

Amir answered, "You made me feel something, but it wasn't fear."

Kareen said, "What did you feel?"

Amir asked, "Are you ready that answer?"

Kareen said, "I'm ready for the answer and what comes with it."

Amir asked, "You're sure you're ready?"

Kareen said, "Oh! Mr. Hill, I'm ready!"

Amir said, "I feel desire for you. I feel love for you. I feel compassion for you. I feel need. Can you handle all of that?"

Kareen said, "I can handle you, your emotions, your needs, and your desire."

He said, "Can you handle me as a man, as your man?"

Kareen answers, "Definitely!" Kareen's hand continued to rub him.

He said, "Are you saying you are ready to be in a committed relationship with me?"

She said, "Amir, I am unquestionably and entirely prepared to be totally committed and faithful to you."

He said, "I've been waiting for you to say that. Seal the deal with a kiss."

Kareen's touch put him in the mood. After Amir kissed Kareen, he said, "May, I make love to my woman for the very first time?"

Kareen said, "I hope this is your last first time."

Amir said, "I think it will be," as he took Kareen in his arms. He took off the shirt she was wearing. They laid skin to skin, kissing, and holding each other.

Kareen and Amir stared in each other's eyes and became sensitive to each other's touch. They silently exchanged passionate kisses and caresses. Amir slowly and seductively massaged Kareen's thighs and legs as Kareen softly touched Amir's arms and shoulders. Amir turned her onto her stomach to rub her back. Kareen closed her eyes and smiled as she enjoyed the heat of his hands, sending electric pulses flaring through her body. He kissed down her back.

Amir rolled Kareen onto her back. He slowly sucked and kissed her neck down to her breasts. Amir loved her big chocolate kisses, and it showed in the way he touched and kissed them. His kisses made Kareen melt in his mouth and on his hands. Kareen pulled him out of his underwear. As he seductively kissed her, she rubbed him with her hands.

Amir slowly pulled down the shorts she was wearing, revealing her body. His manhood rubbed against her as they kissed. The warmth and wetness of her thrilled him. He caressed her slim, curvy hips as he kissed her cheeks and lips, making Kareen so aroused that she melted on his Egyptian cotton sheets. Kareen inhaled deeply as all of her nerve endings tingled from the sensation of his fingers moving over her.

Kareen watched his big hands touch all over her body as Amir slowly went down to softly kiss her other lips. Kareen caressed Amir's bald head as his tongue made circles in and over her. Through her labored breathing, she called out to him, "Ah! Amir, baby!" Kareen's love potion made Amir's lip shimmer in the dark.

Amir could tell Kareen was enjoying herself. Feeling she was nearing an orgasm, Amir inserting two fingers in her and slowly moved around until he found her g-spot. Amir sucked her as he rubbed her g-spot until she gushed all over his fingers.

Kareen's arms and legs were wrapped around him as he whispered in her ear: you with me is all I ever wanted."

Kareen said, "I wanted that, too. I was scared."

Amir said, "You'll never have to fear me. I won't hurt you."

Kareen said, "I won't hurt you!"

Amir said, "Emotionally or mentally, I won't hurt you, but right now, I want you so badly it may hurt."

Kareen said, "I bet it will with that boulder hanging out your underwear." They laughed.

He reached into his nightstand to get a box of Trojan Magnum XL condoms. Kareen said, "May I ask a personal question?"

He said, "Of course!"

She said, "Have you been with anyone since that night?"

Amir said, "No, I've been waiting for you."

Kareen said, "Really, you've been waiting five months for me?"

He said, "I haven't dated anyone, called anyone, approached anyone. I felt like I was supposed to be with you."

She said, "I haven't been with anyone either." As he put on the condom, Kareen said as she rubbed on his chest, "Since that night, you've invaded my thoughts, my daydreams, and my dreams. Your touch; your cologne; my hands all over your rock, hard chest and abs; your eyes staring at me; your deep voice whispering and moaning in my ear; and that big ass dick fucking the shit out of me. It all stays on my mind."

Amir and Kareen kissed as their bodies gently, slowly winded. Amir whispered in her ear, "Put me where I belong!" Kareen reached down between her legs, taking ahold of him. She widened her thighs as she slowly pushed Amir inside of herself. She bit her lip as he parted her like Moses parted the Red Sea. Amir whispered, "You feel so good." Amir enjoyed the snug, warm wetness of Kareen surrounding him.

Once inside of her, Amir took over. Amir wrapped one arm around her neck and the other around her back. Amir lay chest to chest with Kareen holding her so tightly there was no end or beginning to them. Amir said, "Kareen, you feel so good." Neither one of them could stop verbally showing their adulation as Amir touched Kareen in deep hidden places.

Kareen fingers tightly held on to Amir's back with her legs wrapped around his waist as she felt every millimeter of Amir inside her. Kareen's whole body was under Amir's spell.

When Kareen begins to feel overwhelmed, she subconsciously closed her legs a little. Amir whispered in her ear, "Baby, give it to me!" Kareen realized she was tensed. She relaxed her body, so Amir could get to every part of her. Amir changed positions to relieve her discomfort.

Amir grabbed Kareen's leg and went down between her legs, seductively licking Kareen. He held her feet in his hands, tilting her pelvic area. Amir eats just like he beats. His tongue is just like his manhood: a heavyweight champion. His lick is just like his stroke: fascinating.

Amir pulled Kareen to straddle him. Kareen wrapped her arms around his neck as she slowly lowered herself onto him. Kareen was so engaged that she zoned out. Amir made her feel so good; she said, "Amir, baby, you feel so damn good. I'm cuming again!" Amir let Kareen enjoy herself.

Amir said, "I will keep you cuming all night, every night!"

Kareen loudly moaned as she rocked and rolled Amir into her g-spot. Amir had her whole body bouncing and rocking. He loved the sight of her big kisses bouncing, so he rocked her body even more. Kareen tried to move, but he finally had what he wanted, so there was no stopping him. He said, "Kareen, baby, isn't this what you want?"

She said, "Yes, baby, I want this!"

Amir asked, "So, I can get it how I want it?"

She answered with a cracking voice, "Yes, baby!"

Amir asked, "Do you feel good?"

Kareen said, "Yes, Amir! You're making me feel so good!"

Amir asked, "Are you cuming for me?"

Kareen said, "Yes!" He felt the tension building in her body, but he didn't stop. He made her cum so hard that her body jumped and jerked into a curl on the bed. He positioned her on her elbows and knees. He arched her back. She stretched out her arms and gripped the sheets. He grabbed her hips.

Amir explored Kareen's body, switching strokes to measure Kareen's response. Amir went straight ahead, diagonal, and left to right. Finally, he hit the spot, Kareen said, "Baby! Right there! Ah! Right there! Amir put all the energy he had into getting to that spot. Kareen said, "Oh! Baby! Just like that!" Kareen sighed, out of breath, as she clawed the sheets. Amir rocked and rolled Kareen's body, making her cum again. He soon followed her. Amir wore Kareen out. When her body hit the bed, she fell asleep.

Consolidation

On Kareen's birthday the following year, she and her friends plus Vanessa, John, Bishop, and Michael met for dinner at Kareen's favorite restaurant. Amir gave Kareen an excuse to cover why he was running late. Amir was actually meeting with Mr. and Mrs. Caine at their home, asking for their blessing to ask for Kareen's hand in marriage. They were thrilled and gave their blessing.

Everyone at the table was eating and catching up when a deep male voice lowly said, "Kareen!" Everyone stopped eating and talking, instantly. They looked up to see Amir. Every eye in the restaurant was on him as he stood, holding a dozen long stem red roses and three small gift bags. Dressed in an Italian-tailored suit, he sat the gift bags on the table, knelt on one knee, and confidently professed his love to Kareen as he laid the roses at her feet one-by-one.

He said, "From the first moment, I saw you. I knew you were the woman I wanted to spend my life loving. I knew because there was a bright light shining around your spirit that drew me to you like a moth to a flame. I said to myself, Amir, that's your wife and she's absolutely beautiful. Maybe, it was wishful thinking, but I had to take a chance, so I sat next to you. Somehow, we started to talk, and I fell in love with you right then and there. When I got a chance to get to know you, I was convinced that I was right. "When I get a chance to hold you, I don't want to let you go. When we are together, I never want you to leave. When we're apart, I can't think straight. I get caught in a loop of wanting you and thinking about you. I can't wait until you're in my arms again. I have come to the conclusion that I cannot live without you. The thing is I don't think I should have to.

"I will be all the man you need. I will support you in everything you do. I will love you, unconditionally. I will provide all your wants and needs. Wherever you go, I will follow you. If you want to try something new, I will be your biggest cheerleader. I will be your partner in life and love. I guarantee you that no one can or will love you more or better than me."

He pulled a box out of each of the gift bags. He opened the first box. It was a diamond bracelet. He put the bracelet on her wrist and locked the clasp; he said, "It seamless. When it's clasped together, you can't see a beginning or an end. This bracelet represents our love. Like infinity, our love has no beginning or end."

The next gift was a diamond necklace. He said, "The chain represents eternity. That's how long I will love you," as he put the necklace around her neck.

Lastly, Amir grabbed the ring box. He opened it and pulled out the ring. Holding the ring between his fingertips, Amir said, "This diamond represents the promise and the purity of our love," as he placed the ring on her finger. Amir said, "Dr. Kareen Caine, will you be my wife?"

Kareen excitedly said, "YES!" The entire restaurant erupted in applause and cheers as Amir and Kareen stood up and embraced. Everyone at the table stood up and celebrated. The men shook Amir's hand and congratulated him, while the woman doted on Kareen and her ring. Destiny secretly helped Amir pick out the ring. Amir and Kareen looked at each other and, said, I love you.

(Present Day) Lexington fills her heart with courage as she soaks in the tub. She takes off her makeup and wraps her hair as she prepares herself to talk to her daughter. Lexington puts on pajamas and goes to knock on her daughter's bedroom door. Anniston tells her to come in. Lexington gets into bed with her daughter; she says, "Some things are not easy for a mother to tell her daughter."

Lexington leans against Anniston's headboard. Anniston says, "Man, it must be deep. I've never seen you nervous."

Lexington says, "Do not tell your father we had this conversation. He knows I am going to talk to you about sex, but he doesn't know exactly what I'm telling you," as she makes her daughter pinky-promise to keep their conversation a secret and to not act out any of this story.

Lexington says, "Now we've come to the hardest part of the story."

Anniston asks, "What's the hard part?"

Lexington answers, "My revelation year!"

Just as Lexington is about to tell her story, Khryssa walks in, she asks, "Mommy, what are you doing in here?"

Lexington says, "Baby, come sit with us. We're talking," Lexington pats the mattress and Khryssa walks over to the other side of Lexington.

Khryssa snuggles in her mom's arms, and asks, "What are you two talking about?"

Lexington answers, "Me and sex. Your father would not like me telling his daughters this story, but I think it's necessary, so you don't make the same mistakes I made."

Khryssa says, "Mommy, I understand. I won't say anything."

Lexington says, "After I tell you this, remember I'm still your mother, and you are to love and respect me the same. I'm giving you my story as a woman, and hopefully, my story will help you craft a better story for yourself. Believe it or not, I had a life before I met your father. I made some mistakes with men that I regret. I got hurt, and I hurt people."

Chapter Six: Lexington

Lexington says, "When I was a teenager, I did everything right until I made one bad decision: Camren Wright, star college athlete, and engineering student. I met Camren, a junior at the time, at the beginning of my sophomore year. Camren was my first boyfriend. By the end of my junior year, his senior year, we were happily engaged with our entire future planned.

"Camren was perfect on paper. He came from a good family. He had a good job waiting for him, so I knew he would be a good provider. The relationship seemed perfect. When he asked me to have sex, I didn't want to, but I did it to keep him happy. His logic was we were getting married why does it matter if it happens tonight or our wedding night.

"One morning, I went to make him breakfast like I always did. When I walked into his bedroom, I found him in bed with two naked females. Not two random females, but two females I knew. These females and I partied together. We went to games together. I felt betrayed. My friends slept with my fiancé in the bed that I lost my virginity in just a few nights before."

Khryssa says, "Mommy, I feel bad that he did that to you."

Lexington kisses Khryssa's forehead. She says, "I was not mad at him. I was mad at me for not following my first mind. My mother warned me. She begged me not to be with him. Who had to dry my tears after he broke my heart? My mother was so disappointed, but she was there for me.

"After Camren, I was single for a long time. One day, one of my friends introduced me to Raymond. He was a gentleman, very smart, very successful, well-mannered, respectful, tall, and cute. Raymond was very disciplined in his role as the man in the relationship, so he did a lot for me without me wanting or asking. His mother and father loved me. All of that made me feel obligated to stay with him.

"My mother begged me not to move in with him, but I did because he begged me. I lived with him for four long years. I felt trapped. One day, he expressed he wanted more, and that pushed me to leave. It took me a year to get the courage to leave. I had been secretly furnishing my apartment and planning my escape for months.

"As I walked out the door, he cried like a baby and begged me to stay. As much as I hated to hurt him, I had to save myself. After I moved into my own apartment, he called every night trying to get me to come back until one day he called and said he was marrying his ex-girlfriend.

"After I broke up with Raymond, I met Roman. Roman was tall, wealthy, and smart. He was bi-racial: black and Italian. He was physically perfect, just fine for no reason. We met at a club. He chased me for three years. Can I take you out, let's have dinner, come hang with me, and the answer was always no.

"He randomly sent flowers to my office, phone calls out of the blue, he would send gifts on my birthday and holidays, and he flirted every time he saw me out. Three years of no, but he did not give up. He always knew where I was and what I was doing. He had to know someone I knew.

"One night, we bumped into each other at a club. From the moment he walked through the door, he was all over me. I went to the restroom, and some of his fans were in there. As soon as they saw me, they started talking about Roman loud enough for me to hear. When I left the restroom, I noticed they were watching us. Just to be petty, I let him touch and kiss all over me.

"I can't lie, I enjoyed the attention. The music was blasting, he was whispering in my ear and kissing all over me. The females were watching. They were mad. If looks could kill, the whole club would be dead.

That night I realized, I was attracted to him, and the females talking and hating made me curious. Before I never even entertained the thought. But with him all over me, and females watching with envy and jealousy written all over their faces, I was interested. Days after that night in the club, I could still feel him all over me. But, when he asked me out, I said no.

A few weeks later, we happened to run into each other on vacation in Cancun. I was sitting with my friends, having dinner one night. I looked up and right into his smiling face."

Inhibition

Roman walked to the table; he said, "Lex, baby! What's up!"

She asked, "What are you doing here?"

He said, "Trying to have some fun in the sun." She knew this was not a coincidence; he followed her. He spoke to her friends, and Akera invited him to sit down.

He asked, "Lex, when are you going to let me spend time with you?" She put her head down.

Akera didn't give Lexington a chance to speak; she asked, "What's up with you and Lexi?" As Roman answered, he stared at Lexington. He went on and on about how she's his dream girl, how much he likes her, he promised he'd be good to her, and take care of her.

Lexington was embarrassed, she asked him, "If I say yes, would you please end this conversation."

Roman said, "Say yes, and I'll leave."

"Okay, Roman," she said.

Roman said, "I'll see you tomorrow night."

"Roman, do you know where I am staying," she asked.

Roman said, "I know where to find you! I'll pick you up at seven."

She said, "Okay! Now go!"

The girls ate up everything he said. As he got up, he winked at Lexington. After he walked away, her friends swore Lexington watched him with seductive eyes. She swore it was an irritated face.

Kareen said, "Lexington, you say you don't like him, but that night at the club. I mean, you two were all over each other and now tonight the way you looked at him. I think something is happening."

Lexington shook her head no; she said, "He was on me at the club."

Akera said, "You were dancing on him, hugging him, he was kissing all over you, and his hands were all over your booty. And don't think we couldn't tell you were enjoying it."

Kendra said, "Biggest Sister, would it be so bad to give the brother a chance?"

She said, "Baby Sister, not happening!"

Akera said, "That's what your mouth is saying, but your eyes are saying something different. The way you looked at him, you're trying to fuck."

Kareen asked Akera, "So you peep that look, too?"

Lexington said, "I am not!"

Destiny said, "Best Friend, he's going to get it, and you gave him a look like you want to give it to him."

"Leave me alone, Destiny," Lexington replied.

Kendra said, "If nothing, have a little fun."

Lexington said, "It's one dinner. That's it!"

The next night, Lexington put on an all-white, knee-length dress with spaghetti straps. The dress was so form-fitting that it could attract a blind man's attention. Since he wanted to see her so badly, she set out to show him something. Roman dressed in white linen pants with a black t-shirt under his unbuttoned linen shirt. When she opened the door, she was instantly pleased.

They went to dinner, dancing, and for a walk on the beach. She had a surprisingly nice time. Roman was attentive, funny, engaging, interesting, and a gentleman. She enjoyed herself way more than she expected.

The moment came when she had to decide if she was going to let Roman make a move. They stood at her hotel room door as she internally debated. She thought maybe I could let go and enjoy myself. On the other hand, she thought Roman was not a smart choice. Roman stood there, smiling and talking. He slowly, got closer and closer. Roman caressed her hair as he leaned in to kiss her, but she leaned back, grabbing the doorknob. She asked if he wanted to come in.

Embarrassed that she broke the flow of the kiss, he happily accepted the invitation. Lexington unlocked the door and walked in. Roman followed her into her room and locked the door behind him. Roman got further than he anticipated.

As she took off her shoes, Lexington said, "Make yourself comfortable; I have to go to the restroom."

Roman sat on the couch. When she returned from the restroom, she sat next to him. She asked if he would like something to drink. He said whatever you're having. She poured two glasses of wine. She sat back on the couch and handed him a glass of wine. She sipped her wine then sat it on the table.

She went over to the television. She asked, "What kind of movies do you like?"

Roman smiled; he said, "I like all kinds of movies." When she cut the on tv, the movie she was watching the night before started to play.

He said, "Let's just finish watching this." He told her to hit the light.

She said, "I have popcorn."

Roman said, "That sounds good!" She grabbed the popcorn, cheese dip, and bottles of water before she cut off the light.

They sat on the couch, watching a movie and eating popcorn. Roman noticed Lexington dipping her popcorn in cheese. Roman said, "Let me taste that."

Lexington reached to hand him the cheese, but he grabbed the other hand, holding the dipped popcorn. He ate the popcorn and licked the cheese from her fingertips.

As he sucked her fingers, he stared into her eyes. The wet warmth of his lips and tongue on her fingers turned her on and lowered her inhibition. He said, "That tastes good, but I bet you taste better," as he continued to suck her fingers.

Lexington was frozen with shock but intrigued by the message his soft pink lips sent: I aim to please. Her senses received the message loudly and clearly. The read receipt was her soaked panties.

He grabbed her thighs with a firm grip and pulled her to him, "Let me taste you," he whispered in her ear.

She felt his warm breath on her ear and neck, making her saturate her panties even more. He pulled her closer to him, kissed her neck then her ear, he whispered: "Can I taste you?"

He kissed from her neck to her breasts. He said, "Say yes, and I'll do anything, everything you want me to do," as he kissed up to the other side of her neck.

He took the popcorn and cheese from her hand and sat it on the table. He laid Lexington on the couch and wrapped her legs around him. He lifted her dress above her belly button. He caressed her abs as he leaned forward to kiss her through her panties; he said, "Say yes. (She felt the heat of his breath through her panties.) Let me hear you say yes. (He kissed her panties again.) Lex, come on, say, yes!"

Lexington shyly whispered, "Yes!" and that was all Roman needed.

He pulled her panties off, sat them on the table, and firmly gripped her hips holding her in place as he stared at her Brazilian wax. He spread her lips with his fingers; he said, "Your pussy is so pretty. It looks like a beautifully bloomed rose." He rubbed her thighs as he continued to admire her; he said, "Looking at you like this is like watching the sunrise in a clear blue sky: it's amazing."

Roman laid on his belly. He began to intensely lick and suck her as he stared in her eyes. Lexington had never felt anything like Roman, and her body responded immediately. Lexington tenderly breathed as her body experienced changes she never felt before.

Roman rolled on to his back and sat Lexington on his face. He locked his arms behind her lower back with his elbows on her hips. He had Lexington riding his tongue backwards like she was driving a luxury European automobile. She moaned as she rolled and rocked her hips, and proof of her pleasure poured all over Roman.

Roman picked her up and carried her to the bed. He slowly pulled her dress over her head. After she was undressed, she got under the cover. She watched him undress. He asked, "You like what you see," as he rubbed himself.

"I must say it's a nice view from over here," she said.

He picked his pants up off the floor, reached into his pants pocket, and pulled out his wallet. He grabbed three condoms from his wallet; he said, "Girl, it's going to be a long night." As he got into the bed, she lifted the cover so he could get on top of her. He laid between her legs. He kissed her breasts as he put on the first condom. He kissed down from her chest to her stomach down to the middle of her thighs. Roman's tongue had Lexington gasping for air as if she was drowning.

He used the tip to tease Lexington. They moaned from the pressure of Roman entering her. Roman wrapped his arms around her. So happy to have a chance to feel her, Roman began taking slow, long, deep, rhythmic strokes into her soaking wet body. Lexington dug her fingertips into his shoulder blades.

With Lexington's bent legs resting on his sides, Roman touched Lexington in places that had never been touched by a man. Lexington moaned as she felt lust travel through her body. Lexington hands rubbed all over Roman's abs and chest. They stared into each other's eyes, feeling euphoria as they lived out the moment they fantasized about. Roman put his hands on her waist and went to work.

Roman turned Lexington over onto her stomach in the center of the bed. Roman rubbed Lexington's back with one hand as he used the other hand to guide himself inside her. Once inside her, he held her hips. He started slow, but it was so good that his strokes became faster and more forceful. He said, "Lex, baby, work that ass like you danced on me at the club."

Lexington, catching his rhythm, started throwing her body back against him. Roman said, "Hell yeah Lex, baby, throw that ass back just like that! Good girl! Yes, Lex, keep it arched, just like that. Shit! Girl! Throw that shit back. Yes! Lex! Just like that, baby! You feel so good!"

After the third condom was full and Lexington soaked the bed, the sun was breaking through the dark sky. They watched the sunrise in each other's arms. Roman kissed her forehead and said he would go, so she could get some sleep. As he put on his clothes, he said, "You know I wanted you for a long time!"

Lexington said, "Is that so," and smirked.

As they walked to the door, Roman said, "You're more incredible in person than in my dreams."

Lexington replied, "So, you dreamt about us being together?"

Roman said, "Only two hundred million times." They laughed. He added, "But, nothing beats you in person; you're amazing."

Lexington smiled and said, "Thanks, as are you." Roman hugged her before he walked out the door. Lexington locked the door and went back to bed.

Retribution

After spending the day with her friends, Lexington returned to her room completely exhausted from the previous night. After she showered, she put on lotion. She slipped on a camisole, some yoga pants, and white socks, then laid in the bed. She lowly played music as she drifted into a light sleep only to be awakened by a knock at the door.

She thought it was Akera trying to get her to go to a club. She was surprised to see Roman dressed in a white t-shirt, gray sweatpants, and a pair of Jordan's. "Oh, hey," she said.

"You were expecting someone else," he asked.

"I thought you were my sister. Come in," she replied.

"I wanted to see you before I flew out in the morning," he said as he walked in the door.

She closed the door and said: "That's sweet!"

He grabbed her hand and pulled her close to him. He said, "Can you handle a round two?"

"What's in it for me," she asked.

He picked her up; he said, "Trust me, you will get yours." He kissed her neck as he carried her to the bed.

She said, "Roman, I was sleep. I'm so tired."

He said, "Don't worry, I will put you back to sleep, a deep sleep."

He laid her on the bed; he said, "I've been thinking about you all day," as he took off her shirt. He kissed her from her neck to her navel.

She rubbed his face and back as she asked, "What were you thinking?"

He kissed her breasts as he answered, "I thought about kissing you," his hands slowly slid down the curves of her body; he said, "I thought about touching you." He licked her from her navel to her neck.

He said, "I thought about tasting you," as he pulled her pants and panties off. As he kissed her neck, he said, "I could smell you, taste you, hear you all day. I couldn't get you off my mind. The truth is I was supposed to leave this morning, but I changed my flight, hoping to spend some more time with you." Lexington said, "Awe! Roman, that was sweet."

Roman said, "Purely selfish!" When she was undressed, he stared at her, lying naked.

He pulled her closer; he said, "Come here with your fine ass!" He kissed her from her knees to her hips. He wrapped his lips around her, and he sucked her like a fresh, ripe, dripping pink slice of seedless watermelon. He firmly placed his hands on her butt and pulled her toward him as he slid his tongue into her.

He repeated that motion until Lexington achieved her first pleasure victory. He sucked the cum out of her like a hungry seafood lover slurps an oyster, making her moan like he wanted. She had one hand on his head and the other hand gripping the sheets. She felt a rush of warm energy from all over her body to the core of her being. Lexington's feminine calls of pleasure encouraged Roman's performance.

He flipped her over and smacked her ass. He took his underwear off and put on a condom. He said, "I'm about to fuck the shit out of you." He pinned her left shoulder to the bed with his left hand, and he gripped her right hip with his right hand. Her face was tilted to the right against the sheets. She had a beautiful view of the full moon, illuminating the night sky.

He let the tip sit in her for a moment. Filled with desire for him, Lexington squeezed him. Roman said, "Uh, huh! That's the shit I like right there." Then he pulled himself out. He rubbed himself against her before he slowly pushed into her until he was completely engulfed in her silky, soft, tight flesh.

Once he was all the way in her, he said, "I'm going ocean floor deep all night."

Lexington said, "Just don't drown. I don't know CPR."

Roman said, "Don't worry, I'm an excellent swimmer."

He began to aggressively stroke into Lexington like a construction crew breaking the pavement with a jackhammer. Lexington gripped the sheets with one hand and clawed the headboard with the other hand.

The room was full of the sound of his body slapping against hers while Lexington's music continued lowly playing. He was captivated by the sight of her ass bouncing on him. he said, "Damn girl, the way your ass bounce warms my heart. It makes my eyes water." She would have laughed, but she was preoccupied with eight inches of his rock-hard body knocking into hers.

Roman had a whole different energy tonight. Last night, Roman was alluring, attentive, and gentle. Tonight, he came to get revenge for making him chase her for three years. He was in the position of power tonight. He had one goal: knock the bottom out.

It didn't take long for him to find the spot where Lexington wanted him to be, and when he did, he beat it like a store owner beats a thief with a bat. Lexington cried out: Oh my God! Lexington reached back to push Roman away, but he took her arm and laid it across her lower back. She said it again, "Oh my God!"

Roman said, "He can't help you now."

He smacked her ass twice really hard, and said, "Can you make it dance on me?" Lexington gathered herself, took a deep breath, and adjusted her body. She made her ass pop and jiggle as requested. Roman said, "Hell yeah! Take all this dick, Lex, baby!"

Roman said, "You're squirting again, girl, you are drowning me!" Lexington rocked her hips as she pushed back on Roman as she rubbed herself. Roman said, "Oh, you're trying to cum, huh?" Roman let her take over. He said, "Look at you! Come get what you want!"

He closed his eyes. He said, "Yes, Lex, baby, fuck me." Lexington continued pushing back on Roman. Roman said, "You're cuming for me! (He smacked her ass twice.) I feel it coming."

Roman slowly started to move again. He hit the right spot. Lexington said, "Right there! Roman! Right there!"

Roman said, "I feel it coming." He stayed on that spot. He made Lexington cum so hard that she momentarily lost her eyesight. She was exhausted, but she took Roman until he was done. Lexington took a moment to rest as Roman put on a new condom.

He laid on the bed next to her. He said, "Tomorrow, you're going to feel this. Every time you sit down, every time you take a step, you're going to think: Roman beat it up!"

Lexington asked, "And, what will you be thinking?"

Roman said, "I knocked it out, and she liked it,"

Lexington said, "How do you know I liked it?"

Roman said, "I feel everything when I'm inside you."

Lexington, laying her head on her pillow, said: "Roman, for the record, I did like it!"

Roman (lifting Lexington from the pillow) said, "Oh no! Don't get comfortable; we are not done. Baby, I'm about to go knee-deep."

Lexington said, "Now, you're just talking shit!"

Roman said, "I can back my shit up, though!"

Lexington touched his chest with her fingertips. Roman pulled her arm and said, "Get your pretty ass over here." Roman literally rocked Lexington to sleep.

When she woke up in the morning, Roman was putting on his pants. The sex was incredible, but she still wasn't into the idea of pursuing a relationship with Roman. She wasn't even sure she wanted to see him in the states. Roman noticed she was awake and said, "I tried not to wake you up. I have to catch my flight."

Lexington said, "Have a safe flight!"

Roman kissed her forehead and told her, "I really want to see you again."

Lexington said, "You have my number."

Roman said, "I am serious. I really want to see you."

"Roman, I'm not hard to find," she said.

He said, "I know where you are always. I will always find you." She smiled. Roman said, "I got to go. Go back to sleep, I'll talk to you when you get back to the states."

She said, "Ok!"

He grabbed her hand; he softly kissed the back of her hand. As he left the room, he said: "See you, Lex!" Lexington waved, rolled over, and went back to sleep.

(Present Day) Lexington says, "It was supposed to be a one-time thing. When I came home from Cancun, my plan was to avoid him, but somehow, he talked his way into my life."

Anniston asks, "Mommy, what made you do it?"

Lexington says, "Boredom! Temptation! I wondered what it was like to be a bad girl for once and take a chance to experience pleasure."

Khryssa asks, "Mommy, it sounds like things were serious with him."

Lexington says, "Maybe, it could've been if Chad didn't enter the picture." Both of her daughters looked at her with shocked faces.

Khryssa asks, "Mommy, you cheated on him?"

Lexington says, "We weren't officially a couple, but at one point, he begged me to promise I would not see other men. Chad made me break that promise. A year into the thing with Roman, I was leaving the gym when Chad approached me. For a rich, white boy, Chad had style from the way he walked to the way he spoke to the way he dressed to the cologne he wore to the way he wore his hair and beard. He was so sexy.

"Chad was tall, handsome with an Ivy League education, and a body so chiseled that it could've been in a European art museum. Every part of him had muscles. He had the clearest, brightest blue eyes I've ever seen. I was very attracted to him. When he introduced himself, I was struck by how polite and well-spoken he was. He asked for my number. I gave it to him. He called. We went out a couple times. He made me feel comfortable. I enjoyed the innocent attention he gave me.

"One night, Chad called to ask if he could stop by my apartment. It was weird because we had never visited each other at home, but I figured we would just have some harmless conversation. Chad had my favorite food from my favorite restaurant and my favorite wine. I was shocked that he paid so much attention to me. We ate and talked. The conversation was nice. Chad, like always, was a total gentleman."

Satisfaction

Chad looked at his watch and said, "It's getting late, I better go." Lexington unassumingly walked him to the door. When they hugged, Chad put his hands on the small of Lexington's back. He turned her to face the wall, and he kissed the nape of her neck. Lexington was shocked because that was the most physical contact they ever had.

He lifted her shirt and kissed from her neck to the edge of her pants, making sure his lips and tongue softly touched every inch of her spine. Chad knelt and he pulled Lexington's pants down. He caressed her lower body as he slowly kissed from her lower back to the back of her knees. He wrapped his arms around her waist to touch her with two fingers.

Lexington was entirely caught off guard. Chad didn't give her a chance to consent or reject him. It happened so quickly that she went with the flow. Lexington put her hands on the wall to support herself as Chad licked her repeatedly like she was soft serve ice cream.

Each time he reached a hole, he gently inserted his tongue then puckered his lips to suck her, and it drove Lexington crazy with pleasure. Lexington breathed and clawed the wall as his tongue caressed her most sensitive spots, making her spritz like the first break into a juicy orange. Her reactions turned Chad on and gave Chad confidence to do what he wanted.

Chad picked Lexington up and carried her to the couch. He put her on all fours with her knees on the arm of the couch and her hands on the seat of the couch. He spread her butt cheeks and pulled her toward his face. He had Lexington bouncing back on his tongue. She looked back at him and was struck by his sharp blue eyes staring at her as he licked her.

When it seemed like Lexington couldn't take any more in that position, Chad laid on the couch, and he sat Lexington on his face. Chad had her riding his face like a skilled biker.

Chad used his fingers to find Lexington's g-spot, making Lexington rain like a thunderstorm all over Chad's face. He could tell by her reaction that she loved what he was doing. Chad kept going and going. Lexington kept cuming and cuming. Chad wasn't a saint, but he had Lexington calling on the

Lord as she lightly rocked her hips, making circles on his tongue. The softness of his moist tongue, his super-soft fingertips, the tenderness of his soft, thin lips, and the gentle warmth of his breath made her excited from head to toe.

He laid her on the couch. She couldn't speak or think as her body spasmed in the aftermath of pleasure. He stood up and wiped his face with her panties. He looked at her with a smile on his face; he said, "Are you okay?" She nodded, yes. He asked, "Are you sure?" She gave him a thumbs up.

Chad said (looking at Lexington with a smirk on his face), "I'm going to let myself out."

Lexington couldn't move because she was still having an orgasm, so she said, "Ok!"

Chad said (as he put on his coat), "Thanks for having me over."

Lexington responded, "Thanks for coming!"

Chad said, "Maybe next time." He said, "Don't forget to lock the door," as he walked out of the door full of pride.

(Present Day) Lexington says, "When I walked him to the door, he was all over me. I wasn't expecting that from him. We never even kissed before. After that night, we felt more comfortable, and we made out more and more until we had sex. For two years, I juggled Roman and Chad. Trying to keep them both secretly satisfied was a lot of work, time, and energy."

Khryssa asks, "Mommy, who did you like more?"

Lexington says, "Honestly, I liked them both for different reasons."

Anniston asks, "Do you ever missed them?"

Lexington answers, "When I come home to my husband, look at my husband, or think about my husband, I know I will never ever need another man, so, no, absolutely not."

Khryssa says, "Annie, you noticed Mommy only dated tall, rich, handsome men."

Anniston said, "That is a common thread."

Lexington said, "If you're going to be with a man, you might as well have something to look at and he should be able to afford it."

Khryssa asks, "What made you end it if you were having so much fun?"

Lexington says, "When the consequences kicked in, the fun ended. There is a consequence for every action, good or bad. The day came when they wanted more from me. More than I could give. More than I ever wanted from either of them."

Termination

Chad called to say he had something important to talk about and asked if he could come to her apartment. She replied, "Of course." When he arrived, he was visibly upset. She offered him a glass of wine, but he said no. She asked, "What's on your mind? You seem upset."

Chad said, "My father basically forced me to propose to a family friend. She accepted. In return, I get controlling interest in the family business, but I'll throw it all away if you say you'll marry me."

She almost choked on the wine she was drinking. He continued, "I really want you. My heart is here with you." He pulled a huge rock out of his pocket and said, "Marry me!" He got on one knee and slid the ring on her finger.

She said, "I am the wrong age, the wrong color, and from the wrong social circle. There are too many differences between us to make it work."

He said, "Lexington, I want to be with you. We can make this work. I don't care about any of that." She tried to take the ring off, but he wouldn't let her. He said, "I want you to think about it before you say no. Please!"

She said, "Chad, I can't,"

He cut her off and said, "Just take a day or two to think, before you say no."

Lexington said, "Chad, that's not right. A woman is walking around so happy to be engaged. She's showing all her friends, family and co-workers the ring you gave her, and you're here saying this to me. Chad, that's not fair to her. It's not fair to me. I don't want to be my husband's afterthought. You thought about me after you proposed to her."

Chad said, "I didn't buy or give her a ring. My father gave her my grandmother's ring." Chad was disappointed. She felt bad, but she couldn't entertain his proposal even though the diamond was huge. She tried to give him the ring back, and he said, "I can't believe you're saying no. You know that I would love you, take care of you, cherish you. How could you say no?"

She said, "One day you will wake up, and you will resent me and regret marrying me because you gave up so much to do so. I can't live like that. I can't wake up every morning under that pressure. I won't be enough to replace your family and their money."

Chad said, "Fuck them and their money. I can make it on my own. I have built a name for myself. I can build my own wealth. All I need is you by my side, and everything else will fall into place."

He tried to kiss her, but she moved, "Chad, you're engaged to another woman," she said.

"But I was dating you first," he replied.

She said, "Chad, no! Please, stop!" She struggled to get away from him.

He said, "Since I can't have you for life, just give me one last night."

"Chad no, that's not right. We can't do that to her," she said.

(Present Day) Lexington says, "You see how he played me. He made me feel obligated."

Khryssa says, "He was all the way wrong."

Lexington says, "Right! The ring, perfect, but what kind of proposal was that."

Anniston says, "Mommy, it seemed like he really wanted to be with you."

Lexington answers, "But, that's not how the game works, you cannot switch up or change the rules on someone. He couldn't expect me to feel the way he felt."

Lexington goes back to that night; she says, "I was trying to get away from him, and he cornered me on the couch. I tried to push him away, but he was stronger than me. He towered over me, begging, and he wouldn't let me go."

Conclusion

"Let me make love to you with my tongue, then fuck you until the sun comes up," he said.

He tongue-kissed the back of her knee and made his way up her thigh under her shorts. She tried to push his head away.

She repeatedly told him no and stop, but he said, "Lexi, please, don't stop me. Don't push me away," as he grabbed both of her wrists with one hand and held them over her head and pushed her thighs back and apart with his shoulders.

He had her restrained, so she couldn't physically resist him. He moved her panties to the side with his mouth. He used his elbows and forearms to hold her thighs in place. She tried to reason with him, but he refused to listen.

Chad licked her end to end; he said, "I promise this is the last time, and you won't regret it," as he stared in her eyes and slowly continued licking her. She tried to break free, but his grip was too strong.

He told her, "Lexi, don't fight it." He asked, "Don't you want to be with me?"

Lexington said, "Chad, doing that to me, engaged to her is wrong. Chad, let me go."

Chad stopped talking and argued his position with his tongue. He licked her so sensually that he calmed her rebellious spirit. It felt so good that she relaxed. Chad let her go, and she let him go. He gently pulled her shorts and panties off and sat them on the couch.

He rolled her onto her side. He laid on his side, facing her, making a pillow of her thigh. He held her other thigh straight up and put her knee over his shoulder. He closed his eyes and sipped from her like she was a water fountain. He brought her thigh down to rest on the side of his head. He wrapped his arms around her hips so tightly that she couldn't move. Chad kissed, sucked, and licked her so sensually that she left shimmers and glimmers of black girl magic all over his face.

He rolled her on her back as he firmly gripped her hips; her knees were over his shoulders. He whispered to her, "I'm going to miss you!" Chad lifted

Lexington from the couch with the backs of her thighs seated on his shoulders. He supported her with his forearms across her lower back. She held on to his head. Lexington never felt so close to the ceiling. It was exhilarating sitting atop Chad as he pleasured her. He gave her deep French kisses to the lips below her belly button as he walked around to the back of the couch.

When he reached the back of the couch, he gently and slowly let her upper body fall down against the back of the couch. He stood behind the couch, hanging her upside down over the back of the couch. He repeatedly pulled her up to his face inserting his tongue into her. He lifted her like he was curling weights. Lexington went from begging him to stop to never wanting him to stop.

Like a well-digger, Chad's tongue dug and dug until he found a source of water. Drizzles of her lust dripped over his tongue and dripped down onto his Adam's apple and chest. Lexington moaned as the guilt merged with pleasure. She didn't want to be with a man that was taken, but what Chad was doing felt so good she didn't want to stop. Chad could sense her reluctancy.

Chad put all his energy into willing her into seeing things his way. Chad lifted her up from the couch. Chad let Lexington slide down his smooth, soft hairless chest. Letting her fall into his arms. He carried her to the bedroom. He laid her in the bed. He went into her nightstand, pulled out her stash of Magnum XL Trojan Condoms.

He said, "Ride my face while you put the condom on me!" He got completely naked and laid down. He sat her on his face. Chad could barely breathe with his nose between her butt cheeks, but he was determined to win her over. Lexington made circles with her hips, riding Chad's tongue like a surfer riding a wave. She massaged his manhood as she reached for the condom, opened it, and gently slid it onto him.

He let her slide down his hairless, smooth chest. She enjoyed the titillating feeling of the ridges of his abs, slowly rubbing against her soaking wet, stimulated flesh. He held her in an obtuse angle position with his palms against her back. They moaned as they made each other feel good. Chad let

Lexington lean all the way back, placing her back against his chest. He caressed her breasts with one hand and caressed her with the other hand.

Their bodies grind against each other at the same pace, making each other feel pure pleasure. When Chad felt Lexington climbing the heights of passion, he pulled her back to his tongue. He didn't sip from her cup; he drank it all.

Chad wanted to feel more, so he positioned Lexington on her stomach and pulled her to the edge of the bed. He stood between her legs and gripped her thighs. Chad slowly slid into her body. His slow, deep strokes into her made her coco-smooth cream. Chad lifted Lexington to lick her like the cream on top of a cup of hot cocoa. He laid her down and slowly pushed into her.

The pleasure was paralyzing. Chad breathed heavily as he used all his might to please Lexington. He drew energy from every fiber of his being to put into every stroke until they climaxed. He fell on the bed, breathing heavily. He reached to touch her; she caught his hand, she said, "Chad, baby, I can't take anymore. (She pushed him out the bed.) Let's go, take a shower, so you can go home."

"Will you miss me," Chad asked while Lexington washed his hair.

Lexington answered, "Yes, I will!"

Chad said, "I will definitely miss you. I've never met a woman like you before. There's something about you that I've never seen in another person," as Lexington washed his face.

She said, "That's sweet. You're a good, gifted man. It's all going to work out. You'll see it! You're doing the right thing," as Chad washed her back.

He said, "Even if my heart and mind are with you," as he rubbed her body with her soapy loofa.

"You're twenty-five, you're going to meet so many women in your lifetime. Your heart or mind won't be here long," she said, washing his chest.

He said, "Not one of them will make love to me like you do or make me feel the way you do," as she gently rubbed him with the soapy towel.

She said, "Your whole life is ahead of you. There's going to be women at every stage."

"You think I'm too young to get married," he asked.

Chad rubbed Lexington's legs with the soapy loofa as she answered, "I'm just saying you're a great, attractive guy; there will be plenty of women wanting to be with you."

"Thank you for tonight, for the last two years. It all has been an incredible experience," he said as he rinsed the soap off her body.

After they showered, they dried each other off and brushed their teeth. Lexington told him, "Be good to her and yourself. I know you'll be a huge success, and you'll make your father proud," as she buttoned his shirt.

She asked, "How are you going to explain taking a shower before coming home?"

He said, "She's not like you; she doesn't pay close attention to me. She's only doing this for the money, you know."

She said, "I know!"

Chad said, "She doesn't love me or care about me. She is not going to love me or take care of me like you would. And she definitely can't do it like you."

Lexington said, "I know, and I feel bad for you, but I am powerless against your dad. You're smart Chad, you'll figure out how to make it work."

Chad looked so sad as he walked toward the door. Lexington said, "Chad, it's for the best."

He asked, "The best for who: you, my father, her? Definitely, not me." They hugged one last time. Chad said, "Would you at least kiss me, goodbye?"

Lexington slowly stood on the tips of her toes and lightly put her lips to his. Chad closed his eyes and enjoyed the goodbye kiss.

Chad said, "Lexington, don't ever forget me!"

Lexington said, "Chad, I won't forget you. Take care of yourself."

He said, "You do the same," and he walked out of Lexington's apartment for the final time.

(Present Day) Lexington explains, "After it was over, I regretted it in a way, but I also thought the connection we had was beautiful. It was never my intention for things to go the way they did. After that night, I realized I liked Chad way more than I thought I did. I knew we couldn't be together. I wished he hadn't got hurt.

"It made me say to myself it is time to break away from Roman. I didn't have the heart to say it to him, so I avoided him and his call for weeks. I was done, and I was hoping the silence would tell Roman how I felt. About two months after Chad's proposal, Roman finally tricked me into answering my office phone by using a number I didn't recognize. He convinced me to have dinner with him at his house."

Anniston asks, "Mommy, did you miss him?"

Lexington answers, "I did!"

Khryssa says, "Did you want to go?"

Lexington says, "No and yes! Roman had a way of making me feel conflicted. I had a lot of work to do, so I really needed to go home. On the other hand, I did have an affection for Roman."

Khryssa asks, "What made you go?"

Lexington answers, "As much as it wasn't ideal to be with Roman, it was like living out a fantasy when we were together. I got to feel adored and desired without any responsibility. We always had a lot of fun. He always spoiled me and made me feel good. But mainly, I went because, like everyone else, he made me feel obligated to spend time with him."

Limitation

When he opened the door, Lexington asked, "The coast is clear, right? You've cleared out all the little things your girlfriends left behind to let other women know they were here."

Roman said, "Girl, I told you no other woman comes here. Now get your ass in here." Roman pulled her into the house.

When she walked into the house, she said the food smells great. He took her jacket and purse and hung them up in the closet. Roman said, "You know you're at home here, so make yourself comfortable. I'm almost done with dinner."

She took off her shoes and went to the restroom. When she came back to the kitchen, she asked, "How have you been?"

Roman answered, "Missing you! How have you been?"

Lexington said, "I've been well, thanks for asking."

Roman asked, "Where have you been?"

Lexington said, "Work, home! You know me."

Roman asked, "Why haven't I heard from you?"

Lexington said, "I have just been to myself."

Roman said, "You know you are a trip. I see what you're doing."

Lexington asked, "Roman, what am I doing?"

Roman answered, "I see what you're doing. I perfected those moves. You're pulling a me on me. It's cute!"

Lexington asked, "What am I doing to you, Roman?"

Roman said, "Don't do that! Don't play me!"

Lexington said, "Roman, I'm not trying to play you or do anything to you."

Roman said, "I play this game with women all the time. I guess God sent you as karma."

Lexington said, "Roman, I don't know what you are talking about."

Roman said, "Yeah! Okay!"

When Roman was done cooking, they sat at the table to eat. They talked over dinner. When they were done eating, they washed the dishes together. Lexington was going to leave after washing the dishes, but Roman wanted her to stay.

"Please, stay with me tonight," Roman asked.

"Roman, I really need to go home," Lexington said.

"Spend the night with me, Lex. Please! I'm begging you, don't let me sleep without you. I've missed you so much," he said, holding Lexington's hand.

Roman pulled Lexington close to him, and he whispered in her ear, "You have no idea how I feel when you leave me. I hate sleeping without you. Don't go, Lex! I need you tonight," he gently held Lexington in his arms and kissed her neck, he whispered, "I need you here with me."

As he pulled Lexington into his bedroom, he said, "If you stay, I'll make you a relaxing bath, I'll wash your back and feet, I'll oil your whole body. I'll massage your whole body, and I'll let you sleep in peace. I want to hold you through the night, watch you sleep, feel you next to me. Is that alright?"

Lexington asked, "You promise, you're going to let me sleep?"

Roman said, "Scouts honor."

Lexington asked, "You were a Boy Scout?"

Roman answered, "No, but I'll still honor my word."

Lexington said, "Yeah, right! I never get any sleep when you're around. Think of one time we were in a bed together, and I actually slept."

Roman said, "Can you blame me for being all over you when I'm close to you?"

Lexington jokingly said, "I'm that bitch, huh?"

Roman said, "You're the only drug I use, and I'm addicted."

Roman led Lexington to his master bath. The tub was surrounded by burning candles. He ran a warm bath, and he turned on the spa jets to help her relax. As he undressed her, he told her: "Look in the mirror, Lex, you make me look good! You with me is picture perfect," he kissed her and helped her get in the tub.

He gave her a glass of wine. She sipped the wine as he washed her back and her feet as he promised. He sat next to the tub and watched her. She noticed him lost in thought, she curiously asked, "What's on your mind, Roman?"

When he came back to reality, he said, "You!"

"You're getting in here?" She asked. He undressed and got into the tub with her and sat between her legs. She began washing his chest and abs. She said, "This has always been my favorite part of you."

He said, "That's what you like?"

She said, "Roman, you are beautiful!"

He slowly washed her legs as she washed his head, neck and back; he said, "You are beautiful!" She washed his arms. As they finished bathing, Roman continuously kissed her.

When they stepped out of the tub, he dried her body, and she dried his body. She wrapped a towel around him, and he wrapped her in a towel. He led her to the bed. He laid her down. He softly caressed her thighs and legs with his fingertips covered in massaging oil. He used his palms and fingers to massage her neck and back.

He said, "Tell me your little girl dreams."

She asked, "You really want to hear about my childhood dreams?"

He answered, "Yeah, tell me all the things you wanted for yourself when you were a little girl."

"Really?" she asked.

He nodded and said, yes.

"Okay, well, I pretty much live my professional dreams I always wanted to follow in my dad's footsteps, but I wanted a family like my parents: a loving husband, a few kids, a long, happy marriage. I thought I'd be married by now. What about you," she replied.

Roman, still massaging her, answered, "I wanted to play football, but I hurt my knee in high school, and no college would take a chance on me. Senior year I took econ, and that began my journey here."

"Did you want a family," she asked.

"I do want a family," he answered.

After he was done with the massage, he handed her one of his t-shirts. She said, "Let me wear a pair of your boxer-briefs."

He said, "Oh, you want to wear my underwear?"

She said, "Are you kidding, those things are so comfortable!"

He asked, "How do you know?"

She said, "I just know?" They laughed as he handed her a pair. He put on a pair and crawled in the bed with her.

She grabbed the oil and said, "Your turn." He laid on his stomach and she sat across his lower back. She massaged his back as they continued talking. He said, "So you want to be a wife and mother? You're willing to cut back on work to have a family?"

She said, "Absolutely when my husband and children come, I will gladly give up work to be a mother. Right now, I have no reason not to work hard, so I do."

He asked, "What do you want in a husband?"

She answered, "Someone kind, caring, faithful, loves me, values me, considers me, takes care of me, supports me, protects me, encourages me, respects me, and I will do the same for him. What do you want in a wife?"

He turned to look at her and said, "You!"

"Stop playing, Boy, answer the question," Lexington said, thinking Roman was joking.

He rolled over with a serious face, he said, "I wasn't joking." Lexington was stunned. Roman lifted her up, he got out of the bed and walked over to the dresser. He pulled a ring box out of the top drawer and walked back to the bed. Lexington watched him in complete shock.

He sat down on the bed at her feet and opened the box. "I want you to be my wife," he said, looking straight into her eyes to show he was not joking.

Lexington looked at the ring then looked at him. "Roman, I don't know what to say," she said at a loss for any other words.

"Say, yes," he calmly said.

"Roman…" she started to speak, but he stopped her.

"Is there someone else?" he asked.

"No, there's no one else," she said.

Roman asked, "So why can't you say yes?"

Lexington answered, "I'm trying to comprehend what you've asked me. I'm trying to figure out if you're for real, and where this is coming from. You're talking marriage when you haven't even talked about being my boyfriend. In three years, you haven't mentioned commitment."

Roman said, "I've thought about it for a while, now. I look at you, and I see everything I want. I know I can be what you want if you give me a chance. In these three years, I have been committed to you, and I think of you as my woman."

She said, "Roman, so you're saying in three years, you've been with no one else?" He got quiet. She said, "That's not a commitment."

Roman said, "Okay! When we first started talking, I was in a thing with this female, but once I saw you were feeling me, I told her it was done. A couple times, I was out here bullshitting with her, but that's it, Lex. I don't want her; I want you."

Lexington put her head down and rested them in her hands. Roman knew that meant no. He was disappointed. He got out the bed with his feelings hurt and shattered on the floor. Lexington reached out to grab his arm, but he snatched away. Lexington, not knowing what to say, got up to leave. Roman turned to stop her; he said, "Don't go, please! Come here!" He pulled her into his arms. "Don't go, Lex," Roman said, holding her in his arms.

He kissed her forehead, "Don't leave like this."

Lexington started crying and said, "Somebody already broke my heart. I don't know if I even have any heart left to give you. I just know I can't risk it with you. The things about you that attract me are the very same things that make me want to run. It would be dangerous for me to give you my heart and mind. I give you my body, but I keep those two pieces of me locked away from you to protect me. Roman, I'm not trying to hurt you, but I have to do what's best for me. You and women, I can't go there. I can't take being hurt or betrayed again."

Roman said, "I would never hurt you or cheat on you. I swear I'm not who you think I am, and my life isn't what you think. I understand why you would have that perception, but Lexington, since you and I have been kicking it, I cut all that out. I'm not out here like you think I am. It's hard to trust after you've been hurt. I've been hurt before. I know it's not easy.

"I know a couple times you've seen me talking to women, but I promise you I did not have sex with either of those women. I promise you; I am not the man you think I am. I will be the caring, loving, faithful husband that you want. Just give me a chance to prove to you that I am ready. I promise, you won't be sorry or regret it. Lex, you're the only woman I want to be with, I swear. There is no other woman in my life. You can check my phones, my house, my cars, computers, and my office, there's no one else."

Lexington cried as Roman spoke. She was visibly upset. Lexington said, "Roman, I hear you, but I don't know if that means we are ready to get married."

Lexington said, "I should go."

Roman said, "I don't want you to leave. I didn't mean to upset you. Please, stay! I ask just one thing: allow me to prove my love for you and show you who I really am and what I am really about." Roman added, "I can love you how you want to be loved. I can give you everything you want. All you need is right here in me. I love you. I always have."

Lexington said, "Is love enough? I don't know. It's not just you. I don't even know if I'm ready. What kind of marriage will we have if I have no trust in you?"

He replied, "I hear you. Time, you need some time," as he wiped her tears with his thumbs, "Let's go back to bed, and enjoy the rest of the night. Don't cry! I never meant to make you cry."

He put the ring on her finger, he said, "Can I pretend tonight that you're my girl, and watch you sleep with my ring on your finger? Is that too much to ask of you?"

Lexington said, "No, I can give you that much." Roman picked her up and carried her back to bed. Emotions were running high between the two of them. She laid next to him, looking at the ceiling, thinking maybe I could settle for Roman. He does love me in his way, but the other part of her brain said there's something more out in the world for me.

Roman looked at her and asked, "When you're alone at night, do you think of me?"

"I think about you often," she answered.

"What about that white boy," he asked.

She asked, "How do you know about him?"

He said, "Lex, I know everything you do."

She asked, "How do you know what I'm doing when we are not together?"

Roman said, "Just know, I know every move you make. When it comes to you, I will always make a way."

Lexington asked, "Have you seen us with your own eyes, or someone told you about us?"

Roman said, "Both! Is the relationship serious?"

"It's over," she answered.

Roman asked, "Did you like him?"

Lexington thought about it before she answered, "I did. We had a good time."

Roman asked, "So you messed with him, messed with him?"

Lexington laughed and answered, "I don't want to talk about him."

Roman asked, "That's a yes. Who is better?"

Lexington laughed. Roman said, "Answer the question: who is better?"

Lexington said, "Really, Roman?"

Roman said, "I want to know what I'm up against."

Lexington shook her head and said, "I don't want to have this conversation. The thing with him is over. Besides, you don't talk to me about your women."

Roman said, "Ask me anything."

Lexington said, "I don't want to know."

Roman said, "Well, I want to know. Who was better?"

"Roman, you are," Lexington answered.

Roman asked, "What makes me better?"

Lexington asked, "You really want me to answer that question?"

"Yes, I want an honest answer," Roman answered.

Lexington said, "Well, he gave the most incredible head, but your stroke makes you reign as king."

Roman asked, "Who's bigger?"

Lexington laughed and answered, "You are, Roman. Now can we talk about something other than him?"

Roman said, "Just so you know, no one compares to you in any way!"

Lexington asked, "What makes you say that?"

Roman answered, "You have no idea that you are perfect. You're everything I want in a woman. You're beautiful and smart. Everyone thinks so highly of you. You engage and intrigue me mentally and physically. You stimulate and satisfy me, mentally and physically.

"You're classy and cultured. I can take you to the most exquisite, expensive places, and you know how to carry yourself. You're well-educated, well-spoken, and well-traveled. You don't even understand what you're working with, that little body of yours is perfect. You're this beautiful, quiet lady when we are out and about, but when we get in this bed, you're exactly what I need you to be. The way you call my name drives me crazy. When you say Roman, I'm cuming, I'm in heaven.

"You have the wettest, fattest, sweetest, deepest love. I want to live in it. The way your sexy little ass throws it back on me amazes me. You can't imagine what it's like to be a man and to be with you, inside you. You drown me, and I'm consumed by you.

"You're the coolest female I've ever kicked it with. You don't sweat me. You don't trip out on me. You can cook. You grind and hustle just as hard as I do. You make your own money. I know, if we were together and I needed you, you would hold me down and have my back. I would not even have to ask. You're loyal and genuine. You can get whatever you want from me, but you never ask me for anything. And all of that makes me want to be with you."

She smiled, "Roman, that's really sweet, but all that hasn't kept you from other women."

He replied, "Woman! I kicked it with one female. Every female in my space, including my mother, knows how much I care about you. Since we've been talking, I do not approach women. When they come at me, I tell them hoes from rip nothing is popping because I have a girl, Lex."

Lexington asked, "You told your mother about me?"

Roman said, "I told my mother about you the day after I met you. She asks about you all the time."

Lexington asked, "What did your mother say when you told her about me?"

Roman answered, "She said she has never seen me smile about a woman or heard me speak so highly of a woman. She thinks I'm in love, and she wants to meet you."

Lexington asked, "What about the girl I saw you having dinner with?"

Roman answered, "For the record, she has been my friend since high school, I'm her kids' godfather, and she knows all about you."

"If you're so faithful to me, why did a chick try to check me," she asked.

He asked, "Someone came up to you asking about me, when?"

She answered, "She thought it was me, but it was my sister. It was like a year ago."

He said, "I'm so sorry, but I don't know who that could've been."

She said, "Clearly, she wanted a position that was already filled."

He said, "Look at you, talking cocky."

She said, "You know what's up!"

He said, "I surely do!"

Roman asked, "Did the female tell Akera her name?"

Lexington answered, "If she did, my sister didn't mention it. I was actually with you that night. My sister and our friends were at a club, and they said she came up to them asking which one was Alexa, and well, you know my sister; that was like lighting a detonator on a bomb."

Roman said, "Probably was someone that got mad when I turned her down." Roman (putting his sexy voice on) said: "Let me ask you something."

Lexington said, "What?"

Roman asked, "When you lay in the bed at night, do you touch yourself when you think of me?"

Lexington said, "Well, with you doing what you do so well, I usually have to give her a break."

Roman asked, "Well, do you ever touch yourself?"

Lexington said, "Isn't that why I have had you around for the last three years?"

Roman said, "Let me see!"

Lexington said, "What?"

Roman said, "Let me see you make her cum on that ring."

Lexington asked, "Are you serious?"

Roman said, "Touch her while you tell me about your favorite memory of us. Then I'll tell you about my favorite time we spent together."

Lexington said, "My favorite memory of us was two or three months after Mexico. I came over late on a Friday night, and we stayed in the whole weekend, and you had me drinking pineapple and cranberry juice all day every day."

Roman seductively said, "Touch her and tell me what you liked about that weekend." Roman kissed and touched all over her body as he listened.

Lexington felt kind of shy, but she took her hand and slid it into the boxer-briefs she was wearing.

Roman said, "Think about that weekend. Tell me what I did that you liked."

Lexington said, "You cooked for me. We talked and laughed a lot. I fell asleep in your arms while we were watching *Love Jones*, and you woke me up with your tongue in my panties." Lexington softly and slowly rubbed herself as she talked.

Roman asked, "Did you like that?"

Lexington said, "I did!"

Roman said, "I liked it too. You tasted just like so sweet."

Roman started kissing and rubbing her thighs. "The gushy was so thick and sweet. I was slurping it like I was at seven-eleven. You kept squirting. It was all over my face and neck. It slid down my throat. I think you tried to drown me," Roman said.

Lexington said, "I think I came twenty-five times that first night. You wouldn't let up."

Roman said, "And that river wouldn't stop flowing."

Lexington said, "By Monday, my entire body hurt from having so many orgasms, even my arms and feet were sore." The conversation and stimulation turned them on.

Roman lifted the t-shirt she was wearing to kiss her stomach and breasts, he said, "What else did you like that weekend?"

Lexington said with her voice cracking on the verge of an orgasm, "You were incredible. That's the night I named you: Loch Ness: The Pussy Monster. You hit the spot over and over and over again,"

Roman asked, "You nicknamed me The Pussy Monster to your friends," he smiled. Lexington nodded her head, yes. He said, "I like that."

Lexington said, "After that weekend, I started a ritual of drinking a cup of pineapple juice every morning and a cup of fresh organic cranberry juice every night."

Roman said, "Oh, so you stay ready for me."

Lexington said, "I have to."

Roman said, "Don't think I didn't notice. You definitely keep it right and ready for me." He asked, "Are you cuming for me, Lex?" He continued kissing and rubbing her breast.

Lexington whispered, "Yes!"

Roman seductively said, "Tell me the way I like to hear it!"

Lexington softly said, "Roman, baby, I'm cuming!"

Roman kissed and rubbed her thighs; he said, "Push it all out for me," as he watched her push herself over the edge of satisfaction.

When Lexington pulled her hand out of the boxer-briefs, Roman took her hand and sucked her fingers. Lexington watched him sucking her fingers; she said, "Now, you have to tell me about your favorite time."

Roman pulled off the boxer-briefs Lexington was wearing, he said, "I love every time, but the weekend we went skiing is my favorite time. Well, we went to the lodge; we never did ski." Roman slowly kissed from her inner thigh up to the center.

He slowly licked her; he said, "You, me, and that blanket in front of the fireplace." He licked deep into her love as he stared into her eyes. He said, "Chante` Moore was playing in the background." He slowly licked her again; he said, "We were drunk from all that champagne."

She made love faces as he licked her most intimate spaces and touched her most sensitive places. He said, "I hit it in every position. You took all of me all night." He slowly licked her again.

"You were moaning, screaming my name, and scratching my back," he said as he licked her again even slower. He said, "I can still hear you calling my name. I love it when you say my name."

He used two fingers to rub inside her as he rolled his tongue over her. Already full of emotion and sexual energy, Lexington reached for Roman's shoulders as desire overtook her. She relished Roman's touch as her satin secretions covered Roman.

Lexington, with lustful eyes, watched as Roman slithered on his belly like a snake sucking her like she was the sweetest mango. Roman looked at her and said, "So your little, young boy gave you the best head? Not after tonight!" He flipped her over, pinning her upper body to the bed and lifting her torso and lower back. He pulled her toward his face.

He dove tongue first into her like an Olympic swimmer diving into the pool, aiming to win the gold medal. The touch of his soft, wet tongue gliding over and in her sent electric energy through her body. Roman's tongue moved through and around her like a speeding car weaving through traffic.

Roman slowly traced the brink of her with his tongue before slowly gliding his tongue into her. He swiveled his tongue, making circles in her. In and out, back and forth, went his tongue. Lexington gently gyrated her hips smoothly soaring over Roman's tongue.

Roman wrapped his arms around Lexington's lower back to restrict her movement keeping her firmly pressed against his lips as he slurped and sucked, compelling Lexington beyond the margin of elation. She called out, "Roman, baby, ah, I'm cuming," as the build-up of tension hurriedly surged through her body.

Roman went into his nightstand drawer to grab condoms. He said, "After tonight, you'll say, Roman, you're the best I had at everything. I'm going to beat that box and eat that box like no one else can. I'm not leaving any pussy for your little, young boy or no one else."

Lexington looked into his eyes, biting her bottom lip as he put the condom on, kneeling between her legs. Roman bent Lexington's right leg, and he tightly merged with her body, leaving no space between them. He slowly slid himself into Lexington, making her quickly gasp. She smacked his chest when she felt a burst of tingling pleasure throughout her midsection.

Roman's strokes were slow, impassioned, and deep, hitting every minuscule part of Lexington. The sensation of her soaking wet, tight flesh squeezing him and surrounding him got to him, urging him to take it easy, but he pushed through because he wanted to love Lexington longer. Both of their breathing rates increased as Lexington's feminine calls of pleasure turned Roman on even more.

She tried to push him, but he grabbed her hands, he said, "I can't move! Baby, not now!" As soon as he took the next stroke, his efforts culminated into an explosion of her love all over his chest and abdomen. "Damn, girl, you're like a super soaker," he said.

"Because you're a super stroker," she said, smiling.

"Is that right?" he asked.

"I think the proof is on your chest," she said.

Roman rolled onto his back in the middle of the bed, and Lexington climbed on top of him. She slowly lowered herself onto him, knighting his manhood to enter the royal court. Lexington rolled her hips encircling and encompassing all of Roman inside her. Roman sat up and smacked her ass twice; he said, "Ride that dick," he smacked her ass two more times, "Hell yeah, Lex! Baby, fuck me," he said.

Lexington leaned back, supporting her weight with her hands on Roman's thighs. Roman said, "Yes, Lex! Ride that dick like you know it's yours!" Roman held Lexington's ankles as she continued to rock and roll her body back and forth, up and down, left to right. Roman grunted, as the presence of Lexington touching all over him, produced a pleasure so great that he could no longer contain himself.

Roman laid back and rested Lexington's feet on his chest. He grabbed her arms, and she held on to his arms as he took her on a boat ride atop violent, bumpy waters. Roman stroked upward into Lexington. Roman held Lexington's feet in his palms. Lexington rubbed and caressed his chest. He arched his back and bent his legs to leverage the position of power from the bottom. Lexington did Kegels on him until he filled the condom with his unborn children.

Roman sat up, pulled himself out of Lexington to put on a new condom. He rolled her onto her back to the other side of the bed. Like a tidal wave crashing onto the shore, Roman crashed into Lexington, rocking the bed. He wrapped one arm around her neck and the other arm around her shoulder, ensuring she couldn't move him, push him or run from him. She whispered, "Ah! Roman! Baby!"

He said, "Lex! Baby, I feel it too."

Lexington clawed Roman's back as every muscle in her body tightened. She said, "Roman, baby!" Her toes curled as her fingertips pushed into Roman's back. Blood rushed to her feminine organs. Her shoulders and chest moved as if she were in a state of trepidation. Roman held her close to him as he continued stroking deeply into Lexington.

Roman asked, "You like it?"

She said, "Yes!"

Roman asked, "You're cuming for me?"

Lexington said, "Yes!"

He said, "Tell me, baby!"

She said, "Roman, baby, I'm cuming."

Roman said, "That's what I love to hear!" He felt the warm blood hurriedly flowing through his body. His body trembled as he moaned out, "Ah! Lex, baby!" Roman hugged Lexington.

Lexington looked at the ceiling as she caressed Roman's back. She didn't have the heart to tell him she couldn't marry him. She woke up early in the morning to make her escape. She hurried to get dressed. She sat on the bed to say goodbye to Roman.

She handed him the ring; she said, "Thanks for inviting me over. I had a good time, but I need to go home to get ready for work." Roman refused to take the ring, he said, "You're always welcomed here. That is yours, keep it, and every time you look at it, think of the time, you said no and broke my heart."

"Roman, I can't keep this; it's so expensive," she said.

Roman said, "I bought it for you. (He slid the ring on her finger.) It's yours. You are an amazing woman. And, for the record, I do love you, always have. Lex, the man that wins your heart, is a lucky man, but I am not that man, am I?" She smiled and reached out to embrace him.

As they hugged, she told him, "Roman, you're an amazing man, and the woman that gets you will be abundantly blessed." Lexington kissed his forehead.

Roman said, "Call me!"

Lexington said, "Go back to sleep!" Lexington got her jacket, purse, and shoes, and that was the last time she saw Roman in that way.

(Present Day) Lexington says, "He proposed. I said no. His feelings were hurt. I felt bad. He was mad. I was crying. He felt bad for making me cry."

Khryssa says, "What happened?"

Lexington answers, "We had sex, but that was the last time I was with Roman."

Khryssa asks, "Why were you with him in that way if you didn't want to marry him?"

Lexington says, "I wish I could give you an intelligent answer, but I don't have one. It shouldn't have happened."

Anniston asks, "Why were you so sure Roman wasn't the one?"

Lexington answers, "We had a special connection, but I knew he wasn't the man I was supposed to be with for the rest of my life. Roman was too risky. I knew he had feelings for me, but I knew he wasn't ready to be with one woman. For a tenth of a second, I thought about saying yes, but my mind said absolutely not. I told myself, the man that will love me the way I need to be loved is coming; be patient."

Khryssa says, "Mommy, you're a heartbreaker under that sweet, innocent act."

Anniston says, "Mommy, I always thought you've only been with Daddy."

Lexington says, "Well, ladies, you learned a lesson: a lady stays classy and clean even when she has done a little dirt."

Anniston says, "Poor Roman and Chad!"

Khryssa says, "Don't forget about Raymond."

Lexington says, "If I went to Roman or Chad asking for something more, they would have treated me the same way. It is never okay for the woman to catch feelings and change the rules, so why should it be okay for men? I was tired of men making me feel obligated. I didn't want to hurt them, but I had to do what was best for me."

Anniston says, "Mommy, I still can't believe you had a bad girl side. You're like the perfect mother and wife."

"Lexington says, "You think I'm perfect?"

Anniston says, "Yes, I do!"

Lexington kisses Anniston, she says, "Thank you, Baby Girl!"

Khryssa says, "I don't know how you said no to them. They were cute, rich, and would have done whatever you wanted."

Lexington says, "I had to take a page from Kendra's book and walk on faith that love the way I wanted and deserved was coming. Either of them would have done whatever I wanted, and they would have given me material things that I could have acquired for myself. And that was part of the problem, material things were not what I needed. I needed something that money couldn't buy. I needed more in a husband than fun, stuff, and sex.

While everyone else had been so easy, Michael challenged me. He made me think. He made me grow up and change. I wanted to marry him and have his babies. Roman nor Chad couldn't pray for me like Michael; lead me through life like Michael; inspire me to recommit to God like Michael did; or give me five beautiful children like Michael did."

Lexington cuddles up with Khryssa and Anniston in her arms. Lexington says, "When I look at my children, I know I made the right choice. I love you all so much."

Khryssa and Anniston say, "We love you too, Mommy." Lexington falls asleep.

Khryssa and Anniston whisper. Anniston asks Khryssa, "Do you think you'll ever be in love like Mommy and Daddy?"

Khryssa says, "I hope so!"

Anniston says, "Me too! I never would have guessed in a million years that Mommy was going to tell us that."

Khryssa says, "Me neither!"

Anniston says, "It makes me wonder about Daddy and his life story. Do you think he was married before Mommy? He never really talks about himself."

Khryssa says, "I don't know, he'll probably never tell us. I could hear him now. (Khryssa mocking her dad's voice.) What? Why are you asking me that?" (Anniston laughs and joins in mocking her dad's voice) "Did you ask your mother? What did your momma say?"

Khryssa laughs; she says, "That's him!" The sisters whisper about their parents and their future until Khryssa falls asleep.

Anniston plays on her phone with her head on her mother's shoulder, thinking about what they talked about all day. Michael comes into the room. He reaches for Lexington, but Anniston catches his hand. She asks, "Daddy, can she stay just for tonight. I haven't slept with Mommy in a long time, please?"

Michael asks, "Is everything ok? Do you need to talk?"

Anniston says, "I want to hug Mommy while I sleep."

Michael asks, "Are you sure everything is okay?"

Anniston answers, "Daddy, everything is good, I promise, so can she stay here with us, please?"

Michael says, "Of course she can stay!"

Michael showers and climbs into bed. Michael tosses and turns. He can't sleep without Lexington. He pulls out his MacBook to do some work. At about three-thirty in the morning, Lexington wakes up and carefully eases out of bed. She walks into her room where Michael is typing, she says, "What are you still doing up?" Michael sits his MacBook on the bed.

Michael says, "I couldn't sleep without you."

She asks, "Why didn't you wake me up?"

He answers, "The girls wanted you to stay." Lexington crawls in the bed with him and straddles his lap.

She says, "Awe, it feels so good to be wanted."

Michael says, "Baby, you're always wanted."

She asks, "You still want me after all this time?"

Michael says, "I want you every minute of every day." They kiss in a way to relieve the strain of not seeing each other all day.

Lexington hands seductively move across his chest and shoulders. Michael's hands slowly move up his wife's thighs. Lexington kisses Michael's neck. She says, "In twenty-one years, I've never wanted anyone else." Michael kisses her.

Lexington smiles and caresses Michael's face, she asks, "How was your day?"

Michael, with his hands on her hips, says, "It was good!"

Lexington says, "That's good!"

Lexington kisses him and gently bumps against him.

Michael, trying to resist the temptation, says, "Anniston begged me to let you sleep with them."

Michael peels Lexington off of him. He says, "Mommy duties call tonight, but tomorrow we are taking the day off, and I get to have you to myself all morning."

As Lexington reluctantly crawls out of bed, Michael smacks her on her butt. Lexington smiles and waves at him as she leaves the room.

Lexington quietly goes back to her daughter's room and eases between her two daughters. Anniston snuggles right in Lexington's arms, and Khryssa rolls on her side, putting her back to Lexington's back. Lexington wraps her arms around Anniston and holds her until she falls back asleep. They sleep until Anniston's alarm goes off for school.

Lexington says, "Good morning, my lovely daughters." Lexington tightly hugs Anniston and rubs Khryssa's back, she says to Anniston, "It's Thursday, are you nervous?"

Anniston says, "A little."

Khryssa says, "How cute, your Michael is going to meet your Michael."

Lexington says, "Go get ready for school." Lexington goes to make breakfast and lunch for her four kids. When the kids come down to the kitchen to eat, they notice she's not dressed for work.

Nexen says, "Mom, why aren't you dressed for work?"

Lexington says, "I'm not going."

Jaxon asks, "If Dad is still sleeping, who's going to take us to school?"

Lexington says, "Your beautiful sister over here can take you."

Khryssa says, "Why aren't you going to work?"

Lexington says, "Because I'm grown, and I have something to do. Is that ok with you?"

Khryssa says, "I bet it's six-feet and three-inches tall!" Anniston laughs.

The boys looked confused because they didn't understand the joke.

Lexington says, "Take these kids to school!"

Khryssa says, "Fine, I'll take the rugrats to school, but I better enjoy this dinner tonight."

Lexington says, "That's why I love you. Now, eat, and get out. Have a good day at school, I love each and every one of you," as she leaves the kitchen.

Khryssa says, "Go run upstairs to Michael!"

Michael is sound asleep. She sneaks into the bathroom to brush her teeth and comb her hair. She lightly crawls into bed and onto Michael's chest. She whispers in his ear, "Michael, baby, wake up," she kisses him as he opens his eyes, she says, "Good morning, baby!"

He says, "Morning, baby, where are the kids?"

Lexington says, "They're in the kitchen eating. Khryssa is taking everyone to school."

Just then, they heard the door close. Lexington says, "It seems like we are home alone. What are you going to do with me all morning?"

Michael says, "Somehow, I think you already know the answer. Now, take those pajamas off."

Michael goes into the bathroom to relieve himself. He watches his wife in the bathroom mirror as she undresses, he says, "You still look as good as the first time I saw you." As he brushes his teeth, he says, "I was absolutely taken by you. I was standing there thinking, who is this woman. I dare she make me fall in love like this."

She asks, "Baby, you fell in love that day?"

He says, "It was a takeover. One minute, I was in control. The next minute, I was surrendering to you."

She says as she lays down, "I fell in love the first time you called me. The moment I heard your voice, I knew you were the man for me."

Michael asks, "What do you know now?"

Lexington says, "I know I was right."

Michael asks, "What do you know right now?"

Lexington says, "I know I want you and your hands all over me. I know that right now."

Michael comes back and gets into the bed next to his wife and says, "That's what you know?"

He pulls Lexington onto him. She says, "Yeah, that's what I know, and I bet you want the same thing."

Michael says, "You know I want the same thing," as he rubs up and down her soft body. He says, "Remember the first time you let me touch you this way?"

Lexington says, "I remember. I came to spend the weekend with you, and you put me back in the guest room."

Michael laughs and says, "I was a gentleman, and making sure you were comfortable."

Lexington says, "You were a gentleman, but you happened to have a brand-new box of condoms in your nightstand."

Michael says, "I was a gentleman with wishful thinking."

"I'm glad you were thinking and prepared," Lexington says.

Michael says, "You came knocking on my door, acting innocent, saying I'm bored, and I can't sleep," as he kisses her neck in the irresistible way that he knows will entice her.

Lexington says, "I needed to be near you just like I do now," as his charming ways enchants her.

Michael says, "It was obvious what you needed when I saw that purple lingerie," as his hands hold her hips. He kisses her breasts in her black lace bra.

Lexington says, "Yeah! That was on purpose. I had to give you something to look at."

Michael says, "Mission accomplished!"

Lexington says in her alluring, sexy little girl voice, "But you loved giving me what I needed, right?" She fondles him under his boxer-briefs to tempt him and attract all of his attention to her.

He says, "More than you know," as his tongue slowly flirts with her body.

She says, "Baby, before that night, I had never seen or felt one so big."

Her hands stroke up and down his manhood as his hands, lips, and tongue tease her body. Michael says, "That night, knocking on my door, crawling in my bed, you didn't know what you were getting yourself into, did you?"

Lexington says, "I expected it to be amazing because I wanted to be with you so badly. When you pulled that thing out, I was thinking, what is he going to do with that?"

Michael says, "Give you what you wanted," as he kisses her.

As she takes Michael's shirt off, she says, "You're still the finest man I've ever seen," as she rubs his chest.

She says, "Michael, I love you so much." She licks the outline of his abs then kisses up his chest to his neck.

Michael says, "I appreciate that I never had to doubt or question your love."

She whispers in his ear, "You never will, I guarantee that."

Michael's fingertips gently and slowly move over his wife's soft exposed skin, fascinating her senses.

He says, "I knew you loved me before you said it. I felt it in your touch, I heard it in your voice, and I saw it in the way you looked at me. I recognized the way you felt because I felt the same way."

Lexington asks, "Why did it take us so long to tell each other how we felt?"

Michael says, "I don't know because we both knew. Maybe, we were being cautious." Michael kisses her drawing desire from her.

Lexington says, "When you finally said it, my whole being melted."

Michael lays Lexington down and massages her back, and he says, "When you crawled into bed with me that night, I felt it then. I was so in love with you. It was like my dreams became reality and laid right next to me. How blessed am I that I get to experience my dreams in reality night after night, day after day!"

He caresses and kisses her thighs as she says, "That night while we were laying there talking, and you started touching and kissing my thighs. It was so amazing. I felt like I finally began to live that night. Remember what you did next?"

Michael says, "The same thing I'm about to do now."

Lexington says, "You know I love when you do that."

Michael says, "I love that you love it," as he rolls onto his back. He lifts her up and sits her on his face. Lexington closes her eyes and grips the headboard as she thinks back to the first time that she and Michael made love.

Copulation

She knocked on Michael's bedroom door. He opened the door. His eyes almost popped out his head when he comprehended Lexington's lingerie. Michael had to concentrate on her face to conceal his interest in her undergarments. With an innocent look on her face, she told him she couldn't sleep. He asked, "Is everything okay?"

She said, "Yes, I'm bored all the way down the hall by myself." He opened the door and told her to come in. She walked into the room.

Michael closed the door behind her and walked over to his bed. She asked, "Were you sleeping?"

Michael said, "No, I was looking for something to watch." Michael got in the bed. She took off her purple, silk robe and purple, feather slippers. He quickly got a glimpse of her body as she crawled over him. She purposely brushed against him. He was intrigued by the sight and smell of her as she crawled over him, but he played it cool.

Once in the bed, she sat right next to him; she asked, "So, what's on?"

Michael said, "Nothing interesting!"

Lexington said, "You feel like talking?"

Michael laid back and said, "What's on your mind?" Lexington turned to face him. From his position, he got an eye full of her breasts nearly popping out of her purple and black lace bra and her hips and butt bulging out of her black lace panties with purple trim.

Lexington asked, "If a genie granted you three wishes, what would you wish for?"

Michael thought about it, and said, "I guess I would wish for world peace, an endless supply of food for the hungry, and shelter for everyone homeless."

Lexington pushed his shoulder; she said, "Those were noble answers, but that's not what I meant. What would you wish for yourself?" Michael caught her hand and held it as he thought about his answers.

Michael said, "For myself, (He rubbed her fingers against his as he thought.) three wishes for myself, I guess, maybe a ridiculous sports car or a huge yacht. I really don't know what I would wish for. I'm pretty satisfied with life."

Lexington asked, "You wouldn't wish for a night with a beautiful actress or model?"

Michael said, "Why would I do that when I got you?"

Lexington smiled at him and said, "That was cute!"

Michael said, "That's real! I don't need anyone else."

She rubbed his arm and then laid next to him. Michael asked her what she would wish for if she was granted three wishes. Lexington rolled on her side, putting her body right against him. The scent of her sweet perfume filled Michael with desire. Lexington said, "I don't need any wishes with you next to me. I'm good."

Michael said, "Cute," as he touched her nose. She smiled at him. He knew she was trying to seduce him, but he didn't make a move.

As Lexington reached for the remote, her breasts slowly brushed across his chest. She said, "Can I try to find this movie I want to see?"

Michael said, "Help yourself!" Lexington laid her head on his shoulder. He rested his hand on her thigh. Lexington found the movie. Michael cut off the light. As they watched the movie, Michael's fingertips gently rolled over her thigh. Lexington softly caressed his chest. When the actors in the movie started kissing, desire built between the two of them.

Lexington looked at him. She slowly moved close to him and softly kissed him. They looked at each other before kissing again. Michael's hands gripped her hips and back, pulling her on top of him as their lips and tongue exchanged a passionate flow of energy. Her hands rubbed from his arms to his face. Her body gently rolled against his as they kissed. Her tongue traced his lips as his hands invaded her panties.

He firmly gripped her butt and hips as if to say I finally have what I have wanted for so long in my hands, and I'm never letting go. His fingers slowly slid down her. With Michael's hands on her, she was overcome with heat. She never kissed a man the way she kissed him. Lexington took off her bra, and then she pulled Michael's shirt over his head. Wanting access to more of her,

Michael rolled on top of her. He sucked her neck with passion as she held him close.

His big hands touched all over her as he slowly kissed from her neck to her breasts. Lexington wrapped her legs around Michael as he softly kissed her breasts. Lexington lovingly ran her hands over Michael's shoulder blades and down his arms as they looked in each other's eyes. At that moment, their eyes spoke everything that needed to be said.

Michael slowly pulled her black and purple lace panties off. Michael stared in her eyes as he gripped and kissed her thighs. His tongue slowly slid down her thigh. His pink tongue emerged from his soft lips to make Lexington melt with the first lick. His tongue slowly but strongly stroked up and down her until he covered all of her with his lips and sucked, causing her to cry out, "Michael, Baby!"

(Present Day) As she reflects back to the first time Michael tasted her, the excitement of Michael is making her melt just like it did that first time. Michael's hands rub all over her soft body. She puts one hand on his salt and pepper brush waves, and she leans back, resting the other hand on his chest. Her whole body reacts to the warm, soft sensation of Michael's tongue in her sweetest place. She cries out, "Michael, baby," just as she did that night.

She says, "Look what you do to me, my whole body is shaking. Husband, you feel so good."

She takes his hand from her breast and rubs his index and middle fingertips against her lips. She slowly sucks his fingers seductively rolling her lips and tongue over his two fingers as she rubs his chest. She's finding it hard to contain herself with Michael's tongue moving in and out of her and his lips firmly encasing her.

Michael rolls her onto her back and bends her thighs back. As she lays there, she continues to think about the first time they made love. She remembers how in the heat of their first time, Michael made her feel something she hadn't felt before. She felt real emotion. It was as if she and Michael already had a lifelong bond. Michael made love to her, unlike anyone before.

Jubilation

Michael was finally touching her, kissing her like he wanted to touch her and kiss her since the day they met. He refrained from crossing over the line for four months, and it was not easy. Before that night, Michael daydreamed about her, nights he dreamt about her, and every morning he woke up thinking about her. The moment finally arrived, and Michael was in it to win it.

He put forth a noteworthy effort. Lexington gently rolled her hips, grinding herself against his tongue and lips as she moaned: "Ah! Baby!" Michael tasted her passion for him, and he felt the love she had for him. With his big hands firmly on her hips, she surrendered to him, totally letting go of all inhibitions. Michael's tongue worked the middle so intensely that Lexington felt her life change.

The pleasure felt so good that it hurt. She said, "Michael, baby, that feels so amazing," as Michael sucked her. Michael manhandled her thighs, preventing her from moving. With a clear path to where he was headed, Michael went all in, tasting every part of her. Lexington couldn't be quiet. Michael had her whining like a bad little good girl having a temper-tantrum.

Lexington's body quivered and tremored as she cried out in pleasure. **(Present Day)** As she recalls that very first orgasm with Michael, she feels that familiar fever rushing in like the ocean's tide during a storm. Her body shakes just as it did that night. Feeling Lexington's pending reaction, Michael pulls Lexington down to meet his immense manhood wrapping her legs around his hips.

Michael sucks and kisses her breasts as he makes up for their night apart. Michael feels the wetness of her covering him as his manhood gently slides through her lips. Even though it's been twenty-one years, Michael still is stunned by the exhilarating, exciting energy that shoots up his nerves as he enters his wife. He can never get enough of that feeling.

As they make love. She thinks about the very first time he entered her.

Implementation

It was so big that she ran from him before the first stroke. As she quickly scooted backward, Michael grabbed her and held her, he said, "Come here, Lexi, don't run from me."

He whispered in her ear, "Breathe with me." He sat up and sat her across his thighs. He wrapped his arms around her back. She wrapped her arms around his neck and put her forehead against his.

Breathing in their nose and exhaling out their mouth, they closed their eyes and breathed each other's air. Michael caressed her back as they sat chest to chest, breathing and caressing each other. He didn't want to rush it, but he wanted her so badly.

Lexington put her hand on Michael's chest, so she could feel Michael's heartbeat. She could tell he wanted her as much as she wanted him by the look on his face. She relaxed. Michael passionately kissed her from her neck to her lips as his fingers rolled over her hips. Her curvy, tight body was so alluring to him.

With their arms wrapped around each other, Michael slowly, gently moved against Lexington as he kissed from her lips down her neck to her breasts and slowly caressed her back with his big, soft hands. Lexington lightly bumped against Michael as she caressed his head and back. She told herself, Michael was the man for her. She made up her mind that she was going to take the pain and pressure with the pleasure.

He laid her down. He laid on top of her, kissing her passionately. Lexington took his cheeks in her soft, little hands. The energy between the two of them was the most intense either of them had ever felt. The connection and chemistry were too compelling for her to give up.

Michael asked, "Have you ever felt this way about anyone before?" Lexington shook her head no. Michael said, "Me either!"

Michael put a pillow under Lexington's head, back, and knees. Michael stared into her eyes and told her to relax and breathe deeply and slowly. Michael slowly but sensually massaged Lexington's thighs. His hands slowly massaged her using the ancient tantric yoni massage method.

Michael said, "I've never wanted anyone as much as I want you. (He whispered in her ear.) You are perfect! Absolutely beautiful."

Lexington smiled at him; she said, "Thank You!"

Michael talked her through the experience by teaching her to control her breathing. He told her to keep looking into his eyes. He said, "Relax, enjoy the feeling. Don't think of anything except the sensation you feel. Don't feel pressured to make something happen. Let things be, just let the energy flow through your entire body, and trust me." Michael kissed her forehead, then each cheek. He stared in her eyes as he continued to massage her yoni.

After the massage, Michael knelt before Lexington and wrapped Lexington's legs around his waist. Preparing herself mentally for what was about to happen, Lexington got lost in Michael's eyes. She took a deep breath, and mentally encouraged herself.

Michael added, "Keep breathing, baby, I got everything else."

He slowly and gently slid himself into Lexington. Lexington whimpered as she exhaled than inhaled, she said in a voice marked by shock and awe, "Baby, it's so big!"

"Do you want me to stop," Michael asked.

Lexington said, "No, baby!"

Michael asked, "You're sure?"

Lexington nodded her head, yes.

Michael said, "We can wait!"

She said, "I want you, right now, and I want you to want me."

Michael said, "You have no idea how much I want to be with you. I'll take it slow and be gentle."

Lexington said, "No, I want to feel the real you and how you really feel. When you want to be sweet and gentle, be so. If you feel like being aggressive, do so."

Michael said, "If you promise to do what I tell you, I promise I can be myself, and you will enjoy the entire experience."

Lexington said, "I promise to do as I'm told."

Michael leaned over to passionately kiss Lexington as he let himself rest peacefully inside her, he reminded her to keep breathing and asked, "What do you feel when I kiss you?"

Michael kissed Lexington again, she said, "I feel passion and desire."

Michael caressed her thigh, he asked, "What do you feel when I touch you?"

Lexington said, "I feel scorching heat. I feel need. I feel butterflies in my stomach. I feel desire in my chest."

Michael said, "I feel the same way. You read us well, so you definitely will know how I feel after tonight."

Lexington said, "What do you feel when I touch you?"

Michael said, "I feel the touch of an angel."

Lexington said, "Your words are always so sweet."

Michael responded, "You inspire my words, and I truly mean every word I say to you."

Lexington said, "I feel the sincerity." Michael seductively kissed her again.

Michael slowly pushed himself into Lexington as far as he could fit, he said, "Keep your eyes open," as he continued to slowly thrust himself in and out of Lexington.

She said, "It's so deep, baby. The pressure is hitting all the way up my rib cage." He coached her breathing by telling her when to exhale and inhale. Lexington began to tighten up from the pressure and pain of Michael overwhelming her sensitivity.

Michael told her, "Breathe! Relax your whole body and let the energy flow from me to you up to your head then down to your toes. Feel the sensation of me inside you and enjoy the pleasure." Lexington closed her eyes to relax and breathe. Michael said, "Keep your eyes open. Look at me!" Lexington opened her eyes and continued to breathe.

When she relaxed and focused her attention on the pleasure, and she breathed through the pain, her body began to respond sharply to every touch of Michael. Electric sparks flooded her abdomen and back, her eyes watered as her heart and pulse raced from the excitement of being so close to him.

Lexington got lost in Michael's eyes as she continued to breathe as instructed. Heat and ecstasy rushed over her body, she said, "Michael! Baby! Oh! Baby!"

Lexington continued to breathe and moan. Michael felt her muscles beginning to contract, he asked, "You're cuming, baby?"

Lexington said, "Yes!" He slowly pulled himself all the way out.

Michael whispered in her ear, "Breathe and calm your body down. Let the energy flow from your pelvic area throughout your body. We are going to build up the energy until it overflows, and it will blow your mind. Trust me."

Michael kissed and sucked her bottom lip. Lexington's fingernails scraped across his back. He told her to breathe slowly. Michael hugged Lexington tightly. Michael sucked her breast as their bodies seductively moved sending electrifying energy pulsating through both their bodies.

Lexington expected Michael to be good, but she had no clue he would have her creaming, screaming, running, crying, and cuming with barely five minutes passing into the sex. Lexington's body put a satin covering all over the condom that amazed Michael, she said, "Baby, I'm trying to hold it, but you're knocking into the spot."

Michael said, "It's okay, baby! It takes practice. Let it come down. I will still get you there and blow your mind."

Michael and Lexington lay skin to skin as he took slow, deep, controlled strokes as far as he could go into her body. Lexington moaned, unable to control her body's reaction, she said in a quivering voice, "Ah, Michael! Baby!" Her words encouraged Michael, who was working hard to contain and control his own reaction. He no longer aimed to have her hold the energy. Now, he wanted to drive her to another orgasm at full speed.

With years of practice with tantric methods to control his ejaculation and using his breath to sustain his energy and prolong his performance, Michael was able to present a cool, calm and collected front externally, but on the inside, Michael was like a kid in a toy store Christmas shopping with a limitless budget. Michael's powerful strokes hit harder and faster, getting Lexington where he wanted her. Michael enjoyed seeing the look of pleasure on her face.

Lexington cried out, "Yes, Michael, baby," as her muscles contracted, making her body vibrate against his body. Lexington felt a surge of warm energy flow through her body that made her toes curl, her body jerk, and her eyes twitch. She grabbed his chin and pulled his lips to her lips. She passionately kissed him as if she were saying thank you without speaking.

Michael gently laid her on her stomach. He put two pillows under her to leverage her lower body. He placed his hand on the back of her neck and used the other hand to guide himself into her. Once inside her, he placed the other hand on her hip. He said, "Remember to relax, breathe, and enjoy yourself. Don't think about anything but how you are feeling. I got the rest."

Michael looked at her with amazement in his eyes. Her femininity, her intellect, her drive, her sex appeal, her voice, her body, the feel of her, the scent of her perfume, her beauty, and the way he felt inside of her all had him in awe of her. Everything Michael wanted in life; he had in his hands. Michael had the girl of his dreams naked in his bed, and he was soul deep inside her love. Michael felt serenity.

The moment was so mentally exhilarating for him. He was thrilled by her naked body in his bed; her soft skin in his hands; her body grinding against his; the sounds of her filling his room; her scent all over his sheets; and her essence dripping down his body. Michael was set on making a lasting impression that they both would remember for the rest of their lives.

Michael watched as Lexington's butt bounced against him as he stroked her from behind, Lexington moaned as Michael strokes became more aggressive. Michael was so turned on that he had to pace his own breathing. He rocked Lexington's body like she was a crying baby. The sight of her bouncing body was his own personal wonder of the world.

The sound of their bodies colliding coupled with the sensation of Lexington's warm, juicy body engulfing his manhood made Michael excited. He said "Baby, you feel so good. You look so good. You smell so good. You sound so good. You taste so good. Damn, I wish I could have this night forever."

Lexington said, "If I can't give you forever, I will give you all the time I have."

Michael said, "I'll take it."

Lexington moaned, "Baby! Oh, my God! Look at what you're doing to me," he felt so good she couldn't stand it.

He said, "I can't help it."

She said, "Michael, baby!"

He said, "I promise, you will feel this way every time we're together!"

She asked, "You always love women like this?"

Michael answered, "I have to admit, you give me special inspiration."

Lexington slowly inhaled in her nose and exhaled out of her mouth. Michael felt her muscles contracting and a surge of silky, warm liquefied love splash onto him. Lexington's paralyzing orgasm was so explosive that it was like she was struck with ten thousand volts of lightning. She was speechless. Lexington's jerking body squeezed him as if she was making fresh orange juice out of him. Michael didn't move. He watched her and was so turned on by her reaction.

(Present day) Michael's head is between her thighs with her legs laying across his back. The memory of Michael and the touch of Michael has Lexington extremely turned on. She looks at his salt and pepper hair as she rubs from his head down to his back. She smiles at the memory. She smiles at the now. Michael still had the same effect on her. Her body begins to jerk and shake as the love stored in her core begins to release.

They have grown older in twenty years of marriage, but little has changed, she says, "Twenty-one years since the first time, and you still make me feel the same way."

Michael says, "I was thinking the exact same thing. You still look good. You still smell good. You still feel good. You still sound good. You still taste good, and I still want you forever."

Lexington says, "I will still give you all the time I have."

Michael says, "I'm going to cherish every moment."

With his fingers interlocking with hers, Michael slowly enters his wife. He kisses and nibbles on her ear and neck as he strokes deeply into her love. Lexington says, "Oh, Baby! You're so incredible."

Michael asks, "You like that, Baby?"

Lexington replies, "Yes!"

Michael asks, "That's where you want it?"

Lexington answers, "Yes, Baby! Keep it right there." Michael slowly glides over the spot where the "g" is nestled. Every stroke sends desire through her body.

The sound of his body smacking against hers keeps Michael focused. The warmth of her soft, wet body surrounding his makes him feel as if the kingdom has come. Her scent and essence soaking his skin entice him. The warm, wet feeling of every ripple, ridge, and the smoothness inside her brings heaven to earth for him every time they are together.

Michael says, "I can never get enough of you."

Lexington says, "I feel exactly the same!"

Caught in the paralyzing and gratifying moment, Lexington feels euphoric bliss emanating throughout her abdomen. The feel of Michael kneading her treasure produces electric tingles from her scalp to her feet. Her eyes water. She could feel her pulse throbbing in her ears. Her fingertips grip his shoulders as Michael rocks her body and blows her mind.

Michael feels her body calming down. He softly kisses her; he asks, "Are you good?"

She answers, "Yes!"

Michael says, "Good because we're just getting started!"

Lexington laughs: she says, "In twenty-one years, I have never outlasted you."

Michael says, "You know, you always come first in every part of my life."

Lexington hugs Michael: she whispers, "I love you, so much."

He says, "I love you more!"

After making love all morning, Lexington spends the afternoon preparing for their special dinner guest. Even though Michael is against the idea, he helps her prepare for the night. She wants everything to be perfect for Anniston's sake.

When Lexington picks the twins up from school, she warns them to be on their best behavior. She lays down the rules, which makes the boys unhappy because they have to wear suits to meet someone they don't want to meet.

They try to be excused from the dinner since they have no interest in meeting Anniston's friend. Lexington tells them they should be interested in their sisters' dates.

She says, "As men in this family, you have a responsibility to look out for your sisters and protect them. You need to be present when they bring men around, so men know they have male protectors. They're your big sisters, but it's your responsibility to protect them and keep them on the righteous path."

As Lexington and Michael dress for the occasion, Michael is visibly unhappy about his youngest daughter dating. Michael says, "Lexington, I don't like this. We are supporting our daughter in breaking a rule. She should wait until she's sixteen like the other girls did."

Lexington says, "Michael, you know as well as I know girls will do what they want when it comes to boys. Think back to when you were a teenager." That statement terrifies Michael.

Michael thinks about all the naughty things girls did with him as a teenager. Michael is visibly upset at the thought that some boy may do his daughter what he did to girls as a teenager.

Michael says, "Hell, no! Not my baby girl! You know what teenaged boys want and think! You know what boys expect when they go to dances! I don't want that for my daughter."

Lexington says, "Then you need to talk to her, tell her, so she knows what boys want and think."

Michael says, "The other kids will think it's okay to break the rules. We are undermining our own authority."

Lexington says, "We are adjusting our authority to meet the needs of the individual at hand."

Michael says, "If she breaks this rule, she may break others."

Lexington says, "Clearly, she already likes him. If we say don't see him, she'll sneak to see him."

Michael says, "Giving in to her makes us look weak. The girls will think they can play us."

Lexington says, "Khryssa is on her way to college. Michelle is already gone. We can't control them, Michael. We have to teach and prepare them to make wise decisions. We have to trust them to make good choices. We've never given the boys an age to start dating. The girls could say that's bias, but they understand there's a difference between the girls and the boys. I will talk to Khryssa and Michelle, so they understand we're doing what's best for Anniston."

She kisses Michael. She says, "Husband, trust me! Anniston is my mini-me. All the other kids look like you, think like you, act like you, and they are tall like you. Anniston thinks like me, she acts just like me, she's short like me, and she looks just like me. I have to deal with the monster I created and telling her to wait is not dealing with her. Telling her to wait will make her sneak to do what she wants. We are doing the right thing. We are informing her, empowering her, relating to her, listening to her, and we are showing interest in her interests."

Michael says, "Ok! You're right, but he better not touch my daughter."

Lexington says, "We'll pray about it, baby, (she adjusts his tie) be nice tonight," she kisses him and says, "I'll do that thing you like, tonight."

Michael smiles, he says, "The thing!"

Lexington says, "The thing, but you have to be nice."

Micheal says, "I can be nice."

The Moore family congregates in the kitchen. They gather around the table with Michael at the head of the table. Lexington sits across from him. Anniston sits quietly to the left of her mother, and Khryssa sits at Lexington's right. A twin sits on each side of Michael, and there is an empty chair next to Anniston. The doorbell rings. Lexington tells Michael to go with Anniston to answer the door. The twins look bored, but Lexington warns them to be engaged.

As Michael walks with his daughter to the door, he says, "Daughter, I will always support you no matter what, and I will always love you. I don't like this, but I'm going to do this for you." Anniston hugs Michael and says, "Thanks, Daddy, I love you, too."

Michael smiles at his daughter; he says, "Baby Girl, go open the door for your friend."

Anniston asks, "Daddy, can we talk tonight? I need to ask you something."

Michael says, "Of course, whenever you need me."

That was exactly what Lexington was hoping for. She wanted Anniston and Michael to talk. Michael goes back into the kitchen, and Anniston continues to the door. When she opens the door, she and Michael Bateman smile. Michael waves bye to his mom and dad in the car. She invites him in, and she shows him where the restroom is to wash his hands. After he washes his hands, they walk to the kitchen. Anniston introduces him to her family.

Lexington welcomes him to their home. Michael Bateman thanks Lexington, and says, "Mrs. Moore, you have a lovely home," just like his mother told him to do. Lexington thanks him. Michael Bateman firmly shakes Michael's hand, just like he practiced with his dad. Michael already knows Khryssa, but he shakes her hand anyway. Khryssa smiles at him. He shakes each of the twins' hands. Lexington invites him to sit down. Michael says grace to bless the food.

Michael starts passing the food. He wants to interrogate and threaten Michael Bateman, but for Anniston's sake, Michael carries on like it's a normal dinner with his family. Michael checks in with each of his kids about school and their personal interests. Lexington asks Michael about his parents and siblings. He explains that his parents are lawyers and that he is the middle of three boys. Michael, Michael, and the twins talk basketball as they eat.

After dessert, Michael Bateman offers to help Lexington wash the dishes. Lexington tells him thank you, but declines. His parents call to tell him they are outside. Michael walks him to the car. Michael thanks Mr. and Mrs. Bateman for allowing the introduction to happen. Michael compliments the Batemans for raising such a respectful and intelligent son. Mr. Bateman says he and his wife are more than willing to drive the two teenagers to the dance and back home.

When everyone settles down for bed, Lexington goes to check on Anniston. She asks if she was happy with the way dinner went. Anniston says, "It went way better than I anticipated. I'm happy that Daddy is okay with this."

Lexington says, "He just wants to protect his daughter."

Anniston says, "I understand that."

Lexington says, "He knows what boys want. You are going on a date, and that scares him. It scares me because I can't protect you. I don't want my baby to get hurt."

Anniston says, "I will be responsible, Mommy. I promise!"

Lexington says, "I know you will! Have a good night's rest!"

Anniston hugs her mom, she says, "Thanks Mommy, goodnight!" Before Lexington leaves, Anniston asks what she thought about Michael Bateman.

Lexington says, "He's adorable!" They smile at each other.

Lexington walks into the master bedroom, she kisses Michael, who is lying in bed watching television, she says, "Thank you for tonight."

Michael says, "You know I'll do anything for you."

Lexington kisses him again, she says, "You know I love you, right?"

"I know, I love you, too," Michael says.

Lexington says, "Thank you for having my back even though it went against what you believed to be right."

Michael says, "Whatever I have to do for my wife, gets done!"

Lexington gets her MacBook and gets into bed. Michael whispers, "Come here; the kids have all gone to bed."

Lexington says, "I can't right now; I have to get a few things done for work."

Michael said, "You promised, remember! The thing! Come here!"

Lexington said, "Baby, give me twenty minutes, and I'll be all yours."

Michael says, "Don't make me wait! Come here!" Michael pulls her close to him, sits the MacBook on the bed and kneels between her legs.

He says, "Baby, give me thirty minutes," he kisses her.

Lexington laughs, and says, "Baby, what are you going to do with thirty minutes? You need at least three hours to get enough."

Michael replies, "I can't believe you're making me wait. You don't know what happens to me when you lay next to me. I can't wait!" He kisses her neck and says, "Don't make me stop."

Michael softly kisses her lips while he pulls her panties down. Lexington says, "Baby, you're so bad."

Michael says, "Only because you're so good," as he continues kissing and touching all over her body.

Lexington says, "Well, you've started something, now, you have to finish it." Michael's enthusiasm is like a kid walking in a candy store as he kisses his wife. Lexington forgets all about her MacBook and starts feeling the scene Michael is setting.

Just as they're getting carried away, Michael receives a text from Anniston asking him to meet her in the kitchen. Michael says, "I guess you get to work."

Lexington asks, "Where are you going?"

Michael says, "I promised Annabelle we would talk."

Lexington says, "Daddy duties call."

Michael says, "Wait up for me!"

Lexington says, "Hey! Do something with that!"

As he puts on his robe to cover his erection, Lexington winks and says, "Baby! You still got it!" Michael smiles.

Michael meets Anniston in the kitchen. She's sitting at the counter eating cookies and drinking milk. She says, "Hi Daddy!" as he enters the kitchen.

He says, "Baby Girl, what's good with you?"

She says, "Do you want milk and cookies?"

He says, "No, I'll get a water."

Anniston says, "Can we talk now?"

Michael says, "What's on that pretty mind of yours?" Michael was secretly nervous about talking to Anniston because he has no clue what she wants to talk about.

Anniston says, "First, our conversation stays between us, right? No one not even Mommy will know what we talked about."

Michael says, "Ok, so what do you want to talk about?"

Anniston says, "You!"

Michael asks, "What about me?" Michael immediately feels hot and pressured and not in a good way. It is safe for him to take off his robe, now. He uncomfortably sits in the chair.

Anniston says, "Everything! I want to know you as a man, not my father. You never open up with us and tell us anything. I want to know how you think; why you think the way you think; why you do what you do; and what made you the man you are. I want to know all that and much more."

Michael says, "My life is simple. I work, I love my wife and kids, and I faithfully serve the Lord."

Anniston says, "Daddy, come on, that's not a good answer."

Anniston asks, "Ok, let me be specific. Why mom? What made her the one for you?"

Michael answers, "Well, when I was young, I had a vision of the woman I'd marry, and your mother is everything I envisioned. From the way she looks to the way she thinks to the moves she makes. She is all I ever wanted."

Anniston says, "Mommy feels the same way about you. She is crazy about you, but don't tell her I told you."

Michael smiles at his daughter and says, "I won't tell."

Anniston asks, "You like having kids?"

Michael says, "I love it. Each one of you is a blessing to me. I hope you know that."

Anniston says, "You're always so quiet that it's hard to tell if you're really happy. Sometimes, I wonder if you're happy."

Michael says, "You never have to question if I'm happy with my family. I am beyond happy. Quiet is a result of being an only child. I never really had anyone to talk to, so I learned to operate inside my brain."

She says, "That makes sense, but do you think we could talk more often?"

Michael says, "I'll definitely put forth an effort to be more vocal."

Anniston says, "It'll be nice to know how you are feeling and what you are thinking."

Michael says, "I'll keep that in mind."

Anniston asks, "You spend all your free time with the boys. Khryssa and I want to hang with you too."

Michael says, "I am sorry if I made you feel left out. I will plan more daddy-daughter time." Anniston smiles.

She asks, "How many women have you been with, what age did you start…you know…being with girls in that way?" He almost chokes on his water.

He says, "I never planned to have this discussion with my daughter. I'm ashamed of the answers to those questions. I was thirty-eight the first time I was with your mother, and she is the only one that counts."

She says, "Good try, but not good enough. You don't have to worry, Daddy. I'm not going to have sex early because you had sex early. I'm not going to try to match your number. I just want to know you."

He asks, "Why do you want to know that?"

She says, "You are my example of what to expect in men. I am trying to figure out what's normal, what men do, and want."

Michael says, "I was twelve the first time I had sex."

Anniston says, "Woah, Daddy, you were getting it in at a very young! How old was the girl?"

Michael answers, "She was sixteen."

Anniston asks, "What was a sixteen-year-old doing messing with you at only twelve?"

Michael said, "She was making me a man. She was fine."

Anniston asks, "Dad, how did you know about sex at twelve?"

Michael says, "I didn't, but I figured it out."

She laughs and asks, "Who started it?"

Michael says, "She did. I thought she was cute, but I didn't think she paid much attention to me. I came to visit her brother, who was my friend at the time, but he wasn't home. She convinced me to come into the house. When she took me upstairs to her room, I didn't know what was about to happen. She did things to me in that room that I had never heard of before that day."

She asks, "Did anyone ever find out?"

Michael says, "No one knows but her and me. I kept my promise not to tell anyone."

She asks, "Did it happen more than once?"

Michael says, "Maybe about ten more times that summer. I would sneak out at night to visit her when everyone was asleep. When school started back, her boyfriend came back, so that was the end of that."

Anniston asks, "How did you figure out what to do?"

Michael says, "I responded to her! Instinct did the rest."

Anniston asks, "Do you ever see her?"

Michael says, "You see her every Sunday, and I am not telling you who it is, so don't ask?"

Anniston says, "OMG! Does Mommy know?"

Michael says, "No! We don't talk about my past."

Anniston says, "Why don't you tell Mommy about your past?"

Michael says, "I don't want her to know the dirt I did. She met me as a grown man who had changed. I don't want to ruin her perception of me. She may think my truth is ugly."

Anniston asks, "Are there other women at church you, you know?"

Michael says, "I was single for a long time before I met Lexington."

Anniston says, "So what you're saying is you ran through the church before you were married?"

Michael answers, "I've been many places."

Anniston is shocked; she asks, "How many women between the first and Mommy?"

Michael says, "I can't answer that."

Anniston guesses, "More than twenty! More than fifty! More than one hundred! Daddy, am I close?"

Michael says, "I don't want you to know. I don't want you to think I used women because I didn't. I don't want you to think I don't respect women because I do. I've been with a lot of women, but ninety-nine per cent of them approached me.

"It's been like that since the day that sixteen-year-old girl took me to her room. You could talk to each one of them, and not one would say I was abusive or that I used them. Did I do everything right? No! A few times, I didn't consider a female's feelings, but I never lied about what I did.

"I never misled a woman. And I never did anything with a woman she didn't want to do. I learned from all my experiences, and it prepared me for your mother. I promise you, by the time I met your mother, I had already put away all my childish ways. I was ready to settle down and be a husband."

Anniston says, "So you never cheated on Mommy?"

Michael says, "I cheated on women in past relationships many times, but never on your mother."

Anniston asks, "Why?"

Michael says, "Lexington is all I want and need."

She asks, "Why did you cheat before?"

Michael says, "They weren't Lexington. It's that simple."

Anniston says, "Do you notice how Mommy looks at you?"

Michael answers, "Probably the same way she looks at you: with a lot of love."

Anniston asks, "Do you know how much she loves and trusts you?"

Michael says, "Not as much as I love and trust her, but I do know I am blessed to have her as my wife."

Anniston says, "She looks at you like she loves you more than any woman ever loved a man."

Michael says, "I love her even more than she loves me."

Anniston asks, "If you love mommy so much, why do you boss her around so much?"

 Michael asks, "You think I'm bossy toward your mother?"

Anniston says, "You always tell her what to do, and she does it."

Michael says, "Give me an example of what you mean."

Anniston says, "The other day, Khryssie and I were in the kitchen talking to Mommy, and you told Mommy to hand you a bottle of water now, and she said alright, alright."

Michael asks, "You didn't like that because it seemed like I was telling her what to do?"

Anniston says, "I want things to be fair for her."

Michael says, "I promise you that your mother is loved and appreciated. I would do anything for her. Your mother is safe and protected with me. I will be mindful of the way I speak to her in front of you because that's not the perception of us I want you to have. I guarantee you things are not the way you perceive them.

"It's harmless flirting. The words we were speaking weren't necessarily the messages we were communicating. When she said alright, it wasn't about the water at all. Trust me, your mother knows exactly what she is doing."

She says, "So, you two were really talking about sex?"

He answers, "The whole discussion was not about the water, I promise."

Anniston is shocked. Michael adds, "I would never demean my wife, especially in front of my daughters. I don't want you to think it's acceptable for a man to demean you because you thought my behavior was demeaning toward your mother. I have the utmost respect for Lexington."

Anniston says, "Daddy, all this time, I thought you were a wee bit of an ass, but really my parents are horn balls. I had no idea."

Michael says, "It takes a lot to keep two people engaged in a monogamous relationship."

Anniston says, "I'm coming to understand that. I'm so sorry I thought that about you."

Michael says, "It's understandable. I would think the same thing if I were in your position."

Anniston says, "It's a good thing we are getting to know each other. Is there anything about me you don't like or don't understand?"

Michael says, "I love and like everything about you. The understand part, can I think about that and get back to you?"

Anniston nods, yes.

Anniston asks, "Daddy, would you do anything differently in your and Mommy's relationship?"

Michael says, "No, I think our life is perfect."

Anniston asks, "Did you and Mommy wait until marriage to you know?"

Michael said, "When a woman makes up her mind, you can't stop her. When a man desires a woman, and she knows it, she gets her way. Baby Girl, your mom always gets her way."

Anniston says, "She is special. When I look at Mommy, I see my mother, but there's this beautiful, humble, happy, pleasant woman filled with this light."

Michael says, "I see that, too!"

Anniston asks, "I definitely understand you and Mommy a lot more. I am going to change the subject. What led you to a career in real estate?"

Michael says, "It was a booming industry while I was in college studying business. I thought I could make some money as a little side hustle while I was in school. I originally wanted to start a restaurant."

Anniston says, "I want to be a doctor like Aunt Kareen, and Khryssa wants to take over your business when you retire."

Michael says, "Those are both honorable goals, and I know you both will be successful. I know for sure God will bless you both in those pursuits."

Anniston says, "If you could only teach me one thing about men or sex, what would it be?"

Michael says, "The bible teaches the role and responsibility of a man. A man is a provider, a protector, the leader, so he has to think logically, strategically, be wise and make good decisions. A man should be an example to his kids, and he leads his wife on a righteous path. You're going to meet a lot of males and they won't even come close to what a man is supposed to be. "When a man shows you who he really is, believe him the first time. When you first meet a man, he will show you what he thinks you want to see. He can only hold up the façade for so long before his true self comes shining through. Always remember, Baby Girl, like Dr. Angelou, said, 'You teach people how to treat you.' You have to love you and give yourself the best and accept nothing less from anyone trying to enter your world.

"If he cannot fulfill the role of the man in your life, he doesn't deserve you or your body. You don't want to be tied to a man that's weak, needy, incapable of providing or protecting you. As a man, I hope that every day of your life, I have set an example that shows you how a man is supposed to care for his wife and his kids. I want you to find a man better than me. If he cannot protect or provide better than I do, he's not the one for you.

"As your father, I beg you to wait for the man that God has ordained for you, and that may take a while, so don't feel like you have to rush. When you meet him, I hope you wait until marriage to have sex. I don't want you to be out here, giving yourself away. I don't want you to be so eager, vulnerable that you allow men to take advantage of you. I hope you know your self-worth. If you know your value, you will set high standards for any man trying to be with you.

"When a man and a woman join as man and wife, he is taking on her past, burdens, and her baggage. She takes on his past, burdens, and baggage. I pray that the man you marry comes with light burdens and baggage and brings you the happiness and love you deserve. I don't want some young knucklehead ruining your future by placing his heavy burdens and baggage on you."

She asks, "Does the past burden your marriage?"

He says, "I unpacked my baggage and unburdened myself before we met."

She asks, "Did Mommy bring baggage from past boyfriends?"

He asks, "She told you about Roman?"

She asks, "Daddy, who is Roman?"

He says, "The dude she dated before we met. I hate him."

She asks, "Why?"

He says, "I know she loved him."

She says, "I guarantee you she didn't love him as much as she loves you."

He was touched.

Anniston says, "Thank you for being so open and honest."

Anniston adds, "Daddy, I know my going to the dance is not easy for you. I recognize that my growing up is not easy for you to accept, but I promise Daddy, I will always be your baby girl even when I am grown and married!"

Michael says, "You will always be my baby girl, no matter what!"

Anniston asks, "Daddy, what did you really think of Michael?"

Michael says, "I don't like him. I don't want you to be with him. I don't want him touching you."

Anniston says, "As a man, you see something that I don't see. What is it?"

Michael answers, "I see myself. A good-looking, respectful kid from a good, Christian family, but when I was alone with girls, I was a whole other person!

Was I raised to behave like that? No! My parents would've never thought I was doing what I was doing. I never got caught. To this day, my parents think I was a perfect angel."

Anniston says, "You think Michael will try to take advantage of me or hurt me?"

Michael says, "I do!"

Anniston asks, "Why would he do that?"

Michael answers, "Baby Girl, males want sex, and that's all it is to us, just sex. Whatever we have to say or do to get it, that's what we do. We aren't like women. You value the connection you have with him. He values getting between your legs. Males at that age are like animals. They want sex all the time. It's not until we grow up and find that special woman that we see value in the connection and relationship.

"When you asked why I cheated on women before your mother, the reason is I didn't value them. I didn't love them. I was fulfilling my flesh. I met a girl when I was about twenty-eight. We were engaged, but I messed up. I liked her, but I wasn't ready to settle down. I hurt her feelings more than once; other things happened. We broke up. You would've thought that would have calmed me down, but it didn't. It made me worse.

"To make a long story short, it was a long ten years between Kayley and Lexington. I figured I was single and free to do what I wanted. One day, I was ready to settle down. I prayed about it. I prayed for my wife to come into my life. I stopped entertaining women. A few months later, this woman name Lexington crossed my path, and made my whole life complete. The key was I was ready to settle down. I don't care how much he likes you. If he's not ready, it's not happening!

"And, Baby Girl, please, don't let a man tell you twice, he doesn't want you. Baby Girl, his actions will let you know that he is not into you, or he doesn't value the relationship. Anniston, I cannot stress this enough. As beautiful as you are and as good as you are, there is nothing you can do to make it work if the man does not want it to work.

"Kayley was a beautiful girl. She did everything for me. She was good to me and faithful to me. She gave me all she could and did everything she should.

None of that stopped me from hurting her. I'm ashamed to say that to you, but I did something so foul to her that I don't think she'll ever trust men again. I don't want a man to treat you the way I treated Kayley. I want you to be with a man who treats you like Michael treats Lexington. The truth is Anniston, you're going to get your feelings hurt once or twice. Let those be lessons.

"Learn from those experiences. Learn from me and Kayley. Learn from your mother and me. Anniston, you may get some of my Karma, so I need you to be strong and wise. If you ever find yourself in a situation that you can't handle, please, come to me. I will be there for you. I will listen. I will knock a dude out for you. I hope you wait for marriage, but I will understand if you don't. When that time comes, I want you to talk to me. I will not judge you or be mad at you."

Anniston says, "I really appreciate you and your honesty, Daddy. I will talk to you."

Michael says, "I'm glad we had this talk. It was well overdue."

Anniston says, "I hope we can talk like this more often."

Michael says, "We will!"

Anniston says, "This is my last question."

 Michael says, "Go ahead!"

Anniston asks, "What's your private prayer for me that you have never spoken to anyone, not even Mommy."

Michael says, "Baby Girl, I like your mind. I like the things you think about and the things you find important. I do pray for you every night and every morning. I pray that you live a long life in good health, full of happiness. I pray God prospers you, your efforts, and endeavors. I pray you are faithful, strong, brave, and courageous in your walk with Christ. I pray you seek God and build a relationship with Him. I pray for your understanding, wisdom, and discernment.

"I pray you live the life you want. I hope you live the life God has ordained for you. I pray you know very little heartache. I pray you are wise with your choices with men. And I pray that my, your mother's, our parents' and their parents' burdens and demons do not attach to you or manifest in your life. I pray all generational curses and chains are broken. I pray you have God's favor all your life. I pray you have much success and prosperity."

Anniston says, "Daddy, that was really sweet. I pray for you too, Daddy."

Michael says, "Is that so? What do you pray for me?"

Anniston says, "I pray in Jesus' name that you live a long, healthy life. I pray for your marriage, happiness, safety, and salvation. I pray you are fulfilled with your life, your wife, and your kids. I pray you never leave us. So many kids at school dads leave, and I never want to be like them. I never want to live in a separate home from you. I love seeing you every day. I pray that you prosper in all your works and that you are blessed in all you do."

Michael says, "Baby Girl, that warms my heart to know you think of me in such a loving way. Thank you," as he hugs her.

Anniston asks, "Daddy, you promise we will talk like this more often. Just you and me, maybe Khryssa sometimes, but not all the time."

Michael answers, "Of course, I would love to have daddy-daughter time with you."

Anniston says, "Khryssa needs more of you, too."

Michael says, "I'll check in with Khryssa more often as well."

Anniston says, "Maybe we can talk while you teach me to play chess."

Michael says, "Baby Girl, you want to learn to play chess?"

Anniston answers, "I need to become a thinker, learn how to strategize quickly."

Michael says, "I can definitely teach you the game of chess. Now go to bed, so you can be ready for school."

Anniston says, "Okay, Daddy!"

Before she leaves the kitchen, Anniston says, "Daddy, I hope my husband is as good to my kids and me as you are to Mommy and us. And I hope I am a wife and mother like Mommy. I hope we look at each other and love each other the way you and Mommy do. Goodnight, Daddy!" Anniston walks out of the kitchen and goes up to her room.

Michael says, "I hope that for you, too, Baby Girl!" Michael was touched by her maturity, kindness, and intellect. Michael goes back to his room. Michael says, "You're right about one thing."

Lexington says, "What's that, Babe?"

Michael says, "That little fifteen-year-old girl in there is just like you. She thinks like you, she acts like you, she's sweet and kind just like you, and she looks just like you."

Lexington says, "What did she do?"

Michael says, "She almost made me cry."

Lexington asks, "What did she say?"

Michael says, "She said what was on her heart and mind, and it hit me."

Lexington sits her MacBook down, she asks, "Do you want to talk about it?"

Michael says, "No, she and I haven't talked like that before."

Lexington says, "Awe, baby, come here." Lexington wraps her arms around Michael, she says, "Anniston has that effect on me too."

Michael says, "We were talking, and I was struck by her intuition and interest. Baby, I had to fight back the tears."

Lexington says, "We are truly blessed to have our children."

Michael says, "We have five wonderful children, but there's something about her. Remember when you first told me you were pregnant with Michelle, and I said I wanted a little girl who looked and acted just like my wife? Well, that is Anniston."

Lexington says, "Khryssa and Michelle are definitely girl versions of you, and the boys are reincarnations of you. All four of them act so much like you that Anniston says she feels left out. She told me I don't give her enough attention, I am closer to Khryssa and Michelle than her, and you spend all your time with the twins, so she feels like she is always alone."

Michael says, "She said that?"

Lexington says, "It messed me up, too."

Michael says, "I will make an effort to connect with her as an individual. I get why you're fighting so hard for her to go to the dance. The gifts of insight and wisdom you have, you gave to her, and you both use them effortlessly."

Michael says, "Lexington Michon Moore, I love you, and I thank you for our kids. You have been an awesome mother."

Lexington says, "Michael Daniel Moore, I love you, and I thank you for loving our children and me."

Michael says, "You and Anniston have me feeling sentimental. Just hold me, baby." Michael lays his head on Lexington's chest, and she caressed his head until they both fell asleep.

Lexington picks Anniston up from school and heads to the salon. As she drives, they talk. Anniston asks, "So, what did Daddy say about Michael?"

Lexington answers, "He said he was glad he met Michael Bateman. Michael Bateman and his family seemed like nice, decent people and he supports letting you go to the dance. He's concerned about his intentions as any father would be when it comes to a male being in the presence of his daughter."

Anniston asks, "What about you?"

Lexington asks, "I am trusting you because you are my baby. I know you will keep your word, so I'm good."

Anniston says, "Thanks, Mommy, that means a lot."

Lexington says, "I'm glad my trust is valuable to you."

Anniston asks, "Mommy, are you going to tell me how you and dad met?"

Lexington says, "One afternoon, I was sitting at my desk working like every other day. I answered the phone. When the voice on the other end spoke, I was struck by lightning. I was sitting there thinking who is this man. The voice was pleasant, deep, intriguing, intelligent, and it did something to me. After we hung up, I couldn't get the voice out of my head.

"There was something about how he spoke to me, the words he chose, and the sound of his voice. That's the first thing that set him apart from other men. There was something about his voice that calmed and softened my spirit, but we kept the interaction professional. We entered into a business transaction, in which we helped his company acquire and sell a property.

"One phone conversation had me hooked. I was wondering what he looked like, who was he, was he single, and would he like me. I created an image of him in my mind, and it stayed on my mind. I was so attracted to him without even meeting him or talking to him personally. We talked a couple times after that initial conversation. We set a date to meet to sign some papers.

"He made a point of availing himself to come to my office. I thought maybe the attraction in my head is mutual. With him coming to my territory, I had to be fire. I dressed to impress with the most expensive shoes in my closet, a black blazer, a knee-length black skirt so tight I could barely breathe, and a lace camisole. My fingernails and makeup were on point. I wore my most expensive jewelry.

"After two weeks of corresponding over the phone, the time had come for us to meet. Michael was impeccably dressed in a tailored, black, Italian suit with a fresh haircut and shave. His deep brush waves were noticeable from fifty feet away. His cologne smelled so good. He had the sexiest smile I had ever seen. He walked with a confidence that made people attend to him. When your dad steps into a room, everyone stops to take notice of him.

"When Marie called me to let me know Mr. Moore was in the office, butterflies took over my stomach. She must've known how I felt because she winked as I walked past. I took a deep breath before I went to greet him.

"I stared at him. I couldn't think or speak. Both of us were frozen for a moment. Finally, we shook hands; it was electric. Tingles like fireworks shot through my body. I saw him, and I knew he was the one. I felt like he was feeling me, too. As we walked, his cologne pierced my brain. He smelled so good. We exchanged pleasantries and had small talk about his flight and the weather. I couldn't keep my eyes off his lips and those pretty white teeth. I wanted to kiss him.

"We didn't take our eyes off each other the entire meeting. When we walked into the conference room, I noticed how he opened and held the door for me. The meeting lasted about thirty minutes. In those thirty minutes, I was in love. The meeting stayed professional, but it was clear there was something between us.

"When he got on the elevator to leave, we stared at each other until the doors closed. When the elevator doors closed, Marie said, 'Ms. Lear, you can wipe the drool from your bottom lip, now. He's gone!'

"Mike said, 'You see it too! They were googly-eyed and mesmerized by each other. I thought they were going to jump on each other right in front of us. I was going to leave the room because I didn't want anything splashing on my clothes. I just bought this suit.'

"Marie said, 'Brother is on it! Do you hear me? And, by that determined look on his face, he's going to get it. Did you see how he looked at her?'

"Mike said, 'That skirt! Those shoes! Oh, she gave the brother something to look at!'

"Marie said, 'Oh! She knew what she was doing when she got dressed this morning.'

"Mike said, 'Didn't even bother to put a whole shirt on. The girls are out on this cold winter day.'

"Marie said, 'They are probably shocked by all the exposure.'

"Mike said, 'A lace camisole in the dead of winter.' I was speechless standing there listening to the conversation.

"Marie said, 'He didn't have on a ring, Ms. Lear, you should call him.'

"I told them, "You all are bad!" Mike and Marie started making kissing noises and singing Michael and Lexington sitting in a tree. K-I-S-S-I-N-G! First, come love than come marriage, then comes Lexington with a baby carriage."

Anniston jokingly says, "That's exactly how it happened, right?" Lexington laughed, "I know! They didn't have to be so right, though." Anniston and Lexington laughed.

Telecommunication

About two weeks after they met, Lexington sat at her desk, reading a report when the phone rang. When she answered the phone, Michael said, "Hello, Ms. Lear, it's Michael Moore. We met two weeks ago."

She was excited to hear from him, but contained herself and maintained a professional demeanor. She said, "Good afternoon, Mr. Moore."

He asked if she was busy. When she said no, he asked if she was in a relationship. When she said no, he explained he was interested in getting to know her personally. He asked if she could find some time to hang with him soon. She said, "I would love to." That broke the ice. They talked for hours like they were old friends. Before hanging up, he talked her into spending the weekend with him.

When she exited the plane, Michael was the first person she saw. They hugged like old friends. It felt like home in his arms. Michael took her to his grandparents' restaurant for breakfast. The food was great. He introduced her to some of his friends.

He took her sightseeing around the city. They went to the museum where they saw a painting by her favorite artist. What was so amazing is he remembered that she liked that artist, and he bought a painting by the artist for her birthday. That night, they went to a jazz concert and had dinner at a French restaurant. While on their date, they behave like a couple.

Early Sunday morning, Michael cooked breakfast and served her in bed. She was shocked that Michael cooked so well. He told her he spent most of his childhood working in the kitchen at his grandparents' restaurant. After breakfast, they went to church, where he introduced her to his parents and grandparents.

Lexington fell in love with his church home. The congregation was like a huge family. The pastor preached an incredibly moving message on second chances and life changes. She hung on to his every word. Michael held her hand throughout the whole service.

After services, they had lunch with his parents and grandparents. His family was very inviting and polite toward her. That night, before she got on the plane, they had their first kiss. She hated getting on that plane because she didn't want the date to end. They were both already in love by the time she got on that plane.

(Present Day) Lexington and Anniston sitting in the massage chairs while the nail artists began their pedicures. Anniston asks, "What made you say Daddy was the one?"

Lexington said, "Michael then is not different from Michael now. He is and has been a gentleman since we met. He is a protector. He is honorable and respectful. He is slow to anger and quick to love. He is head and shoulders above the rest like Saul. He is faithful, observant, and strong like David.

"He is wise and prosperous like Solomon. He never complains. He's never down. He hasn't had many bad days. He never takes without giving. He honors his word. He is calm and quiet. He brings me peace. He brings me joy. His heart is full of goodness. Like Absalom, he has charming manners and ways that captivate the hearts of people. He lives in great style and is the most handsome man in the room no matter where he goes."

Anniston says, "Mommy, that was beautiful. I hope I can say that one day."

Lexington says, "I pray that for all three of my girls."

Anniston asks, "Mommy, when did you and dad say this is a committed relationship, and I want to be with you and no one else?"

Lexington says, "After our first date, we agreed to not date anyone else. We faithfully dated for a little over a year before we verbally acknowledged we were in a committed relationship; it was his birthday the next year.

Declaration

Saturday morning, Lexington met Kendra at the salon. Lexington was planning to reveal her secret until Kendra told her about Rodney. Lexington was devastated by Kendra's news. Lexington felt bad because Kendra was having man trouble, and Lexington was sitting in the clouds, head over heels in love. Lexington didn't want to rub her happiness in Kendra's face, so she told Kendra she was visiting her parents.

Michael arrived to escort Lexington to the airport. He knocked on the door. When she opened the door, the sight of him amazed her. She stared at him in awe. She always got lost in her thoughts when her eyes met his eyes. They simultaneously reached out to embrace. Michael lifted her off her feet. She wrapped her legs around his waist and her arms around his neck.

They engaged in a passionate kiss. Lexington caressed his face. She said, "Hey, Birthday Boy! I missed you."

Michael replied, "I missed you too!" He asked, "Did you pack your passport?"

Lexington curiously smirked as she said, "I need my passport? Give me a second."

Michael kissed her again before putting her down. She ran to grab her passport, and Michael grabbed her luggage, sitting next to the door.

As they walked onto the elevator, she asked, "Where are we going?"

"I told you, it's a surprise," Michael slyly said.

She said, "It's your birthday, but you're surprising me."

Michael replied, "Any day is a day to surprise my woman because she deserves it."

She didn't say anything, but that was the first time he referred to her as his woman. She kissed him until the elevator doors opened.

When they got in the car to go to the airport, Michael asked, "Do you really want to know where we are going?"

Lexington says, "Yes, even though it doesn't matter where I am when I'm with you, I always have a great time."

Michael says, "We are spending seven days in the beautiful St. Lucia!"

"Are you serious," she asked.

"I'm serious," he answered. Michael said, "I've wanted to go for some time. I said when I find her, that's where we're going. I found her, so that's where we're going."

Lexington said, "You found her?"

Michael looked directly in her eyes; he repeated, "I found her!" He kissed her lips.

Lexington asked, "And, you don't need anyone else?"

Michael said, "No one else!"

Lexington said, "She doesn't need anyone else, either."

When they arrived at the hotel, Michael checked in while Lexington looked around the hotel in awe. They went to their room to shower and dress for dinner. Michael tied his tie as he watched Lexington admiring the view from their room. He saw how her dress clung to every curve of her body, he thought to himself: she is so sexy. They dressed for dinner as if they were going to the Oscars. When they sat down at their table, Michael ordered a bottle of champagne.

The waiter poured each of them a glass; he asked, "Are we celebrating something special?"

Lexington said, "It's my man's birthday," staring in Michael's eyes.

When the waiter left the table, Lexington said, "I know it's not your birthday for a few more hours, but I want to give you your birthday gift."

She presented him with a gold box with a red bow from her purse. He stared curiously at the box. She put the box in his hand and said, "Happy birthday, baby."

Michael opened the box; he said, "Wow! Lexington...This is...Wow!" (It was a fully iced, eighteen karat, white gold Rolex with the inscription on the back: All the time I have is yours.) Michael read the inscription, he said, "This is really sweet! This is the best gift anyone has ever given me." Lexington reached for the watch. He handed it to her, and she put it on his wrist.

As she put the watch on his wrist, she said, "You have everything, but I noticed you never wore a watch. I hope you like it."

He said, "I love it, and now I will always wear a watch."

"And I will always give you time," she said.

He said, "Thank you, baby," as he kissed her hand.

He said, "I really appreciate you, the gift, and you being here to celebrate my birthday."

She said, "I wouldn't be anywhere else. I'm glad you like the watch."

He said, "I love it. It's amazing!"

After dinner, they took a walk on the beach. They admired the bright moonlight sparkling across the calm water. They kissed under the moonlight as the water lightly rolled over the shore. Lexington looked Michael in his eyes; she said, "I love you so much!"

Michael said, "I love you more!" That was the first time they spoke their love.

(Present Day) Lexington tells Anniston, "In St. Lucia, we had deep conversations about us, our feelings for each other, and our relationship."

Anniston asks, "Do you have pictures from St. Lucia? I don't think I ever heard of St. Lucia."

Lexington says, "They are on my MacBook."

Anniston asks, "May I see them?"

Lexington answers, "I'll show you when we get home."

That night, Anniston walks into Lexington's room; she says, "Mommy, may I look at your pictures, now?"

Lexington says, "Come in, Baby Girl!" Lexington grabs her MacBook and opens up her photos. She finds the pictures from St. Lucia and hands Anniston the MacBook.

Anniston looks through the pictures and is impressed by her mother's beauty. She says, "Wow, Mommy, you're so beautiful. Look at you, all blinging and glistening. Look at those diamonds! It must feel amazing to be that beautiful."

Lexington says, "Awe, thanks, Baby Girl, but you should know because you're that beautiful. If you saw me at age fifteen, you would think you were looking in the mirror."

Anniston says, "Mommy, why did you stop wearing all those diamonds to wear pearls?"

Lexington says, "I earned the pearls I wear. Pearls are a symbol of wisdom gained through experience. Everything I've been through and the changes I made are represented in the pearls I wear."

Anniston is totally consumed by the pictures of her mother, she says, "Mommy, you've had an amazing life."

Lexington says, "Only because I have you."

Anniston says, "I'm serious. Every girl wants to be desired like you are. Daddy loves you. Roman and Chad loved you, wanted you more than any other woman. That has to feel amazing."

Lexington says, "It's amazing to be loved and desired by my husband. If I had to describe that feeling, I would say it feels like good music.

"It's rhythmic, timeless, and everlasting like jazz. It's deep and sultry like soul music. It's soft and romantic yet rugged and fatal like R&B. It's meaningful, spiritual, strong and deep like Neo-Soul, and it's joyous and uplifting like gospel. It's definitely amazing to be loved by Michael."

Anniston asks, "How do you do it? How do you get men to fall in love with you so easily?"

Lexington says, "I can't say that those other men loved me or were in love with me. I don't know that to be true. As far as Michael, God did that. Our whole relationship is more than anything I could have done on my own. "When I'm with a man, I am always myself. I've always been true to myself. I am the lady, the woman my mother raised. I am comfortable and happy with myself. I am a decent person. I like to have fun. Maybe it's a combination of those qualities, but honestly, I don't know what in me made Michael like me or love me. For sure, I don't know what the hell Roman wanted. Chad was young. He didn't know what he wanted at twenty-three or twenty-five."

Anniston is fascinated by her mother's beauty and style as she continues to browse through the pictures. She asks, "Why haven't you put any of these pictures around the house? They are beautiful."

Lexington says, "Pictures of my children are all I need to see."

Anniston comes across a picture of a young Lexington hugging a man that wasn't her father. She whispered, "Mommy, who is that?"

Lexington says, "That's Roman."

Anniston says, "Mommy, he's fine."

Lexington says, "Don't ever tell your father you saw that picture. He hates Roman."

Anniston said, "I guess this is Chad," pointing to a picture of Chad and Lexington hugging.

Lexington says, "Yes, that's him, and you didn't see that, either."

Anniston laughs, she says, "I didn't see anything, but he's super cute. I see what you mean. Chad's eyes are a beautiful blue."

Anniston looks at pictures of Lexington with her friends as teenagers; she says, "Mommy, I do look like you."

Anniston finds more pictures of Lexington with Roman, Chad, Raymond, and Camren. Anniston says, "Mommy, I admire you, not just because you're beautiful or because you're my mother. I admire the person you are, how you love, and how you lived your life."

Lexington says, "Anniston, I appreciate that so much. That makes me so happy and proud because everything I've done and been through has been to be my best for my children."

Anniston says, "What advice would you give to a young woman about attracting men like the ones you have dated: successful, handsome, respectful, classy?"

Lexington answers, "Be unattainable, be extremely selective, be mysterious, and be a lady all the time. Most importantly, honor your own truth. No matter who is around, be unapologetically you. Be the girl in the room that every man wants but think they could not possibly get.

"You cannot give it away and think it still will have value. You cannot be a girl that everywhere you go, some man can say I hit that. Be quiet about what you do and whom you do it with. Pick a man that wherever you go, he stands out among all the other men in the room. Make choices that you can live with."

Anniston says, "I can see that you lived by that philosophy. Chad, Roman, and Daddy stand out among other men."

Anniston shows her mother a picture of herself in her twenties; she asked, "What advice would you give her?"

Lexington says, "Listen to your mother! That picture was taken about the time I moved in with Raymond. The two times I didn't listen to my mother turned out to be the worst mistakes of my life. I was miserable, and my mother was the one who was there for me.

"(Lexington points to the picture.) She had a tendency to stifle herself and dim her light. She did what Camren and Raymond wanted and disregarded what she wanted. I would tell her to be comfortable and secure enough on her own. I would tell her to stand up for herself and be brave enough to say no. I would tell her to be clear and vocal about her desires in relationships.

"If I had stated clearly what I expected and wanted from Roman and Chad very early in the relationships and remained clear throughout the relationships, maybe the relationships would've ended without anyone getting hurt or the relationships wouldn't have happened at all."

Anniston says, "Mommy, I will always remember what you said. That's great advice!" Anniston adds, "Mommy, if anyone ever asks how I feel about your story, your life, I'm going to say incredibly proud."

Lexington says, "Awe! Baby Girl, you mean that?"

Anniston says, "If I'm half the woman you are, I will be satisfied with my life."

Lexington hugging Anniston says, "You'll be ten times the woman, I am. You will accomplish all your goals and dreams. There are no limits for you, Baby Girl. You already make me so proud."

They come across more pictures of Lexington and Roman. Lexington says, "That seems like a lifetime ago."

Anniston asked, "Did you ever see him again?"

Lexington says, "We spent a week at Destiny's house when you were one. I took you and your sisters to our favorite pizza place."

Recognition

Lexington had Anniston strapped to her chest as she pushed her other two sleeping daughters in the stroller. Lexington walked into the restaurant and immediately heard someone call her name. She turned her head and looked right into Roman's eyes.

Roman, smiling at her, said, "Lex, you're a mommy, now."

Lexington said, "Hello, Roman!"

Roman said, "Like mother, like daughter. She was definitely made in your image. You're looking finer than ever. Motherhood looks good on you."

Lexington said, "Thank you! You look well and happy."

Roman asked, "What are you doing with yourself these days?"

Lexington said, "I'm raising these girls and caring for my husband."

Roman said, "I knew you would be that kind of wife and mother. God has blessed you, Lex. The love of my life is somebody else's wife."

Lexington said, "Roman, don't do that."

Roman asked, "I'm guessing you married chocolate thunder."

Lexington said, "His name is Michael, and yes, that's my husband."

Roman said, "I heard you moved."

Lexington said, "Yeah! I'm a southern, churchgoing, stay at home mother, now."

Roman said, "I am not mad at you!" Roman peeked in the stroller; he said, "Three beautiful little girls."

Lexington said, "Yes! I'm working on a boy, hopefully soon. What about you?"

Roman answers, "I'm married with kids now. Our oldest, Roman, is three, and Siena is two. Nico is on the way."

Roman pulled out his phone and showed Lexington pictures of his family. Lexington says, "You have a beautiful wife. Your son looks just like you. Siena is adorable. I'm happy for you."

He said, "Why, because someone took me off your hands? I'd rather be with you."

Lexington said, "Roman, don't disrespect your wife."

Roman said, "I told her how I felt about you, how you broke my heart and left me devastated."

Lexington said, "That is not what happened."

Roman said, "That is exactly what happened, but I guess it depends on who is telling the story."

Lexington said, "Everything worked out."

Roman said, "Everything did work out. She holds me down. I love my children."

Lexington said, "You seem really happy."

Roman said, "Well, I can't really be happy if another man is married to my wife."

Lexington said, "You are married to your wife. I'm happy for you and proud of you, Roman."

Roman said, "You should be proud. You taught me to do better. I took her home to meet my mother. I told her from the start she was my woman. I always tell her the truth. I go home every day on time. I pray for her. I'm faithful. I support her in everything she wants to do. I cheer her on when she starts something new. I take care of her every need. I said to myself, don't fuck this up! Be the man Lex wanted you to be, and this will work out. I told her all about you and how fucked up I was when you dumped."

Lexington smiles, "I'm so happy you found her, and you're doing right by her!"

Roman couldn't handle talking to her as Michael's wife; he said, "I better let you feed these pretty, little girls. You take care of yourself and these three beautiful girls. What's this one's name?"

Lexington said, "This is Anniston."

Roman touched her cheek, "Anniston, be good to your Mommy for me. (He pulled out a one-hundred-dollar bill and handed it to Anniston.) Pay for sister's pizza for me, but not your mother's. Her husband can pay for her pizza."

Lexington said, "Roman, take your money."

He said, "I can buy lunch for my should've been daughters. Besides, pretty women should never have to foot the bill."

She said, "If that's the case, you're paying for my pizza, too." He laughed.

He reached out his hand, he said, "Stay blessed!"

When she took his hand, it broke his heart all over again. She said, "Goodbye, Roman."

(Present Day) Anniston says, "Mommy, he still wanted you back after all that time, what did you do to him?"

Lexington says, "I will never figure men out. I hope my husband never tells a female anything like that. It would be demoralizing to know he married me because he couldn't have the woman he really wanted."

Anniston says, "I know for a fact that you are the woman of his dreams, and he married you because he loved you."

Lexington says, "How do you know?"

Anniston says, "I asked." (Lexington smiled at her daughter.)

Anniston asks, "Did you tell Daddy we saw him that day?"

Lexington says, "I told him right after it happened. He said, 'I'm on my way.' I asked if he trusted me, and he said, 'It's not you that I'm worried about.' By sundown, he was knocking on Destiny's door."

Anniston scrolls to the more recent pictures and comes across a picture of a tiny baby, she asks, "Mommy, whose baby is this? I don't recognize it at all."

Lexington says, "That's my baby."

Anniston's mouth drops: she says, "Mommy, that doesn't look like any of us."

Lexington says, "That's Micah."

Anniston asks, "Where is he?"

Lexington couldn't bring herself to verbalize the answer; she just shook her head. Lexington says, "When Michelle was a baby, I found out I was pregnant again. When the doctor said it was a boy, I was so excited. I felt like I was going to give my husband what he always wanted. About five and a half months into the pregnancy, I woke up in the middle of the night in pain."

Devastation

"Michael, Michael! Wake up," she whispered, hitting his shoulder. He opened his eyes and asked what's wrong. She told him something was wrong with the baby. They got dressed and rushed to the hospital. When the doctor examined her, he told her the baby's heart was no longer beating. He said she would have to deliver the stillborn baby. She and Michael were both devastated. Michael's parents came to the hospital to get Michelle. Mrs. Lear took the first flight.

The nurse gave her medicine to induce labor. The whole thing felt terrible. It was not the same as her first delivery. It was cold, quiet, and dead of energy. Michael cried and held her the entire time. She had never seen Michael cry or show that kind of emotion. She was so stunned by his grief that she locked hers inside. She had to play tough because he was so fragile.

From the moment they met, Michael had been a pillar of calm and strength. He was literally weeping from his soul. He kept kissing her and saying, "I'm so sorry! I never wanted this to happen to you." He thought it was his fault. Only God knows why he makes the decisions that he makes, but she surely didn't think it was Michael's fault.

They had to bury the baby. Lexington's heart was broken. It was the hardest thing she ever had to do. She put on a brave face and hid her emotions. She had to stay strong for him, so she cried to herself when she was alone. She didn't want to hurt him more by showing her true feelings. She wanted that baby boy so badly, but she accepted that God had other plans. Mrs. Lear took care of Michelle until Lexington was physically and emotionally healthy.

They prayed through it, and God blessed them for it. Khryssa came the next year. Anniston came two years after Khryssa. Two years after Anniston, the twins were born. Lexington prayed with all her heart for the twins. They ended up with six kids, just like Michael said they would.

(Present Day) Anniston says, "Mommy, I'm so sorry that happened to you. That had to be hard for you."

Lexington says, "It was, but it was harder for your father because that was the second baby boy he lost."

Anniston asks, "Daddy was married before you?"

Lexington says, "No one knows I have this picture, but this is your father's ex-fiancée and their stillborn son, Michael Jr."

Anniston asks, "How did you get this picture?"

Explanation

Grandmother Upshaw walked Lexington through the front room, looking at photos. Lexington stared in shocked at a photo of a woman. Mrs. Upshaw asked, "Are you ok?"

Lexington asked, "Who is that?"

Grandmother Upshaw said, "That's my mom. She loved Michael. She and I raised Michael. He spent most of his childhood at the restaurant with us." Grandmother Upshaw pulled out a picture of twin boys.

Lexington said, "They are so cute. Who are they?"

Grandmother Upshaw answered, "Michael and his brother. His brother was stillborn. In our family, sometimes the male child doesn't make it. Michael, didn't tell you he was a twin?"

"No, Michael did not," she said.

"I guess he didn't tell you about this either, huh?" she asked as she pointed to a picture.

She grabbed the picture from the fireplace of a woman holding a baby in a hospital room. Grandmother Upshaw said, "This was Michael Jr. and his mother, Kayley. Michael Jr. was stillborn. It was so devastating that Michael and Kayley broke off their engagement. Michael really never dated anyone seriously after that until you came along."

"Michael doesn't talk much about what bothers him," Lexington said.

Mrs. Upshaw said, "He never did even as a child. Come on in here, so we can eat. I think you're going to enjoy the food."

"I am sure I will," Lexington said. When Grandmother Upshaw left the room, Lexington secretly took a few pictures of the photos.

That night, Lexington tried to talk to him about the pictures. She said, "You know you can tell me anything, and it'll be okay."

He said, "I know I can. Grandmother showed you the pictures?"

"That's why you said no to naming a boy Michael Jr.," she asked.

"I really don't want to talk about him, Kayley or the brother. I dealt with those things and put them away," he said.

(Present Day) "We never spoke of any of them again," Lexington said as she shows Anniston the picture of Michael and his brother.

Anniston says, "OMG! They look just like the twins."

Lexington says, "Yeah, they do."

Anniston says, "Man, so the twins broke a generational curse. They both survived. They are thriving and succeeding."

Lexington says, "We serve a mighty good God."

Anniston says, "Mommy, that is an amazing testimony."

Lexington replies, "It taught me the power and importance of prayer. I pray before I make a decision. I cover all I do in my marriage, as a mother and in my work in prayer."

Anniston continues looking at the pictures. She came across a picture of Lexington with three-year-old Michelle and one-year-old Khryssa. Anniston says, "Mommy, look at you, Michelle, and Khryssa."

Lexington looks at the picture, she says, "That was a very crazy day."

Anniston asks, "What happened that day?"

Indignation

Lexington and her daughters visited Michael at his office. He asked his wife to get him a cup of coffee while he showed off his daughters. When Lexington went into the breakroom, there was a group of men sitting at a table, talking. They spoke. She spoke. As she made the coffee, they got up to walk out of the breakroom. As they walked out, one of them said Michael's wife has a fat ass. The other men laughed. They left, and she left. She didn't think about it again.

The next day, she was in the kitchen, making a snack for her daughters when Michael came home. She could tell something wasn't right because he was home so early. She could hear his unhappiness in his footsteps. His pace and the heaviness of his footsteps were not normal. She looked at him as he walked into the kitchen; she said, "Hey, Babe!"

With a stern face, he said, "So you weren't going to tell me that someone disrespected you at my workplace?"

"Baby, I didn't want to start anything," she said.

"You should've said something," he said.

"You couldn't possibly think I paid him any attention," she said.

"It's not about him. It's about you not talking to your husband," he said.

She said, "I didn't think it was a big deal."

When she said that, it made him more upset. He backed her against the kitchen counter. He had never treated her like that. He had never touched her in anger or yelled at her.

He was so mad that she really didn't know how to handle him. They had never had an argument. He started yelling at her, and pointing his finger in her face, he said, "That's the problem, Lexington, you didn't think. You didn't think about me. You were going to let me go on thinking he was my friend, and he disrespected my wife. Unacceptable, Lexington!"

He started pounding his chest, "Lexington, you tell me stuff like that and trust that I, the man, can handle myself. You know how stupid I looked when someone told me something happened to my wife, who I slept with last night, and she didn't mention it. Don't let me find out about my home in the streets! Do you hear me?"

She answered, "Babe, I hear you." He turned to leave.

Before he could get to the door, she started crying. He paused, turned, and came back. He wrapped his arms around her, and said, "I'm not mad at you. I'm just saying you should have told me." When he left, the babies were screaming and crying. Through her own tears, she had to calm them down. She was so hurt that he yelled at her.

That night, when Michael came home, there was a fierce thunderstorm. The thunder rumbled in the sky and shook the whole house. Lexington pretended to sleep just to avoid him. Even with her back to him, she could see his every move, the look on his face, and the anger in his heart by every sound he made, his footsteps, the water running as he showered, and the movement of the bed when he laid down.

As the thunder rumbled and lightning crackled through the sky, she could feel his eyes on her. She felt like they were burning through her flesh like fire. There was tension between them like an invisible barrier. She felt him roll over just as a loud boom rolled through the sky; she called his name. When he calmly said, "Yes, Babe," she felt she could talk to him.

She rolled over, and he turned to face her. They stared into each other's eyes. She said, "Michael, I am so sorry. You're right, I didn't think. Don't be mad at me." Tears rolled down her face. Michael grabbed her and pulled her over to him. He wiped her tears.

He wrapped his arms around her and said, "Lexington, come here, I'm not mad at you. It's okay. Stop crying." The thunder boomed so loudly that she jumped from fear. Michael comforted her.

Lexington snuggled in his arm and rested her head on his shoulder, she said, "Baby, I can't stand you being mad at me."

He said, "I should've handled that better, for that I am sorry. When we have a difference of opinion, we talk about it, and we come to an understanding. I shouldn't have touched you in anger or raised my voice. Baby, I promise that will never happen again."

Michael kissed Lexington on the forehead and asked, "We're good?" She traced his lips with her fingertip, she nodded yes and said, "Thank you for loving me the way you do."

Michael said, "I do love you, but that doesn't mean we will always agree. From now on, we wait to talk until we can talk calmly."

"You were so upset, it scared me," she said.

"I didn't mean to scare you. I was hurt, not upset because I felt like you didn't think about me," he said.

"Let's make a deal. I will think about you in all my decisions, and you always deal with me calmly and peacefully," she said.

Michael kissed her hand. "Deal," he said.

Michael and Lexington embrace each other. He held Lexington so tightly to his chest that she could hear and feel his heartbeat mixed with her own. The storm continued to rage outside, but the closeness of Michael soothed and comforted her.

The rain tapped on the windows, the thunder rolled through the sky, and lightning crackled through the surrounding atmosphere. Michael's hands slowly caressed up her back then he tapped down her back to the rhythm of her pulse. Lexington's head and hands were on his chest. With his other hand, he used his nail like a rake to lightly scratch up and down her side. The gestures of love melted away all the tension between the two of them.

Michael and his wife passionately kissed as he continued wiping her tears; he said, "Baby, I'm so sorry. I don't like it when you cry. Stop crying!" They continued kissing to express their apologies physically. Michael was ashamed of his behavior. He never meant to deal with her in anger.

Michael rolled on top of Lexington and rested his face on her chest, listening to her heartbeat as she traced the shape of his head. She whispered, "I love you so much." He looked at her and kissed her like he never wanted to stop. As they kissed, she rubbed his back and shoulders as Michael massaged her thighs and worked his way to her calves.

Michael looked in her eyes and said, "I love you. I promise this will never happen again."

She softly caressed his arms as he softly caressed her hips. He said, "You know I never want to hurt you. That's not the kind of husband I am. I will never act like that again. When I confronted him, things got so heated that people had to restrain me. I was mad at him and took it out on you. Baby, say you forgive me." Chest to chest, they could feel each other's heartbeat as Michael talked.

As she inhaled, he exhaled, and as he inhaled, she exhaled. They were so close; they could feel the air entering and exiting each other's body. Michael kissed her neck, begging for her forgiveness. He said, "Forgive me, baby," as he wiped her tears. He added, "Baby, I feel so bad. I hate that I made you cry. Say you forgive me."

Lexington said, "I forgive you, Michael." Michael kissed her.

Michael took his index and middle finger to pull her panties to the side. He slowly slid himself into his wife. Lexington nails scratched across his back as he entered her; she breathlessly said, "Baby!"

Michael kissed her neck, he said, "I feel it too!" Michael, full of emotion, made love to his wife with the intensity of the raging storm, still rumbling in the sky to prove to her that he was truly sorry for the way he handled things.

(Present Day) Lexington says to Anniston, "You know what happened that night: you," as Lexington touches Anniston's nose.

Anniston says, "Mommy, how did you two go from arguing to making a baby," as she continues to look at the pictures.

Lexington winks and says, "We made up, and made one of the best things that ever happened to me."

Anniston says, "Awe, Mommy!"

Lexington says, "When I was pregnant with you, Destiny was pregnant with Serenity, Kendra was pregnant with Mallory, and Kareen was pregnant with Akeem. What a coincidence!"

Michael comes into the room, and Anniston quickly closes the photo app and MacBook. Anniston says, "Hi, Daddy!"

Michael says, "Hey, Baby Girl!" He hugs Anniston and goes to kiss Lexington.

Anniston sits the MacBook on her mother's side of the bed, and says, "Goodnight, Love Birds."

They say in unison, "Goodnight, Baby Girl."

Lexington tells Michael, "There's a warm bath awaiting you, and your plate is in the microwave."

Michael says, "Thanks, baby, you're the best," as he went into the bathroom.

Lexington puts the MacBook in her nightstand and crawls into bed, lays down, and closes her eyes. By the time Michael comes to bed, Lexington is sound asleep. After he eats, Michael gets in bed and wraps his arms around her until he falls asleep.

Saturday finally arrives, Lexington being the proud, supportive mother takes her daughter to the salon to get glammed up.

Anniston says, "I can't get over those pictures. Why didn't you tell us about Micah?"

Lexington says, "It'll hurt your father too much to talk about it. It's easier to pretend it didn't happen than it is to deal with the devastation."

Anniston asks, "Why did he die?"

Lexington says, "I don't know!"

Anniston asks, "What did the doctor say?"

Lexington answers, "That it happens for many different reasons."

Anniston says, "Mommy, I am sorry that happened to you. I couldn't imagine how terrible that was for you. It's sad just knowing you were hurt."

Lexington says, "Awe! Thank you, Baby Girl. That definitely helps me feel a million times better."

Anniston says, "Mommy, you are beautiful now, but you were so gorgeous back then. Roman and Chad were all over you in those pictures. I can tell they really liked you. Did Roman or Chad ever try to get you back?"

Lexington laughs: she says, "Chad no, but I guess you can of say Roman did."

Anniston asks, "What did he do?"

Retrospection

Michael and Lexington were on the couch, wrestling and a watching movie. Michael began tickling Lexington, she laughed so hard that she had to relieve herself. She said, "Okay, okay, you win," and took off running to the restroom in the hallway. As she ran into the restroom, there was a knock at the door. Michael said, "Lexi, there's someone at the door. Are you expecting anyone?"

Lexington responded from the restroom, "No, would you get it for me?"

Michael opened the door, there stood a shocked Roman. They stared at each other for a moment. "May I help you," Michael asked.

Roman replied, "Is Lexington home?"

Michael yelled, "Lexi, baby! Someone is here to see you." Roman and Michael stood there, sizing each other up with their eyes but never spoke a word.

Lexington said, "Just a sec! Honey, I'm coming." She finished in the restroom and quickly came running to the door.

When she reached the door, she was shocked. "Roman," she said.

Roman said, "Hey, Lex!"

"What are you doing here," she asked, very uncomfortable with Michael watching her talk to Roman.

Roman answered, "I'm checking on you, Lex. Making sure you're okay in person since you won't answer the phone."

There was an awkward tension as the three of them stood there. Michael interrupts, "She's been very busy, Light Skin," as he wraps his arms around her.

Lexington placed her hands on Michael's arm wrapped around her neck while she responded to Roman, trying to keep both men pacified, she said, "Yes, I've been very busy, but I'm well. I hope all is well with you."

Roman replied, "All is not well, I lost my friend. I was hoping to find her."

Michael said, "I think that crackhead is still on Main Street, right, Babe? We saw her on our way home. You might catch your friend if you hurry." Roman faked a smirk.

Lexington tried to get Michael out the doorway, but Michael wouldn't move. Roman wanted to ask her to come to the hall to talk, but he decided not to do so. Roman grabbed Lexington's wrist, and Michael pulled her arm, removing it from Roman's grip. Lexington said, "Roman, you have plenty of friends. I'm sure you're fine."

Roman said, "But not the one that matters."

Michael tells Roman, "Okay! You can go now!" Roman ignores him and stares into her eyes.

To escape the awkward energy, she said, "Roman, thanks for checking on me. Stay well," as she tries to close the door. Roman looked like a kid who lost his puppy. He stuck his foot in the door, he said, "That's what friends do. They check on each other. They have consideration and concern for each other. You're my friend, Lex. You haven't checked on me. It's like you never cared."

Michael said, "She checks on me every day, as my woman, my friend, and my lover."

Roman sarcastically said to Michael, "Aren't you lucky!"

Lexington felt bad, she said, "Roman, I..." She stopped talking. She couldn't find the words.

Roman never took his eyes off her; he said, "I guess, I'll let you go get back to your chocolate thunder lover."

Michael smirked and said, "Chocolate thunder makes it rain." Roman eyes pierced through Lexington like a swordsman slicing his opponent; he said, "I know those showers very well."

Before he walked off, Roman and Michael had a war with their eyes (Lexington was trying to push Michael away from the door.) Michael said, "Correction: you knew those showers, but it's all over for you now."

Roman stopped walking, turned, and said, "Remember, I hit it first. I taught her everything she knows. You're enjoying the fruits of my labor. You can thank me later. Don't get caught slipping because I'll be right back on it."

Michael said, "I got a good woman. If I slip, she'll catch me before I fall. Oh and, I got that ass last. It hits really different after it's been hit right."

Lexington said, "Boys!"

"It was hitting perfectly fine, the three years I was knocking it back," Roman said.

Michael responded, "And, yet she left you for me."

Roman said, "I never heard her say she was done with me."

Michael said, "I'm telling you, now, she's done with you, so don't come back here."

Lexington said, "Boys, boys, let's play nice," as she struggled with Michael to close the door. Lexington was finally able to close the door, and said: "Wow, did you really engage in that conversation."

Michael said, "Yes, I did!"

Lexington said, "You and him, just gave my neighbors an earful about my sex life."

Michael said, "I couldn't help myself."

Lexington said, "You're so bad."

Michael said, "You're so good."

Lexington said, "I didn't invite him here. I didn't know he was coming; I swear."

Michael wrapped her in his arms and picked her up. "I know," he said as he carried her to the couch with her legs wrapped around his waist.

Lexington asked, "How do you know?"

Michael (hugging Lexington as she straddled his lap sitting on the couch) said, "I can tell he hasn't seen you in a long time by the look on his face. That was the look of a man missing a woman. That would be the same look on my face if you left me. I would be just like him, at your door trying to get you back. That's the price you pay for having that good, good: men don't want to let you go."

Lexington said, "It better not be anyone knocking on your door trying to get you back."

Michael said, "She won't get in. I'm taken."

Lexington said, "Yeah, remember that!"

Michael said, "You're the one with an obsessed fan at your door."

Lexington laughed; she said, "He is not a factor. The thing with him was over before I met you."

Michael said, "You didn't get the memo?"

She asked, "What memo?"

Michael said, "The one that said: I got this (pointing to Lexington than himself) on lock."

Lexington asked, "How can you be so sure?"

Michael said, "Months before I met you, I told God I was ready. I prayed that the woman he had for me was prepared for me. I prayed that he would remove any and all obstacles blocking my way to her. The moment I saw you, I said that's her. I prayed before I called you. I asked God to open your heart to me and turn your heart and mind away from any/all other men pursuing you. I asked the Lord to make you mine. My God answers prayer, so I know he is not a factor."

Lexington said, "I cannot question that. That was beautiful, Michael. You really prayed for me?"

Michael said, "I pray for you every day. I cover you head to toe every morning and every night. You're with me now, and with me, you will always be covered in prayer, you will never be alone, you'll never struggle or carry a burden alone. I'm preparing to spend my life supporting you, loving you, pleasing you, making you smile, making you laugh, and making you happy. "When tough times come, I'll be there covering you, supporting you, and protecting you. So, no, we are not thinking about him or anyone else. We are focusing on figuring us out and preparing for our future."

Lexington said, "Michael, (He looks in her eyes.) I'm ready, Baby." She rubs his arm.

Michael responded, "I know!"

Lexington asked, "What are?"

Michael cuts her off, "Trust me, I'm working on it."

Lexington let it go and said, "I trust you!"

Michael said, "Thank you for trusting me," just before the phone rang.

Michael said, "Babe, my car is here."

Lexington pulled his arm and said, "Baby, no! I hate it when you go. Please stay one more night. Please! Please!"

Michael hugs her; he said, "I would, but I have a meeting first thing in the morning. Come, walk me to the car."

Lexington walked Michael to the car. Michael leaned against the car, and Lexington leaned against Michael. Lexington wrapped her arms around Michael, and said, "I'm so lonely when you're so far away."

Michael says, "I'm lonely without you, too!"

She said, "I'll see you next weekend."

Michael held her hips as they kissed. Michael said, "I can't wait!" They kissed again.

Roman sat in his car, watching them passionately kiss as they said goodbye. Roman thought to himself: she never kissed me like that. He watched as Michael hit Lexington on her butt before getting in the car. Lexington waved at the car before she walked back into the building. When Roman figured she was back in her apartment, he called from a new number, knowing Lexington wouldn't recognize it.

When she said hello, Roman's heart broke. "So, she finally answers the phone," Roman said with a melancholy voice.

Lexington said, "Hello, Roman."

He said, "You know I love it when you say my name."

Lexington said, "What's on your mind, Roman?"

Roman answered, "I miss you for one. Two, you cut me off. You cut me out of your life after three years, like I meant nothing to you. And three, I want my girl back.

"Lex, we're friends. That's not how you were supposed to do me. We're better than that! I should mean more to you than that. It hurt my feelings. You just kicked me to the curb and didn't tell me anything. You didn't give me a chance to do something. How could you do me like that? That was heartless and cold, Lex, but I know you didn't have the heart to tell me it's over because you really didn't want it to be over."

Lexington said, "You're right, Roman, I'm sorry. Roman, I didn't mean to hurt you. I knew I couldn't give you what you wanted, so I thought it would be best to leave you alone. I'm sorry. Nothing that happened was purposely done to hurt you."

Roman said, "Is he why you said no that night?"

Lexington said, "No, Roman, I didn't meet him until months after we stop speaking."

Roman said, "We didn't stop speaking. You stopped speaking to me. There's a difference Lex!" Roman asked, "Are you happy? Is this serious?"

Lexington said, "Yes, I'm happy, and yes, it's serious."

Roman replies, "That's all that matters. I want you to be happy. You deserve to be happy even if it's with someone else."

Lexington said, "Thank you! Roman, you deserve to be happy with someone who loves you."

Roman asked, "May I ask a question before you hang up?"

Lexington said, "Ask your question."

Roman said, "Why him and not me?"

Lexington said, "Roman, don't do that."

Roman said, "No, I want to know what I couldn't do that he could. What did he do, Lex? Why do you love him and not me?"

Lexington said, "Roman, that's not a fair question."

Roman replied, "Lex, tell me, explain to me how he's different. You knew I wanted you. You didn't even try to make it work with me. I've loved you for seven whole years. You just met him, and he gets you. Please, Lex, tell me why him and not me."

Lexington said, "My being with him is not a reflection of you or a result of your doing or not doing something. I'm with him for him. It has nothing to do with you. I never thought you would want more than what we were doing until that last night. I had to stop what we were doing before it got too deep."

Roman said, "It was already deep. The first night you gave yourself to me in Mexico, it got deep."

"Roman, that's not fair. You got exactly what you wanted and what you asked for," she said.

"So, I'm good enough to fuck, but not love? Is that it, Lex," he asked.

She said, "Roman, don't say it like that. You know I don't think of you like that."

Roman asked, "What does that mean, Lex? You fucked me over and over, and you fucked me so good I didn't want to be with anyone but you. And, when you were done fucking me, you just left like you never cared for me."

Lexington said, "Roman, I did care for you."

Roman said, "I saw you kissing him, and I thought she never kissed me like that. Just know, I always wanted you to kiss me and love me, but I see you never planned to do so.

"I would've done right by you. I would have loved you because you're that special to me. I have never met a woman like you. Tell your boyfriend he's the luckiest man in the world, but if he ever fucks up, I'll be right here. I better not ever catch him slipping. I want my woman back, and I'm not fucking around this time. When I get you back, I'm locking you down. If you ever need me for anything, I'm just a phone call away. Take care of yourself, Lex."

"You too, Roman," said Lexington. They hung up.

About ten minutes after they hung up, there was a knock at the door. She opened the door and said, "Roman, what are you doing here?"

He said, "I just want to talk."

She said, "Roman, we just talked."

Roman said, "I need you to look me in my face and say it's over."

She reluctantly let him in, "Come in, Roman. I don't need my neighbors getting another earful," she said.

Roman said, "You're right. I wasn't respectful earlier. I was in my feelings. I apologize for that."

He sat on the couch. She stood leaning on the wall. "Are you going to sit down," he asked.

"I'm good here," she said. "What's on your mind, Roman," she asked.

"Lex, I'm not going to bite you. Come closer! I need to ask in person what happened. I proposed, and you ran away," he said.

"Roman, don't make this into a thing," she said.

"It is a thing, Lex. I'm supposed to let someone take the one great thing I had. I love you, Lex, I want to be with you," Roman said.

Lexington said, "Roman, you don't love me."

Roman said, "You couldn't feel that I loved you when I touched you, when I tasted you, or when I was inside you three hundred twenty-five times? You had to feel it, Lex!"

Lexington said, "We liked each other a lot. We were very attracted to each other. We had a lot of fun and shared some good times. I had to move on, and you needed to as well."

Roman said, "Nope! I haven't moved on, that's why I am here."

Lexington said, "You had other women…."

He interrupted, "But, I wanted to marry you."

Lexington continued, "I've been out and seen you with other women the day after you were with me more than once, and I never said anything because I knew what it was, and I accepted what we were. You were chilling with a bitch in my face. Do you know how that shit made me feel? It was like you were saying I was not good enough."

Roman said, "Never on purpose, Lex. Never did I mean for that shit to happen. I wasn't fucking them. I never fronted on you. Those were not intimate relationships. They were just friends."

"Roman, I just don't believe you," she said.

Roman said, "So you think I'm just a hoe, huh?"

Lexington said, "I know you were with other women more than the one you told me about."

Roman said, "You were fucking someone else!"

She replies, "You did it first."

Roman said, "How can you be so sure there was someone else?"

Lexington said, "I know you and what you feel like. I could tell the difference in you when you were with someone else. I never said anything because I knew we were just having sex."

Roman said, "That's not true, I was with you. You were my girl!"

She asked, "If you were trying to be with me, you wouldn't let a chick in your space or in your face."

Roman said, "You're misreading the situation."

Lexington said, "There was only one way to read the situation. So, No! You don't deserve me now. You had six years to do right by me, and you didn't. Now, I have the man of my dreams, and you want to show up talking about you love me. You should've done that four or five years ago when I might have bought the shit you're selling.

"If you loved me, Roman, you would've been with me one thousand ninety-five nights, and no other woman could have kept you away. After we came home from Mexico, you continued as if nothing changed for you."

Roman said, "Lexington, that's not true. I cut off so many women for you. I curbed so many women for you. I thought we were working toward something.

"Okay, before Mexico, I was out there, but when we came home, I changed. I will admit, I did mess with my ex more than I led you to believe the last time we talked, but she was it. I was caught between you and her for a while. Truthfully, I did struggle with whether I wanted to go back to her or pursue you for the first year. But she knew how I felt about you. I thought about it, and I realized it was you I wanted, so I cut her off. It was just you from that point on. I was working on building our relationship."

Lexington said, "You thought three hundred twenty-five nights, which is less than thirty per cent of three years, was working toward something?"

Roman said, "We were, Lex!"

Lexington asked, "So, what were you doing those seven hundred seventy nights that you weren't with me, and I didn't hear from you?"

Roman said, "Not what you think! You mean so much to me that I am here begging you after a year and a half of you not speaking to me. I miss you so much. I sit back and think about how I had you, and I let you get away. I regret that. Whatever I did or didn't do, I am sorry. I want my girl back."

Lexington said, "Roman, Honey, you don't love me, but he does. He shows me that he loves every day, even from another state. His life is completely open to me. He shares everything with me. He shows up for me. He prays for me. He checks on me. He shows an interest in my life and the things that are important to me. He takes care of me. If I catch a cold, he will fly all the way here just to make soup for me. He made me a priority in his life on day one.

"When I call, he answers or calls right back if he misses the call. You know why I always waited for you to call me, and I never called you, Roman?"

Roman asked, "Why, Lex?"

Lexington answered, "Because I couldn't deal with the possibility of you not answering. There's always too much possibility of the wrong shit with you, Roman. And you are sitting here lying like a mother fucking carpet. You know damn well you didn't stop messing with that chick.

"Roman, she called me. She told me everything. Oh, yeah! And I know about the bitch with the blonde hair. While you were telling bitches about me, they were plotting to mess up what we had. Your friend with the blonde weave called me, too. I listened to what they had to say, but I told them, I'm just a squirrel trying to get a nut. He's not my man, and he can do what he wants. Why keep lying to me, especially since I know the truth.

"Roman, I did love you, but I had to bottle it up because you're so fucking sloppy and messy. But with Michael, life is peaceful. I know what I'm getting into. He took me to meet his family and said this is my woman. He took me to meet his friends and said this is my woman. He took me to his workplace and said this is my woman. And he has the decency not to flaunt other women in my face. He doesn't have to cut his phone off because females are calling all night. And you're right Roman, we had a lot of incredible sex.

"I learned a lot about sex from you, but Michael taught me how to make love. There's a difference. Michael makes love to my whole body, and I feel loved. He made it clear very early what he wanted and what his intention was with me. He, as the man set the tone, and I as the woman followed his lead.

"Roman, you made it seem like our relationship was just sex for you. You never sat me down and said, Lex, I was messing with a girl before I met you, let me clean this up, and I'll get right back to you. You never said, Lex, it's really you that I want to be with. You should have said, Lex, let's make this work.

"You popped up with a ring right after I just ended things Chad. And, for the record, there would have been no Chad if you had not been with someone else after Mexico. That's on you, and you can't be mad at me.

"In regard to kissing you, I never kissed you like I kissed him. Really, Roman, really! I didn't kiss you because you weren't my man to kiss. The way you gave me head, I can only imagine what you did with that ex. I know you're lying about only messing with the ex the first year. You moved out after Mexico, but you kept fucking her and the female with the blonde weave. You didn't know I knew that!"

Roman thought about what Lexington said. He had to concede and admit she was telling the truth. Roman said, "I'm not mad at you, I'm mad at me. I can't believe I let another dude come steal my girl. You're supposed to be my girl. But I get it, I was dragging my feet when I should've been building something with you. I don't know what the hell was wrong with me.

"Damn, man, I guess I lose, but I don't want to, though. You're the most incredible woman I've had the pleasure of spending time with. Damn! Man, I fucked up." Roman stood up and faced Lexington sitting on the arm of her couch. He grabbed her hands.

She said, "Roman, you're a good dude. We had a good time. I'll forever appreciate the time we shared."

"It was all good," Roman said, rubbing her thigh and leaning in closer, "It was really good," he added. Roman lifted his eyebrow and winked at her, he said, "Did you tell your boyfriend about all the times I fucked the shit out of you on this couch and in your bed?"

Lexington said, "Until today, he never heard of you."

He said, "Oh, so you had some explaining to do when I left."

Lexington said, "Roman, we talked a little bit."

Roman said, "Trust me, he's curious, and he will find a way to bring it up again. Any man would be if a dude showed up at his girl's house."

Roman whispered in her ear, "I miss you." He said, "Girl, you have no idea how I miss you, how I miss us. You got me walking around the house singing love songs, missing you."

Lexington, feeling awkward, turned her head to look away. Roman leaned in even closer with his hands on the couch between her legs and said, "Let me taste it one last time. Your boyfriend won't know."

She pushed him away and said, "Roman, my man was just in there, and you want to taste it?"

"I'll tear into that mother fucker like it was a Snickers, right now. I don't give a fuck about him," he said as he rubbed the crotch of her jeans. He leaned closer and tried to kiss her, but she moved. He added, "I will kiss it, lick it, suck it, and stick my tongue so far in it I'll taste your thoughts and emotions. Just say, yes."

Lexington finally broke the bond she shared with Roman when she said, "No, Roman." Lexington moving his hand and avoiding his face, said: "No, Roman! The thing we had is over."

He tried to kiss her again, but she pushed his forehead, and she moved from the couch. She walked him to the door, pushing his arm. He said, "You said no to me. You have never said no to me."

Lexington said, "Bye, Roman!"

Roman said, "You're really saying no!"

Lexington laughed as she opened the door, she said, "Roman, I said no. I mean, no."

Roman said, "I guess it really is over," as he walked out the door, he turned to face her. Roman sadly said, "For the record, I did love you. I do love you! I will always love you, no matter what or who comes into the picture. That dude better do right by you."

Lexington says, "He will! And, Roman, I loved you, too, in a special way. You'll always hold a special place in my heart."

Roman reached out to hug her. Lexington pushed him out the door; she said, "Roman, go home."

Roman said, "I can't even get a hug, goodbye?"

Lexington said, "Quickly, Roman!" He gripped her butt as they embraced. She pushed him away.

Roman said, "Saying goodbye and leaving here to never see you or talk to you again is the hardest thing I have ever had to do."

Lexington says, "Roman, it's for the best. I know you'll be fine."

Roman said before he walked away, "I won't be fine ever. I'll live, but I won't be fine. Your dude is a blessed man. I hope he knows that."

Lexington said, "He knows!"

"I'm going to miss you, Lex," Roman said as he kissed her hand and then walked away. She closed the door, hoping that was the last encounter she'd ever have with Roman.

(Present Day) Anniston asks as they drive from the salon to Anniston's favorite restaurant for lunch, "Were you tempted at all by him?"

Lexington says, "Roman couldn't compare to Michael in any category."

Anniston says, "Give me an example of something Daddy did that made you believe Michael was the better choice."

Lexington says, "There are so many things, but I can give you the perfect example.

The day Roman showed up, we had a conversation after Roman left. Michael said, trust him in regard to our future. I had no idea what he was doing, but I did trust him. A month later, he proved he was trustworthy. Keep in mind, I messed with Roman for three years, he chased me for three years, and we didn't speak for a year which makes a total of seven years. I dated Michael for a year and a half, and in that time, was ready to build a future with me."

Liberation

A month after meeting Roman, Michael surprised Lexington on a Thursday evening as she was ending her workday. He hadn't called all day, so Lexington was anticipating hearing from him. As Lexington put her laptop in her bag, there was a knock on her office door. She grabbed her phone to check for messages or missed calls, as she said, come in. The door opened, but she was still preoccupied with her phone.

A deep, familiar voice said, "Hey, baby," as the door closed. She looked up and saw that it was Michael. She smiled a big, happy smile filled with love. She sat her phone on the desk and rushed over to hug him, saying, "Hey! What are you doing here?"

He said, "I couldn't go another minute without seeing you," as they embraced. He kissed her forehead.

"Is everything okay?" she asked.

"Everything is good. Sorry, I got tied up and couldn't fly out to see you," he replied.

"It's okay. Things happen," she said.

"I don't like breaking promises to you, you know that right," Michael asked.

Lexington said, "You keep the ones that matter. I'm grateful you're here now."

He kissed her hand. "Thanks for being understanding," he said. She touched his cheek. He asked, "Are you hungry?"

She said, "Yes, I'm starving!"

He said, "Come, take a ride with me."

As they approached his car, she asked, "Michael, this is not a rental. Did you drive all the way here?"

Michael said, "I needed to see my woman is that alright with you."

Lexington said, "It's more than alright." He opened her door, and she sat in his car. As they drove, she tried to get Michael to tell her where they were going. Michael refused to give any hints.

They drove into the driveway of this big, newly renovated house. Michael got out of the car and walked over to the passenger side and opened the door for Lexington. "Whose house is this," she asked.

Michael answered, "Just get out of the car." Once they walked through the front door, Lexington was immediately hooked.

A white piano and bench sat adjacent to the fireplace. They continued to the dining room where the table was set with expensive crystal dinnerware. Lit candles and champagne sat on the table.

Michael said, "Why don't you take a tour of the house, while I finish preparing dinner."

As she went from room to room, she felt a connection to the house. The bedrooms were decorated as if she did it herself. In the master bedroom, she saw Michael's personal things all over the room. His laptop was on the bed. His shaving kit and toothbrush were in the bathroom.

She walked through the closet touching his clothes and looking at his shoes. Lexington thought Michael moved here, but she wanted to hear it from him. She went back downstairs, and the piano caught her eye.

The white piano near the fireplace was just like the one in her childhood home. For years, Mrs. Sheraton came to her house after school on Mondays and Wednesdays for lessons. She was saddened when her parents sold it before they moved to Florida. She returned to the dining room, where Michael sat at the table. When Michael saw her, he stood up. He escorted her to the table, pushed in her chair, and sat a napkin in her lap. Michael went back to his seat.

He asked, "What did you think of the house?"

She answered, "It's really beautiful."

Michael said, "I'm glad you like it."

Lexington asked, "Whose house is this?"

He said, "Can we enjoy the meal that I worked so hard to prepare; afterward, I'll answer your questions?" Lexington agreed.

They talked as they ate. Lexington told him, "My parents want to meet you, maybe we could fly down for a weekend."

Michael said, "Definitely!"

After eating, they went into the kitchen to wash the dishes. He looked at her and said (drying the dish he was holding), "I love this."

She curiously asked, "What?"

He said, "You, me (pointing to her then himself) together. Being close to you. (She dried her hands to listen to him.) Being able to reach out and touch you. (He set the dish down that he was drying and embraced her.) Being able to smell your perfume as I look into your eyes and say I love you.

"I love being with you and being near you. It's getting harder and harder to leave you and go home to be so far away from you. At night, I lay in bed, and I can't sleep because I want you next to me. When I do sleep, I dream about you. I wake up and reach for you, but you're not there. I really couldn't take one more night."

Lexington was so touched by his words, she said, "Awe! Baby, I hate being away from you, too!"

He turned to the drawer, opened it up, and pulled out a key. He slid the key on the counter toward her, he said, "So, you want to know who owns this house: we do. I'm done with flying back and forth. I want to see your face every morning and hold you in my arms every night. Do you want that?"

She said, "Yes, baby, I do, but you're sure you want to leave your everything?"

He grabbed her and said, "My everything is right here."

Lexington picked up the key. "Baby, we're moving together?"

Michael responded, "All my stuff is already here. All I need is my woman to take her place beside me, and I will be content."

"So, this is why you've been asking me what I like and what I would want in my dream house," Lexington asked.

Michael smiled; he said, "I nailed it, didn't I?"

Lexington said, "You did! I love it, baby. I love the house and everything in it."

Michael replied, "I'm glad you love it because I did it all for you."

Lexington said, "Michael, you're unbelievable! Thank you, baby!"

When they were done with the dishes, Michael said: "Baby, play something for me."

Lexington asked, "What do you want to hear?"

Michael said, "Play the first song that you learned to play because you loved the song and not because your music teacher made you learn it."

Lexington sat on the bench. She touched the keys. She said, come sit with me. She began to play the Intro to "Lead Me into Love" by Anita Baker. She said, "I loved the instruments in this song. I played the intro over and over until I got it." She sang and played the intro.

When she was finished, Michael said, "Baby, that was unbelievable. I'm blown away."

Lexington said, "Thank you, baby, the music stopped after college."

Michael asked, "Why?"

Lexington said, "Long story!"

Lexington leaned onto Michael; she said, "You're so good to me, and you're so good for me."

Michael said, "Everyone we meet serves a purpose. Every experience helps shape us. If my presence impacts you in a positive and meaningful way, I am serving my purpose. It's my pleasure and my honor to serve."

Lexington touched his face, she said, "Thank you for loving me."

Michael said, "I do love you!"

Lexington said, "I love you! Wow! Michael, this is like a dream!"

Michael said, "I'm glad you're happy."

Lexington said, "I never knew love and life like this."

Michael said, "It's only going to get better."

Michael reached out his hands, he said, "Give me your hands!" Lexington placed her hands in his. Michael began to pray, "Heavenly Father, I pray for your blessings as we begin our journey together. Bless our path and guide our decisions. Give us patience and acceptance for one another so that we always deal with each other with kindness. Bless us with a long, healthy life together full of joy and new experiences. Bless our bodies and keep us well. Bless us with prosperity. Help us be fruitful.

"Remind us of joy when there is pain. Comfort and guide us through any trials we face. Let us always remember to walk this walk of life with faith and as a cohesive unit. I, the man, as the head and Lexington, the woman, as the heart letting no outside forces penetrate, break, or destroy our bond with you or each other. Putting you first and submitting to your will. I pray in Jesus' name, Amen!"

Lexington followed, Amen! Lexington and Michael kissed, she said, "Baby, there's like seven bedrooms in this house."

Michael said, "One for us, and one for each of our six kids."

Lexington said, "Woah, six kids."

Michael said, "Yeah! Six kids! Keep the house noisy and busy. I can't wait to see you waddling around." They laughed.

Lexington said, "How about we settle on two kids and a dog?"

Michael said, "Six, kids!"

(Present Day) Sitting in the booth looking at the menu, Lexington explains how she revealed her secret to her sisters, she says, "With us moving together, I had to come clean with my sisters. I couldn't move in with him and continue to keep him a secret."

Admission

Her friends were looking through the racks. Lexington was looking at herself in the mirror when she announced she had a secret. Her friends froze and stood, staring at her.

Lexington calmly said, "In my Toni Braxton voice (She got excited), I got a boyfriend. He is absolutely amazing. Before you all say anything, I want you all to come to our new house for dinner on Sunday to meet him. You all are going to love him."

Akera said, "I knew you were secretly seeing someone. So, this is what we are doing. You're keeping secrets from me."

Lexington said, "It's not like that."

Destiny said, "This is serious, Lexi, you said (Destiny gestures air quotes.) our new house. You are moving in with him, or you've already moved in with him."

Lexington said, "Yes, I am moving in with him."

Destiny said, "How long have you been seeing him?"

She answered, "A year and a half."

Kareen said, "When did you two decide to make this move?"

Lexington said, "Last night, he picked me up from work and took me to this amazing house that he secretly purchased, renovated, and decorated all by himself. He's been at my apartment all day packing and moving my stuff."

Kareen asked, "Who is he, and where did you meet?"

Lexington said, "His name is Michael. I met him at work."

Akera asked: "Wait a minute! He purchased and renovated a house all by himself; moved without your help; he packed your stuff all by himself, so you could go to work then come hang out with us. Okay, let's review he's rich, he's smart, he can think and plan, he has good, common sense, and he's compassionate. Did Jesus come back?"

Lexington added, "He's incredibly gorgeous, every piece of his chocolate body was made perfectly, he cooks, he cleans, and he is unlike any man I've ever known."

Akera replied, "Jesus did come back, and he found you out of all the millions of women in the world. That isn't fair."

Kendra said, "Best Friend, favor isn't fair. Can't be mad at Lexi because she's favored."

Kendra said, "I am so happy for you, Biggest Sister."

Kareen said, "Me too, Lexi!"

Akera added, "I'm so happy for you, Sister."

Destiny said, "He is definitely your husband. You'll be married by next year."

Lexington said, "You think so?"

Destiny answered, "I know so! A good man makes sure things are in order before he marries. You're both educated, secure financially, so providing a home was the last step."

Lexington said, "I hope you're right!"

Kareen said, "You got a winner, Lexi!"

Lexington said, "I do!"

Akera anxiously asked, "Okay! I hear all that, but how is the sex?"

Lexington said, "It's not just sex with him. It's a mind-blowing experience of intimacy. When we make love, it's like the gentleness of spring, the heat of summer, the excitement of autumn, and the harshness of winter all mixed into one experience."

Akera said, "Damn! That sounds so sexy."

Kendra said, "He sounds amazing, but why did you wait so long to tell us about him?"

Lexington said, "From the beginning, I knew I liked him. I felt like he genuinely liked me. He came at me so differently than any other man. I felt something real, but I wanted to make sure before I spoke on it. I wanted the commitment to be there. I wanted to make sure that when I presented the relationship, I was sure and confident in the relationship I was presenting."

Lexington's statement made Kendra think about her relationship with Bishop. She thought to herself: maybe I should follow Lexington's footsteps with this one. Maybe if I patiently gave the relationship time, it would be different from the relationships of the past. If I'm sure before I introduce him to everyone, at least that would save me the embarrassment of another breakup.

Kendra asked, "Lexi, how did you know it was real? What did he say or do?"

Lexington explained, "Back in the spring, I told you I was going to see my parents. I really spent the week with him in St. Lucia for his birthday. The conversations we had, the love we made, the energy between us said it's real. During that trip, we spoke out loud the emotions and commitments that had gone unspoken year. We took our time and let things happen naturally. He stayed consistent. He kept his word. For the first time, I'm really in-love."

Akera said, "Big Sister, you got that magic. Even though Camren messed up, he loved you. Every dude, you kick it with falls head over heels in love with you. It's like you hypnotize and mesmerize them. Like you have some kind of hypno-pussy-merizer. Whatever you do to men, I need to know, so I can bottle it, book it and sell it. I'll have an Oprah special. I'll be like you put it on him, you put it on him, and you put it on his ass."

Kareen said, "Lexi, you do have all your dudes wrapped around your finger."

Kendra said, "Men do love you; hence, the collection of engagement rings in that jewelry box of yours. Think about it: every man you ever slept with has proposed and let you keep the ring."

Kareen said, "That's so true, so one can guess Michael will follow suit."

Akera asked, "What the hell do you have in that thing of yours. I need to figure this out, right now."

Kendra said, "I want to know, too."

Akera said, "It's probably the pretty face, fat ass, and big titties. Men aren't that complicated, and they are visual creatures. They like to make them big titties and that fat ass bounce and jiggle."

Kendra said, "Ignore her, Biggest Sister. She doesn't play with a full deck." They laughed as Akera danced, making her breasts and butt bounce.

Lexington said, "I don't know. I don't do anything outside, be myself."

Kendra said, "Than I need to be more like you."

Lexington told Kendra, "I hate to tell you this, Kendra, but you are me. We are so much alike that people always think you are my sister, and, Baby Sister, you have never had a shortage of men pursuing you. See, just being you is enough."

Akera said, "I don't buy that at all. I never told you this, but after you broke up with Raymond, he called me crying. I mean, he was bawling his eyes out. I wanted to laugh, but I listened. He begged me to ask you to come back to him. He told me a little bit about your sex."

Lexington said, "He did not."

Kareen said, "He called me, too!"

Destiny said, "Me, three!"

Lexington said, "You all are lying, right now."

Kareen said, "He was crying so hard, I couldn't take it. I hurried him off my phone."

Destiny said, "He begged me to talk to you. I pretended I was calling you. When he called back, I sent him straight to voicemail."

Lexington laughed; she said, "I can't believe it."

Akera said, "He was rambling and talking about what he missed and what he couldn't live without."

Lexington asked, "What did he say?"

Akera said, "Enough to blackmail your ass if I have to, but seriously I definitely got the impression that you put it on him like no one ever had before."

Lexington said, "I don't know what men want."

Akera said, "You know something."

Lexington said, "I'm just trying to figure out what I need to do to get Michael."

Akera said, "Sounds like you got him, Sis. He is unpacking your shit while you chill with us. The man is got."

Destiny said, "Yes, men are visual creatures, and yes, Lexington is aesthetically pleasing, but she is blessed with an awesome spirit and personality. She's incredibly bright, gentle, and loyal. Men look at her, and yes, they are attracted to her, but it's the substance of who she is that makes them want to be with her. You need more than a pretty face to really intrigue a man. A woman has to have something to say and be able to think.

"Her intellect, spirit, and heart tell men she will be a good mother, a good wife, a good life partner. The pretty face, sexy body, and good sex are the very good buttercream icing on a very delicious cake. Lexington, you are everything a man wants in a woman internally and externally, and I promise you, Michael will be proposing very soon. Just watch what I say."

Lexington said, "Awe, Destiny, that's so sweet!"

Kendra said, "I see you're still wearing the Rolex Roman brought."

Lexington said, "He had to go, not the jewelry."

Destiny said, "That's right! The gifts stay!"

Akera said, "She earned that shit throwing that ass back."

Akera said, "That's the complexity of you, Big Sister, you are a lovely lady, wonderful woman, good girl, and a bad bitch all rolled up into this sweet, little five feet of a beautiful, feminine, sophisticated ray of sunshine. If you weren't my sister, I'd hate you, but, since you're my sister, I love and admire you."

Lexington said, "Awe! I love you!"

(Present Day) As Lexington helps Anniston put on her dress. Lexington pushes her hair behind her ear, exposing the scar on her forehead. Anniston touches it and says, "Mommy, how did you get that scar?"

Lexington answers, "I was driving home at about two o'clock in the morning. The music was blasting. Michael had sent sweet texts all day, hinting that something special was happening when I got home, so I was trying to get home to be with him. The light turned green. I pressed the gas. BOOM!

"A truck driver had fallen asleep while driving, he ran the red light and crashed into my driver's side. For some strange reason, the fully functional airbags delayed, so I hit my head so hard on the steering wheel that I was immediately knocked unconscious. My eye was swollen. The cut on my forehead hurt. The first time I looked at my face, I saw ruin, but later I learned God's intention was reconstruction. I had to rebuild my life and do things differently."

Revelation

Michael walked what seemed like the green mile to the reception desk. He asked the nurse about Lexington. The reception nurse asked his name and relationship to the patient.

He said, "I'm Michael Moore, and she's, my girlfriend." The nurse said I can only release information to the immediate family. He said, "But we live together."

The nurse said, "I'm sorry, Sir, but I can only release information to the immediate family." Just as she finished the sentence, Akera walked up to the counter. Michael was about to get angry. Akera touched his arm; she said, "Hey, Brother!"

He replied, "Hey, Sister!"

"I'm her sister," Akera said to the nurse.

The nurse replied, "The doctor is with her now."

Akera asked, "Is she awake? How bad is she hurt? Can you tell me anything?"

The nurse replied, "It's really best to wait to talk to the doctor." Akera reluctantly accepted that.

The nurse said, "Please, go to the waiting room. When her name comes across the screen, next to her name will be the floor and room number. Go to that floor and check-in at the desk. The doctor will meet you in the room."

Akera and Michael sullenly walked to the waiting room. Kareen came in with tears in her eyes. She hugged Akera and Michael; she said, "She hit her head. They can't wake her up." Akera burst into tears. Michael wrapped his arms around both of the crying women.

Akera said (crying on Michael's arm), "She's fine, right, Brother."

"She is," Michael said.

Kareen (drying her eyes) said, "I'll check on her every chance I get." Kareen hugged Akera and Michael before leaving the waiting room. Akera and Michael watched the monitor like it was a movie. Michael's leg shook vigorously as Kendra and Destiny came running into the waiting room. They all hugged. Akera told them she hit her head, and she won't wake up. They sat for an hour before her name appeared on the screen.

They went up to the floor, and the reception nurse directed them to the room. When they walked into the room, Michael almost fainted at the sight of Lexington injured. The look and sound of the machines and tubes connected to her took him by surprise. He was overwhelmed by the sight of the bandages on her forehead and under her eye.

Akera caught him, she asked, "Are you okay, Brother?"

Michael had to steady himself. "Yeah! I'm good," he answered.

They gathered around Lexington's bed, consoling each other when the doctor walked in and asked for Akera. Everyone listened intently to his every word. He said, "We ran an MRI and CT-scan. We saw no broken bones, internal swelling, or internal bleeding. She has a wound on her forehead. We used an adhesive to close it. She has a bruise under her eye. It is swollen and probably will turn black in a few days. Besides that, we do not see any other injuries.

"All of her vitals are normal. She's breathing on her own. The breathing tube is just a precaution. She is medicated to control any pain. Honestly, I don't know why she hasn't woken up. In the morning, we will do another CT-scan. Hopefully, she will be awake by then."

The nurses rolled an extra bed into the room. When Kareen's shift was over, she crawled into bed with the women. Michael slept in a chair next to the bed.

An hour before sunrise, everyone was asleep, an older nurse with a southern accent walked in the room. She checked Lexington's vitals. Lexington felt a throbbing and spinning pain in her head. She couldn't talk with the breathing tube in her mouth. The nurse said, "How are you feeling this morning? You bumped your head." Lexington touched her head and face.

The nurse handed her the button; she said, "Press this when you need some pain meds." The nurse said, "Don't worry, you're alive and well. The Lord was just trying to get your attention. You're such a blessed and beautiful woman, kind of stupid to be so smart." Lexington looked at the nurse with a confused expression.

The nurse said with a convicting tone, "Yes, stupid. The Lord has given you a lot. What have you given him?" Lexington couldn't think of an answer. The nurse continued, "No answer, just like I knew. That's why I said stupid. You have worldly knowledge, but that won't serve you in the kingdom of heaven. Right now, you are more concerned about celebrities and your girlfriends than you do your one true, living God, and that is a crying shame. Your husband over there hasn't moved all night. The man needs to pee, but he is so afraid he'll miss the moment you wake up that he refuses to move."

Lexington thought to herself he's not my husband. The nurse said with a raised eyebrow, "And, whose fault is that...yours...you shut off your heart so afraid you'll be hurt again. Girl, you ought to use your mouth to tell him how you really feel, or some other girl will. You use it for everything else. Nasty butt!

"He's fine and rich. Plenty of women would take him. So many women have searched for a good man for years. They would kill for a man like him. I knew loneliness after my Harold. Harold would do anything for me. He always took such good care of me until death did us part. Michael looks just like my Harold. Harold was tall, strong, faithful, smart, successful, and wise. I could always trust his decisions. He never let me down.

"Harold was a good man. Oh, how he loved me! Just like Michael loves you. You need to secure this relationship with marriage, now! You're going to regret it if you don't. That's a good man right there, and he is everything you ever wanted in a man. We both know he is. You're ready, and he's ready, so it is time to stop living in sin. Neither of you were raised to live in sin.

"This generation is so blessed with so many more worldly opportunities than generations passed and take so much for granted. You have your expensive things (she pointed to Lexington's purse) you have your friends (she pointed to the sleeping women in the other bed) you have the men, you know the ones you call when you want a little nookie. You all think that life is about things and sex. That's idolatry to covet and worship things and sex.

"Life is about love. Love from God to man to woman to the children to family to the community, and back to GOD. Love is what life is about! (With disdain in her voice, the nurse said) All the sex you gave to Chad and Roman, you could've saved for your husband."

The little voice in Lexington's head asked, how does she know about Chad and Roman.

The nurse said, "Yes, I saw it, and so did the Lord. He sees everything. He sits high and looks low. The Lord sees everything you do. He hears your thoughts. He knows your desires and secrets. He knows what's in your heart. Wherever you go, he is watching Proverbs 5:21. He's not mad at you, just disappointed because he knows you know better. You knew all along you were to wait for your husband. But no, oh no, you were too impatient to wait on the Lord! Look who he sent you (pointing to Michael) did the Lord disappoint? No! Did you thank him? No!

"You're smart in business and stupid in life! That's what I meant when I said you're stupid. You're ignoring the Lord and taking him for granted. Take time to thank him for all he has given you, send him praises, and do something for him to celebrate all the love he has given you.

"Get yourself right with him! Get an understanding! Get your life decent and in order! I know one thing, you come to him correctly before he comes for you. It won't be pretty, Care Bear, if you make him come to you." The nurse turned to walk out.

Lexington thought, "Care Bear," no one has called me that since my grandmother died.

As the nurse reached for the doorknob, she yelled, "Take that weave out your head." The nurse shouted, "Wake up!" as she exited the door.

Lexington woke up and realized it was a dream. Every word the nurse spoke stung Lexington with shame because it was the truth. The nurse left Lexington feeling disgusted with herself. She turned her back on God after Camren. She hadn't thanked God for Michael or her success. She wondered why God continued blessing her even though she lost her way.

(Present Day) Lexington tells Anniston, "Just after sunrise, I woke up attached to machines with pain in my head and face. As I reached out to touch Michael, I said to myself I should be married to this man. When I touched him, he jumped up out of his sleep, startling the girls in the other bed. 'Baby, you're up,' he said. He pushed the button for the nurse. The girls rushed over to me. Everyone was trying to embrace me, but all I wanted was Michael."

Submission

A nurse came in to remove the breathing tube. The nurse said, "I'm glad to see you're awake, Ms. Lear, I'll go get you some ice to soothe the irritation from the breathing tube."

Lexington said, "Ok!"

The nurse said, "I'll be right back."

Lexington said, "Thank you!" Lexington grabbed Michael's wrist.

When the nurse left, the girls all leaned in to hug Lexington. "Hey, everyone!" she said.

She turned to Michael still clenching onto his wrist, she said, "Thanks for being here. You slept there the whole night," as she reached out to hug him.

"I wasn't moving until you woke up. I wanted to be the first person you saw," he said while he embraced her.

Lexington said, "I love you so much."

He kissed the center of her forehead and said, "I love you, more!"

The nurse came back with the ice. She said as she handed Lexington the ice, "We're going to take you down for a CT-scan. The doctor will be in to talk to you after the scan." Lexington thanked the nurse. Michael went to the restroom. Lexington watched Michael as he walked into the restroom. She smiled at the thought of the nurse in her dream. When her friends asked why she was smiling, she said, "No reason, I'm just happy to be alive."

Lexington encouraged her friends to go home. She assured them she was fine and promised Michael would stay with her. Her friends were reluctant to leave, but Lexington insisted they go because she really wanted to be alone with Michael.

Lexington said, "I'm good. I promise Michael will call each of you if anything goes on. Destiny needs to get the kids to school and everyone else needs to go to work. Now go!"

When Michael returned from the restroom, he and Lexington were alone. As he walked toward her, she reached out her hand. Michael took her hand; he said, "Baby, eat your ice. It will help your throat." He put his forehead on hers and said, "You scared me. Don't ever scare me like that again. I am so glad you are okay."

She smiled. She said, "Thank you, baby! My face hurts. Does it look terrible?"

Michael said, "You're always beautiful and perfect in my mind," as he lightly kissed the bandage under her eye.

She said, "You're so sweet. All I remember is a big boom and waking up to see you sitting there. I'm so glad the Lord spared me. Lord knows I want more time with you."

He gently kissed her forehead; he said, "The thought of possibly losing you." His eyes watered as he talked, "I cannot lose you. I never want to lose you. When I walked into the room and saw you hurt, I couldn't take it. I told myself to be strong, so I can be here for you." Tears rolled down her face, he wiped her tears, and kissed her.

She said, "I never want to lose you." She asked, "What did I ever do to deserve you?"

Michael grabbed her hand and held it to his face; he said, "Maybe, I am the one who deserves you. Maybe my tithes, my service, my prayers, and my faith earned you. A man is made whole when he takes his bride. Don't ever forget you're the jewel to be treasured. I am the treasurer. It's my job to treasure you."

She said, "Wow, that's powerful. Thank you. I won't forget." They hugged as two nurses walked into the room.

The first nurse said as they walked toward Lexington, "Ms. Lear, we are going to take you for a CT-scan." The nurses began to prepare the bed and machines to be mobile.

The second nurse said, "Sir, you can wait here, and we will bring her back as soon as the scan is completed."

Michael sat down in the extra bed, and he and Lexington stared at each other as the nurses rolled her out of the room. Just before they exited the door, she blew him a kiss. He caught it and put it on his cheek.

When they returned, Michael was asleep. The first nurse said, "He's sleep."

The second nurse, "He has to be tired."

The first nurse said, "It was a long night. I felt so bad for him. He was so worried about you, Ms. Lear."

The second nurse said, "Remi said he almost fainted when he saw you."

The first nurse said, "You could see the panic on his face. He loves you, Ms. Lear."

Lexington looked at him and said, "I love him!"

The second nurse said, "Invite us to the wedding."

The first nurse said, "I know that's right, and if he has a brother, sign me up."

The second nurse said, "We are going to remove all the machines, and hopefully, you can go home."

The first nurse said, "The doctor will be with you shortly."

The doctor came to talk to her about an hour later and told Lexington everything looked fine on the CT scan, and she could go home. He told her, "Take it easy for a few days. Give yourself about three to five days before going back to work. I will give you a script for pain meds. Take them only if you need to and follow up with your primary care physician in about two weeks."

The nurse came in with a pair of scrubs, a bag of bandages, and discharge papers, she said, "Sorry, Ms. Lear, but your clothes were ruined. Here's something you can wear home."

"Thank you," said Lexington. When the nurses left, she woke up Michael, she said, "Baby! Baby! They said we can go home."

Michael woke up. He said, "Really, that's good, Babe." He saw her struggling to change her clothes. He rushed over to help her.

She said, "Baby, my entire body hurts, especially my chest and back."

He said, "It's going to hurt for a few days from the impact. I'll take care of you, so you can rest."

Lexington said, "You're going to take care of me?"

Michael said, "I'll cook for you, run your bath, massage your body, and clean the house. All you have to do is heal."

Lexington said, "Awe! Thank you, baby!"

On the way home from the hospital, they stopped to get Lexington's things out of her car. Michael specifically told her to stay in the car, but she didn't listen. She walked into the junkyard and almost passed out when she saw the car. She shouted, "My car!"

Michael said, "That's why I told you to stay in the car. Lexington, go to the car, you don't need to see this."

She said, "But, Michael!"

Before she could say anything else, he said, "Lexington, I will get you another car, but I can't get another you. Let's just stay thankful that you are alive and well. Go, get in the car." She knew he was right, so she went back to the car.

When he came back to the car, he looked at her. He touched her forehead with his finger; he said, "You're hard-headed! Listen to me, I'll never tell you anything wrong. Stay focused on what's important!"

"You're right, Michael, I'm sorry," she said.

As soon as they got home, Michael cooked, and she fell asleep. Michael woke Lexington up, saying, "Lexi, wake up, Babe, and eat your food." After she ate, Lexington called her mom to tell her about the accident and assured her that all was well. One by one, her friends called. They chatted for a bit, but she wanted to rest in Michael's arms. After a bath, she went to bed. She laid in bed, listening to Michael moving around, on the phone, and on his laptop. She didn't want to rush him, but she wanted him in bed with her.

Finally, he got into bed. She snuggled in his arms. She said, "This is my very favorite place to be."

Michael knew exactly what that meant, he said, "I'm glad to hear that."

She laid in his arms, thinking about the dream. She thought: All the things the nurse said were true. I have my own beautiful hair, but I cover it up with expensive weave. I haven't thanked God or did anything for him. Lexington realized just how vain and selfish she had been. She felt ashamed of herself.

He asked if she needed anything. She said no but thanked Michael for taking care of her. She said, "You've taken such good care of me. I appreciate you."

Michael said, "I know you're independent, so it's probably hard for you to accept being taken care of. But I am the man, and I will always be the man in this relationship: sickness or health, poverty or wealth. Do you hear me?"

"I hear you," she said.

She grabbed his hand and said, "Marry me." Michael wasn't expecting that response. She said, "If you love me and want to take care of me, marry me." He didn't speak, he reached into the drawer of his nightstand. He grabbed a small golden gift box. He handed it to her.

She opened the box and was shocked. Michael took the ring out of the box. He said, "I will marry you today, tomorrow or yesterday. He slid the ring on her finger. I was going to ask last night." As she listened to Michael, her eyes filled with tears that slowly streamed down her face. He said, "There's nothing more I want than to be your husband."

She said, "A fall wedding in Niagara Falls would be cute. Taking pictures by the waterfall."

Michael asked, "Are you sure you don't want a big wedding?"

She told him, "I just want to be your wife. It's not the wedding I want, it's you. Just give me you, and I'm good."

The next morning, she went to the salon. The stylist did a great job of styling her natural to cover her forehead and eye. She was about to marry the love of her life. She was on top of the world. She took a moment to thank God for all the blessings. On the flight, she asked him where he wanted to go for the honeymoon. He said, "I want to go to Paris. Going to Paris with you as your husband would be a dream come true."

She said, "Paris it is."

When they made it to Niagara Falls, the first thing they did was apply for a marriage license. Lexington said, "I can't wait!"

The clerk said you can apply for the 24-hour waiver and get married today. They looked at each other, and Michael said, "Let's do it!"

In the excitement, she forgot to change her clothes. They got married in jeans and t-shirts, but they were so happy. Being Michael's wife was amazing, but a week in Paris as Michael's wife was magical. The honeymoon was so magical that God made a miracle.

Three weeks after they came home, she thought she caught the flu until the doctor said, "Good news, Mrs. Moore, you're going to be a mommy."

When she got in the car, she was full of emotions: happiness, fear, and joy. When she got home, she walked into Michael's arms. He asked, "Is something wrong? What's wrong?" She started crying. He sat her down; he said, "Lexington, talk to me!"

She said, "I'm pregnant!"

She fell into his chest, sobbing. Michael had this huge smile on his face. He was calm and at peace with the ideal of being a daddy. He said, "Baby, it'll be okay, the baby will be fine, we're going to be fine. I've already covered us in prayer. Stop crying! This is a good thing. I promise!"

She said, "But we just got married, we didn't get a chance to enjoy us."

Michael said, "It's more of us to enjoy."

She said, "Who gets pregnant on their honeymoon?"

Michael said, "Blessed people who marry the one ordained for them!" Michael said, "Just so you know, and this may sound selfish, I want this. I want this baby and five more. I want a little girl who looks just like her mother, who acts just like her mother, who thinks just like her mother, and is sweet just like her mother."

"That's cute, but, baby, five more. That's a lot of kids," she said.

He said, "It's going to be so cute when my daughter gets here. She will follow me around the house calling me daddy. She's going to be so spoiled. I've got to pray about a name."

She said, "Michael, who's paying for six kids to go to college? Who going to cook for and clean up after six kids?"

Michael said, "We will! We will make it work!"

"Maybe it will be a boy, Michael Jr. My father will love a grandson," she said.

He said, "It's a girl. I specifically prayed for a girl."

"When did you pray," she asked.

He answered, "Our first night in Paris. I told the Lord I was ready, and we were now living in the covenant of marriage. I asked him to bless us with a beautiful baby girl. Michelle, that's her name."

"Michael, I know nothing about babies," she said.

"Me either, we will learn together. Let's pray," he said.

Benediction

Michael bowed his head, and began to pray, "God, I pray our baby and my wife will stay in good health. I pray our baby girl is strong and developing appropriately. I pray you keep a close eye on both mother and baby and make this pregnancy as easy as possible for my wife. I pray you catch her fears, wrap them up, and discard them.

"God, I pray you give our baby a clear, strong understanding of you and the word. I pray our baby is blessed with a spirit full of wisdom and discernment. I pray she will follow your word and have your protection and favor all of her days.

"God, I pray she will feel and know our love every day of her life. We love her so much already. Let nothing interfere with our familial bond. I pray she loves us as much as we already love her, and she enjoys our presence in her life daily.

"God, I pray she will learn the true meaning of love and make you her first love. I pray that she will love you all of her life with all of her heart, soul, and mind.

"God, I pray our baby has a good, joyous spirit bearing all the fruits of the spirit: love, joy, peace, forbearance, kindness, gentleness, goodness, faithfulness, and self-control. I pray she grows into a discerning, obedient, and wise teenager. I pray you prosper her works, and she lives the life you ordained for her.

"God, I pray our baby is an advent student and reader of the word. I pray she is faithful with prayer and service all her life. In Jesus' name, I pray, Amen!" Lexington said, "Amen!"

(Present Day) Anniston looked in the mirror, admiring her hair, makeup, and dress. Lexington says, "Wait, I have something to complete this outfit." Lexington goes into her room and comes back with some of the jewelry Roman brought: a bracelet, a pair of earrings, and a necklace. Lexington says, "Baby Girl, diamonds complement every outfit."

Anniston says, "Mommy, that's your jewelry from the pictures."

Lexington puts the jewelry on Anniston. Lexington says, "You are so beautiful!"

Anniston asks, "Mommy, these are gorgeous. Why don't you wear them anymore?"

Lexington says, "Basically, your father told me I couldn't."

Anniston asks, "Why? What's wrong with them?"

Lexington says, "Roman!"

Confession

Michael was on his laptop. Lexington was leaning on Michael's shoulder with one hand on his chest and the other holding the book she was reading. He asked a question that Lexington wasn't expecting.

Michael looked at her hand on his chest; he asked, "Did a man buy any of the jewelry you wear every day while you are wearing my wedding ring and carrying my baby?" Lexington was thinking damn, no he did not. She hesitated to answer, but she eventually said yes.

Michael said with a tone of disdain in his voice, "So, you make love to me in our marriage bed, carrying my baby, and wearing my wedding ring all while wearing another man's jewelry? (Lexington's face could have fallen on the bed and slid to the floor.)

"May, I ask you to take off any piece of jewelry another man gave you. My wife doesn't need to wear anything from another man. I'll replace every piece of jewelry with something new and one hundred times better. If you take off the old, you make room for the new."

Lexington said, "Baby, I never meant to be disrespectful. Of course, I will take all of it off." Lexington took off the bracelets, the rings, the necklaces, the Rolex, an ankle bracelet, and the earrings. As Roman predicted, Michael found a way to ask about the past without asking directly. When she was done removing the jewelry purchased by her former lovers, she was only left with her wedding ring. She felt light without the weight of the jewelry.

Michael said, "Damn, Lexington! Who bought all that?"

She answered, "Raymond bought the ankle bracelet, the two diamond bracelets, and a ring. That guy Roman bought the Rolex, the other rings, the earrings, one of the necklaces, and a bracelet. Chad gave me the diamond necklace and a bracelet, and Camren gave me the other necklace."

Michael picked up the watch. He asked, "So, that dude Roman gave you this? How serious were you two?"

She answered, "When I broke up with Raymond, I was single and celibate for a long time. One day, I met Roman. He tried to talk to me; I wasn't hearing him. He chased me for years: sending flowers, candy, and gifts with cute cards to my office.

"We ran into each other on vacation. Knowing Roman, he purposely followed me to Mexico. We had sex. He said we spent three hundred twenty-five nights together over the next three years. It was just sex. We weren't committed. When he tried to get serious, I cut it off months before I met you.

"The jewelry was courtesy gifts. Roman sent a jeweler to my office every year for six years on my birthday and said I could pick whatever I wanted.

He didn't even care enough to select the choices; the jeweler did. I put the jewelry on and never took it off. He gave me purses for Christmas and shoes for Valentine's Day.

"Raymond and I were in a relationship for about four years. Raymond was a decent guy. We had a pretty calm, quiet relationship. He was generous to me, so I felt obligated to stay with him. When he wanted more, I ended it because I didn't want more from him.

"Camren was my first boyfriend. We met in my sophomore year of college. By my junior year, we were engaged until I caught him in the bed with two naked females.

"Remember a little while back, we were eating at a restaurant, and there was a young, white couple, and the man kept staring at me. That was Chad. Chad, well, Chad and I met up every now and then over two years, and he did nice things for me."

Michael asked, "Like what?"

Lexington said, "Trust me, you don't want to know. The jewelry was birthday gifts. Now you know my entire sexual history. I've been with Camren, Raymond, Roman, and Chad. Take the jewelry because I don't want you to feel a way every time you look at me. None of it is worth disturbing our marriage."

Michael took the jewelry and walked over to her jewelry box. Lexington said, "Wait before you open that! There are a few engagement rings in there that you've never seen."

Michael said, "How many engagement rings?"

Lexington said, "Four!"

Michael, shocked, asked, "You were engaged four times?"

Lexington says, "No! Four men asked, and I said yes once and no three times. I proposed to the only man that matters, and he's standing right there (Lexington points at Michael)."

Michael put the jewelry in the jewelry box and locked it in the safe in the closet. As he walked toward the bed, he said, "Now, all that is put away for good. I will dress and adorn my wife with fine clothes and jewelry."

Lexington asked, "How do you feel about what I just told you?"

He said, "I don't! I never want to hear it again. I never want to talk about you and another man. I don't want to think about another man's hands on you, whether I knew you or not. You got it off your chest, and now it is put away, and it shall stay put away."

Lexington touched her bare earlobes, looked at her naked wrists and fingers, and glanced at her unadorned ankle. With only her wedding ring on, she felt naked and exposed. She laid in the bed, stripped of her secrets, weave, and jewelry.

(Present Day) Lexington says to Anniston, "It was like Exodus 33:5. Somehow, he knew my sins by the jewelry. I don't know what made him ask, but I guess it was all in divine order. If you don't wait, you have to tell your husband, my body is your home, but here's a list of squatters and previous renters. When I told Michael about Camren and Raymond, I felt used. But telling him about Roman and Chad, I felt worse. I was expecting Michael's eyes to change when he looked at me, but they never did. He never threw my past at me to hurt me or belittle me. As he promised, he put it away, and we never spoke about it again.

"After that night, I was stripped of my jewelry, my secrets, I had given up my weave, and wore very little makeup. There was nothing between him and the real me: no barriers or boundaries for me to hide behind. He saw the real me, all of me, and still, he loved me. His affection toward me never changed, and that has made me feel safe, beautiful, loved, and desired."

Anniston says, "Mommy, that's beautiful. I love the way Daddy loves you."

Lexington says, "Me too!"

Anniston is all dressed and adorned with her mother's old jewelry when the doorbell rings. She smiles at her mother. Lexington says, "He's here, Baby Girl!"

Anniston asks, "How do I look?"

Lexington says, "Like the most beautiful girl in the world. I'll grab the camera and meet you downstairs."

When Lexington gets downstairs, Michael is talking to Michael, standing at the door. Lexington stands by her husband and greets Michael Bateman.

As Anniston comes down the stairs, Lexington takes pictures. Lexington notices Michael's face when he sees his daughter wearing some of Lexington's old jewels. Lexington grabs his hand; she whispers, "Baby, smile at your beautiful daughter."

Michael said, "We'll talk about this later."

Lexington and Michael take pictures of Anniston and Michael Bateman before they leave. As soon as the happy couple is out the door, Michael says, "I can't believe you put that jewelry on my daughter."

Lexington says, "She's a young girl. Those are real diamonds. It doesn't matter to her how I got them. She feels like a beautiful, little, proud girl wearing her mommy's jewels. When she comes home, they'll go back in the jewelry box. Besides, they're going to be hers one day. A mother passes her jewelry down to her daughters."

Michael says, "I better be dead the next time you pull any of that mess out of that box. I told you I did not want to see that stuff again."

Lexington says, "I know, but you don't let the girls wear expensive jewelry, so she didn't have anything nice to wear, and she's way too young to wear my jewelry that you bought. I figured she could wear the old stuff, and if she loses anything, it's okay. I just wanted her to feel pretty on her first date."

Michael says as he turns to walk upstairs, "Next time, tell me, and I'll buy jewelry that she can call her own."

Lexington follows him up the stairs; she says, "Baby, don't be mad," as she wraps her arms around him.

Michael says, "Oh, I'm mad alright, and you are about to feel it as soon as we get in this room. I'm all over you. And that little boy better not touch my daughter, or that's your ass."

Lexington laughs, and says, "He won't be touching that thing tonight. She had her first Brazilian bikini wax. That thing is sore and swollen."

Michael laughs, he says, "You think you're slick!"

Lexington says, "I'm a mommy, I have to be resourceful."

As soon as Lexington walks into their room, Michael throws her on the bed. Michael says, "I thought we had an understanding about you disobeying me," as he pulls her leg to the edge of the bed.

Lexington asks, "Did we have that understanding? What did we say was the consequence of me disobeying you?"

Michael grabs her thighs and says, "I get to spend an hour or two in your penalty box."

Lexington says, "I do not remember agreeing to that."

Michael says, "You didn't. I just made it up, but you agreed to consider me in your decisions."

Lexington says, "You are right! I knew you would be mad, but I figured I could make it up to you."

Michael asks, "How are you going to make it up to me?"

Lexington says, "Letting you spend an hour or two in my penalty box."

Michael whispers in her ear, "I'm going to beat the bottom out of your penalty box."

Michael kisses his wife, passionately. Lexington says, "Baby, not right now, the boys will hear us." Michael picks his wife up and begins walking toward the bathroom.

Michael says, "The shower is the perfect place to get wet. You know your hair is about to get wet."

Lexington says, "Michael, baby, not my hair."

Michael says, "Oh yeah! That's the price you pay for disregarding me."

Lexington says, "I just got my hair done."

Michael says, "Khryssa can flat iron your hair tomorrow."

Lexington says, "If you wet my hair, you're going to mess up my makeup."

Michael says, "You're definitely going to mess up that lipstick on Daddy?"

Lexington licks her lips and says, "I can do that for you, Daddy."

Michael carries her across the threshold as she kisses his lips and rubs his chest. Once in the bathroom, Michael puts Lexington on her feet. Michael kisses Lexington as he takes off his shirt; he says, "Those lips are so pretty," he rubs her lips with his right thumb. Lexington walks backward as Michael walks forward. Her hands rub all over his arms and chest, as she asks, "You like my lips?"

Michael reaches into the shower to cut the water on and says, "I love those lips; that's a pretty color," as he backs Lexington into the side of the tub. Lexington sits on the edge of the tub. Michael caresses her hair, and says, "Let, Daddy, feel those pretty lips."

Lexington pulls him out of his pants and rolls him across her lips. She softly kisses him; he says, "Those lips feel as good as they look." Michael pulls his pants and underwear off.

She firmly grips him with both hands as she sucks the tip of him. She lets saliva run down him, and she rubs it all over him. He watches holding her hair. He asks, "Do you remember the first time you did that?" Lexington smiles and nods yes as she continues sucking him.

He whispers to her, "Baby, make it disappear." She inhales then exhales. She closes her eyes and pushes him all the way into her mouth. He says, "Look at me while you do it."

She looks at him as she begins to think back to the first time that she let him feel her lips. They spent a week in Hawaii to celebrate one year of dating. Lexington mentally prepared herself. She spent weeks researching, reading books, and watching videos to learn how to perform.

Reverberation

Lexington stood on the balcony of their hotel room, enjoying the night sky. Michael got out of the shower, wrapped a towel around his waist, and joined her on the balcony. He wrapped his arms around her. He asked, "Are you enjoying the scenery?"

She answered, "It's so beautiful, even in the dark."

He said, "It isn't nearly as beautiful as you." Michael sat down in the chair, he said, "Lexi, I needed this vacation. I'm so tired. Plus, I get to be with you six more nights."

Lexington said, "Let me give you a massage." She walked behind the chair and began to massage his neck and shoulders.

Michael said, "That feels good." Michael relaxed and enjoyed the touch of Lexington.

She asked, "How is everything with work?"

Michael said, "Busy, but good busy, so I'm appreciative. How about you?"

Lexington said, "I can't dare complain. We must be each other's good luck charm."

Michael said, "You're more like a blessing: my biggest, best blessing. I thank God every day that I have you in my life."

Lexington said, "Awe! Honey, that so sweet," as she walked to the front of the chair. She knelt between his legs to massage his legs and thighs.

They stared into each other's eyes. Lexington noticed Michael's nature rising under the towel. She moved her hands slowly up his thighs until she reached him. She firmly held him with both hands as she slowly slid her lips and tongue over him. She rolled her tongue around and around and around the tip of him. With both hands holding him, she sucked the tip of him like she was sucking the juice from a sour pickle.

She sucked so hard that Michael temporarily lost the ability to speak. Lexington slowly pulled him out of her mouth as her lips and cheeks maintained a firm grip. Pop went the weasel as she pulled her lips back. Lexington winked at him as she slowly put him back in her mouth.

Slobbing and bobbing all over Michael, it was like she was slurping Campbell's soup and it was mmm-hmm good. Michael gently held Lexington's head as she continued to pleasure him. Lexington impressed herself with her performance. For this to be her first time, she did it so well that she turned herself on.

Michael was so turned on that he had to fulfill the need rushing through his body. He snatched Lexington up and carried her to the back of the chair. Michael bent her over the chair putting her knees on the top of the back of the chair. Michael lifted her dress and slid her panties to the side. Michael, filled with animalistic lust, slowly pushed into her.

Michael asked, "You feel me, baby?"

She said, "Yes, baby!"

Michael asked, "I feel you, too. How do I feel, baby?"

Lexington said with a soft voice, "Like a miracle, baby." Lexington was in a fit; she said, "Ah! Baby! Ah! You're hitting everything."

Lexington's ass cheeks were bouncing off Michael and popping in all directions. Lexington said in a cracking voice, "Baby, please, take me inside." Michael stopped and picked her up to carry her into the room. He laid her on the bed. She was exhausted.

He sat next to her and said, "You got me so hype."

Michael looking at the condoms on the nightstand, said, "Things popped off so quickly; I didn't use a condom. I didn't mean to dishonor our agreement to wear a condom until we are married. I'm sorry."

Lexington rubbed his shoulder and said, "I know you didn't."

Michael said, "I'm going to get some water. I'll be right back."

Michael came back and sat next to her. He asked if she was ok as he handed her a bottle of water. Lexington put the cold bottle of water on her stomach. She said, "Babe, I think you hit my heart."

Michael sipped his water; he said, "Your performance got me so hype."

Lexington said, "I wasn't done." Lexington crawled over to him and untied the towel around his waist. She leaned over into his lap. Michael watched her as she slowly put him into her mouth.

Michael laid back on a pillow. He pulled Lexington onto his chest. His two fingers and thumb sensually played with her. Michael's fingers were dripping with Lexington's love for him.

Lexington was trying to concentrate, but Michael's sensual touch was distracting. Lexington was so aroused that every fiber of her yearned for him. Her heart pounded so hard in her chest that Michael could feel the reverb in his abdomen. Her pulse and breathing quickened as blood flooded her sugar walls and her nipples. Michael could feel the need in her growing stronger and stronger from his gentle touch.

The more attention he gave her, the more he encouraged her performance. He rubbed and smacked her ass with one hand as he made circles on and in her. She said, "Babe, I'm trying to concentrate, but you are about to make me cum." Michael pulled her up to his face to give her the pleasure she was giving him. Her love covered Michael like glitter. Michael had to have her.

Michael got out of bed and got a condom from the nightstand. He took a pillowcase off one of the pillows. He put Lexington on all fours and pulled her toward him on the edge of the bed. He put the pillowcase under her belly and around hip bones to make a doggy swing. He said, "I'll take it easy."

She said, "We are inside now. You can be you."

Michael asked, "Are you sure?"

She answered, "If you can't be yourself with me, we have a problem. Out of everyone in the world, you should be safe to be yourself with me."

Michael said, "So you're about to take all this dick?"

Lexington said, "I'm a big girl."

Michael controlled the height of Lexington's arch with the pillowcase. He had her just where he wanted. He said, "You know what to do!" Lexington took him in one hand, and she slowly guided him into her. Michael spread her knees a little wider. He said, "No guts, no glory! I'm going all in until I put you to sleep."

Michael held the pillowcase with his fists as he made good on his promise. He enjoyed Lexington's loud, feminine moans as he pitched it like a major leaguer in the World Series, going for a no-hitter. For Lexington, it hurt so bad, but felt so good.

Michael admired the jiggle and bounce of her curvy frame as his body smacked against her body. The swishing sound from him sliding through her rang like music to his ears. He said, "Your little, thick ass is so fucking fine. You bouncing back on me is a work of art: a masterpiece. I love the way you bounce when I'm beating it." As he rocked her body, she felt his deep penetration all through her abdomen. Michael went all in until she fell asleep.

(Present Day) Lexington, sitting on the edge of the tub, says, "You don't know how much research I had to do to do that in Hawaii."

Michael says, "You always were very astute." Lexington had twenty years of practice, so pleasuring Michael now is a lot easier. Michael holds her hair to the side as he watches his wife's every move.

He says, "Your pretty lips are so soft and feel so good."

Lexington says, "I'm glad you're happy." Her lips feel so good that Michael is having a hard time controlling his reaction. Michael wants the intimate moment to last longer, so he stops her.

Michael says, "I'm ecstatic! Come here!" Michael stands her up and undresses her. Michael says, "I love you so much!" He picks her up and carries her into the shower. Michael has her suspended in the air with her legs hanging over the folds of his arms.

Lexington wraps her arms around his neck as her fingertips are pressed into his back. He tells her to put him inside her. Lexington takes him in her hand and whispers, "Ah! Baby," as she slowly slides him inside her.

He places his back against the wall. Lexington kisses him and caresses his shoulders. He repeatedly pulls his wife onto him. The water splashes as her body smashes against his. Lexington bites her lip and holds onto him as she takes in Michael. Michael asks, "Are you good?"

Lexington says, "Yes!"

Michael asks, "Are you sure?"

Lexington says, "Yes!"

Michael says, "See how hype you get me when you do that?"

Lexington says, "I'm glad you enjoy me."

Michael pins Lexington against the wall with her thighs at his hips. Her hands are above her head against the wall as he moves through her. He whispers, "You feel me!"

She whispers, "Yes! Baby! I feel you."

He whispers, "Do you like what you feel?"

She whispers, "I love it!" Michael slides her up and down him until he feels her love coming down. Michael kisses her as he feels the changes in her body.

Michael kisses her lips; he says, "Your lipstick is still perfect."

Lexington says, "It's smear and waterproof."

Michael says, "We have got to mess up that lipstick!" Michael smiles and kisses her again.

Lexington says, "Ok! Baby, put me down."

Lexington lowered to her knees. Michael says, "You look so sexy with the water flowing over you and that long, dark wavy hair. I appreciate how you have taken care of yourself over the years. You're sexier now than the day I met you. The fact that your body carried six children and you still look good amazes me," as Lexington surrounds him with her lips, tongue, and cheeks. Michael says, "Ah! Baby! That mouth is amazing. So amazing!"

Lexington sucks him exactly the way he likes it until his love floods her tongue and drips from her lips onto her breasts. The rushing water washed his love from her body. Michael stands her up and hugs her; he whispers in her ear, "I love you." Lexington resting her head on his shoulders, says, "I love you, too!"

Michael turns her around to touch her hair; he says, "Your hair is beautiful," he grabs her shampoo and lathers her hair. Michael washes her hair. Lexington enjoys the attention from her husband, as he massages her scalp and detangles her hair; she says, "You spoil me!"

Michael says, "That's my job."

He rinses the shampoo then saturates her hair with conditioner. After he rinses her hair, she washes his body. She says, "Husband, you're so perfect. No one could love you more or desire you more."

He says, "God blessed me when he brought you into my life. I cannot lie about that. The past twenty-one years have been great, and the next twenty-one will be even better."

Lexington says, "Amen!"

He says, "Baby, you're the perfect one. Absolutely perfect."

She says, "Thank you!"

Michael lathers her body with soap. He rinses her off and asks, "Do you need me to do anything else?" She answers no. He says, "I'll get you a towel." He wraps her body in a towel.

He grabs another towel to dry her hair. "Thank you, baby," she says.

Lexington puts lotion on Michael, he says, "See, you spoil me too."

Lexington says, "You're a good man. You deserve it!" After brushing their teeth and getting dressed, Michael checks on his sons playing video games in their room while Lexington blow-dries her hair.

Michael sits on the bed watching the clock until he hears the front door open, they look at each other. Lexington says, "Your daughter is home alive and well, but don't let her know you were worried. We want her to think we trust her, and we have faith in who she is as a person. This whole thing will be fruitless if there is no trust. Sit back in that bed and look nonchalant when she walks through that door."

Michael says, "Yes, Ma'am!"

Khryssa has a later curfew, so she's hanging out with her friends. Anniston goes straight to her parents' room. Anniston knocks on their bedroom door and says, "Mommy, Daddy, I'm home."

They invite her in. When she comes in, she sees Lexington on the couch working on her MacBook and Michael relaxing in bed watching television. She says, "I wanted to say goodnight before I went to bed."

Lexington sits her MacBook down. Michael sits up. They ask about the night. She tells them the dance was fun. They tell her they're glad the dance was fun. She hugs her dad and thanks him. She goes to hug her mother but stops to ask, "Mommy, you washed your hair and took off your makeup already?"

Lexington says, "Long story!"

Anniston says, "Thank you for everything. Good night, Mommy and Daddy."

They say, "You're welcome! Good night, Baby Girl!"

Chapter Seven: The Temptation

On the Tuesday after the dance, Lexington is sitting at her desk when she receives a text.

Anniston: Mommy, are you busy?

Lexington: Never too busy for you!

Anniston: Don't get mad! Today, I did something you wouldn't approve of.

Lexington: Baby Girl, what did you do?

Anniston: Promise, you won't get mad or tell Daddy! Please! Mommy, don't tell Daddy!

Lexington: My heart is racing, tell me!

Anniston: After practice, I didn't come straight home like you told me.

Lexington: What? Where did you go?

Anniston: Michael's house

Lexington: Were his parents at home? Were you alone with him?

Anniston: No! Yes!

Lexington: Baby Girl! No, you did not! I'm not ready for that. Where is your sister?

Anniston: She's here. I told her you said I could go to Charly's house after school to study. Mommy, I am so sorry.

Lexington: Why did you do that?

Anniston: I don't know! He asked me to come over, so I went.

Lexington: What did you do?

Anniston: Are you mad?

Lexington: No, shocked! I can't believe you lied. I don't like you lying and not being where I expect you to be.

Anniston: Mommy, I'm sorry.

Lexington: I know Baby Girl. That's why you're confessing. But what happened?

Anniston: Mommy, I did nothing.

Lexington: What did he do?

Anniston: Mommy, he was all over me. It was like he was a totally different person.

Lexington: Did you, you know?

Anniston: I promise! He begged, but I said no. I thought about you and what we talked about. I could not do it. He said if I liked him, I would do it. I didn't, so we broke up. I walked all the way home by myself in the dark. He wouldn't even walk me home because I wouldn't have sex. I thought he liked me. He was mean to me and mad at me when he didn't get what he wanted.

Lexington: Baby Girl, I'm so sorry that he did that to you, but that's how males are when they don't get what they want. They turn into big, mean babies. Daughter, do you trust me?

Anniston: Yes, Mommy, I trust you!

Lexington: Baby Girl, next time you want something, just ask. You don't have to sneak or lie!

Anniston: Deal!

Lexington: I promise we will always work something out.

Anniston: Please, don't tell Dad!

Lexington: What did you think Michael wanted to do?

Anniston: He couldn't possibly think I wanted to have sex because we went to a dance.

Lexington: That's exactly what he thought.

Anniston: Mommy, I get it, and I don't want it like that.

Lexington: So, you can wait?

Anniston: Mommy, I'm going to wait!

Lexington: Why did you agree to go to his house?

Anniston: I wanted to be with him, kiss him and make out a little, but not go all the way.

Lexington: You see how quickly things get out of hand and how manipulative males can be when it comes to sex. Did you get what you wanted?

Anniston: Yes!

Lexington: Was the experience enough for now?

Anniston: Yes, I'm not ready.

Lexington: Did you learn something?

Anniston: Yes!

Lexington: The man God has for you wouldn't let you walk alone in the dark. Were you scared?

Anniston: Yes, but I felt like it was my punishment, so I just pushed through it. I couldn't tell Khryssa I lied to go to Michael's house. She would kill me. She's more protective than you.

Lexington: I love you so much! Thank you, Baby Girl!

Anniston: I love you too, but why thank me?

Lexington: Thank you for being my daughter, heeding my warning, and being honest with me.

Anniston: Am I in trouble?

Lexington: No, but what if something happened to you? Baby Girl, if I don't know where you are, how can I protect you or come get you. You should've called me to come to get you. I don't care what you do. I will always show up for you. I need to know where you are. I don't want to think of what could've happened while you were walking by yourself. Baby Girl, it's not good for such a young, beautiful girl to be outside alone in the dark.

Anniston: I know! Mommy, I'm so sorry, please don't tell Daddy. I promise, I won't lie again. Please! Please! Don't tell Daddy. He'll be so mad at me. I promise, I did not have sex.

Lexington: Do not tell anyone else what happened. Go, delete this text thread on my MacBook. You better cover your tracks. You told Charly to cover for you if Khryssa mentions it, right?

Anniston: She knows! Thank you, Mommy!

Lexington: Don't ever lie on me again, and don't ever locate yourself at any location that you do not have my permission to be located. When you are grown, and on your own, you can make your own decisions, but for now, you follow my rules.

Anniston: Yes ma'am! Mommy, I will make sure you know where I am, always. (Anniston immediately enables sharing her location with her mother.)

Lexington: Thanks for telling me.

Anniston: Thank you for loving me!

Lexington: You're the best daughter!

Anniston: You're the best mommy!

Anniston deletes the text thread on both their MacBooks and her phone. Lexington cries as she sits at her desk. She bows her head, and thanks God. She prays so hard for her daughters and their futures. She asks God to keep and protect her daughters. She repeats, "Yes, yes!" in a whisper. She packs her things to go home. She says, "God is good." She looks at her children's pictures on her desk, she says, "Thank you, God!"

When Lexington gets home, she goes into Anniston's room. Anniston hands Lexington her phone and laptop. Anniston, who has never been disciplined or grounded, says, "I know, I'm grounded."

Lexington says, "You're not grounded. We talked about it, and it is over. That doesn't mean I condone what you did, but your confession is penance enough." Anniston hugs her mother and apologizes again.

Lexington asks, "Are you telling the truth, that didn't happen?"

Anniston looks her mother in the eyes and says, "I promise, I did not have sex."

Lexington asks, "What did happen?"

Anniston smiles and says, "Mommy, stuff happened, but I swear his thing did not go in my thing."

Lexington says, "You let stuff happen? Like what kind of stuff?"

Anniston was too shy to answer. She says, "Mommy, I would rather you take my stuff than answer that question."

Lexington asks, "Did you?"

Anniston answers quickly before Lexington could finish the question, "Oh no! Absolutely not!"

Lexington says, "If I took you to the doctor tomorrow, he would say your still a virgin?"

Anniston says, "He would!"

Lexington says, "You're sure that didn't happen?"

Anniston says, "I am sure that didn't happen!"

Lexington says, "You'll talk to me if you want to do that before you're married, right?"

Anniston says, "I promise!"

Lexington says, "Anniston, you better not be lying to me, and don't take yourself to another boy's house until you no longer live in my house. Do you hear me?"

Anniston says, "I hear you!"

Lexington says, "If your father finds out about this, you, Michael Bateman, and I will be murdered. I'm going to keep your secret, but you better make sure Khryssa doesn't find out and snitch on us. You owe me big time!"

Anniston says, "I owe you, huge!"

Lexington says, "When I said I will always be there for you, help you and keep your secrets, I meant that with my whole heart."

Anniston says, "I believe you!"

Lexington says, "Nothing or no one can ever come between us. I don't care what anyone says or what you do. Whether you are wrong or right, I will be there for you. Nothing can stop me from getting to you when you need me. I know what it's like to be in your shoes. I understand the risks you take and the mistakes you make when you're young, and you think you like a boy. I know how it is to want to be with a boy so badly it doesn't matter what your mother says.

"I see you like him, but what we like at fifteen, twenty, twenty-five isn't necessarily what we like at thirty or forty. When you make the decision to give yourself to a boy for the first time, ask yourself, can I live with this choice at thirty, forty, or fifty? My answer is no, and I don't want that for you. My mother begged me not to be with Camren, and she had to dry my eyes when he hurt me. You don't know Mr. Bateman well enough to make such a permanent decision.

"That text hurt my feelings, and I'm disappointed that you chose him over me, but it doesn't change anything. You're still my beautiful, perfect baby girl. We won't always like each other's decisions, but we have to talk so we can grow. Don't worry about Mr. Bateman, he showed you his true self and feelings. I hope that's not the kind of person you want to be with." Anniston swears she's done with Michael Bateman.

Anniston apologizes a million times for hurting her mother's feelings.

Lexington asks, "So what did he do to you that you are not telling me?"

Anniston says, "Mommy! We just made out."

Lexington interrogates her daughter until she admits to everything that happened. They talk about what happened, the things Michael Bateman said and did, and how Anniston felt about what happened. Lexington wanted to get an understanding of Anniston's thinking and feelings.

Chapter Eight: The Redemption

Anniston texts her mother to ask for permission to visit Aunt Kareen at the hospital after school and visit her grandparents before bible study. Lexington thought it was a strange request, but she agrees and tells the girls to be safe. Anniston pays Khryssa ten dollars to take her to the hospital. Anniston walks into the hospital while Khryssa waits in the car. Kareen meets Anniston in the main lobby. Kareen says, "Hey, Niece!"

Anniston happily says, "Hey, Aunt Kareen! How are you?"

Anniston and Kareen hug as Kareen says, "I'm good. I've missed you."

Anniston says, "I've missed you, too."

Kareen asks, "Annabelle, how are you?"

Anniston says, "I am good. How is Uncle Amir?"

Kareen says, "He's good."

Anniston says, "Tell him I said hello!"

Kareen says, "I will."

Anniston says, "I saw the boys at school, today."

Kareen said, "They told me how cute you were at the dance with the captain of the junior varsity basketball team."

Anniston says, "Well, he dumped me seventy-two hours later, but it's okay."

Kareen said, "Baby Girl, you're your mother's daughter, truly."

Anniston smiles. Kareen says, "So, Annabelle, what brings you to the medical center?"

Anniston says, "Well, I came to ask a favor."

Kareen says, "What's on your heart, Annabelle?"

Anniston says, "Mommy and I have been talking, and I found out that Mommy and Daddy didn't have a real wedding. I was wondering if you would help me surprise them with a wedding on their twenty-first wedding anniversary, so granddad can walk Mommy down the aisle and give her away properly."

Kareen says, "You know why I call you, Annabelle?"

Anniston answers, "No!"

Kareen says, "Not because you're physically beautiful, but all your life you've been kind and caring to everyone, and that makes you beautiful. Of course, I'll help you!"

Anniston says, "Your job will be the dress. I'll trick mom into picking out her own dress, and you can pick it up and keep it at your house until the wedding day."

Kareen says, "I can definitely do that!"

Anniston says, "Thanks, so much, Aunt Kareen."

Kareen says, "You're welcome, Annabelle. This is the sweetest thing ever. Your parents are going to love this."

Anniston says, "One more thing, would you and Uncle Amir be willing to stand as the maid of honor and best man?"

Kareen answers, "We would be honored."

Anniston says, "Do you think Uncle Amir would mind picking up the tuxedos and keeping them at your house? I know where dad and the twins get their suits tailored. I will talk to the owner. He and Daddy are really cool. He'll look out for us. I'll text you when the dress and the tuxedos are ready."

Kareen says, "Okay! Annabelle, we will handle the dress and the tuxedos. Let me know if you need anything else."

Anniston says, "Thank you, Aunt Kareen!" When Anniston gets back in the car, she asked Khryssa to take her to see Michael's parents before they go to visit Lexington's parents. Khryssa reluctantly agrees for five more dollars.

Khryssa asks, "You're up to something. First, you need to talk to Aunt Kareen. Now we're going to see both Grandmothers. Why do you need to see them?"

Anniston says, "It's a secret. You can't tell anyone, especially Mom or Dad."

Khryssa asks, "What are you up to?"

Anniston says, "I'm reconciling the past."

Khryssa says, "What are you talking about?"

Anniston says, "I want to give Mommy and Daddy a real wedding as an anniversary gift. Aunt Kareen is going to get mom a dress. I need to talk to grandma about the food for the reception, and I need to see Bishop tonight to ask him to perform the ceremony."

Khryssa says, "Okay, Sis, I like your idea. It's lovely. What do you want me to do?"

Anniston answers, "You are in charge of the invites and guest list so grandma will know how much food to order from the restaurant. We also need to go see Nanna, so she can get Papa fitted for a tux." The girls visit both grandmothers, who are more than happy to help.

Before Bible study, Anniston knocks on Bishop's door. Bishop Wright invites her in his office.

Bishop Wright asks, "Little Annabelle, how may I help you," as he gestures for her to sit down.

Anniston says hello before explaining her idea, "My mom and dad's anniversary is in a few weeks. I want to surprise them with a wedding and reception here at the church because they never had a wedding, reception, or wedding pictures. I would like you to officiate the ceremony, and to let us have the reception in the hall."

Bishop Wright says, "Little Annabelle, I would be honored to officiate the ceremony. It's very commendable to see a young girl do something so great for her parents. Annabelle, your life is so blessed, and blessings will overflow your life for years to come. You have such a good spirit, and your light shines so brightly. I hope, I'm around to see you receive all God has in store for you. What are you planning to study in college?"

Anniston answers, "Pediatric medicine, I want to be a doctor like my Aunt Kareen."

Bishop says, "Amen, Amen! The Moore family has raised some ambitious, blessed young ladies. So what date are you looking to do this?"

She says, "Friday after next at three o'clock, but we will start setting up in the morning."

Khryssa texts Michelle and Akera to explain the plan. Akera's job is to make sure Destiny, John, Kendra, Bishop, Vanessa, and the kids fly down for the wedding and to keep the secret from Lexington and Michael. Michelle's job is to sing Lexington's favorite song for the first dance. Michelle is an extremely talented singer, but she is very shy. Despite her fear, she agrees.

Khryssa sits the twins down to explain the plan and swear them to secrecy. The four of them combine all the money they have laying around the house, they withdraw all the money from the bank, and pawn all their electronics to buy their parents an anniversary band set and to pay for the ceremony. When Akera hears how much they're sacrificing to try to cover the growing bill, she sends money to cover the expenses.

Anniston arranges for Charly's mom, a professional party planner, to decorate. Anniston calls the salon where her mother took her to get ready for the dance. She arranges for a few stylists and make-up artists to come to the church on the morning of the ceremony to do the females' hair and make-up. Anniston calls her dad's barber, who will come to the church with a few barbers to cut the men's hair.

Over the next week, the girls hire a deejay and photographer, and set the menu. Khryssa finalizes the guest list. Anniston writes vows for their parents to read at the ceremony. Kareen gets all the tuxedos and the dress for Lexington. Kareen gets a dress for herself. Amir buys his sons the same tuxedo. Khryssa and Anniston buy dresses to wear to the wedding.

Akera, Destiny, Kendra, Vanessa, Bishop, John, and their kids fly in on Thursday night. They stay at Kareen and Amir's house. Michelle drives in on Thursday night and also stays at Kareen's home. Khryssa and Anniston tell their mother they are taking the boys to eat dinner at Aunt Kareen's house to give Lexington and Michael a chance to be alone. They have a huge feast as they talk and catch up. They are all excited as they wrap wedding gifts.

Finally, it's Friday, Khryssa pretends to take everyone to school for her mother as an anniversary gift, but they go straight to the church. Charly's mother, Sylva, and her staff are decorating the sanctuary and the reception hall when they arrive.

The restaurant workers arrive to cook breakfast for everyone. After the decorations are complete, the photographer begins capturing photos, and the videographer begins filming. The family sits down to eat and talk. Two-by-two the women get their hair and make-up done. The boys and men get their hair cut. By two o'clock, the cooks are working on dinner, everyone is dressed and ready to put the plan into action.

Lexington and Michael are at work when each receive a text from one of their daughters stating it's an emergency and please come to the church immediately. Lexington calls the school and finds out the girls didn't go to school. They both rush over to the church so quickly that they don't think to call each other.

When Michael walks into the church, he runs into Amir, John, Bishop, his father, and father-in-law all dressed in tuxedos. They shout happy anniversary. They can tell Michael is worried about his daughters. They assure him the girls are fine. Michael asks, "What is going on?"

Amir tells him as he hugs him, "You're getting married in a half-hour."

Michael says, "Married?"

John says (as he and Michael embrace), "Today is your wedding day, and we are all here to celebrate you."

Michael embraces each of the men, he says, "What a pleasant surprise?"

Bishop says, "We wouldn't miss this for the world."

Michael asks, "Lexington planned this?" The men say no.

John says, "Lexington has no clue what's going on."

Amir says, "Your daughters planned this." They escort him to the men's dressing room.

John says, "You have to put on your tux!"

When Lexington walks through the door, she runs into Destiny and Kendra elegantly dressed with their faces perfectly adorned with makeup. She says, "Destiny, Kendra, what are you doing here?" They wrap their arms around her.

Destiny says, "We're here to see you!"

Kendra says, "Happy anniversary, Biggest Sister!"

Lexington says, "For real, what's going on?"

Kendra says, "Come in here."

Destiny says, "You need to get ready for your wedding," as they push her toward the women's dressing room.

Lexington says, "Wedding?" When she walks through the door, she's surprised to see her three daughters, Destiny's daughters, Kendra's daughters, Vanessa's daughter, her mother, her mother-in-law, Akera, Vanessa and Kareen.

Anniston walks over to her and says, "Mommy, we wanted you to have a real wedding and real wedding pictures to hang on the wall."

Lexington started crying and hugged her daughter; she says, "You're so sweet."

Michelle walks up to Lexington and Anniston. Michelle says, "Mommy, this was all Anniston's idea," as Lexington pulls Michelle into the hug. Khryssa joins the hug from the other side. All the women in the room join the group hug.

Anniston says, "You have to stop crying, so they can do your hair and makeup."

Lexington says, "You all are so sweet!" Lexington closed her eyes and says, "I love all of you so much."

Akera says, "Sis, don't make us cry, and mess up this makeup. We still have to take pictures."

Mrs. Lear says, "Baby, pull it together, so you can begin this beautiful day that your daughters have worked so hard to give you. Come on, baby, breathe!"

Lexington breathes, still hugging her daughters. Lexington whispers to her daughters, "Thank you so much for loving me. This is the most beautiful thing anyone has ever done for me." Her daughters squeeze her and tell her they love her because she's been a good mother.

Michelle says, "Okay, Mommy, you have to hurry up." Kareen comes over with the dress.

Lexington says, "That's the dress. Anniston, you really got me. You all really got me good."

Anniston says, "Thank Aunt Kareen. She bought it for you." Lexington hugs and thanks Kareen.

Kareen and Destiny pull Lexington into the bathroom. Destiny says, "Girl, we've got to get this on you now." The rest of the women go down to the sanctuary.

Once they're in sanctuary, Anniston tells her sisters she wants to play the piano as their mother walks down the aisle. Khryssa and Michelle are shocked because since they were small children, Anniston has been the most reluctant to play the piano. Michelle says, "You hated when Mommy gave us piano lessons."

Anniston says, "I've been practicing at school with my music teacher. I am super nervous, but I want to do this for Mommy."

Khryssa says, "Little Sister, I'm so proud of you. You can do it! You did all of this, and you can sit at that piano to play your heart out for your mother."

Michelle says, "Khryssa is right, Annabelle, you can do whatever you set your mind to do. Mommy always wanted you to play and sing like her, so she's going to love to hear you play as she walks down the aisle."

As the girls huddled together discussing Anniston playing the piano, Michael walks up, he says, "My three daughters!"

Michelle turns around, and excitedly says, "Daddy!" She jumps in his arms.

He asks, "You've been good?"

Michelle answers, "Yes, Daddy, school is going really well."

Michael says, "I'm so glad to hear that. (He kisses her forehead.) I miss you, but I am proud of you!"

Michelle says, "Awe! Daddy, Thanks. I really want to make you proud!"

He says, "You always do!"

Michelle says, "Daddy, I was accepted into this program. It is a big deal. Three hundred people apply every year, but only five get in. Can we talk about it while I'm here this weekend?"

Michael says, "Absolutely! I'm very proud of you. I will support whatever you want to do?"

Michelle says, "I have to take summer classes, so it'll be more money."

Michael says, "Don't worry about that! You focus on making A's. I will worry about the bill."

Michelle says, "I love you, Daddy!"

Michael says, "I love my girls. You girls are amazing to do this for your mom. She deserves it, and it's well overdue."

Anniston says, "It's not only for her, Daddy. It's for you and Papa, too. I know you really wanted a church wedding twenty-one years ago. Papa always wanted to give Mommy away, so this is his chance, and this is your chance to properly ask for Mommy's hand in marriage."

Michelle says, "She's right. You know Papa feels a way still. You need to make it right before the bride is ready."

Khryssa says, "Daddy, we'll go with you. Come on!" As everyone in the sanctuary is waiting on Lexington, Michael and his daughters approach Mr. Lear.

Michael says, "Pops!"

Mr. Lear says, "Son!" They hug.

Michael says, "It has been a pleasure and an honor to be your son-in-law for twenty-one years. I hope I have proven myself as a man, husband, father, provider, protector, and as the head of my household. I'm asking for your blessing to marry your daughter, which I should've done twenty-one years ago."

Mr. Lear puts his hand on Michael's shoulder and says, "Son, I appreciate that more than you know. You have become my son over the years. I am so proud of you as a son, father, and husband. There's nothing about these twenty-one years that I would change. When it comes to Lexington, I rest well, knowing she is in your care. You have been such a blessing to my wife and me. We love how you lead your household. You have my blessing wholeheartedly, Son." The two men embrace. The girls celebrate their dad's success.

Destiny comes to get Mr. Lear, she says, "Mr. Lear, your daughter is ready." Everyone takes their seats. Michael's and Lexington's friends from the church and their workplaces are in attendance. Michael's relatives are in attendance. Everyone is excited and happy for the couple.

Anniston sits at the piano with her heart pounding out of her chest. Everyone stares at her waiting for the music to start. Anniston takes a deep breath and starts playing the piano.

Amir escorts Kareen down the aisle followed by Michelle and Jaxon, then Khryssa and Nexen. The men stand beside Michael at the altar. Everyone is watching the door. When Mr. Lear and Lexington are visible, everyone stands to watch Mr. Lear escort Lexington to the altar. When Lexington makes it to the altar, the song ends. Bishop asks, "Who gives this woman to this man?"

Mr. Lear says, "I do!"

The twins say, "We do, too!"

Lexington smiles as faces her husband. Bishop Wright begins the ceremony: "Dear Beloveds, we are gathered here today to witness the recommitment of this man, Michael Moore, and his wife, Lexington Moore. They have shared a life of mutual commitment, love, understanding, respect, and friendship in this union. It is clear how these two have made it. Early on in this relationship, they built a sturdy, durable foundation.

"The proof of their love and hard work is in the five children that they have raised. Even when they were babies, the Moore children stood out as stellar children. Most importantly, these two have faithfully kept God at the center of their household. Very rarely has this married couple missed a Sunday service. They faithfully tithe and serve in the Lord's house, so He faithfully tithes and serves in their house.

"The abundant blessings that have nurtured this marriage over the past twenty-one years will overflow onto their children as they follow in their parents' footsteps in serving the Lord. Now we are going to let the couple exchange their vows." Anniston hands each of them a card. Bishop Wright says, "Michael, you can begin."

Michael reads the card: Lexington Michon Moore, twenty-one years ago, today, you became my wife, my life partner, and my best friend. On that day, you made a commitment to love me, honor me, support me, and you have kept your word. (Michael fights back the tears. The men encourage him. The women are touched by his emotions.) As my wife, you've never faltered or flickered. Your love light has shined for me with the consistency and intensity of the sun. I appreciate all you have done as my wife, my best friend, and the mother of my children.

"When we met, you were a complete, whole, successful woman. You gave up life as you knew it to be in this marriage and raise our family. I recognize that it could not have been easy for you. You selflessly sowed into our family, and for that, I am eternally grateful.

"The past twenty-one years, I have loved you with all my heart, and I promise to continue loving you with every fiber of my being. I promise, I will never take you for granted. You, your happiness, your security, and your needs will always be my first priority. I am grateful for our past, and I look forward to our future."

Bishop says, "Lexington, you may begin."

Lexington, with tears streaming down her face, begins to read her card, "Michael Daniel Moore, twenty-one years ago, today, you took me as your wife and gave me life. Before you, I thought I had everything, but the day I met you, I realized I had nothing. (Lexington smiles and looks at Anniston.) I was alive, but I wasn't living. You taught me how to live life right and fully.

"From the first time I heard your voice, I knew you were my husband. I came into this marriage very clear in my intentions as your wife. I came into this marriage wanting to give to you, support you, take care of you, fulfill your desires, and to be a good mother to your children.

"I have never questioned or doubted your love. You have been an amazing husband and father each day of our marriage. I wouldn't change anything about our love story. I appreciate all you have poured into me. I am grateful for the first twenty-one years, and I look forward to the next."

Bishop Wright says, "Now, you two have recommitted yourselves to this union. You two have taken vows in front of your God, your children, and your family and friends. The boys are only four years away from leaving home, which will leave you two alone in this union for the first time since the very beginning.

"In the quietness and stillness of your home, remember you stood in front of us and promised to cover each other in prayer; to be each other's peace amid any storms; to walk together and never be alone in this life; to weather all storms in each other's arm; to provide each other with warmth in the coldness, and to be stable and consistent with your presence and participation."

Bishop says, "Rings, please." Nexen hands Michael Lexington's ring. Jaxon hands Lexington Michael's ring. Bishop says, "Michael repeat after me. Take this ring as a symbol of my never-ending love. It is perfectly round with no beginning or end. Nothing or no one can penetrate or break our love."

Bishop says, "Lexington repeat after me. I give this ring as a symbol of continued faith, love, and commitment. Faith because God brought us together, and he'll keep us together. Love, because I love you, and I have since the first time we spoke. Commitment because I am and will always be totally committed to our marriage. Nothing will come between us or break us apart."

Bishop says, "Let me say, the vows spoken by Michael and Lexington were written by their daughter, Anniston. Her insight, wisdom, and preparation of this event here today is living testimony of what greatness lives in this union. Together they have raised five committed, intelligent children with manners and kindness. That alone says to me God is all in this union, and what God brought together, no man shall undertake it. Amen!" The onlookers say Amen.

Bishop Wright says, "I, now, reaffirm you, man and wife. Michael Moore, kiss your woman, Brother."

Michael picks Lexington up to passionately kiss her. Lexington places her hands on his face. The audience cheers and claps.

While still holding her in the air, Michael says, "Lexington, "I love you."

Lexington replies, "I love you."

After the ceremony, the guests move to the hall for the reception, while the wedding party pose for pictures. The videographer records messages from the guests as they eat and socialize.

After taking photos, the wedding party enters the reception except for Lexington and Michael. Michelle takes the stage to sing her mother's favorite song. The room is so quiet that you could hear a pin hit the floor.

The photographer takes pictures as Michelle stands at the microphone. The beat drops. Michelle starts singing. Michael leads his wife to the dance floor. As Michael and Lexington dance, the twins and the other kids raid the candy table while all the adults are preoccupied with watching the dance floor.

When it's time to catch the bouquet, the women gather on the dance floor. Lexington turns her back to the women. She flings the bouquet over her head, and it lands right in Michelle's hands. When Lexington turns to see who caught it, she is shocked to see her oldest daughter with the bouquet.

After dancing and enjoying the evening with their families and friends, the crowd blows bubbles as Michael and Lexington leave the church. The kids stay behind to clean the church before going to hang out with their aunts, uncles, and cousins at Kareen's house. At about two in the morning, they make it home.

When the girls are dressed for bed, they decide to visit their parents to say goodnight. Michelle knocks on the door, "We want to say goodnight." Their parents invite them in. Michelle and Khryssa crawl in the bed between their parents, making Michael and Lexington move apart.

Anniston crawls straight into her mother's arms; she says, "Mommy, I hope you enjoyed today."

Lexington kisses her forehead, "I loved today. I feel so loved. I'm so grateful to you all."

Khryssa and Michelle hug their parents. Michelle says, "Daddy, did you like today?"

Michael answers, "I loved it. The entire day was absolutely amazing. You three young ladies really did an excellent job. I am so proud and so thankful."

Khryssa asks, "So, Lexington and Michael, where are you going for your honeymoon this time?"

Michelle adds, "Yes, darlings, you have to go on a second honeymoon. I'll come home and watch the kids for you while you spend a week in Italy or Spain."

Anniston says, "Mommy, Italy sounds like a good choice, just don't come home pregnant."

Khryssa says, "Yes, Lexington Moore, one oops on a honeymoon is forgivable, but two would be a sin."

Lexington responds, "One, my name is Mommy for the rest of your life. Two, my big girl was not an oops."

Michelle asks, "Daddy, was I a oops baby?"

Michael says, "No, you were planned and prayed for by me."

Michelle asks, "Mommy, you didn't want me?"

Lexington says, "Michael, don't make her think that. It wasn't like that at all. Come here!" Lexington hugs Michelle. Lexington says, "I've always loved you, and I always will."

Anniston says, "She wanted you. She was scared and under a lot of pressure as a new wife. That's all."

Lexington says, "Thank you, Baby Girl. That's exactly what was going on."

Michael says, "She cried every day for two weeks after the doctor said she was pregnant; then she cried for another two weeks when she found out it was a girl. I was good because I was getting exactly what I wanted: a beautiful baby girl named Michelle."

Anniston says, "But Daddy, you are a whole human older than Mommy, so it makes sense that you were more prepared emotionally for parenthood."

Lexington says, "Thank you for sticking up for me, Baby Girl." She hits Michael as she tells Michelle, "When you're pregnant, anything can make you cry, and I loved you even through the tears don't ever doubt that, Big Girl."

Anniston says, "Michelle, Mommy gave up her whole life for you. She grew up and did right by you and Daddy, so that alone says she wanted you and loved you."

Michael asks, "Anniston, how do you know all that?"

Anniston says, "Because she is my mommy, I love her, and I pay attention to everything she does."

Lexington says, "Baby Girl, I love you, and I pay attention to everything you do."

Khryssa adds, "I know one thing for sure. We are the most favored girls in the world to have you two as our parents. You have given us everything. And the best gift you both have given us is love."

Lexington says, "Awe! Middle Girl, that's so sweet!"

Michelle says, "I second that! Today was a small token of our appreciation for all the sacrifices you two have made for us."

Anniston says, "I wish I could do more to show you how much I appreciate you."

Lexington says, "Girls, I love you so much. We appreciate today, and today was more than enough. Akera told me how much you all gave up to pay for today. We'll get your stuff back."

Khryssa says, "No, Mommy, we don't want our stuff back. We wanted you to have a beautiful day, and that's worth more than anything we gave up."

Anniston says, "Just get our MacBooks back, please! We need them to do homework."

Michael says, "You girls have given us so much just by being who you are and doing what you do. We are the most favored parents in the world to have three beautiful daughters."

Anniston shyly says, "Mommy, Daddy, I have a confession. I sort of pawned that jewelry you let me wear to help pay for the ceremony. Planning a wedding is very expensive. But Aunt Akera is going to go get everything back tomorrow."

Michael says, mocking Roman's voice, "It's okay. Right, Lex!" Lexington immediately recognized what Michael was doing. No one ever called her Lex but Roman.

Lexington says, "Michael, don't start! (She says to Anniston:) Baby, it's okay! Akera told me."

Khryssa says, "Daddy, I know it's your wedding night, but we are sleeping in here with our mother."

Michelle gets under the sheets and lays next to Michael, she says, "Scoot over, Daddy, make more room for Khryssa." Just then, the twins walk in.

Jaxon asks, "What's all the laughing going on in here?"

Nexen says, "The whole family is in here, and no one invited us."

Khryssa says, "Daddy, make room for the boys."

Michael says, "I can't even see my wife way over here."

Michelle says, "But you can see us, your beautiful children."

Khryssa says, "Just in case you were trying to pull another one over on Mommy, we are blocking that because no one wants another boy running around here."

The twins say, "Hey!"

Jaxon says, "Boys are better than girls."

Khryssa says, "Only in your imagination."

Lexington says, "Children, be nice. You're all wonderful. Our family is complete, so there will be no more babies until you all are married and decide to have your own."

Michelle says, "It's been so long since we all slept in here together. Remember when we were little, and we would sleep so wild that Daddy would go sleep on the couch."

Khryssa says, "Yes, I remember those nights. Daddy would be irritated in the morning."

Michael says, "A man doesn't want to be separated from his wife."

Khryssa says, "You have to share, Buddy."

Michael says, "Maybe, I should have cried for two weeks."

Khryssa says, "Daddy, you know you couldn't live without us."

Michael says, "Middle girl, you're right about that!"

Lexington and Michael fall asleep, surrounded by their children. Anniston lays on her mother's chest, wrapped in her mother's arms. She sees her mother's journal on the nightstand. She gently opens it and begins reading. It's so interesting that she barely sleeps.

The next morning, Michael takes Lexington to breakfast, leaving their five children home alone. Anniston sneaks to read her more of mother's journals. She finds a few entries that are interesting. Anniston calls her siblings to her parents' bedroom.

She says, "Listen to this," she reads: "Blessed is our union. Blessed are his hands and his heart. Blessed is the day we met. I cherish the day he realized I was the one. I cherish the day he thought to himself, I can't live without Lexington! Blessed are the vows we took. Thankful for every step we took and trial we overcame to make it to the day I took his last name. I was blessed to live my destiny when he said, I do!

"My love for him is as far and as wide as the sky. It is as deep and as beautiful as the ocean. He brings peace with his calm and quiets storms with his wisdom. His heartbeat is music to my ears. I can listen for hours and never tire of the repetitive sound. He makes me strong with his strength. I appreciate him, all he is and has done. He works hard to provide for his family.

"I am the one he needs day and night. I am the first person he calls when he has good news. I am the one he reaches for when he is sad. I am the one to calm him when he is angered. I can listen to him talk for hours because he intrigues me with his candor. I am the one he desires. He leads and teaches me in the life of Christ. I perfectly prepare his meals. He relishes the attention and comfort I give him. I am the one to run his bathwater and wash his back.

"I am the one to rub his feet when he is tired. I am the one to fulfill his desires. I am the one to walk into his dreams at night. I am the one in his visions in the day. I am a pillar in his spiritual temple. I support his dreams and pursuits. He pushes me and makes me a better woman. He rests in my arms in the evening and clings to my back through the night. When I crawl into his embrace, I put my head on his right shoulder, and I finally have peace.

"We love, laugh, pray, cry, and eat together! Our marriage bed is blissful! His love is strong, tender and forceful! I am encouraging! I am pleasant and peaceful! We have all we ever needed, wanted, and desired. I love him, and he loves me. We trust each other. We are faithful. We're thankful for each other. We are submissive to and supportive of one another. We will never feel lonely again. We don't deny the other. We encourage each other. We share with each other.

"He covers me with special prayers day and night. He prophesies over my future. He knows my every flaw. I accept him as he is. Despite all circumstances, we have survived. I am the proverbs 31 woman. He is the man. He allows me to be a woman. He encourages my pursuits and development. He shares his wisdom with me as his wife.

"He is head and shoulders above the rest like Saul. He is faithful, patient, and strong like David. He is wise and prosperous like Solomon. He is as protective and watchful as Boaz was with Ruth. He is as charming as Absalom. He is dependable and trustworthy. He is complete and full of the

Holy Spirit. He is for me. He never takes without giving. His truth is your truth, Lord! He is obedient and submissive to you, my Lord.

"He honors his word. He lives in happiness. He's calm and quiet. He's slow to anger and quick to love. He never makes me feel less or low! I appreciate him day and night in my words, thoughts, and actions. I pray in Jesus' name that we never part. Amen!"

Khryssa says, "That's deep!"

Michelle says, "It's like I got to look into Mommy's head and heart."

Khryssa says, "She really loves Daddy."

Anniston says, "I found something she wrote about each of you. Listen to what she wrote about Michelle," she reads: "Michelle Moore, I met you for the first time today. I never knew I could love someone or something so much. You're so perfect. When the doctor laid you in my arms, you looked at me and took my heart. I can tell you love me already by the look in your eyes. Such a special bond we have already: I need you and you need me. I will love you forever and always.

"As I cradled you in my arms, I felt the softness of your skin and saw innocence in your eyes. You have your father's eye, but you have my nose, lips, and hair. I see so much of the man I love mixed with me in you. You're the culmination of our love. You are the best thing we've done.

"You are made of goodness. I have so many hopes and dreams for you. My biggest hope is that you will always love me. I pray you dream and believe big. Whatever you desire, it shall be yours. Not even a day old, and I already believe in you. You're a conqueror.

"When your father held you for the first time, he fell in love with you. You will have him wrapped around your finger. I have never seen a man so happy as he was when he greeted and held you. You love him too. You stared at him as he talked to you. He said you are his miracle. I have to agree, you are a miracle. The labor pain, the morning sickness, the fears, and tears were all worth this moment. Welcome to the world, Michelle Danielle Moore, my miracle."

Michelle says, "Awe, that's so sweet!" Michelle's heart melted for her mother.

Anniston says, "I found this about Khryssa," she reads: "Today, Khryssa, you said out of nowhere, love you, Mama, for the first time. You kissed me and hugged my neck. You didn't want anything. You weren't crying. You're just beginning to walk and talk, so I was so shocked. It made me smile. I felt so happy. It is so amazing to be loved by my babies. Khryssa, you sat in my lap and rubbed my hair and cheek. When I said I love you, Khryssa, you smiled. You gave me your favorite toy before you went to play with your sister. It's those moments that make me understand love and life.

"Khryssa, I love you more than you will ever know or understand. I look at you and see the love of my husband reflecting through you and back to me. You look and act just like your father. The most handsome man in the world gave me the two most beautiful girls in the world.

"Michelle is reserved like your father, but you are strong-willed like your father. I love how much you two girls love each other. You share with your sister, and you hug your sister. I love that about you. You're the baby, but you're going to be her protector, I can tell already.

"Khryssa, I am so happy and proud that I am your Mommy. Out of all the women in the world, your soul chose my soul to come shining through. I will never mind that you are a daddy's girl because I know you love me. I will always remember the day you told me. I promise to never let you down. I promise you will never regret choosing me. I will work my fingers to the bone every day to prove my love and live in a way that will earn your heart until my dying day. I love you so much, Khryssa."

Khryssa says, "Mommy is so sweet! I wish I remembered that day."

Michelle says, "Mommy, was right, Khryssa, you are the protector. You are strong like Daddy, and you have been a great sister."

Khryssa says, "Awe, Michelle, that's so sweet." Michelle and Khryssa hug.

Anniston says, "Listen to this," she reads: "My kings, my sons, Nexen and Jaxon, you both are growing up so beautifully. I'm learning to be a mother to boys. Letting you play rough was hard for me. Letting you play tackle football was so scary for me. I don't want to see you hurt, but I need to let you be boys. I want my boys to grow up to be men. I had to learn to deal with my fear and separate it from you. I pray for you instead of worrying about you.

"Having three girls, I've had to learn to communicate and talk to you, boys. Sometimes, I ask you to do things, and you don't. I learned you are not disregarding me, but it hurts my feelings when you don't listen to me.

"I'm used to girls who move immediately. Your father used to step in to say, Son, listen to your mother, or don't let my wife tell you again. Although we have a long way to go, we have come very far. I so appreciate the growth in you boys. Now that you are big boys, we have this incredible bond. I love being your mother.

"I used to sit at your football games and cover my eyes when one of you got hit. Now, I'm your biggest cheerleader. My boys have grown into great athletes. You play every sport so well, and I'm so proud of you. It's time to start preparing for your manhood, and I hope I'm doing my part well. I pray you are watching your father and understanding his thinking. One day, you two will sit at the head of the table. You will have wives and children of your own. You will be the leaders and protectors of our family.

"My kings, my sons, Nexen and Jaxon, you are more than capable. Always remember to look out for my girls. I will always be so grateful and thankful that I'm your mother. I love you so much. No matter how many times I have to say clean your room, do your homework, take the trash out, or put your shoes in the closet, I will always be grateful that I'm your mother."

The boys sit quietly, thinking about their mother's thoughts. Nexen says, "Jax, sometimes we don't listen to Mommy. I never thought I was hurting her feelings."

Jaxon says, "We have to be more responsible. I don't want to hurt or disappoint, Mommy."

Nexen says, "It feels good to know someone loves you so much even when you don't deserve it."

Khryssa says, "You two aren't that bad. The problem is neither of you order your priorities. You do things, but not in order of importance."

Michelle says, "You're going to high school next year, it's time to learn to set your priorities. Sports are important, so are chores, homework, and bible study. Video games are your hobby. We all need hobbies to give us a break from life, but if all you do is your hobby, you aren't living life responsibly."

Khryssa says, "Balance things out, Little Brothers."

Jaxon says, "We'll do better now that we know what to do."

Anniston says, "Mommy, will appreciate that so much." Anniston says, "I want to read what she wrote about Micah, but you have to promise to never mention him."

Jaxon says, "Who is Micah?"

Anniston says, "Micah is our brother. He died as a baby."

Nexen says, "Wow!"

Anniston says, "It happened when Michelle was one year old."

Khryssa says, "Mommy never told me we had another brother. I feel so bad for her."

Michelle says, "That had to be devastating. I am glad I don't remember that."

Anniston says, "She doesn't say anything because it's too hard to talk about him. I think you all should know how hurt she was when she had to bury her baby." Anniston swears them to secrecy before she reads the journal entry about Micah, "Today was the most devastating day of my life. I had to say goodbye to you. I'll never get a chance to hear your cry, listen to you call me Mommy, or change your diaper. I had so many hopes and dreams for you. I really wanted to give my husband a son. I can only imagine the son you would've been. I can only imagine how much you would've loved your daddy. I can only imagine you and him playing, laughing, watching sports, and wrestling on the living room floor.

"I wish I could've watched you take your first steps, hear you say, Dada and Mama, give you a bath and wash your hair. I hate that I'll never teach you to write your name, say the alphabet, or count. I'll never know your favorite snack, movie, song, color, or television show. I wanted to be your mother. I hope you know that you were loved and wanted, but I guess God wanted you more. Be a good baby for him and serve your purpose in heaven. Make me proud!

"I wonder, do you know who I am. When I get to heaven, will you be there waiting for me? Do you want to hold me and hug me like I want to hug and hold you? I wonder, do you know my voice and what I look like? Only God knows why he chose to take you away from me. I pray the angels care for you and love you the way I would have. Always remember, I love you, Micah."

Michelle says, "That was heartbreaking. I never realized how much the little things matter to a mother."

Khryssa says, "We have the best Mommy in the world. We don't give her enough credit."

Jaxon says, "Now that we know what Mommy really thinks of us, we have to live up to her dreams for us."

Michelle says, "It does add to the pressure to make her proud." The kids look at each other.

Khryssa says, "Imagine being the one out of six to disappoint her."

Nexen says, "Not one of us can fail. We all owe it to her to fulfill her dreams for us. We all have to promise right here, right now, that we will live up to her expectations for us, and we will always do the best we can to make her proud." Nexen puts his hand in, and all the others follow.

Michelle asks, "Annabelle, what did Mommy write about you?"

Jaxon looks out the window; he says, "Mommy and Daddy are back."

Khryssa says, "Annabelle, you better put everything back exactly the way you found it, or Mommy is going to kill you. We are not supposed to touch mommy's journals." Anniston rushes to put everything back.

Michelle says, "Let's go distract Mommy and Daddy while Anniston puts the journals back." They run downstairs to the kitchen. When their parents walk in the door, they surround them with hugs and kisses, professing their love. Anniston comes into the kitchen and joins in the hugging.

The kids notice Michael is holding bags of food from their grandmother's restaurant. The kids take the bags from Michael and rush over to the table. Michael and Lexington sit down and talk to the kids while they eat. The twins have a football game followed by basketball practice in an hour.

Jaxon says, "Mommy, we are going to score for you."

Nexen says, "When we make it to the pros, Mommy, we are going to take care of you and your daughters."

Lexington smiles and says, "Thank you, Sons! I appreciate you already." She kisses her sons and goes to pack snacks and lunches for them.

Michael whispers in Lexington's ear, "You, them, and moments like this is what life is about."

She smiles at him; she says, "I definitely get why you wanted six children."

The End

www.ingramcontent.com/pod-product-compliance
Lightning Source LLC
Chambersburg PA
CBHW040520170726
48295CB00012B/273